# The Purpose of Erie
## Curve Ball

*Jane Neagley*

The Purpose of Erie - Curve Ball

Copyright 2025 by JaneNeagWrites

www.janeneagwrites.com

ISBN: 979-8-9990352-0-2

Cover Art by RD Creative Strategy

Interior Design by MWilbur Designs | www.mwilburdesigns.com

Editing by Elyssa Warkentin | www.elyssawarkentin.com

# Chapter 1

*June 1987*

Cassidy Banker pulled her blue Toyota Corolla into a second-row spot in her apartment complex's parking lot. She turned off the ignition and sighed, leaning her head back against the headrest. Her long, wavy, dirty blonde hair pressed into the fabric behind her. She gazed out into the clear, June night sky.

After sitting for a long moment, she took a deep breath, collected her keys and dark grey purse, and climbed out of the car. She quickly locked the car door with her key before turning and walking into her complex.

Cassidy swiftly scaled the stairs to her second-floor apartment and let herself in.

"I'm back," she called out, hanging her purse and key lanyard on the coat tree to the right of the door.

"Hey," her roommate, Marissa, called out from the direction of the kitchen. Cassidy made her way down the entry hall and into the large living room which connected to the rectangular galley kitchen. Marissa was standing at the counter chopping

1

a block of cheese into snack-sized slices. Marissa was petite and thin with dark brown hair that was almost always set in two French braids along the sides of her head.

Cassidy kicked off her white Nikes and padded over to the kitchen to help herself to some of Marissa's cheese. Cassidy was about three inches taller than her friend. And while Cassidy was nowhere near overweight, she had an athletic build – twelve years of competitive softball will do that to you. She always felt large next to Marissa, twinging a bit of jealousy, especially on their nights out to meet guys. However, Marissa herself never made Cassidy feel insecure, and Cassidy comfortably grabbed a handful of cheese slices from the cutting board before walking back into the living room and plopping down on the sofa, stretching her legs out to the middle cushion.

"Stress eating?" Marissa asked as she cut the final two slices and put the knife in the sink.

"Mmmm," Cassidy agreed, taking a bite out of a slice of cheese. Marissa collected her cheese slices into a bowl and made her way to the living room. She took a seat on the opposite side of the sofa and stretched her legs out in front of her, her ankles resting atop Cassidy's feet.

"How'd it go tonight?" she asked, casually popping a piece of cheese in her mouth. It was the first Friday of June, and in the Banker family, the first Friday of the month meant family dinner night. Cassidy and her four brothers all returned home to their parents' house for a family meal.

Cassidy's parents, Art and Lynne, had started this tradition when their eldest left for college. The monthly dinner had been routine for nine years now. Both Art and Lynne were nearing retirement, and with all five children out of the house,

2

they looked forward to it more than ever. Their children, on the other hand, had mixed feelings. Some months they loved it, some months, they would have rather stayed home.

Cassidy's brother Alex was the eldest of the Banker children. Twenty-eight, now, with medium height and a slightly stocky build, his dark blond hair rested just atop his ears. He dreamed of being a novelist, and spent most of his free time scribbling away on his notepads. However, wannabe writer doesn't pay the bills, so Alex put his creative writing skills to work at his job with the Erie Times Newspaper where he wrote the "Household Hints" and personal advice columns. Cassidy always found it amusing how much stock people put in the paper's advice. If all those women that wrote in only knew they were getting their relationship tips from a chain-smoking, day-sleeping, twenty-eight-year-old man, they'd die of embarrassment. She had to admit, Alex gave surprisingly good advice, though.

Next was twenty-seven-year-old Matty. Tall and thin with short, light brown hair, Matty was a math teacher at the high school in Cambridge Springs, just two towns over from Erie, where they all grew up. Matty was loud, sarcastic, and funny. He made friends wherever he went, yet he had a knack for putting his foot in his mouth. Lucky for him, he could win people back pretty quickly, or at least defuse the situation with a well-timed joke.

Technically, Cassidy was next born. However, she only held that place by a twelve minute margin. Cassidy was a twin. She and her brother Eric were twenty-five. Both had wavy, dark blonde hair and stocky builds. While they were obviously not identical, there were striking similarities between the two of them – much to their mutual dismay.

Twins were expected to be best friends, close companions: two peas in a pod. Cassidy and Eric were not. They didn't hate one another, but they definitely weren't close. They'd never shared a friend or even a secret. When spending time with family, they always gravitated to their other brothers, all of whom they were much closer with than each other. This was an unfortunate fact of their lives. Neither were thrilled about it, but neither wanted to put in any effort to fix it.

They'd both graduated college three years ago – class of 1984. Eric from the University of Pittsburgh and Cassidy from Edinboro University. Eric was back in Erie now, working as an HR assistant for a computer training facility. He'd always been into computers. Cassidy was a Certified Public Accountant at a small accounting firm downtown. She'd always loved numbers and was very organized. Accounting was her dream career.

Finally, there was Ben, the youngest Banker at twenty-one. Ben had the lightest blond hair of the five kids, and he always wore it long, to his chin – much to the intense disdain of their mother. Ben was currently on summer break before his senior year at Mercyhurst University in Erie, studying to be a therapist. Cassidy couldn't understand how he'd selected psychology as a major. Ben couldn't listen to a shopping list before going to the store; how on earth was he going to listen to his clients? Yet Ben remained on the Dean's List every semester and played varsity soccer for the school.

But Ben was not Cassidy's concern at the moment. She was thinking about how to answer Marissa's question.

"Hmm? How did it go?" Marissa prodded, gently tapping her heel on Cassidy's foot.

"Well," Cassidy began, letting out a loud breath. "Eric's

engaged."

"What?" Marissa squawked, completely bug-eyed.

"Yeah," Cassidy said in a low, long drawl.

"That Laura girl?"

Cassidy shook her head as she munched on her final piece of cheese.

"Laura is Alex's girlfriend," she corrected. Alex and Laura had been together for eight years, since their sophomore year at college. She was an art teacher at the vo-tech school and worked part-time painting and designing sets at the Erie Playhouse. The two of them lived in bohemian bliss in a loft downtown.

"Oh, that's right."

"Eric is with Ellie," Cassidy clarified.

"Eric and Ellie," Marissa said in a mocking tone. Cassidy smiled.

"I've met her a few times, she's not bad."

"Sure about that?" Marissa raised an eyebrow. "You're not super convincing."

"Honestly, she's fine. You know, it's just… it's Eric. It's hard for me to be happy for him. Especially for him getting married before me. You realize the entire planning, preparing, showers, and wedding itself will just be people asking, 'When are you getting married?' 'Your twin got married before you, how do you feel about that?'" Cassidy ended with a huff.

"Ugh, yeah, people suck."

"They do," Cassidy agreed, resting her head on the back of the sofa.

"You just have to remember, it's Eric's day."

"It's not Eric's day, it's Ellie's day. Eric's just along for the ride," Cassidy replied bluntly. Marissa laughed out loud.

"How long have they been dating?" Marissa asked, once she had stopped laughing.

"A little over a year, I think."

"Did your mom flip?"

Cassidy rolled her eyes hard. "Oh, my gosh, yes. She went absolutely crazy."

"Well, at least it'll only be pure chaos until the big day. Have they set a date?" Marissa asked.

"Eric mentioned that Ellie wants a snow-free wedding, so they need to hurry up and do it now, or it'll be next May, probably," Cassidy said with a shrug.

"Ahhh, the joys of Erie weather," Marissa mused.

"Yeah, it's fantastic." Cassidy replied, though she honestly did love the area.

"You're really upset, aren't you?" Marissa asked gently after a long moment of silence. Cassidy shrugged.

"I guess I always just assumed that I would be the first to get married, because I'm the girl. Or, I don't know, maybe Alex would have been first, but no matter what, it definitely wouldn't have been Eric."

"Well, Eric marrying before you may not be the worst thing…." Marissa suggested. Cassidy lifted her head and raised an eyebrow. "Your mom can get all her crazy out on him, and then when it's your turn, she'll be calmer."

"Calm is not one of my mother's functions," Cassidy retorted.

"Well, it'll give you a preview of what she gets upset about, then. You can learn how to avoid it."

Cassidy rolled her eyes. "If you say so,"

The girls changed the topic to their workdays, movies, celebrities, and everything in between. They chatted away happily for over an hour.

Cassidy had met Marissa their freshman year at Edinboro University, a small state university outside of Erie. They lived in the same residence hall, and both were plagued by horrible roommates in their freshman year. The two girls bonded quickly and ended up rooming together the next three years of school. After graduating, they both got jobs in Erie and happily jumped at the chance to get an apartment together on the edge of the city.

The girls departed to their respective bedrooms to go to bed a little before eleven. Cassidy flopped back on her bed, feeling a bit more relaxed than she had when she first got back from dinner at her parents'.

A loud, shrill ring roused Cassidy from a deep sleep. Again, the noise rang out. Cassidy gave a disoriented sigh and rolled over onto her back. A few seconds later, the sound echoed once more. Cassidy had the groggy realization it was the telephone in the living room. She strained to open her eyes and glance at the digital alarm clock on her bedside table. 1:33 glowed back in large red numbers. Cassidy swore. Suddenly she heard the sound of a door opening and determined steps down the hallway. Marissa had gotten up to end the ringing.

"What?" Marissa answered the phone sounding equally annoyed and exhausted. Cassidy lay motionless, waiting to hear Marissa slam the phone down and stomp back to her room. Unfortunately, that's not what happened. A few unintelligible grumbles later, and Marissa let out a bellow.

"CASSIDY!"

Cassidy leapt out of bed faster than she thought possible and dashed to the living room where Marissa stood looking disheveled, exhausted, and very irritated.

"It's your stupid brother." She set the receiver down on the table and stomped back to her room, slamming the door.

"Sorry," Cassidy called as she tried to think who could be on the phone.

'Stupid brother' could easily apply to any of the four of them.

"Hello?" Cassidy put the receiver to her ear and plopped down on the oversized chair in the corner of the room, crossing her legs underneath her.

"Hey." The breathy, unmistakable voice of her eldest brother, Alex, answered. He had clearly just taken a drag off his cigarette.

"What do you need?" Cassidy asked, stifling a yawn.

"You don't want to talk to me?" Alex asked, sounding slightly offended.

"Do you know what time it is right now?"

"Of course. It's 1:34," Alex replied coolly. Cassidy rolled her eyes and decided not to explain to him that some people sleep at this time of night. It was pointless, and she wasn't awake enough for that conversation.

"Okay. What's up?"

"Just wanted to check in," Alex replied sweetly. Cassidy bit her tongue to keep herself from telling him to call her at normal hours. She knew he was honestly trying to be nice.

"Um, well, I just saw you a few hours ago," Cassidy chuckled.

"I know, but I thought Eric's engagement might have thrown you. You looked like a ghost when he told mom and

8

dad." Cassidy smiled to herself as she heard him take another drag. Her eldest brother was always the most observant of all of them. And while he and Cassidy led very different lifestyles, they loved one another fiercely. Cassidy never felt she had a favorite brother, but Alex was forever her champion.

"I didn't mean to make it obvious, but I was surprised," Cassidy admitted.

"It surprised the hell out of all of us," Alex said with a chuckle.

"Really? Eric didn't tell you guys anything?" Cassidy knew Eric talked to their brothers more than her. Granted, the bar of communication was pretty low between the twins…

"Naw," Alex said. "He never mentioned anything about engagement. He told us when they started dating, when they started sleeping together, meeting her friends and family. So, I guess it was coming, but he really never said anything. Not to me, at least."

"I guess that makes me feel better," Cassidy said with a shrug.

"Are you sad? Or pissed?"

"I don't know. Still processing, I guess."

"Processing what?"

"The whole thing."

"Do you hate Ellie?" Alex asked abruptly.

"I don't really know Ellie," she said honestly. "I guess I don't really know Eric, either."

"Cassidy," Alex said in a warning tone. She heard him let out a smokey breath.

"What?" she asked, irritated.

"You know Eric, you guys just don't get along. You need to stop feeling sorry for yourself that you're not best friends with him. That ship sailed a long time ago and you've both already milked it for all it's worth. Pick another battle."

Cassidy felt her jaw tighten. His words were annoyingly true, which only made them sting harder.

"Fine," she said quietly.

"Cassie—"

"What do you want me to say?" Cassidy asked.

"I want you to say what you're feeling!"

"I'm – I'm feeling… terrible," she admitted.

"Why don't you tell me about it?"

But Cassidy couldn't explain. She suddenly felt a rage boil up in her. Every thought and feeling, fear, shock, and annoyance, all seemed to bubble up into one big lump inside of her. She was going to explode. She could feel it. But she didn't want to. She wasn't prepared to face her emotions yet.

"I don't want to talk about it! It's the middle of the night! I'm done!" she snapped.

"Cassidy," Alex protested.

"Go to bed, Alex!" She slammed the phone down with a satisfying click. But she was instantly filled with regret and guilt. She bit her bottom lip as she leaned forward over her crossed legs and let out a low groan. She swore under her breath at her ridiculous childishness before getting to her feet and stomping back to her bedroom, closing the door behind her, and face-planting onto her mattress. She willed herself to fall asleep before the tears came.

# Chapter 2

Cassidy ran her eyeliner pencil gently under her left eye and blinked twice as she leaned closer to the mirror to make sure her left eye matched her right. She set the pencil down and grabbed her dark pink lipstick, applied it liberally before smacking her lips and smiling back at her reflection.

She and Marissa were going out that night. They'd decided they both needed to let loose. They used to go out often in college, but since graduation they only seemed to go out once a month at the very most. They were due a night of fun – especially after last week's family dinner. After sliding her make-up back in her top dresser drawer, Cassidy walked over to the full-length mirror on the back of her bedroom door. Her teal strapless party dress fit her toned body perfectly. The flared hem rested about an inch above her knees. Her long, dark blonde hair had been curled and teased, making it look stylishly feathered, but not overly big. She couldn't understand why that was the style now. Seemed like way too much work. Cassidy smiled at herself, feeling pleased with her appearance. She thought she'd get at least one free drink that night. Perfect.

Marissa was in the galley kitchen pouring a pre-game shot for each of them. Her dark brown hair was tied up in a perfect bun and her petite frame was covered in a light pink dress, cut similarly to Cassidy's except Marissa's had thick shoulder straps. Only someone Marissa's size could pull that off and still look sexy.

"Heyyyy!" Marissa said as she walked the shot glass over to Cassidy. The girls were eye to eye tonight since Marissa wore three-inch white heels. Cassidy had no idea how she could walk, let alone dance in those things. But Marissa wore high heels every chance she got. Cassidy stuck to her flat black strappy sandals.

"You look great!" Cassidy remarked as she took the glass. She really did – but then, she always did.

"You, too!" Marissa said, raising her shot glass. Cassidy clinked hers against it and they both downed the strong liquid.

"Phew!" Cassidy gasped. Marissa shook her head and laughed.

"I just called the taxi; should be here in a few minutes," Marissa said.

"Great!" Cassidy picked up her purse to make sure she had everything. Wallet, ID, house key, two condoms, and a box of Tic-Tacs. She was ready.

"How much cash are you bringing?" Marissa asked. She was digging through her little black purse, as well.

"I have $28. That should cover two drinks and the taxi. That means I need to find some guy to buy me one or two,"

Cassidy explained with a smirk. Marissa chuckled.

"I'm taking $15 and it's all for the taxi. I want men to buy all my drinks. It's been a long few weeks. I deserve it."

Cassidy rolled her eyes. She had no doubt all of Marissa's drinks would be bought for her. Marissa was petite and pretty, and filled with confidence. Her bold manner is what drew Cassidy to befriend her all those years ago – she was confident, yet not conceited. A fine line to walk, but Marissa danced across it beautifully.

Two loud honks rang out from the parking lot outside the apartment window.

"That's us!" Marissa gushed. The girls quickly grabbed their bags, turned off the lights and departed the apartment, locking the big red door behind them.

They headed down the complex stairs, through the small, nondescript lobby and out the door to the waiting yellow taxi out front.

"Hello!" Marissa called as the girls approached the taxi. The driver rolled the window down. A large puff of grey smoke from his cigar billowed out.

"Yeah?" the gruff middle-aged man asked.

"Taxi for Marissa Solomon?"

"That's me; get in." The driver coughed and rolled his window back up. Marissa and Cassidy climbed into the dark back seat.

"Where to?"

"Revolution – the club downtown," Marissa instructed. The gruff man simply nodded, pressed the button to start the toll, and the taxi lurched forward. The girls talked as they weaved through the streets of Erie. Before they knew it, they were being dropped off on the narrow sidewalk in front of the large, tan building. A neon red sign glowed above the entryway. Two large men stood framing the doorway.

"Thanks," Marissa and Cassidy said to their driver. They handed him the $8 cash, clambered out of the yellow car and walked over to the bouncers.

"ID, ladies," the black-shirted man on the right side of the door said in a surly tone. Both girls handed him their licenses. He eyed both IDs and both girls for about fifteen seconds, really making a meal out of it, before handing the licenses back to the girls with a curt nod. The bouncer on the left side opened the door to let them in.

Two steps inside and the door thumped closed behind them. All of their senses were stimulated in an instant. The inside of the club was as dark as it was outside, but without the benefit of street lights or car headlights. The music rang through the air. An old Pat Benatar song was being spun by the DJ on the other side of the large room. Their nostrils were filled with an overwhelming mixture of cigarette smoke, spilled beer, and gallons of perfumes. Cassidy and Marissa gave each other a quick side glance before bursting into large grins. Memories of fun nights out as college students were flooding back. They were both very much looking forward to tonight.

Cassidy led the way to the long, dark wooden bar along the right side of room. They weaved through the high tables that were almost all occupied, past the row of circular booths along the wall until they reached the corner of the bar.

While it was a Saturday night, it was also the beginning of summer and ninety-five percent of Erie's college students had gone home for the summer. Erie had four universities right in the city center, and several others in the surrounding suburbs, including Edinboro University, where Cassidy and Marissa

14

had attended. During the winter, this club would have been completely packed at this hour, with a long line out the door. But it was summer and there were less than a hundred people there that night. Oh, well. The lines were shorter!

"Hi, ladies," The bartender, a tall man with short black hair, greeted them as they rested their forearms on the bartop.

"Hey," Marissa replied with a sultry smile. Cassidy bit her lip to hold in a smile.

"What can I get yinz?" the bartender asked.

"What are you offering?" Marissa asked, leaning forward. Cassidy couldn't help but let out a small giggle. The bartender smiled back at Marissa knowingly.

"Drinks," he replied with a smirk. This was definitely not the first time a pretty girl had flirted with him.

"We'll take two shots of B52," Cassidy interjected. She had no doubt that Marissa could get flirt long enough to get them free shots, but she was ready to dance.

"Sure thing, sweetie," the bartender nodded as he quickly got to work. Marissa leaned to her right and brought her lips to Cassidy's ear.

"I had this!" Marissa whispered, sounding slightly discouraged.

"I want to dance. We'll get free drinks later," Cassidy insisted.

"We'll get them now," Marissa insisted. Cassidy chuckled at her friend.

"Here you go, girls," the bartender said, pushing two filled shot glasses in front of them.

"Thanks," Cassidy said.

"That'll be $6." Cassidy reached for her purse.

"Come on, really?" Marissa asked, reaching out and resting

her hand on his forearm.

"I think so," the bartender replied, clearly enjoying the attention of a beautiful young woman in a tight pink dress. Marissa slid her hand down his arm to entwine their fingers before pulling his hand towards her and placing a soft kiss on his knuckles.

"Please? I'll save you a dance," Marissa pleaded, kissing his fingers once more. The bartender let out a sigh.

"Fine. $2. But I'm getting my dance. My shift ends in forty-five minutes."

"I'll be waiting," Marissa replied with a smile, slowly pulling her hand from his. Cassidy watched and shook her head. The girls reached into their purses and each took out $1.

"Your tip comes later," Marissa said with a wink before picking up both shot glasses and walking to the nearest high table.

"You're unbelievable," Cassidy told her, taking one of the shot glasses from her hands.

Marissa shrugged. "I don't know what you're complaining about. I just saved you two bucks! And I'm the one that has to dance with that weirdo later."

"I thought you liked him?" Cassidy asked with a laugh. Marissa frantically shook her head.

"Ew, no! He's way too full of himself, and I can already tell that he's going to be grabby."

"Well, shit…" Cassidy said with a sigh.

"Here's to more free drinks and getting too drunk to be aware of the disaster dance that awaits me!" Marissa proposed, raising her glass.

"I'll drink to that!" Cassidy agreed. The girls clinked their glasses and downed their shots in one gulp.

They both gasped as the alcohol hit their systems. They set their empty glasses down on the table.

"We need to dance!" Cassidy told Marissa.

"Absolutely!" Marissa agreed. The girls linked arms and weaved their way onto the small dance floor in the back of the club. During the school year, you could barely move on the dance floor with all of the packed bodies – which sometimes had advantages. However, with maybe sixty other people on the dance floor, the ratio was near perfect. It didn't feel empty by any means, yet there was room to actually move.

Duran Duran cried out from the speakers and Marissa and Cassidy began dancing and jumping along with the beat as they made their way to the center of the crowd.

Cassidy felt her entire body loosen up as she danced, her mind focused only on the music blaring around her. It was one of her favorite feelings. Nothing else in the world mattered at that moment. Nothing but dance.

They jumped, danced, swayed, and twirled to four more songs without missing a single beat. As a Tiffany song started, Marissa grabbed Cassidy's arm and pulled her close so she could talk in her ear, the only way to be heard over the speakers.

"Those guys over there have been watching us," Marissa pointed. Cassidy glanced over. She was right. There were two 20-something guys leaning against the DJ booth smirking at the two of them.

"Hmmm," Cassidy mused as she smiled back. They were both good looking. One was thin framed with curly brown hair while the other was a bit more muscular with very short hair, just longer than a buzz cut.

"Should we wave them over?" Marissa asked.

Cassidy shrugged. "Why not?"

The girls smiled at each other before each raising an arm and waving a "come here" motion. The guys smiled and began weaving through the dancers as they made their way to the center where Cassidy and Marissa stood.

"Hi there," the muscular guy with very short hair said as he reached the girls. He was a good six inches taller than Cassidy in her flat sandals and Marissa in her heels.

"Hello," Marissa said happily.

"What are your names?" he asked.

"I'm Cassidy."

"And I'm Marissa." The guys nodded at them.

"Who are you two?" Cassidy asked them.

"I'm Pete," the short haired guy replied, "and this is my buddy, Brandon." The thin, curly haired man waved and smiled sheepishly.

"Hey," Marissa said, her focus solely on Brandon. Cassidy quickly realized that Pete was going to be hers, which honestly did not bother her in the least. Pete was a very good-looking guy.

"You guys wanna dance?" Cassidy asked eagerly.

"Yeah," Pete and Brandon agreed in unison.

Without hesitation, Cassidy took Pete's hand in hers and pulled him a few feet away, while Marissa took a step closer to Brandon. A Michael Jackson song was now blaring out of the speakers and the four of them began moving to the beat.

Pete pulled Cassidy close to him as they danced. The scent of his aftershave was thick, but Cassidy found it alluring. She brought her arms up to rest her hands on his shoulders while his large hands came to rest on her hips. She felt a tingle shoot up her spine. She had not had a boyfriend, or any romantic contact, in almost a year. Strong, firm, male hands grasping

18

her hips, with fingertips resting on her butt, felt like a jolt. A good jolt.

Cassidy and Pete's eyes locked as they moved to the beat. They were lost in their own little bubble, unaware of how long they danced. Cassidy was vaguely aware of people jostling around them, and the sounds of many different artists playing through the many speakers, but her focus was on Pete. His touch, his smile, his smell. Cassidy felt elated.

"Want a drink?" Pete asked, his lips right next to Cassidy's ear. She shivered involuntarily.

"Yeah," Cassidy said with a big nod. Pete took Cassidy's hand in his and led her through the crowd and over to the bar. They quickly ordered their drinks, a Budweiser for Pete and a Midori Sour for Cassidy, and they found their way to one of the high tables.

"Tell me about yourself," Pete asked over the music with a smile as he took a swig of his beer.

"What do you want to know?" Cassidy asked with a giggle, chewing on the tip of the black straw in her drink.

"Where are you from?" Pete asked.

"Meadville, but I've been living right in Erie since graduating college," Cassidy explained.

"Where did you go?"

"Edinboro, so I've always been in the area."

"You've never left Western Pennsylvania?" Pete asked.

"Oh, we've gone on vacations around the country, and I did a semester abroad my junior year."

"Edinburgh, I'm guessing?" Pete teased.

"Yep," Cassidy chuckled. "Edinboro has an exchange program with Edinburgh in Scotland. EU students can go to other places, but most of us go to Scotland, as the application is easier."

"Did you like it?"

"I loved it! I went fall of junior year and came home for Christmas. It was perfect," Cassidy told him, smiling as she thought of her time in Scotland.

"That's really cool."

"What about you? Where are you from?" Cassidy asked, taking a large sip from her straw.

"Lorain, just outside of Cleveland," Pete told her. Cassidy nodded. She could have easily guessed northern Ohio or further in the mid-west. His accent was much thicker than hers. Erieites had a mix of a diluted Pittsburgh and a diluted mid-west accent, creating a dialect of their own.

"What brings you to Erie?" Cassidy asked him curiously.

"I'm looking to get a coaching job. Didn't have any luck in Cleveland, so I'm going to try Erie," Pete explained.

"What do you coach?"

"Baseball. I played for Ohio State. I love it. I know I won't make it in the majors but would love to coach," he told her.

Cassidy's face lit up. "Ahh! I played softball!"

"Oh, yeah?" Pete asked, looking amused.

"Yes. Started in third grade and played all through college. Travel teams, tournaments, the works. I loved it! Actually, the only time I didn't play was when I was in Scotland for three months."

"I was the same with baseball! Started young and played the whole way through," Pete said, taking a large gulp of his beer.

"Where are you looking to coach?" Cassidy asked.

"I've put my resume out to a few of the universities in the area. If I don't hear anything I'm going to hit the New England area. I do have a cousin up at UCONN, which would give me an in. I'd be happy to coach for them, but I thought I'd try something closer to home first," Pete explained.

"Wow, well, good luck!" Cassidy said, raising her glass in his direction. Pete smiled and clinked his bottle on her glass. They both drained the contents of their respective drinks.

"Wait here, let me get us a treat," Pete said with a wink. Cassidy giggled, a large smile spreading over her face. She was on cloud nine. She watched him walk back to the bar before starting to look around. The club was filling up a bit more. She gazed around the dance floor for a long moment before spotting Marissa's pink dress. She was energetically dancing with Brandon, and both seemed to be having the best time. They were starting to spin and Cassidy watched, in awe of Marissa's dancing skills in high heels. There was a clink on the table and she saw that Pete had returned.

"What do we have here?" Cassidy asked playfully, looking down where Pete had set a number of shot glasses full of clear liquid.

"I thought we could use some shots before we go back out on the dance floor," Pete smirked.

"Oh, yeah?"

"Come on, I just got three for each of us," Pete said as he divided the glasses and pushed three towards Cassidy.

"Fine," Cassidy agreed. While she had spent the majority of her weekends in college partying, she had slowed down considerably since graduating. These would be shots three, four, and five in the last two hours. Plus her mixed drink. She made a mental note to cut herself off after downing these shots. Her tolerance was not what it used to be.

"Ya ready?" Pete asked, raising the first glass in the air.

"Ready," Cassidy agreed, picking up the glass on her right.

"And, go!" Pete said. Both Pete and Cassidy downed the contents of the first glass and immediately moved on to shots two and three, slamming the glasses down on the table after completing each.

"Ahhhh!" they cried in unison, Cassidy laughing hysterically. Her head was already buzzing.

"Wanna dance?" Pete asked.

"Yeah!" Cassidy extended her hand to him. Pete took it and quickly pulled her through to the dance floor. They immediately started jumping along to the Devo song and Cassidy felt her heart race with exhilaration. By the end of the song, she could feel the alcohol had hit her system. The room was getting a tad blurry and her dancing had become a little wobbly and off kilter, but still in a fun, whimsical way. She was at the point of drunkenness where you believe anything is possible – also, that everything is funny. The sweet spot.

Cassidy and Pete were happily swaying in each other's arms when Cassidy looked up and saw Pete looking down at her. Her heart skipped as their eyes locked. Suddenly the air felt thick. The music faded into a loud hum, and Cassidy felt like the crowd around them had disappeared. Pete slowly lowered his head. Cassidy fluttered her eyes closed in anticipation just before his lips pressed against hers.

A spark shot up Cassidy's spine at the touch of his kiss. His lips were soft yet firm. She gripped his broad shoulders tightly as she felt him wrap his arms around her waist.

Pete's lips moved firmly against hers for a long moment before slowly pulling back. Cassidy involuntarily let out a gasp as they pulled apart. They looked at one another and smiled.

"Wow," Pete said breathily.

"Yeah," Cassidy agreed with a grin. Pete leaned down once more to place a quick peck on her lips before they resumed dancing to Billy Idol.

# Chapter 3

The next hour was a bit of a blur for Cassidy. There was loud music, dancing, and more kissing; however, later she wouldn't be able to remember any specifics. Finally, she started to feel her feet ache from dancing, and the whimsical room-spins of drunkenness morphed into exhaustion. She was ready to leave.

"Hey," Cassidy called to Pete over the music. "I think I need to tap out."

"You okay?" Pete asked, still grooving to the beat from the speakers.

"Yeah, I'm just wearing thin. Time for me to go." Cassidy had spent years at EU exceeding her limits and learning the consequences. She knew when she needed to stop.

"Oh! Well, my place is just around the corner. Seriously, a five-minute walk, tops. I'll get you some coffee," Pete offered, sliding his arms around her waist. Cassidy bit her bottom lip as she thought. She knew exactly what would happen if she agreed to go back with Pete. After a quick moment of internal debate, she decided that was exactly what she wanted to happen.

She gave a small shrug. "Sure," she said.

Pete's face lit up before he quickly composed himself. Cassidy almost wanted to laugh.

"Ready to head out, then?" Pete asked, leaning down so his lips were right next to her ear. Cassidy felt a tingle shoot through her body.

"Let me find Marissa and say goodbye." Cassidy told him.

"Oh yeah, I wonder if she and Brandon hit it off?" Pete took Cassidy's hand and led her off the dancefloor. Cassidy chewed her lip once more. She really hoped Marissa was having as good a night as she was. She would feel like a terrible friend if she found out Marissa had been miserable.

Pete and Cassidy weaved their way through the high tables and people drinking and laughing all around them, their eyes peeled for their respective friends. After a couple minutes of searching, Cassidy spotted Marissa's pink dress out of the corner of her eye.

"Over there," Cassidy said, tugging on Pete's hand and pulling him towards the row of circular booths on the far wall.

Marissa and Brandon were cozied up in the second booth from the left, drinks on the table in front of them. They were talking with their faces very close together. Cassidy smiled. Her friend looked happy. Perfect.

"Hey!" Cassidy called happily as they got to the booth. She dropped Pete's hand and climbed in, snuggling up next to Marissa.

25

"Oh, hi!" Marissa said excitedly.

"What's up, man?" Pete asked Brandon. Brandon simply nodded back at him with a smile.

Cassidy leaned in close to whisper in Marissa's ear. "I'm going to go home with Pete," she admitted with a sheepish grin.

"Who's Pete?" Marissa asked seriously.

Cassidy stared at her. "Him!" she said nodding behind her.

"Ohhh!" Marisa's eyes widened with excitement.

Cassidy smiled at her before glancing up at the guys, making sure they weren't listening – but they had scooted over to the other side of the U-shaped booth and were having quiet discussion of their own. Good.

"How's it going for you?" Cassidy asked.

"Oh, so good! Brandon – is that his name?" Marissa paused, thinking. Cassidy could tell she was even further gone than she was.

"Yes."

"Yeah, Brandon is really nice. I think he's the one," Marissa said in the overly-serious tone that very inebriated people use when trying to make a point.

"'The one' what?" Cassidy asked, starting to giggle.

"The ONE one!" Marissa insisted. Cassidy let out a laugh.

"Uh huh."

"On my wedding day, I'm going to remind you that you laughed at me," Marissa said.

"Okay, you do that." Both girls laughed. Pete and Brandon glanced over at them, causing them to laugh harder.

"Oh, oh, wait!" Cassidy said, trying to settle her giggles.

"What?" Marissa asked, still chuckling.

"Did that bartender ever come by for his dance?" Cassidy

asked. Marissa tipped her head back in exasperation.

"He totally did. Well, we walked up to the bar, and Brandon… that's his name, right?"

"You really need to work on remembering that," Cassidy advised.

"It's a confusing name!"

"It's not."

"Anyway," Marissa continued, "Brandon and I went to get drinks and of course that bartender was there. He starts going 'oh hey, where's my dance?' and I just tried to ignore him, ya know? But he just kept asking. And Brandon is like 'I think she's hanging out with me, mate' which is so sweet, but the bartender dude was not getting the picture." Marissa sighed.

"And?"

"And he ended up charging us like double for the drinks. It was so dumb," Marissa whined. Cassidy rolled her eyes.

"Bartender dude is a douche."

"Major!" Marissa agreed.

"But are you good here with Brandon?" Cassidy asked.

"Oh, yes. You go have lots of fun!" Marissa teased. Cassidy smirked at her.

"Okay, I'll be back home tomorrow."

"And you'll tell me everything?"

"Always!" Cassidy assured her, before giving her a playful kiss on the cheek and scooting out of the booth. Pete glanced over when he saw her get up and stood and wrapped up his conversation as well.

"See ya, man," Pete said to Brandon. The two shook hands and grinned at one another.

"Ready?" Cassidy asked Pete.

"Let's go," he said, taking her hand and leading Cassidy

out of the club and onto the street. The fresh air felt wonderful on Cassidy's face. The club was so very warm and stuffy; the warm summer breeze was a welcome change.

"I love summer," Cassidy mused as she followed Pete down the street.

"Yeah, it's fuckin' A," Pete agreed.

While Cassidy was very happy to be outside at the moment, her feet were really starting to hurt as they walked another block through the city. She was grateful she was wearing flats, at least. She had no idea how Marissa and other girls did this stuff in heels.

"Just up here," Pete said, pointing to the grey apartment building on the block in front of them. Cassidy scrunched up her face slightly. She knew this building, but she had no idea why. More than generally knowing her way downtown, there was something very familiar about this place, but she couldn't quite place it at the moment. She blamed the alcohol. Her head was still buzzing.

"Great," Cassidy said, lost in thought.

"You alright?" Pete asked as they crossed the street to his block.

"Yeah, sorry. I just feel like I've been here before," Cassidy said. Pete shrugged, seeming less concerned about the coincidence than she was.

"Maybe it was some other guy you met," Pete suggested, holding the building door open and letting Cassidy inside. She sighed inwardly. Great, Pete took her for a slut. While she knew he had reason to think so, given that she was going home with him, she'd rather not have had the confirmation.

Cassidy and Pete got into the elevator. Pete pressed the button for the third floor and they started to ascend. It was one of those creepy, black metal, cagy-looking elevators. Cassidy hated them. But it was once again, annoyingly familiar. The elevator car lurched and creaked upward as Cassidy frowned at the open wall and pipes. Then the car stopped, and the door groaned as it opened onto a grey hallway.

Pete led Cassidy to the second door on the left and unlocked the door. Inside was a large, open studio apartment with exposed brick along the exterior wall. Black metal beams across the ceiling gave it an industrial feel.

Adding to the masculine industrial design of the apartment, the whole place felt like a total bachelor pad. Two full cases of beer sat next to the fridge. The sink was filled with dishes. The only pieces of furniture, aside from the bed and a small dresser in the far end of the studio, were in the center living area – a sofa and a chair, both black leather, and a dark wood coffee table covered in girlie magazines, multiple half-filled glasses, and an open pack of cigarettes.

Cassidy felt like she was back in college visiting her then-boyfriend at his frat house.

"Welcome!" Pete said proudly. Cassidy glanced back and gave him a small smile. While she found the apartment filthy, she'd grown up with four brothers. Slovenly males did not faze her in the least.

"Great space," Cassidy lied. Pete walked over to the small, L-shaped counter in the kitchen area.

"Want a drink?" Pete offered.

"Sure, thanks," Cassidy said. "Can I use your bathroom quick?"

"Yeah, just over there." Pete pointed towards the sleeping area. Cassidy nodded and found her way. The bathroom was a decent size and covered in dark green tile. While it was slightly untidy, it was at least clean and free of gross stains or concerning smells. However, the aftershave scent remained thick. She quickly used the bathroom and returned to the kitchen area to find Pete waiting for her with a shot glass. She set her purse on the floor of the living room before joining him in the kitchen.

"What is this?" Cassidy asked playfully, raising an eyebrow at him.

"One more," Pete insisted.

"I'm already in your apartment, you don't need to drug me," Cassidy remarked sarcastically.

"I wouldn't!" Pete said, looking mildly offended. Cassidy ignored him and took the shot glass from his outstretched hand with a sigh. She really had been hoping for some coffee or water. Oh, well.

"Cheers!" Cassidy and Pete said in unison before downing the contents and setting the empty glasses on the counter.

"Come here," Pete whispered. Cassidy couldn't help but smile up at him. He was very handsome, and he had been good to her all night. She took a large step forward and placed her hands on his shoulders. Pete gave her a quick smile before leaning down and connecting his lips to hers.

The kiss deepened, and Cassidy felt a flutter in her belly. She gripped his shoulders a little tighter as his arms snaked around her waist, pulling their bodies together. Cassidy slid her right hand up to the side of his head; his incredibly short hair tickled her fingertips slightly. She liked the feeling.

They kissed until they were breathless, their mouths moving

in perfect synch. Cassidy felt a warmth begin to spread from her core out to her limbs. It had been far too long since she had felt this way.

Pete's left hand slid down from her lower back onto her butt and gave a firm squeeze. Cassidy gasped loudly at the touch. She felt Pete smile against her mouth.

"Come with me," Pete whispered pulling his lips a centimeter off of hers before reattaching them in slow, gentle pecks. Using his hold on her backside, he slowly led her across the apartment towards his bed. Cassidy found herself struggling to walk, and stumbled every few steps. Between Pete's touch, the constant kisses, the alcohol, and walking mostly backwards, she was at his mercy to get there without crashing to the floor.

Cassidy finally felt the mattress against the back of her knees. Pete wrapped his arms tightly around her once more and they resumed their deep passionate kisses. Cassidy again felt sparks shooting up her spine as their mouths moved together. She was on fire.

Without warning, Pete quickly spun them around so he was the one at the mattress and he took a seat, pulling Cassidy close so she was standing between his knees. She pulled back for a moment to look at him once more. In this position, she was almost an inch taller than him. They smiled at one another, and Pete reached up to gently rub his thumb along her cheek. Cassidy bit her lip at his soft touch. She felt like putty.

Cassidy rested her left hand on his shoulder and her right on his cheek. His jaw was strong and firm, clean-shaven. He must have shaved right before coming to the club.

She leaned forward and connected her lips to his. As he kissed her back, she could feel his hands slide up her back

31

to the top of her dress and begin to fumble with the zipper. Cassidy felt a strong tingle of anticipation. Within seconds she felt air on her bare back as the zipper lowered. Pete wasted no time in sliding her dress down her body until it lay pooled around her ankles. Cassidy gave a slight shiver. She was left in nothing but her light pink panties. She felt quite exposed, especially as Pete was still fully clothed.

He pulled back to look at her. Cassidy bit her lip as she felt his eyes on her.

"Holy shit, you're fit," Pete breathed, his eyes locked on her stomach. Cassidy chuckled.

"What can I say? After years of competitive sports, I developed a love of exercise," she said truthfully.

"You're so hot," Pete said, finally looking her in the eye. Cassidy blushed and kissed him again.

Pete immediately deepened the kiss, which Cassidy happily reciprocated. They had only been kissing for a long seconds when Cassidy felt Pete's fingertips on the hem of her panties. She quickly pushed on his chest and firmly shook her head.

"What?" Pete asked, looking confused.

"We're going to even things up first," Cassidy told him. She stepped out of her dress and kicked it a couple feet behind her, kicking off her sandals in the process, as well. Cassidy reached down and pulled at Pete's red shirt.

"Oh!" Pete reached up to help pull off his shirt. He stood and quickly removed his shoes and jeans, tossing them all aside, before reaching down and removing his socks, as well. He returned to his seat on the bed in just his dark blue boxer shorts. Cassidy smiled at his obvious eagerness.

She took a moment to drink him in with her eyes. He was extremely muscular and toned. He had a large tattoo on the front of his right shoulder and top of his chest. Cassidy couldn't quite place what it was, but it looked like something Japanese.

"Ya commin'?" Pete asked with a smirk. Cassidy simply nodded and climbed up on the mattress so her knees were on either side of Pete. He rested his hands on her hips while hers rested on his firm chest and she pressed her lips down on his. They shared three long kisses before Pete tightened his grip on Cassidy's hips and flipped them over so she was flat on her back on the center of the mattress with Pete stretched out on top of her.

"Ooof." Cassidy grunted involuntarily at the sudden movements and the feeling of Pete's weight on her.

Pete tenderly brushed a few strands of her long hair behind her ear before kissing her once more. Cassidy felt a sudden hardness push into her thigh as they kissed. The feeling sent the tingling from her spine down to her toes. She nipped at his bottom lip a couple of times before he crashed his mouth back onto hers and deepened the kiss. Pete's hands freely roamed Cassidy's mostly bare body, her back, sides, stomach and breasts, occasionally slipping down to her thighs.

Cassidy, in turn, ran her hands up and down his back and sides. His entire body was firm and muscular. She had never been in bed with someone as fit as he was. She couldn't decide if she was excited about that or not. What she was excited about was Pete's continued touch on her body with his hands and mouth.

Slowly, both of Pete's hands found their way to her hips and his fingers looped into the hem of her panties. He started to slide them down her legs. Cassidy pulled her mouth off of Pete's to help him remove her final covering and toss them on the floor, before returning the favor and helping Pete remove his boxers.

Within seconds they were both completely naked. Cassidy felt her heart give a weird thud. There was something terrifying, liberating, exciting, and yet overwhelming about being completely naked in front of a new guy. But she didn't have long to process her current situation; Pete quickly leaned back over her and kissed her neck enthusiastically. His need for her pressed firmly into her lower stomach, and she shivered again. They were so close.

"Pete," Cassidy said with a gasp, trying to focus as his tongue slid just below her left ear.

"Hmmm," Pete grunted.

"You have a condom, right?" Cassidy asked.

"Fuck," Pete said as he pulled his mouth off of her and sat up. Cassidy bit her lip nervously. Was that a fuck yes or a fuck no?

He awkwardly crawled over to his nightstand and slid the drawer open, digging frantically inside. Cassidy watched shamelessly. His whole body looked strong – especially his large, protruding member that looked ready to go. Cassidy let a low, deep breath as she stared at it. She quickly shook her head and turned away. She had never been one of those girls that was obsessed with dicks. She liked them, but never went out of her way to see them or got all giddy about them. However, at this current moment, her body wanted his. Perhaps it really had been too long since her last time. 'Get it together, Banker,' Cassidy scolded herself mentally.

"Got one!" Pete said happily, holding up the square package in his fingers.

"Good," Cassidy said, watching him tear open the plastic

with his teeth. He settled down to lie on his side next to her. "Here, let me do that," she offered, taking the condom out of his hands and slowly rolling it onto his dick. She felt him watching her as she gently trailed her fingertips along his length.

"You ready?" Pete asked with a grin. Cassidy simply nodded. Pete pressed his lips to hers and leaned her back onto the mattress as he climbed on top. He used his knee to push her legs apart and settled himself right at her opening.

Without any hesitation, Pete pushed forward and entered. Cassidy gasped, pulling her mouth back from his. Pete quickly found a rhythm and Cassidy dug her nails into his shoulder blades to hold on. He completely filled her, pushing her whole body deep down into the mattress. The faster he moved, the more her breathing began to pick up. She got warmer and warmer, heat spreading from her core. Cassidy started to gasp; Pete placed a sloppy kiss on her lips before letting out a loud groan and giving a hearty shudder.

It was over already. Cassidy gritted her teeth as she felt Pete slide out of her. He collapsed at her side. She glanced over at him; he was clearly lost in post-coital bliss.

"Babe," he whispered, kissing her on the cheek quickly before slowly getting his breathing back in order. Cassidy chewed on her lip a bit longer with a weird feeling in her belly. The moment had gone from hot to cold far too quickly. What an anti-climactic night. After a few long minutes of lying in silence, Cassidy glanced over to her side once more to find Pete's eyes were closed. Was he asleep?

She sat up and gave his shoulder a hard shove. He let out a groan and rolled over onto his stomach. Back to sleep he went. Cassidy rolled her eyes. She hopped up off the bed and went to collect her clothes. She redressed quickly before heading to the bathroom and relieved herself once more before leaving. As she was washed her hands, she glanced at herself in the mirror. She looked rough. Her make-up was starting to smear and her eyeliner had definitely spread, giving her the start of a racoon look. Her hair was frizzy and tangled. She tried to run her fingers through it to fix it, but that only made it looks slightly fluffier. She frowned at herself for a moment.

"Pete," Cassidy called as she walked back to the bed. Pete was still passed out on his stomach, completely naked atop his comforter. She took a seat on the edge of the mattress.

"Hey, I'm going to go," Cassidy said, a little louder as she patted his shoulder.

"Hmmm," Pete grunted.

"I'm going to go," Cassidy repeated.

"Kay. You're hot. Want me to call you, write your name and number by the phone in the kitchen," Pete instructed sleepily without moving or even turning his head to look at her.

"Okay, bye," Cassidy said in a mocking sing-song voice as she got off the bed. She quickly grabbed her purse from the living area. She paused a moment as she looked over at the phone and large pad next to it. After a quick internal debate, she decided to not leave her number. Cassidy let out one last sigh before departing the apartment and closing the door behind her.

# Chapter 4

"I'm an idiot," Cassidy whispered to herself as she walked down the hallway, back to the creepy elevator. It seemed even more ominous now that she was riding it alone. It finally rattled to the ground floor and the door opened onto the lobby. Cassidy glanced at the clock over the closed front desk. 1:45AM. She sighed. It had been an eventful evening. She wandered past the mailboxes to the large payphone hanging on the wall and rummaged in her purse. She found a quarter, then picked up the Yellow Pages to find the phone number for a taxi.

Cassidy had just flipped to the Ts when she was startled by sound of the front door opening.

"What the hell are you doing here?" a familiar voice said in very surprised tone. Cassidy jumped. Her eldest brother, Alex, was standing just inside the door.

"What the hell are you doing here?" Cassidy retorted, shocked.

"I live here!"

Cassidy froze. Everything clicked. This was Alex's building.

She had been here before. That's why she'd recognized it when Pete first brought her there. "Oh, yeah," Cassidy said with a smile.

"What are you doing here?" Alex asked, sounding calmer.

Cassidy blanked. She was not in the mood to tell her brother that she'd just had a one-night stand. Ew. "Oh, just a night out in the city. I knew there was a phone here, so I'm calling for a cab," Cassidy lied. She shrugged up at Alex, never losing her smile.

Alex simply stared at her. He clearly didn't believe her. "Mmmhmmm," he hummed, running a hand through his wavy dark blond hair before crossing his arms over his chest.

"I'm just calling a cab! Everything's fine," Cassidy insisted.

"You don't look fine," Alex said with a grimace.

"What's wrong with how I look?" Cassidy asked, though she fully knew the answer.

"You look like a hooker!"

Cassidy scowled. "I do not," she spat - though he honestly wasn't too far off.

"Oh god, is that what you do now?" Alex asked, mock-horrified.

Cassie sighed. "Really?"

"I don't know what you do with your time," Alex said with a shrug.

Cassidy smacked his arm and he chuckled proudly. "You're an idiot," she grumbled.

"Yeah, but I'm your favorite of the idiots," Alex beamed.

Cassidy thought about it. He was kind of right. While she did love all of her brothers, there was something special about her relationship with Alex.

"I guess," she admitted reluctantly.

"Come on upstairs," Alex offered.

"I'm going to call a cab; I'm ready to go home and crash."

"Come on up and sober up a bit first," he suggested.

"Alex, I'm tired."

"I know, and you can crash here if you want – but just come on up and get some water and food in you. Please," he insisted. "I know you think you still feel okay now, but you get in that taxi and you're going to barf before you get back to your place."

Cassidy thought about it. She did want to go back to her own apartment and bed, but she really could use some food and water sooner rather than.

"Okay," she agreed, closing the Yellow Pages and returning the quarter to her purse. Alex smiled.

"Great! Laura will be happy to see you," he said, walking backwards through the lobby. Cassidy nodded and followed him. She was excited to see Laura, too. And quite grateful that she and her brother were both night owls right now. Alex led them back, once again, to the elevator.

"Oh, no," Cassidy whined. "I don't want to ride the death lift again. Isn't there another way up?"

"There are stairs, but there's no way in hell you'd make it up four flights in your condition," he said.

Cassidy groaned. He was right. The elevator dinged as the door opened and the two Banker siblings entered the cart. Alex pressed the button for the fourth floor and the ascent began.

"Bleh, I hate this," Cassidy sighed.

"Sick already?"

"No! Well, kinda. But I just hate this thing. It's so creepy."

"It's part of the aesthetic," Alex replied haughtily. Cassidy couldn't help but laugh.

The elevator lurched to the fourth floor, the door dinged and opened once more. This grey hallway looked exactly like the floor below it, where Pete lived. Cassidy followed her brother to the last door at the very end of the hall. Alex quickly unlocked the door and led them inside. The apartment was much larger than Pete's. While it had the same industrial loft features, it was a completely different layout with a large kitchen at the entrance of the loft and the living room nestled against the far wall. On the other side of the kitchen was a hallway to two bedrooms and a shared bathroom. Cassidy found it much homier than Pete's apartment.

"Laura, we have a visitor," Alex called, closing the door behind them.

"A visitor?" Laura asked, rushing into the kitchen. She beamed when she saw Cassidy, and Cassidy returned the smile. Laura was tall and thin, about the same height as Alex. She had shoulder-length, dark brown hair with a few streaks of a cool royal blue dyed throughout. She wore a baggy yellow tank top and ratty grey sweatpants covered in paint stains. Only she could make it look good. Laura had an effortless cool that no one could match – especially since it was paired with genuine niceness. Cassidy had always liked Laura. Their lifestyles were incredibly different, but Cassidy still found a kindred spirit in her.

"Hi," Cassidy said happily.

"Cassidy!" Laura gushed as she walked over and gave her a big hug.

"Found this working girl loitering in our lobby," Alex teased. He grabbed a large glass from the cupboard and went to the sink to fill it.

"Shut up," Cassidy sassed.

"I think you'd do a good business. Make some nice money," Laura said with a wink.

"Thanks – I'll update my business cards," Cassidy smiled. Alex groaned.

"Please do not encourage her to be a street walker," he pleaded, handing Cassidy the glass of water.

"You started it," Laura pointed out. Cassidy wanted to make a remark, but she was distracted by the glass of water. It looked glorious. She quickly brought it to her lips and started drinking, draining the contents in less than a minute. It was heavenly. She hadn't realized how dehydrated she was until that moment.

"Can I get another?" Cassidy asked her brother.

"Of course! Help yourself," he said with smile. Cassidy refilled her glass once more while Alex lit a cigarette before reaching into the pantry for a snack.

"Come on over to the living room and take a seat – you look like you need a break," Laura said. Cassidy followed her to the large living room. The far wall was exposed brick, and the room was filled with cozy, mismatched sofas and chairs that all worked together with an eclectic charm. A small TV sat in the corner on an old A/V cart Laura had rescued from a school dumpster the year before. It had lost a wheel, so they used a small block of wood to steady it. The center shelves were filled with Laura's art supplies. Next to the TV cart in front of the large window was an enormous easel with a half-painted canvas resting on it.

Cassidy plopped down on the closest sofa and curled her legs up underneath her.

"What are you working on?" she asked, taking another large gulp of water.

"Sunset over the water," Laura said with a smile. She walked over to her easel and picked up her brush once more, dabbing it in some paint and applying a stroke to the canvas.

"Nice," Cassidy mused. Alex walked past her and plopped down on her right.

"Here," he said, tilting the box of Cheez-Its towards his sister.

"Ooo, thanks." She reached in and grabbed a handful, ungracefully funneling them into her mouth. Alex watched her with a bemused smile.

"So, what are you doing downtown at this hour?" Laura asked casually, her eyes focused on her canvas. She gingerly dabbed her brush in one spot.

"I went to a club," Cassidy replied, her mouth full of crackers.

"And now you're here? Oh, shit! You went home with someone in our building?" Laura cried, spinning around, her eyes wide with intrigue.

Cassidy shrugged her shoulders playfully and took another drink to wash down the crackers. She felt Alex glaring at her and did her best to ignore him.

"Maybe," she admitted with a smirk. Alex made a disgusted groan before taking a long drag from his cigarette.

"Ignore him. I'm happy for you! It's been almost a year since you and Kevin broke up. You needed this."

Cassidy blushed and dropped her head. Her almost-sister-in-law had an opinion on her sex life. Great. "Don't get all weird. It was just tonight. I wanted to go out and blow off some steam, and I did. This is not a new beau."

She reached over to the box Alex was holding. He playfully pulled the box a few inches back, just out of his sister's reach.

42

Cassidy let out a small sigh. Alex held the box out towards her and just as Cassidy reached out he yanked it back again, causing Cassidy to teeter slightly.

"Give me the damn box!" Cassidy said loudly. Alex chuckled and brought the box back towards her. Cassidy grabbed the entire thing and moved it to her lap as she helped herself to another handful.

"So bitchy for a working girl who just got paid," Alex teased.

Cassidy shot him an annoyed glare. "How's the novel coming, Dear Abby?" she jabbed back.

"Alright, guys," Laura cut in, still focused on her painting. Alex and Cassidy glanced at each other and gave a quick shrug. An unspoken truce.

"Where do you guys go when you go out?" Cassidy asked.

"There's a great bar next to the playhouse. It's so much fun. Lots of artists there. Someone's always playing live music, the walls are covered in murals…"

"And they make one hell of a Brandy Old Fashioned," Alex interrupted.

"Ah, priorities," Cassidy said sarcastically.

"What is it with you and that drink?" Laura asked, turning and setting her hands on her hips.

"They're good!" Alex said.

"It's an old man drink," Laura scoffed.

"No, it's not. It's classy."

"Pop Pop drank Brandy Old Fashioneds," Cassidy pointed out.

"Pop Pop was pure class!"

"Pop Pop was old."

"And classy." Alex cocked his head to the side as he looked

at his sister.

"Fine, but the vital fact here is that you drink old people drinks," Cassidy smirked.

"Told you!" Laura chimed in. Alex rolled his eyes and groaned in defeat.

"Oh, hey, we have to remember to pick up the stuff to make curry tomorrow," Alex remarked, perking up.

"Already got it," Laura said, returning her attention to her easel.

"You're making curry?" Cassidy raised an eyebrow suspiciously at Alex.

"Yes!" he replied. "We've made it a few times."

"My old college roommate, Jennifer, and her boyfriend are coming over tomorrow," Laura told her.

"And she loves curry?" Cassidy asked.

"She introduced me to it. I literally had never had it until I roomed with her."

"And Laura got hooked and got me into it," Alex explained, flicking his cigarette into the ashtray beside him. "We decided to try and make it ourselves last year. Seems to get better each time."

"We finally know what we're doing," Laura added. Cassidy chuckled. Cooking had never been Alex's forte; this culinary adventure must have been completely supervised by Laura.

"When did we first have a curry?" Cassidy asked Alex.

"I think I was in late high school... at one of dad's work parties, I think."

"Oh, yeah, what was that Indian holiday? Dibadi?"

"Diwali," Laura corrected.

"Ahh, yes."

"Yeah, and mom was annoyed that people kept trying to put

44

leis and scarves on her because she wore that blue suit that she loved, and hated not showing it off," Alex said with a chuckle.

"Oh, my god, yes. And Ben almost threw a tantrum because there weren't any French fries and that was all he wanted." Cassidy started to laugh at the memory.

"Meanwhile, Matty ate four plates of food and then barfed in the fountain outside in the front courtyard," Alex laughed, shaking his head. Cassidy laughed loudly.

"How have I never heard about this before?" Laura asked through giggles, setting her paintbrush down.

"I don't know! I haven't thought of that night in years," Alex shrugged, his laughter beginning to slow.

"We were in true form, that night. Dad was so embarrassed." Cassidy grinned sheepishly.

"Eh, you, Eric, and I had fun," Alex noted.

"True." Cassidy smiled at her brother, enjoying the forgotten memory.

A comfortable silence fell over the room as the laughter came to an end. Cassidy felt a wave of exhaustion wash over her.

"Can I use your phone?" Cassidy asked with a yawn. She was tired.

"What for?" Alex asked. He made a grab for the box of Cheez-Its, but Cassidy saw him coming and knocked his thigh with her curled up leg. Alex rolled his eyes.

"To call a cab. I'm really tired and I do want to crash. I appreciate the water and snacks; definitely needed them more than I realized, but I'm ready to go."

"Alex, don't let your little sister take a taxi in the middle of the night," Laura said, returning to her canvas. Cassidy scrunched her nose. "Little sister?"

"Wasn't planning on it," Alex said. He stood up from the couch and extinguished his cigarette in the ashtray.

"Are you holding me hostage?"

"Ideally, but you'd be an absolute nightmare to keep locked up," Alex said as he stretched his arms above him. Cassidy smiled.

"So?" she asked.

"So, I'm going to drive you home. Come on, get your shit," Alex said as he walked past Cassidy.

"Really? Thanks!" she said happily. She was honestly thrilled that she didn't have to call for a cab. The late-night drivers were always creeps. She quickly finished the last few sips of her water and stood herself up.

"I'll be back in a jiff," Alex said to Laura, walking over and giving her a quick peck on the lips.

"'Kay," Laura replied cheerily. "Cassidy, it was nice seeing you. We'll have to do dinner sometime, you and me."

"I would love that." Cassidy followed Alex back to the kitchen. She set her empty glass on the counter and picked up her purse.

"Ready?" Alex asked, twirling his key ring on his finger as he waited by the front door.

"Yep."

Despite making a fairly good argument for the stairs, Cassidy found herself bullied back into the creepy elevator for the fourth time that night, which she frankly felt was cruel. The siblings made their way to Alex's white Honda Accord parked in the three-story parking garage next door. Once in the car, they weaved out to the main entrance and onto the street.

"Thanks for the ride," Cassidy said as she looked through the cassette caddy that had been on the floor of the passenger seat.

"No problem."

"Ooo, Billy Ocean!" Cassidy said with a smile, pulling out the cassette and popping it in the tape deck. A few bars 'Caribbean Queen' played before Alex spoke.

"Cassie, are you okay?" he asked seriously as they came to stop at a red light.

"Yeah, why? Do I look green? I promise I won't barf in your car."

"I appreciate that," Alex chuckled.

"Why do you ask?"

"I don't know – you aren't really the type to get shitfaced and sleep with a random guy," he said, accelerating as the light turned green.

"How do you know?" Cassidy asked with a large smirk.

Alex shot her a quick side eye glare. "I know you."

"Alex, I partied all the time in college. You do know I'm not a virgin, right?"

"Ugh, yeah," Alex sighed. "But, you've had boyfriends, relationships. Who the hell was this guy tonight?"

"Are you really asking me this? You wouldn't be happy if I asked you who you're sleeping with."

"The answer would be easy: Laura." Suddenly both Alex and Cassidy started to chuckle. It felt good.

"Are you mad at me?" Cassidy asked finally.

"Why would I be mad?"

"You shouldn't be, but I thought maybe you would be because I hung up on you last night – but honestly, it was late and you woke me up, and –"

"I'm not mad, Cassie," Alex interrupted.

"Oh," Cassidy said.

"I'm just concerned. I don't want you acting stupid just because you're mad at Eric."

"I have no idea what you're talking about," Cassidy replied firmly. "I went out tonight because I haven't gone out in weeks. What happened with Pete was not planned."

"Pete? Is that tonight's mystery man?" Alex teased. There was a hint of venom in his voice.

"Ugh, are we back at my apartment yet?" Cassidy sighed, tipping her head back onto the head rest.

"Pete who?" Alex asked. Cassidy suddenly felt a rock at the pit of her stomach. She had no idea what Pete's last name was. She'd just had sex without knowing the guy's full name. She had never done that before. She couldn't tell if she felt ashamed or liberated. She wanted to feel liberated, but Alex was right – random one-night stands had never been her style. She felt shame start to creep in.

"Do you not know?" Alex pushed. Cassidy could not admit it to him.

"Of course I know!" she lied. "I'm just not telling you. I don't want you chasing the poor bastard down."

"Bastard, huh?"

Cassidy groaned in annoyance and Alex chuckled. She reached forward to turn the stereo up and put her mind to Billy Ocean's lyrics.

The car made two more turns and went down a long street before they reached the parking lot of Cassidy's apartment complex on the southern edge of the city. Alex drove up to the entryway and parked the car, letting it idle. He reached over

48

and lowered the volume on the stereo.

"You're home," he said plainly.

"Thank you, I do appreciate you," she said with a smile.

"Anytime." Cassidy leaned over and gave him a hug, which he happily reciprocated.

"Goodnight, Alex," she said as she pulled out of the embrace and opened the car door.

"Goodnight, working girl," Alex replied, looking smug.

"You're such a dick," Cassidy said, rolling her eyes. She would let him have his fun tonight – but she planned to hit him when she was sober.

"See ya!" Alex said as Cassidy climbed out of the car.

Cassidy yawned as she slowly climbed the stairs. Even though she was exhausted, she was thrilled to not be in the horrible elevator of doom once more. She unlocked her apartment door and closed it quietly behind her. The apartment was dark. It was almost 3 AM; why wouldn't it be?

Cassidy tip-toed to her room. She spent all of ten seconds debating whether she should make the extra effort to properly prepare for bed.

"Screw it," she whispered to herself before tossing her purse on the floor, kicking off her shoes, and flopping down face-first onto her mattress. She was asleep within less than a minute.

# Chapter 5

The incessant beeps from the bedside alarm clock brought Cassidy back to consciousness. She blindly reached around until her hand found the clock and smacked the OFF button. The room was draped in silence once more. She yawned widely and slowly blinked her eyes open. The sun was beaming through the window. She took a few minutes to stretch and roll before heaving herself out of bed. Standing, she looked down and saw that she was still in her party dress from last night. She groaned.

Thirty minutes later, Cassidy was showered and dressed in fresh clothes – a grey T-shirt and dark blue gym shorts – and had brushed her teeth and braided her hair. She made a bee-line for the kitchen for some food. It was 9:30 in the morning, which was late for Cassidy, who was generally an early riser. It had thrown off her usual meal schedule. She was a morning eater. She could happily skip dinner, but breakfast and morning snacks were her lifeblood.

Coffee was brewing, bread was in the toaster, and she was

pouring Corn Flakes into a bowl when Marissa's bedroom door opened.

"Hey!" Cassidy called, but it was not her roommate's voice that replied.

"Uh, hi," a deeper voice said. Cassidy's head snapped up. She was surprised to see Brandon standing at the door.

"Good morning!" Cassidy tried hard to control her expression.

"Morning!" Marissa called, running out from her bedroom and pushing around Brandon. "I'm just walking him out," she added, taking his hand and leading him down the hallway towards the door. She was still in her usual light pink nightdress, while Brandon was in the same outfit he'd worn last night.

"Okay," Cassidy said, returning her attention to her breakfast.

Cassidy was returning the margarine to the fridge when Marissa came back into view, looking sheepish.

"That was a little surprise," Cassidy teased, carrying her breakfast to the living room.

"Uh, yeah." Marissa giggled and poured herself a cup of coffee, joining Cassidy on the couch.

"Was it a good night?" Cassidy asked, taking a large bite of her toast.

"Really good. We stayed at the club for another hour after you guys left, then took a cab back here. I invited him up for coffee. We ended up talking for over an hour, about everything under the sun, then he kissed me, and well… one thing led to another." Marissa grinned.

"Nice!" Cassidy cheered. "Was he good?"

"Oh, yeah."

Cassidy giggled into her coffee. "I'm glad."

"He promised to call me tonight so we can set up a date for this week!" Marissa beamed. Cassidy felt her heart swell. She was very happy for her friend.

"Do you know what restaurant you're going to pick?" Cassidy asked, taking a spoonful of cereal.

"No idea," Marissa laughed into her coffee. "Oh, my god! How was your night?"

Cassidy simply shook her head. "Um, interesting," she said, wincing.

"Please expand on that."

"Well, I went back to Pete's apartment, and things escalated pretty quickly." Cassidy paused to take another spoonful of cereal.

"And how was it?" Marissa prompted.

"Parts were definitely very good. Quick, though."

"Oh, dear." Marissa cringed.

"It's fine. We had a nice, awkward goodbye and I left – only to find out that he lives in Alex's building... when I ran into Alex in the lobby."

Marissa's eyes bugged. "Shut up!"

"Yeah, but it kind of worked out. Alex let me come up and have some food and then drove me home so I didn't have to pay for a cab."

"Yay, Alex!" Marissa cheered. She got up to make herself something to eat.

They were planning to head to the local park for a long walk in the June sun, then spend the rest of the afternoon lounging in front of the TV and ordering Chinese food for dinner. A perfect, lazy Sunday.

Cassidy tapped her pencil on her desk as she proofread the payroll form she was working on for one of her clients. It was the Thursday afternoon before a long weekend and Cassidy was ready to go home. Saturday was July 4th, but her office, and a majority of the city, were closing on Friday the 3rd to observe the holiday.

After confirming that the form was correct, Cassidy enclosed it in a manilla envelope and set it in her outbox to be collected by a mailroom clerk. She looked up at the clock on the wall. 4:45. Only fifteen minutes left until the long weekend. She let out a dejected sigh.

"Any plans this weekend, dear?" Gladys, the secretary, asked politely. Gladys was a small, thin woman in her early seventies. She'd been a secretary with the company since the late '50s and was beloved by all of the employees – beloved and feared in equal measure.

"Not much. My family is having a bar-b-que on Saturday, but that's it," Cassidy said with a small smile. "What about you?"

"We're driving down to Pittsburgh for the weekend to watch the fireworks and do some shopping in the city," Gladys said as she adjusted the leaves of the small, half-dead fern on the corner of Cassidy's desk. Cassidy quickly made note to water the poor thing before she left for the long weekend.

"Sounds wonderful!" Cassidy smiled at the sweet woman.

"Got to get my kicks while I still can!" Gladys winked before returning to her desk. Cassidy chuckled. She hoped she was that witty when she got that old. Although she also hoped she wouldn't still be working – at least not here.

Cassidy got up from her desk, patting her navy-blue skirt straight, before walking over to the large water cooler, filling a paper cup and returning to give her pathetic desk plant some nourishment. After tossing the paper cup in the trash, she started to clear off her desk and ready herself to leave. Filling the time, as best she could.

Once all her files, ledgers, and pencils were put away, she plopped her purse on her desk and pretended to search for something very important inside as the final minutes ticked down.

"Weekend time, Banker!" a male voice boomed as Cassidy stood up to leave for the day. She resisted an eye roll.

"Yep," she replied blandly as the tall, dark-haired man approached. Devon Parks. A sleezy coworker who spent most of his work day making rude jokes and boasting about his sexual conquests. He was probably harmless, but he still made Cassidy's skin crawl.

"I'm going to be spending my time out on the lake," Devon boasted.

"Mmmhmmm," Cassidy replied, scooting past. He deliberately stood in positions that forced her to brush against him.

"You're always welcome to join us. It's going to be great! Beer, bikinis, grilling, more beer – you'd love it." Devon started to walk with Cassidy towards the reception area.

"Quite an offer," Cassidy sighed dramatically. "However, I already have plans."

"Shame. You'd look hot on the lake," Devon said with a wink.

"Goodbye, Devon," Cassidy called as she waved her arm over her head and continued walking towards the door, leaving him behind. "Bleck," she grimaced as she exited the building onto the sunny sidewalk. The July heat smacked her right in the face.

Cassidy readjusted her bags on her shoulder as she strode towards the parking garage two buildings down. Despite being downtown, there weren't any really tall buildings to block out the sun. Normally she enjoyed the summer heat, but after spending the entire day in air conditioning, the sun felt brutal.

She made the walk to her car quickly and rolled the windows down as she started up the engine. Once out on the street, Cassidy cranked up the radio, drowning out the rush hour traffic with The Bangles.

After slowly weaving through the downtown traffic, Cassidy made it to the edge of the city and turned into her complex's parking lot, letting out a loud sigh. She was happy to be home.

Cassidy put her key into the door and let herself inside the apartment, dropping her bags on the floor. "Hi!" she called. Marissa generally got home later than she did, but she thought she'd spotted Marissa's Subaru in the lot. There was no reply, but Cassidy heard rustling.

She walked down the entrance hall and into the living room to find a set of men's feet hanging over the edge of the sofa. She quickly peered around to see Brandon and Marissa laying across the couch, limbs entangled in a full-on make-out session.

Cassidy cleared her throat, amused. Each one of the pair gasped and they scrambled to untangle themselves, the shock causing Brandon to thump onto the floor.

"Hello," Cassidy said with a cheeky smile.

"Hi, Cassidy!" Marissa said, blushing slightly. She and Brandon had been dating since that fateful night at the club the month before. Brandon was now spending one night a week at their apartment, and Marissa was at his once a week. They usually worked in a date night, as well. Cassidy was happy for her friend. Brandon was good to her and they seemed to be having a wonderful time together.

"How's it going?" Cassidy asked in a sing-song voice as she made her way to the kitchen for a snack.

"Well, it was great," Brandon quipped. Cassidy was leaning into the fridge, but she very clearly heard Marissa smack his chest. Cassidy chuckled to herself.

"Poor baby," she teased, emerging with a yogurt.

"Don't worry about him," Marissa said, heaving herself up from the couch and tousling Brandon's hair as she stood. He smiled up at her before moving to take a seat on the sofa.

"Didn't expect you to be home this early," Cassidy said, dipping her spoon in her yogurt.

"I took a half day," Marissa replied, coming over to rest her elbow on the counter next to Cassidy.

"Do you two have something special planned this evening?"

"No. Brandon's leaving tonight," Marissa said glumly. Brandon joined them in the kitchen, casually slinging his arm over Marissa's shoulder.

"Leaving?" Cassidy looked back and forth between the two.

"Driving back to Indiana for the long weekend and spending it with my family," Brandon explained.

"Hmm," Cassidy hummed.

"What?"

"Oh, nothing. For some reason, I thought you were from Ohio."

"No." Brandon shook his head. "I went to Ohio State, but I'm from Indiana. Just outside of Indy."

"Nice," Cassidy nodded.

"It's, like, a six-hour drive," Marissa chimed in, turning to wrap her arms around Brandon's middle, resting her head on the side of his shoulder.

"Just under six; it's not bad," Brandon assured her.

"When are you heading out?" Cassidy asked, downing the last spoonful of yogurt.

"Don't kick him out!" Marissa sassed.

"I'm not kicking him out, I'm just asking!" Cassidy rolled her eyes.

"It's fine," Brandon assured her. "Actually, I need to be heading out pretty soon. I promised parents I'd get in before midnight."

"Traffic is heavier going east. You should have a decent drive," Cassidy told him with a smile. Brandon nodded.

"You're leaving right now?" Marissa asked glumly. She tilted her head up to look at him.

"Yeah. I wanted to be on the road by 5:30 and that's in less than ten minutes. I need to head out." Brandon placed a light kiss on her lips.

Cassidy sighed. They were annoyingly adorable.

"I'll walk you out," Marissa sighed.

"See ya, Brandon," Cassidy said cheerily.

"Until next week," Brandon nodded. He took Marissa's hand and headed towards the door.

"Be back in a couple minutes," Marissa added to Cassidy as Brandon towed her along.

The door shut behind them with a click and Cassidy took a deep breath. She trudged her way to her bedroom and changed out of her work clothes, into a pair of running shorts and a light green tee shirt. After she tossed her hair up and quickly used the bathroom, she returned to the living room and flopped ungracefully down onto the couch. She had just reached for the remote when the apartment door opened and Marissa returned down the entrance hall.

"He left?" Cassidy asked, clicking the TV on.

"Yeah," Marissa said with a sigh. She took a seat on the armrest of the sofa by Cassidy's feet.

"Want to do anything tonight?" Cassidy asked, half-watching the MTV VJ babble on about some new album.

"Eh," Marissa shrugged.

"I want to hit the gym, but after that we can order pizza, if you want," Cassidy suggested.

"The pizza part sounds better than the gym part," Marissa replied, pulling both of her feet up underneath her so she was balancing on the arm of the sofa. Cassidy watched her for a long moment before lifting her foot up and gently tapping Marissa's thigh. Marissa teetered and lost her balance, flailing wildly before she caught herself and rebalanced on the arm, both feet now firmly planted on the cushion below. Cassidy chuckled to herself.

"You don't have to go to the gym," Cassidy assured her. "But we're not ordering pizza until after I'm back."

"Fine by me," Marissa said. "I've got a new book to read."

"Okay." Cassidy stood.

"Oh good, you're going now? Hurry up – I want pizza!" Marissa said, reaching over and smacking Cassidy on the butt.

"Ow," Cassidy whined, though it didn't really hurt.

"See ya," Marissa called as Cassidy exited the apartment. She quickly made her way down the stairs and into the small gym next to the main office and hopped on the treadmill by the window.

# Chapter 6

Cassidy lazily chopped up a large head of broccoli as she waited for her Hot Pocket to finish warming in the microwave. It was just after noon on Saturday, but the long weekend made it feel like a Sunday. Marissa and Cassidy had spent their Friday off going for a long run in the park, shopping at the outlets, and going to the movies after dinner – finally seeing The Witches of Eastwick. They both loved it!

It was the first 'First Friday' in years that Cassidy hadn't spent at her parents' place, and there was an odd freedom to it. However, the freedom wouldn't last long. The only reason Friday dinner had been canceled was to allow for a family Fourth of July bar-b-que today. Cassidy was to be there no later than 3PM, and to bring a salad.

Cassidy brushed the chopped broccoli off the cutting board into the large bowl with her knife just as the microwave dinged. She quickly popped her lunch on a plate to let it cool as she grabbed a bell pepper to slice.

After adding the pepper to the salad, Cassidy took a bite of her lunch just as Marissa emerged from her bedroom, carrying the phone with her to return to its usual spot in the living room. She took a moment to untangle the long cord.

"How's Brandon?" Cassidy asked as she chewed.

"Good," Marissa replied as she set the phone down. "He got to his parents' at 11:45 and was asleep in his old room by 12:15."

"Sounds about right," Cassidy remarked absentmindedly. She was focused on her lunch.

"How's your salad coming along?" Marissa asked, coming to peer into the bowl.

"Not bad. I've got romaine, celery, carrots, broccoli, and bell peppers in there. I just want to add some pine nuts and radishes; then I should be all set," Cassidy said, taking another bite.

"Sounds good," Marissa said.

"Yes – too bad only my mom and I will eat it." Cassidy shrugged.

"The boys don't eat salad?"

"They do, but not if they have other options."

"Well, more for you, then," Marissa said.

"Good point!" Cassidy grinned.

Once Cassidy had finished her final bite of Hot Pocket, she put the finishing touches on her salad while Marissa returned to her room to get ready for the day. She was off to a family party that afternoon, as well.

By 2PM, both Cassidy and Marissa were dressed and ready to go to their separate holiday events; Marissa in a red sun dress and Cassidy in a knee length jean skirt and a white V-neck tee. Both girls sported ponytails as it was extremely hot out. They grabbed their bags, and left the apartment for the rest of the day.

Cassidy drove the forty-five minutes home to her parents' place. The Banker family home was in a small development, comprising a mere five streets in a grid formation, on the west side of town. The Banker's large, red brick house was set on the back corner of the one entrance street off the main road.

Cassidy loved this neighborhood. It had been a wonderful place to grow up. There were lots of other kids to play with and a safe place to ride bikes. There were even two girls Cassidy's age: one a year older and one a year younger. Her neighbor girlfriends definitely made growing up with four brothers easier – at least until they were teenagers and the neighbor girls started to find all of her brothers so cute! Ugh. Cassidy was actually fairly certain her twin had lost his virginity to one of them at sixteen.

Cassidy pulled into the wide driveway. Her parents, Art and Lynne, were both parked in the garage, but there were two other cars parked on the left side of the drive. She instantly recognized them as Ben's Chevy and Eric's Honda. Cassidy pulled up on the right side next to her youngest brother's car. With the large salad bowl tucked securely under her left arm, Cassidy walked to the entryway and let herself inside.

"Hi!" Cassidy called, closing the heavy front door behind her.

"Whatcha bring?" Ben called, bounding down the large, dark wood staircase. His chin-length blond hair bounced as he came.

"Nice to see you, too," Cassidy replied sarcastically as she made her way towards the kitchen.

"Oh, salad," Ben remarked with a grimace as he glanced over her shoulder.

"Wonderful!" Cassidy's mom, Lynne, chimed as they entered the spacious kitchen. Ben quickly pushed around his sister and made his way to the backdoor and outside.

"Hi Mom," Cassidy said, setting her salad bowl on the light blue counter.

"Hi, sweetheart," Lynne said, giving her daughter a quick peck on the cheek. She made her way over to the sink to rinse the potatoes. Lynne's blonde hair was cut short, just below her ears, and was just starting to show a few grey strands. Lynne and Cassidy stood almost the exact same height, but Lynne was slighter than Cassidy's muscular frame.

"What do you need, Mom?" Cassidy asked as she helped herself to one of the Wheat Thins sitting in a large plastic bowl next to the stove.

"Nothing right now," Lynne said. "I think we have everything under control, especially now that you're all old enough to bring stuff. Basically, I am on potatoes, your dad is grilling all the meat, and he picked up two cases of beer last night. We're all set."

"Glad we're all able to finally be helpful," Cassidy said with a smirk.

"Hey, I had five kids in seven years! I'm exhausted, I deserve a break," Lynne teased. Cassidy chuckled.

"So, who is bringing what?" Cassidy asked, popping another cracker in her mouth.

"Ben brought the crackers," Lynne said, nodding toward the bowl Cassidy was picking at.

"A box of crackers? Really?" Cassidy raised an eyebrow. Ben's contributions were always low effort.

"You're eating them," Lynne pointed out.

"Fair enough."

"Eric and Ellie brought dessert, Matty is bringing macaroni salad, and Alex and Laura are bringing fruit and chips."

"Fruit and chips?" Cassidy asked. "Shouldn't chips have been from Ben?"

"He picked up the damn crackers, Cassidy. Move on." Lynne was clearly not in the mood for her daughter's nit-picking.

"Sorry. I'm done." Cassidy sighed apologetically.

"Thank you."

"So, Ellie is here?" Cassidy asked.

"Yes; she and Eric are outside with your father."

Cassidy hesitated.

"Please be nice," Lynne said.

"Mom, I don't have anything against her," Cassidy said. She was only partially lying.

"Really?" Lynne asked. "Because you never seem happy about her."

"I don't really know her. We've only met what – two, maybe three times? No, today will be three," Cassidy counted on her fingers.

"Well, try to get to know her. She's going to be your sister-in-law. You've always wanted a sister!"

"I count Laura as a sister-in-law, even though she and Alex aren't married," Cassidy pointed out. She truly did adore Laura, and had ever since Alex first brought her home for a visit during spring break of their sophomore year at Mercyhurst.

"Laura is a sweetie, but I'm sure you'll enjoy Ellie just as much as the years go on."

Cassidy bit her tongue. "Where are Matty and Alex?" she asked, ready to change the subject.

"They should be here," Lynne said with a small eye roll. Alex was notoriously late. And Matty was a loose cannon – if he was late, he was most likely bringing something they didn't need, like more fireworks. "Why don't you take the big metal cooler from the garage out to the back deck so we can start filling it with ice and get the beers in there."

"Sure," Cassidy agreed. She headed through the side door to the connecting garage and collected the large metal tub. She rested it on her hip as she exited the back door and lugged it out into the yard.

She looked over to the large patio where her father, Art, was lighting the grill. Art was a tall, lanky man with a mat of wavy light grey hair on the top of his head. Both Matty and Ben were built just like him. Cassidy could only imagine that in thirty years, both of them, but especially Matty, would be dead ringers for their dad.

Further out in the grass, Ben and Ellie were playing a game of badminton. Ellie was thin and petite. Her long black hair and tan skin glistened in the bright afternoon sun. Ellie was absolutely gorgeous – gorgeous in that annoying, completely effortless way. Back on the patio, plopped on one of the lounge chairs with a beer can in hand, was Eric. His dark blond hair was greased back and he wore thick black sunglasses. Cassidy couldn't help but think he looked like one of The Outsiders. He glanced over as she made her way to the patio.

"Hi, Dad!" Cassidy called. Art turned from watching the large flames coming off the grill and smiled at his only daughter.

"Hey, Cassidy, glad you made it!" he said happily. Cassidy gave him a one-armed hug before setting the tub down a few feet away from the grill. No need for anyone to get singed when going for a refill.

"Mom said to fill this with the ice and beers. Are they all in the garage freezer?" Cassidy asked.

"Ice should be in the garage freezer, but I think the beers are still in the back of the Subaru," Art said.

"On it," Cassidy said with a smile. She turned to head back into the garage. Out of the corner of her eye she saw Eric leap up and follow her.

"Cassidy," he called as Cassidy reached the garage door.

"Hey," she replied.

"Hey," he repeated, pushing his sunglasses up onto his head. They stepped into the garage.

"What's up?" Cassidy asked, opening the freezer and retrieving two large bags of ice.

"I'm glad you're here early," Eric began.

"Really?" Cassidy asked, handing her twin one of the bags.

"Yeah, I, um – " Eric stuttered. "I wanted to give you a heads up."

"That sounds ominous," Cassidy said.

"I'm going to ask our brothers to be my groomsmen tonight," Eric said.

"Oh, cool."

"Really? I was afraid you'd be pissed."

"Dude, what? They're your brothers, and it's your wedding! I'd be more pissed and disappointed with you if you didn't have them up there with you," Cassidy said.

They stared at each other for a moment.

"I just didn't want you to be caught off guard, so I wanted

to tell you. But thank you for being cool," Eric said with a small smile.

"I'm always cool," Cassidy countered.

Eric scrunched up his face. "You're definitely not."

"Look in the mirror – your hair right now proves you don't know what cool is," Cassidy teased.

"Bullshit. This is in all the magazines," Eric said, pointing at his hair as he slowly walked backwards towards the door.

"What magazine? Boy Scouts of America?" Cassidy smirked.

Eric gave her the finger and Cassidy chuckled.

"Hey! Aren't you going to help me with the beer?" Cassidy called as Eric turned and dashed out of the garage.

"No!" Eric called back.

Cassidy sighed in annoyance, then walked over to her dad's car and opened up the back seat to find a large case of beer. She quickly tossed the bag of ice on top and heaved the case out of the car, kicked the door closed, and departed the garage.

By 4:00 everyone had arrived, the meat was on the grill, and all the other dishes were spread out on one of the large picnic tables. Cassidy was happily lounging on a towel on the grass next to Laura while her brothers and Ellie played poker on the other picnic table. Art carefully monitored the grill while Lynne hopped around, fussing over all the miniscule details and making sure that nothing was forgotten or mislaid.

"Alright, everyone! Burgers and dogs are ready," Art called.

"Now, now, everyone! Grab plates here, and then…" Lynne began, attempting to impose some sort of order on the meal, but she was quickly drowned out by the clamor of the crowd rushing over to the food in a chaotic, ravenous passion. Cassidy and Laura came around to the back of the herd.

"You tried, mom," Cassidy said sympathetically, patting her mother on the shoulder as she and Laura walked past. Lynne let out a defeated sigh. Cassidy didn't know why her mom had not yet learned that the Banker family was completely uncontrollable around food.

In less than five minutes, all seven Bankers, Ellie, and Laura had filled their plates and were all seated at the table, starting to dig in. Cassidy sat at the end of the long table with Alex on her right and Laura on her left. Her father was at the opposite end of the table. He playfully raised his beer can and nodded at her. Cassidy returned the gesture, adding a goofy wink. They chuckled at their own little joke before shifting their attentions to their food and those seated around them.

"So, what are we setting off tonight?" Matty asked. Cassidy rolled her eyes. Matty had a weakness for anything that went 'boom!'.

"Dad and I went 'cross the border to Ohio and got a few good ones – plus the sparklers from 7-11," Ben said excitedly.

"Sweet!" Matty cheered.

"You didn't tell me you bought illegal fireworks," Lynne scolded Art.

"Don't worry, they aren't commercial grade," Art said, his mouth full of macaroni salad.

"And they aren't illegal in Ohio, mom," Ben added.

"But we don't live in Ohio, we live in Pennsylvania!" Lynne said exasperatedly.

"How about tonight we set them off real quick, boom, boom, boom! By the time we're caught, the evidence will be gone!" Matty suggested, taking a bite of his burger.

"That is not a plan," Alex sighed.

"Evidence gone. Boom!" Matty replied dramatically.

"Just put me down for a sparkler," Ellie chimed in. There was a pause as everyone swiveled to stare at the newest person at the table, shocked that she was brave enough to contribute to a Banker squabble. Suddenly, Ben let out a loud guffaw. Everyone else followed suit.

"Well done, babe," said Eric, who was seated next to Laura. He kissed her on the cheek. Ellie looked quite proud of herself. Cassidy hated to admit it, but she was proud of her, too. It must be overwhelming to step into a Banker family function.

"Ellie," Art called from the head of the table once the laughter had died down.

"Yes?"

"What was it you studied, again?" Art asked.

Eric let out an annoyed groan. "Dad, I already told you, she teaches first grade," he whined.

"I knew that!" Matty chimed in obnoxiously. Art ignored him while Ben offered Matty a high five.

"I didn't ask her what she did, I asked her what she studied," Art retorted.

"Honey, she would have studied education," Lynne said.

"It's okay, Mr. Banker," Ellie interjected. "I did major in education, but I also minored in Native American studies."

"That's fascinating!" Art smiled at Ellie before turning to his second son. "I bet you didn't know that."

"I didn't know that," Matty agreed with a shrug.

"What made you want to minor in that?" Art asked.

"Both of my parents are Shawnee. Well, my mother is fully, her parents are, grandparents, and so on. My dad is only half.

68

His father, my grandfather's family is part of the tribe, but my grandma was just a girl from Dayton."

"Shawnee? Like the Indians?" Ben asked.

"Native Americans," Alex corrected. Ben winced.

"Oh, sorry Ellie," Ben apologized.

"It's okay," Ellie assured him.

Cassidy tilted her head to the side in thought. She had never considered the possibility that Ellie was a different nationality before. She knew she was always tan and her hair was a silky, raven black, but the reason for this had never dawned on her. But then, Cassidy never gave much thought to any person's nationality. All people were simply people to her. Come to think of it, though, it should have been obvious that Ellie was Native American, now that she looked at her.

Much to Ellie's relief, the conversation soon shifted from her to old family stories of past holidays. From there, it moved on to movies they loved and from there to former pets – mostly jokes about the Banker's former dog, Domino. He was a dalmatian they'd had when the kids were young, and he'd had the IQ of a meatball sandwich.

Finally, the stories had ended, the food was all eaten, and everyone was ready to get up from the table. After they quickly stacked their plates, Lynne shooed everyone away so she could clean up properly without any interference. Everyone else rushed out to the middle of the yard for a spirited game of volleyball. Cassidy was on a team with Alex, Laura, and Art, while Matty, Ben, Eric, and Ellie took the other side of the net.

Poor Ellie was given a quick crash course into the competitive nature of the Banker siblings. One hour, six skinned knees, a split lip, one bruised elbow, and lots of screaming, arguing, and obscenities later, they called the end of the game. Matty, Ben, Eric, and Ellie's team insisted they had won, though Cassidy verbosely disputed a few of their do-overs due to sun in their eyes or injury – Ben only bled a little bit, anyway.

Now that they had finished their game, they all tromped across the yard back to the patio where Lynne had reset the table for dessert.

"If you're all done killing each other, we can have some dessert," Lynne called.

"Who brought dessert?" Laura asked, resting her knee on the bench of the picnic table.

"We did," Ellie replied.

"What did you bring?" Matty asked.

"I'm starving!" Ben added.

"We just ate," Cassidy pointed out.

"I worked up an appetite," Ben shrugged.

"By cheating?" Cassidy asked, raising an eyebrow.

"Whatever you need to tell yourself – loser." Ben puckered his lips and gave the air two kisses.

Cassidy chuckled and patted his cheek. "Little boy," she cooed before walking past him to claim her spot at the picnic table. Ben rolled his eyes in annoyance.

"Shut up," he whined. Cassidy grinned.

"What did you bring?" Matty asked once more.

"Ellie made brownies and we brought ice cream, too," Eric said.

"Yes!" Matty cheered.

"Come on, everyone, dig in before the ice cream melts," Lynne instructed, and everyone ambled over to help themselves.

As everyone was finishing up their treats, or, in Ben's

case, his third helping of treats, Cassidy saw Ellie whisper something in Eric's ear. He quickly got up from the table and rushed over to the large metal tub, grabbed four beers, and returned to the table.

"Thirsty?" Alex asked.

"I'm sharing," Eric said, passing a can to each of his brothers.

"This is terrible sharing," Art commented, looking longingly at the beers that were not shared with him. "We raised you better."

Cassidy stifled a laugh.

"I'll get you one later, Dad," Eric said.

"What's going on?" Ben asked suspiciously.

"Do you just get us beers now? Because I'm fine with that," Matty smirked, cracking open his can.

"Definitely not. I got you guys these ones because I wanted to ask something," Eric said. He gave a big grin. Alex, Ben, and Matty, who were all sitting across from him, looked confused. Matty took a sip from his can.

"Go on," Ellie whispered, nudging Eric with her shoulder.

"I'd like to ask you three to be my groomsmen," Eric said proudly, raising his beer can in cheers.

"Oh, yeah!" Alex said, a big smile on his face.

"Hot!" Ben cheered.

"Fuck, yes!" Matty added, clinking his beer with Eric's.

"Matthew James!" Lynne scolded. Over the years she had learned to accept and ignore her children swearing. However, she drew the line on a few words, and that was one of them.

"I'm celebrating!" Matty protested.

Cassidy smiled as she watched her brothers toast each other. She was honestly happy for them. Lynne, Art, Laura, and Ellie all started to clap and Cassidy joined them.

"This is so sweet!" Laura smiled.

"Will you each have three people standing up with you?" Lynne asked, wiping a happy tear off her cheek.

"Five, actually," Ellie replied, positively beaming with excitement.

"Oh, wow!"

"It works out great for both of us. I get my brothers and also Derek and Jeremy," Eric explained, referencing his college and current roommate, as well as his best friend from childhood.

"Do you have a big family, Ellie?" Laura asked.

"No," Ellie shook her head. "I just have one sister, Kara. So it'll be her and my friends – I finally have them all picked." Cassidy's ears pricked. There was a weird feeling in her stomach.

"Oh," Laura paused. "No other family?"

"Nope, just Kara."

Cassidy felt like there was a rock in her throat as her stomach continued to churn, harder than before. She suddenly felt Laura's hand come to rest on her left knee under the table and give it a gentle, comforting squeeze. Cassidy glanced over and saw Laura biting her lip. Cassidy sighed. She was not invited to be a bridesmaid in her own brother's wedding. Hell, in her own twin's wedding. She wanted to vomit.

She was vaguely aware of everyone talking around her, but she couldn't absorb a single word. She was lost in a swirl of emotion.

Did she want to be part of the bridal party? No, not really. However, she had always expected that she would be, regardless. You're supposed to invite your future siblings-in-law into the bridal party, right? That's the tradition. Cassidy could not figure out why this hurt her so much. Generally, she hated Eric. Okay, maybe not hate, but they weren't friends. He'd probably told Ellie terrible stories about her to get her to skip her on the invite list. Did Ellie even know that he was a twin? Why did she even care?

Cassidy remained in her zoned-out trance until she felt Laura pulling her plate away from her. She quickly shook her head and brought herself back to reality. Everyone was done eating and starting to get up and gather the dirty dishes.

"Here, I'll take these," Cassidy said, taking the stack from Laura.

"Oh, hey, you okay?" Laura whispered.

"Never better," Cassidy replied sarcastically. She collected more dishes while both of her parents went into the house and her brothers and Ellie headed back to the yard with a soccer ball.

"Cassidy," Laura began, but Cassidy cut her off.

"Laura, please. I can't right now. I'm going to do dishes. Just, go and play soccer with the boys. Please," Cassidy begged. She was moments away from losing her cool, and she didn't want Laura to take the brunt of it. She didn't deserve it.

"Come sit with me later," Laura told her with a sigh.

"I will," Cassidy said with a forced smile before turning and heading towards the back door of the house, her arms full of plates.

After a small struggle with the door, Cassidy got herself inside and into the kitchen where she plopped the pile of dishes down onto the blue countertop. Lynne walked in from the other room and looked surprised to see her.

"Cassidy? What are you doing inside?"

"Thought I'd help with the dishes," Cassidy said. She turned on the faucet to let the water to heat up.

"Dishes over soccer? What's going on?" Lynne asked. Cassidy shrugged and stuck her fingers under the stream of water. Still only lukewarm.

"I'm just… frustrated," she admitted with a sigh.

"With what?"

"With the stupid wedding, obviously!" she grumbled.

"Eric and Ellie's?"

"Obviously," she repeated.

"Cassidy, this is Eric's wedding. He's allowed to talk about it and it's lovely how excited the boys are to be groomsmen," Lynne said with a smile.

Cassidy glared at her. "Of course he's allowed to be happy, and it's great that Alex, Matty, and Ben get to join in the big day, but did you not notice that your daughter is not involved?" Cassidy asked forcefully. She stuck her hand under the water once more. Finally hot. She began shoving plates into the sink.

"What are you talking about? Of course you can't be a groomsman, what are you thinking?" Lynne shook her head.

"I'm not a bridesmaid, either. And if they were each having one person stand up with them, I wouldn't care. But they're each having five people stand up, and I still don't make the cut." Cassidy angrily squirted an obscene amount of dish wash into the sink.

"Well, you don't really know Ellie," Lynne said. It sounded as if she was desperately trying to come up with an excuse.

"But I'm Eric's sister. His twin sister."

"A fact that you normally try very hard to downplay,"

Lynne argued.

Cassidy sighed inwardly. That one stung – especially because it was definitely true. "It's tradition, though," she whined. "Especially in larger wedding parties. You have your fiancé's siblings in the bridal party."

"Not all the time." Lynne shrugged as Cassidy shut off the water and started to scrub.

"If Ellie had four sisters, I wouldn't push, but she has one. She would still have room for three friends if I was there; Eric only gets two."

"Cassidy, this may shock you, but this is your brother's wedding. The day is not about you. Nor are the events leading up to it," Lynne said firmly.

Cassidy wanted to scream.

"I know it's not about me! Stop treating me like a petulant five year old!" Cassidy firmly stacked a plate into the dish rack to dry. She was surprised, though grateful, that she didn't break it with her less-than-gentle movements.

"Well, you're acting a little bit like one. Demanding to be involved."

"I'm not demanding. I'm upset that I'm suddenly not included in a family wedding that the rest of the family is included in," Cassidy argued, slamming another clean plate in the rack.

Lynne sighed, and came to rest her hand on Cassidy's back. "Why is this bothering you so much?" she asked.

"Why wouldn't it? I always assumed I would be involved in my brothers' weddings. If I get married, they'll be in mine."

"Well, now they don't have to be." Lynne shrugged.

"Mom, please stop being so blasé about this. I mean, I know for a fact at your wedding you had both your sister and dad's sister as bridesmaids," Cassidy pushed.

"Well, of course! I had to have Aunt Lucy as my maid of honor," Lynne said, referring to her older sister. "And I had Aunt Marie in because she and your father were close siblings."

"And you had friends. It was all fine," Cassidy pushed.

"But, in Ellie's defense, you and Eric aren't close."

"So you're saying that if Dad and Aunt Marie weren't as close, you wouldn't have invited her? Grandma would have had something to say on that one." Cassidy was proud of the logic of her argument. She put the final plate on the drying rack and unplugged the sink to drain.

"I don't know what I would have done if Dad and Marie weren't as close, but I will say, it wasn't an issue to have her because she was a sweetie," Lynne said.

Cassidy gasped. "What does that make me? Some miserable cow?" She dried her hands on the dishcloth before tossing it on the counter in a heap.

"That's not what I said! Do not put words in my mouth," Lynne said firmly, looking her daughter squarely in the eye.

"You know what, I'm just going to go," Cassidy sighed.

"No, you are not. You're staying here until after dark; I need you here to hold the second fire extinguisher," Lynne smirked.

"Mom, I am obviously not in a joking mood."

"Well, you'd better get in one, because I'm not having you sulk through a family event and ruin the night for everyone."

"I don't intend to ruin anything," Cassidy replied through gritted teeth.

"Okay, well, get your head back on straight, then come back outside," Lynne instructed. "The sun is starting to set and Matty is going to be champing at the bit to blow something

76

up." She was out the back door before Cassidy had a chance to argue.

Cassidy stomped her foot in annoyance. She glowered for a long moment before huffing out of the room and into the hallway. She took a moment to use the downstairs bathroom and splash some water onto her face, hoping it would calm her. When she reemerged in the hallway, she heard a noise coming from her father's study off the foyer.

Cassidy wandered over and found her father sitting in one of his wingback chairs, sipping a glass of bourbon and listening to the radio. Only the table lamp had been turned on for light.

"Knock, knock," Cassidy called, coming to rest on the open doorframe.

"Ahh, someone found me."

"I promise not to reveal your location," Cassidy said with a wink.

"Much appreciated."

"What are you doing in here?" Cassidy asked as she stepped inside the small room and took a seat on the second wingback chair.

"Needed a moment. Love you kids, but I've gotten used to the empty house. This is a lot for me," Art explained.

"You sound like some grumpy old man," Cassidy teased with a smile.

"I'm getting there."

"No, you're not. I saw you play volleyball this afternoon – you've still got it," Cassidy assured him.

"Only in small doses," Art replied with a smirk. Cassidy laughed. "Besides, I wanted a drink," he added.

"There's a tub full of beers outside."

"No, I wanted a real drink, and I have no intentions of sharing the good liquor with your brothers. They'd clear me out." Cassidy grinned and nodded in agreement.

There was a long, comfortable silence between the two as Art sipped his drink and Bobby Darrin crooned from the stereo.

"What are you doing inside? You never miss an opportunity to trip one of your brothers, and on the soccer field you can make it look like an accident," Art said with a smile. Cassidy chuckled.

"Very true. I just needed a break."

"From wedding talk?" Art asked.

"See, even you caught it! Mom didn't!" Cassidy grumbled.

"Cassidy, do you even want to be a bridesmaid?" Art asked pointedly. The blunt question caught her off guard.

"Of course I do," she replied immediately.

"Really? You want to spend your weekends shopping with Ellie and her friends? Oooing and ahhing over every miniscule detail? Gushing with happiness and telling cutesie stories about your brother?" Art asked.

Cassidy grimaced slightly.

"Uhhh…" She hesitated. That did sound dreadful.

"Exactly. That's not you."

"You make me sound like the most miserable person in the world," Cassidy sighed.

"You're not miserable, but you would hate being involved in this wedding," Art said. Cassidy felt a rock in her stomach. "I am sorry you're not included. That has to hurt. But look at it as a blessing in disguise."

"Being left out doesn't feel like a blessing."

"I'm sure it doesn't. But if she had asked you to be a

bridesmaid tonight, you'd be miserable about all the bullshit you'd have to do for that," Art pointed out.

"And we're back to me being a miserable person."

"Pick your poison, Cassidy," Art said, taking a sip from his glass.

"You mean enjoy learn to enjoy being excluded from my brother's wedding?"

"Yep," Art said flatly.

Cassidy chewed her lip. "I'm still mad, but I'll be civil," she conceded.

"That's all we ask."

Cassidy sat with her father for a few more minutes while he finished his bourbon.

"Come on, the sun's setting. Let's go see what the boys want to shoot off," Art said, standing up and switching off the stereo.

"Oh, don't pretend like you aren't leading that charge," Cassidy teased.

Art simply shrugged. "Hurry up, then,"

Cassidy rolled her eyes as they made their way back outside. The soccer game was still going strong as the pinks and oranges of the late evening sky glowed above. Everyone except Lynne and Laura were racing along the grass after the ball. The boys and Ellie were running ragged while Lynne sat at the table chatting with Laura about preparing for the upcoming school year.

Cassidy took a seat next to Laura and listened to them talk, content to just observe the conversation.

As the sun set further, Art carried the large box of fireworks, firecrackers, and sparklers from the garage, which instantly lured Matty and Ben away from the game.

Art, Matty, and Ben spent the next thirty minutes setting up a large array of explosives while everyone else milled around the patio and drank beers. Cassidy sat with Laura the whole time, and actively ignored Eric and Ellie, who seemed to be lost in their own little world, curled up on one of the lounge chairs.

Cassidy remained on the patio with a lit sparkler in hand and watched her father and two brothers set everything off in the yard. They popped, sparked, and in a few cases, let out a loud bang that made everyone jump, as the colors swirled in the air. It was their most impressive display in years.

As soon as everything had been set off, they all cleaned up and collected their things to head home. Cassidy made her rounds of hugs and goodbyes to everyone until she got to Eric and Ellie.

"Hey, I'm heading out," Cassidy said flatly. Much to her surprise, Ellie rushed over and gave her a hug. Cassidy awkwardly hugged her back with one arm, her other clutching her salad bowl.

"Bye!" Ellie said.

"Yep, bye," Cassidy squeaked, pulling herself out of the hug.

"See ya, sometime!" Ellie said with a giddy smile. Cassidy didn't know why, but that really irritated her.

"Sure. Eric," Cassidy nodded at her twin. Eric took a step forward and leaned towards her ear.

"Please stop being shitty," he whispered. A sharp pang of annoyance shot through Cassidy's heart.

"You first," she whispered back firmly. The twins glowered at each other for a moment; then Cassidy felt a hand grip her upper arm and yank her the other direction.

"Come on, Cassidy! We're heading out too, and we parked you in," Alex said cheerily, as if he wasn't separating his siblings from killing each other. Cassidy tried to shake her eldest brother off of her arm, but he held his grip. She finally gave up and allowed herself to be led through the house and out the front door, Laura right on their tail.

Alex finally released his hold when they got to the driveway, and Cassidy instinctively rolled her shoulders a few times before opening the passenger door in her car to set the salad bowl on the seat.

"Don't let Eric get to you," Laura said, patting Cassidy on the back.

"I won't. I just need a moment," Cassidy grumbled.

"Cassie," Alex sighed. "Why don't you come home with us?"

"No, thank you. I just want to go home."

"Is Marissa in town?" Alex asked.

Cassidy nodded. "Yes, she was with family today, too. We should get home around the same time."

"Do you want us to come stay with you until she gets home?" Alex asked. Cassidy raised an eyebrow at him. Alex always tried to be overprotective of her. Cassidy had always loved him, but really needed him less than he liked. She was, however, always highly emotional, and Alex often took those opportunities to get to be her protector. I worked about half the time.

"Alex, I'm a fully functioning adult. I don't need a babysitter. I can stay home alone. It's okay."

"Normally, yes. But you're not in a good mindset right now. I really don't want you alone."

Cassidy felt a warmth around her heart. She appreciated

Alex being so protective and caring. Especially after another brother had left her out in the cold.

"Thank you very much, truly. But Marissa will be home very soon. I'll be okay." Cassidy smiled as she walked over to him.

"Call if you need anything, or just want to call people fucking assholes," Alex offered as he pulled her in for a hug. Cassidy laughed into his shoulder.

"I may take you up on that," she said, pulling back. Laura ran over and gave her a big hug as well.

"Sleep this all off," Laura told her. Cassidy nodded.

"Night, Cassie," Alex said before both he and Laura climbed into his car. Cassidy waved as they started the engine, and walked around to climb into the driver's side of her Toyota. She turned her key in the ignition and glanced at her rearview mirror. Alex and Laura were just turning out of the driveway and onto the street. She shifted into reverse as Matty exited the front door and waved at her.

Cassidy kept her foot on the break as she rolled down the window.

"Hey," she called. "Did you want to pull out first?" While Matty's car was on the other side of the driveway, he was the last car before the street.

"No," Matty replied, coming to lean against her open window. "Just sayin' goodnight."

"Goodnight," Cassidy chuckled. They had hugged goodbye less than five minutes prior.

"Sorry tonight was shitty for you," Matty added. Cassidy's head snapped up.

"You saw that?" she asked.

"You're terrible at hiding the emotions on your face," Matty chuckled. Cassidy groaned.

"I'll work on it," she replied sarcastically.

"I wouldn't. Let Eric and Ellie know you're pissed."

Cassidy thought about that for a moment.

"I'm sorry that you're being excluded. You would have been a lot of fun at the events. But that means we can just get extra shitfaced and dance our asses off at the reception," Matty said with a smirk. Cassidy smiled up at him.

"Thanks, Matty,"

"Alright, enough of this. Get the fuck out of here," Matty said, tapping the hood of her car twice.

"Goodnight," Cassidy laughed as she brought her foot off the break and reversed out of the driveway, onto the street, and sped out of the development.

# Chapter 7

Cassidy made good time getting back to Erie and was thrilled to see Marissa's car in the complex lot when she pulled in.

"Hey," she called as she let herself in the apartment.

"Hey!" Marissa replied from the kitchen.

"How was your day?" Cassidy asked. She set her salad bowl on the counter and collapsed onto the couch.

"Pretty boring, honestly. But the food was good. We only ate and played with sparklers, so I got home early," Marissa explained, coming to sit on the chair next to the sofa, glass of Sprite in hand.

"Glad there was good food."

"Judging by your face, I'm nervous to ask how yours went."

"It was fine, except I found out that I'm not in Eric's wedding," Cassidy sighed.

"Oh, are they just doing a small wedding party? It would be hard for Eric to only pick one brother," Marissa said. Cassidy gave a low chuckle.

"Oh, no, they're having a large wedding party. All my brothers are groomsman, but I am not to be a bridesmaid," Cassidy glowered.

"What? Siblings are always in the bridal party!" Marissa said, looking confused.

"That's what I thought."

"That sucks, I'm sorry."

"My dad kept saying that I wouldn't like to be in the bridal party anyway, which honestly is true, but I'm still mad," Cassidy groaned.

"I think you have every right to be absolutely pissed," Marissa said firmly.

"I'm already there."

"What did everyone else say?" Marissa asked.

"Laura and Alex are upset. Alex has been extra sweet, which I appreciate. Even Matty took my side. But my mom didn't seem to care. She's just in wedding mode."

"Ugh," Marissa sympathized.

"At least I don't have to see Eric for another month," Cassidy said.

"Ellie doesn't come to the monthly dinners, does she?" Marissa asked.

Cassidy shook her head. "She came to one after they started dating, but that was it. Other than tonight, I only saw her once at our grandma's birthday back in February. I hope she doesn't start coming. I mean, Laura doesn't come, and she's my unofficial sister-in-law. She and Alex have been together forever."

"Do you think Eric told her it's just a sibling thing?" Marissa asked.

"I don't think he even told her that I'm his twin," Cassidy

said.

"Jesus," Marissa exhaled.

Cassidy didn't know why, but she suddenly started laughing. Perhaps it was frustration, or the exhaustion, or possibly the few beers she had, but Marissa's reaction cracked her up.

Both girls started laughing and Cassidy began to feel like she might just survive her brother's wedding.

It had been a week since the Fourth of July picnic and Cassidy had only spoken to her mother once since. While Cassidy felt she and her mother were back on good terms, there was still a low brewing frustration that seemed to haunt her thoughts.

Cassidy pulled into the small parking lot across the street from the Mexican restaurant downtown. She quickly shut off the engine, hopped out of the car, and jogged across the crosswalk before a pick-up truck zoomed past. Her light green sundress billowed as she went.

The bell on the heavy wooden door dinged as Cassidy pulled it open and stepped into the colorful interior of the restaurant.

"Hey!" Cassidy cried happily, spotting Laura sitting on one of the benches in the yellow lobby.

"Hi!" Laura said cheerily. She was in faded blue jeans with a black Beatles tee shirt that hung off her right shoulder perfectly. Damn, she was so cool.

"Were you waiting long?" Cassidy asked as they walked to the hostess stand.

"Nope! Less than three minutes."

"Just two?" the hostess asked in beautifully accented English.

"Yep," Cassidy nodded. They followed her through the maze of large wicker and glass tables, and were seated by the windows overlooking the parking lot and the large brick library situated on the other end of the block.

"So, how's it going?" Laura asked casually, sliding the ashtray on the edge of the table toward her and lighting up a cigarette.

"Pretty good. Work is kind of boring; it's our slow season now." Cassidy shrugged. "What are you up to, with school being out for the summer?"

"Well," Laura took a drag, "school is out, but we offer summer camps, so I'm working at a pottery camp for about six weeks."

"Oh, that's cool." Cassidy did not have a single artistic bone in her body, so she found anyone with the ability to create things incredibly talented.

"Yeah, the kids are fun, and they make pretty cool things!"

The server arrived at their table with a basket of chips and a large bowl of salsa. Cassidy waited about .05 seconds after they were set on the table before helping herself.

"Any more dates?" Laura asked after the server took their drink order and departed. She crunched a chip loudly.

"Dates?" Cassidy raised an eyebrow.

"Or, whatever the guy from our building was." Laura smiled widely.

"Pete," Cassidy sighed. She knew full well that her almost-sister-in-law was trying to wind her up. "He was a one-night stand, and just a bad decision. I'm not one of those girls."

"Was he really bad?" Laura asked curiously, popping

another salsa coated chip in her mouth.

"Well," Cassidy blushed, "some of it was quite nice. It just… ended poorly…" She trailed off with a sheepish smile before reaching for more chips.

"Oooof," Laura chuckled.

"Yeah."

"I think I know which guy he is in our building. I see him at the mailboxes," Laura said smugly.

Cassidy rolled her eyes. "Glad to hear it, Sherlock."

"You could have done much worse," Laura smirked.

The server came back with their drinks and the girls quickly ordered their favorites. They had both eaten there many times over the years.

"So, any others?" Laura asked once more.

"Nope."

"That's good. Don't rush anything. But I would suggest finding someone for Eric's wedding – otherwise you'll be miserable," Laura advised.

"You mean more miserable," Cassidy enunciated carefully.

"Exactly."

"I promise I'll find a date for the wedding. Or drag Marissa along."

"Perfect." Laura smiled.

"I have to ask, how on earth have you put up with my family for so long? I mean, we're a lot." Cassidy chuckled nervously. "Like, a lot, a lot. Your family must be a thousand times easier than us."

"Well," Laura laughed, "we have our own quirks."

"Please enlighten me. Because I'm imagining just cool, chill, people, maybe dancing in the rain on holidays?" Cassidy asked playfully.

"Okay, okay, we're hippies, but not that hippie," Laura joked.

"Fair enough."

"I mean, I know I'm an only child, but my family is still chaotic. My parents are high emotion, so they're either passionately in love with each other or passionately screaming at each other. My mom's parents absolutely hate my dad's parents, and vice versa, so we can never do joint family things. I have four cousins between the two sides, but my aunts and uncles all live out of state, so I don't get to see them often."

Cassidy listened carefully, completely captivated. Despite knowing Laura for many years, she was hearing most of this for the first time.

She'd known that Laura was an only child, and that she had artsy parents. Cassidy had met them at Alex's graduation. They were the polar opposite of Art and Lynn, and Cassidy found them fascinating. Laura's mother had actually gone to Woodstock! But somehow that was all she really knew about her almost-sister-in-law's background. Cassidy was starting to feel guilty for never making an effort to learn more about her.

"Are you close with your cousins? I mean, I know you don't see them much, but do you guys get along?" Cassidy asked.

Laura nodded. "Yep. I'm definitely closer with the three that live in Michigan. They're on my mom's side. We're all pretty close in age. The oldest is my mom's brother's son. He's a year older than me. Then her sister has a son and daughter. Beth is two years younger than me and Stephen is two years younger than her."

"Wow, I feel like dick for literally not knowing any of this," Cassidy admitted.

"No, no, you don't need to know my whole family history,"

Laura laughed, snuffing out the tiny nub of her cigarette.

"You've been with my family almost ten years, I should know more about you," Cassidy pointed out.

"You'll learn," Laura smiled.

Cassidy grinned. "I have a stupid question…"

"No such thing as a stupid question," Laura countered, eating another chip.

"You're a teacher to teenagers; you know damn well they have stupid questions," Cassidy pointed out.

Laura chucked and nodded. "Well, yeah."

"I was just wondering … does Alex know all this? Like, about your family? He knows to ask, right?" Cassidy had never given much thought to how her brothers acted in relationships. It was something she's rather not focus on, honestly. However, especially with someone she liked as much as Laura, she wanted to make sure she was treated well. She needed that confirmation.

Laura laughed.

"Yes, Alex knows. He knows my family, my childhood, my life, and I know his," Laura assured her.

"Good," Cassidy smiled.

"Did you honestly think I'd stay with him so long if he didn't take an interest in my family?" Laura asked, raising an eyebrow.

"I told you it was a stupid question," Cassidy sighed. "I just, you know, realized that I don't know as much about you as I should and wanted to make sure you're not putting up with the same shit from Alex. You deserve the best!"

"That's really sweet," Laura smiled. "But yes, Alex is a dream. Kind, thoughtful, always supportive, and so romantic and sexy. Like just last night, I was having a shower and –"

"No! Nope, stop right there," Cassidy insisted, her eyes wide in horror. "I'm thrilled he's good to you but I do not need to know about that."

"Oh, come on," Laura teased. "I'm happy to hear about your date nights! I love to, but I'm willing to share, too. I could give you tips!" Laura winked.

"Ugh! No, no, no, no, I do not want to hear about your 'alone time.' Even if you can teach me things. Especially if you can teach me things!" Cassidy countered, holding her hands up in defense. Laura nearly tipped over she was laughing so hard.

"Shut up," Cassidy jabbed as she started giggling herself.

Their laughter was interrupted by their server appearing at their table with a tray of delicious-looking food.

"Saved by my enchilada," Cassidy beamed as the warm plate was set in front of her.

The girls thanked their server and dug right into their meals: enchilada for Cassidy, fajitas for Laura. Not only did Cassidy love the food, but she loved spending time with Laura. She was so easy to talk to and laugh with. It was the perfect lunch and exactly the recharge Cassidy needed.

# Chapter 8

It was Wednesday afternoon. There was only an hour left in the workday, and Cassidy was leaning against the wall in the conference room chatting with Gladys. The entire office staff was mingling in the conference room for Devon Park's birthday celebration, enjoying a large spread of nibbles, cake, and punch. While Cassidy appreciated the easy afternoon and the free snacks, Devon was her least favorite coworker and his usual obnoxiousness was only amplified with the attention his birthday brought him.

"I didn't think anyone could be that full of themselves," Gladys sighed, watching Devon animatedly retell a story to coworkers that hadn't been standing in front of him the first time around.

"Enter Devon," Cassidy remarked sarcastically, taking a large swig of her punch.

"I hope you're doing something fun after this terrible party," Gladys commented. Cassidy smiled.

"I'm going to head over to MU and watch some of their summer training game."

"What's that?" Gladys asked.

"The school's baseball team comes in over summer to do training and assess the players. They do a bunch of scrimmages. There's one today, so I'm going to go watch." Gladys scrunched up her nose.

"I could get behind going to see the Pirates, but a college scrimmage? No thanks," she said with a playful sigh.

Cassidy chuckled. "I would love to go to a Pirates game, but it's just too far for a weeknight." She shrugged.

"That's true."

"I'm just going to the campus field, grab a sandwich from the food truck, and enjoy a bit of a game."

"Oh, I love those food trucks!" Gladys's eyes smiled.

"My younger brother said they've got two on campus almost permanently. With the athletes back now for summer camps, I know at least one of them will be there," Cassidy said.

"Food trucks on a college campus - they must be doing a hell of a business!"

"Yeah, especially if they're open late nights, which I think they are."

"Well, hell, I'm in the wrong business," Gladys joked.

"Your next job," Cassidy suggested jokingly.

"Ha! Maybe next life. I'm retiring next year. I can't deal with the bullshit anymore."

"Devon is annoying," Cassidy winked. Gladys guffawed.

"You said it." Gladys lifted her cup and Cassidy clinked hers to it. She adored Gladys, and was heartbroken to hear that she would be leaving the office so soon.

93

Cassidy combed her wavy hair with her fingers and pulled it back into a messy ponytail before exiting her car. She was parked in one of the campus lots, only about a block away from the ball field. She brushed the front of her semi-casual knee-length dress. She loved this dress. It was black with tiny white daisies dotted over the fabric. Professional and dressy enough for a day in the office, but comfy and casual enough for the rest of the evening.

She slung her purse over her shoulder as she made her way to the sidewalk and the large, green food truck parked across the street.

"What'll it be?" a grouchy man with a backwards ball cap asked as he leaned on the white counter inside the truck window.

"Uh," Cassidy hummed as she glanced at the menu posted on the side. "Can I have a chicken wrap and a bottle of water, please?"

The grouchy man nodded. "$3.50." Cassidy placed the money on the counter and stepped aside to await her food.

"Why are you here? This can't be the only food truck in the city," a familiar voice rang out. Cassidy turned to see Ben walking toward her, with about six other boys trailing behind him. They were all in black workout shorts and green tee shirts with "Mercyhurst Soccer" written across the chest.

"Hey, kid!" Cassidy smiled at her youngest brother, honestly happy to see him.

"Shut up," Ben sighed.

Cassidy chuckled. "You boys on snack break?"

"No, we're walking to the fields for some drills, then I'm going to have everyone run again," Ben explained. A few groans came from the younger players standing behind

94

him. Ben was starting his senior year in a couple of weeks, and Cassidy realized he was one of the captains leading the summer training. It felt weird to see him as the "oldest" or "in charge". She still saw Ben as her baby brother. She didn't like this feeling.

"Fun," Cassidy replied sarcastically.

"Anyway, we're supposed to be here. This is our school. What are you doing here?" Ben asked, looking down at his sister. He was clearly trying to regain his authority in front of the younger players.

"I'm going to watch the baseball scrimmage. Thought I'd pick up dinner, first."

"You're so weird," Ben sighed, shaking his head.

"I'm not weird, this is a lovely evening!" Cassidy shrugged.

"Chicken wrap!" The food truck man called out.

"That's me!" Cassidy beamed.

"Well, happy chickening," Ben said, nudging the boys to keep moving.

"And baseballing!" Cassidy added.

"Weirdo!" Ben called, moving off with his team. Cassidy rolled her eyes and decided to let him have that win. She'd get him back later.

Cassidy was one of about thirty people seated in the college ballpark that summer evening. Looking around, most of the other spectators seemed to be people involved in the MU baseball organization, a couple of the players' girlfriends giggling and gossiping, with a few overprotective parents sprinkled in.

She took a large sip from her bottle of water before setting it on the concrete and opening her wrap. Cassidy was seated about five rows up along the third base line. A perfect spot. There was something peaceful about sitting at the ballpark in the warm summer evening glow. The clang of the bats, the thump of the ball against the mitts. She was home.

The top of the first inning wrapped up just as Cassidy finished her dinner. She balled up the paper and tossed it to her feet to dispose of later. She heard a bit of a clamoring in the row behind her - someone rushing to get a seat. The place was pretty empty, though; she wasn't sure why anyone would be racing into a vacant row. She ignored the hustle as she watched the shortstop whack a line drive into left field.

"What inning is it?"

Cassidy turned to see a man in his late twenties sitting in the row behind her, about three seats to the left. He had thick, copper-colored hair that rested just above his ears and an oval face. His aviator sunglasses reflected Cassidy's image back at her.

"Um, bottom of the first," Cassidy replied.

"Oh, good! I'm not as late as I thought."

"It's a training camp scrimmage, I don't think this is super high stakes," Cassidy joked, turning back to watch the next player swing and miss.

"Strike one!" the assistant coach called.

"It may not be high stakes, but the guy keeping all the records should be in attendance," the guy joked.

"Records?" Cassidy raised an eyebrow.

"I'm a statistician. I work for the university. I teach Stats 305 and do the books for the MU baseball team," he explained. Cassidy was taken aback.

"Oh!" she said. "That's pretty cool!" The guy looked at her suspiciously.

"I don't think 'cool' has ever been used to describe my job," he chuckled.

"Well, most people don't get it. This is coming from a former competitive softball player and current certified public accountant." Cassidy smirked playfully.

"I think I just fell in love," he quipped.

Cassidy let out a loud laugh. "Happy to help cupid along."

"I'm Jake," he said, extending his right hand.

"Cassidy," she replied, giving a firm handshake. A loud clang from the bat sent a ball over the fence.

"Dammit, I need to pay attention," Jake winced, quickly pulling his notebook from his bag and fumbling for his pen.

"Good luck with the stats." Cassidy turned back around in her seat and faced the field. She couldn't shake the smile off her face. She quickly pulled her sunglasses from her purse and slipped them on, but they didn't hide the slight blush on her cheeks. She concentrated hard on the baseball scrimmage to distract herself.

But after two more innings of focusing on the scrimmage, she was dying to talk to Jake some more.

"How are they looking?" Cassidy asked, turning to look back at Jake, who was scribbling furiously in his notebook.

"Hmmm," Jake hummed. He finished his equation and looked up at Cassidy.

"How are they looking?" Cassidy repeated with a polite smile. Jake looked up and caught her eye. Cassidy felt a thump in her chest. What was happening?

"Oh, um, okay…" Jake said with an unconvincing sigh.

"That bad, huh?"

"Well, there are only two seniors and three juniors; it's a very heavy underclassman filled roster. There's a lot of learning going on," Jake explained, shrugging slightly.

"Ooof," Cassidy grimaced.

"Yeah, but in two years they'll be top of the league."

"Not this year, though?" Cassidy teased.

"No." Jake said firmly. "Not this year."

"So, did you go to school here?" Cassidy asked curiously.

"No, no, I went to Penn State."

"When did you graduate? My soon-to-be sister-in-law went there."

"Eighty-four."

"Her too! Did you know an Ellie Hammond?"

"It's a really big school," Jake replied with a slight smile.

"Yeah." Cassidy grimaced, feeling like a dumbass.

"What about you, did you go to Mercyhurst?"

"Edinboro."

"Pretty small school, right?" Jake asked.

Cassidy nodded. "Yep, but I loved it."

"I get that." Jake smiled. "So, what are you doing here watching MU summer baseball training?"

"I work half a mile away from here."

"Oh?" Jake looked intrigued.

"And my younger brother goes here," Cassidy added, hoping to not sound like some weirdo preying on college boys.

"Shoot, he's not one of the underclassmen I just said needs work, is he?" Jake asked nervously. Cassidy let out a laugh.

"No, no, he's a senior, and he plays soccer. Just saw him on a run with his teammates when I got here, actually."

"I feel much better, then," Jake said.

"You're all good," Cassidy smiled. A loud clink caught their attention just in time for them to turn and see a foul ball whiz mere feet from where they were sitting. They both reflexively flinched. The ball hit the metal bleachers, bounced to the floor, and rolled in the other direction.

Cassidy and Jake burst into laughter. They could hear the players on the field cracking up, as well.

"Guess that's my cue to pay better attention," Jake smirked.

"Okay," Cassidy hummed. She watched him for a moment as he clicked his pen a few times and turned to the next page of his black notebook before she turned around to face the field once more. She felt her heart flutter.

'Come on, Banker,' Cassidy mumbled to herself under her breath. She had had many crushes over the years, but never had one come on so quickly. This was more than finding Jake cute or charming; she couldn't figure out what she was feeling.

The next few innings went by without a hitch, and without any more talking to Jake. Cassidy tried very hard to concentrate on the game, but as the top of the ninth came to a close, she had no idea what the score was. Her mind had been lost in a world of daydreaming.

The first three batters were quickly and consecutively struck out, ending the game. Cassidy let out a contented sigh.

"So," Jake's voice floated behind her. Cassidy turned around to find him stuffing his notebooks and pens back into his bag. He gave her a small smile. Cassidy couldn't help but grin back.

"So, what?" she asked playfully.

"How'd you like the scrimmage?" Jake asked.

Cassidy shrugged. "It was alright. It's just nice to be in a ballpark in summertime."

"Yeah," Jake chuckled, looking amused. Cassidy realized

she must have sounded like an idiot. Her brain was not working properly. She knew the sport inside and out, and she wanted to impress him with astute observations and play analyses. But the honest truth was that she'd spent most of the game in a foggy daydream. Shit.

"What did you think about the game?" Cassidy asked lamely.

"Eh, definitely a rebuilding year." Jake shrugged.

"Yeah, that's right, you had said…" Cassidy trailed off. She was sure her face was bright red. She was off her game and felt like an idiot.

"I gotta get these numbers to the coaches," Jake said. "Maybe I'll see ya at another game - hopefully a better one." He smiled.

"Oh, yeah, yeah," Cassidy stumbled as she watched Jake stand up. "It was nice to meet you."

"You too, Cassidy." Jake nodded as he tucked his notebooks under his arm. He gave her a final flicker of a smile before gracefully shuffling across the bleacher and down the metal steps, making a beeline for the dugout.

Cassidy sighed shakily, annoyed that she was feeling so rattled.

# Chapter 9

"Hi," Cassidy called down the hallway as she shut the heavy red apartment door behind her with a thunk.

"Hey," Marissa called back in a garbled voice. Cassidy could tell she had a mouthful of food. She walked into the living room and found Marissa seated cross-legged on the floor with a Styrofoam container of Chinese food on the coffee table in front of her. The local news was playing on the TV.

"Ooo, what's that? Looks good," Cassidy commented as she flopped onto the sofa.

"Orange chicken and lo mein," Marissa replied, placing another forkful in her mouth.

"Nice."

"I thought you were picking up food, so I didn't order you anything," Marissa said, covering her mouth as she chewed.

"I hit a food truck downtown," Cassidy said, rolling onto her back to look at the ceiling.

"How was the game?" Marissa asked, popping another piece of chicken in her mouth.

"Nothing special. It was nice to be out in the ballpark, though," Cassidy replied, her eyes still on the ceiling. She could feel Marissa's eyes on her. The reporter on the TV droned on about a robbery.

"What's going on? You're off," Marissa commented. Cassidy slowly turned her head to face her friend's big brown eyes and lightly freckled face.

"I was sitting by myself on the bleachers, and this guy sat right behind me…" Cassidy began.

"Hmmm?" Marissa raised an eyebrow, clearly intrigued.

"We chatted a bit; he works for MU. He does the team stats. He's…. he's pretty cute."

"Mmmmm," Marissa grinned. "So, when are you going out?"

"We're not." Cassidy rolled her eyes.

"Why not?" Marissa asked, slurping a lo mein noodle.

Cassidy shrugged, feeling oddly irritated. "I don't know."

"Hmmm."

"What does that mean?" Cassidy pursed her lips.

"I'm just surprised. You're not exactly shy, and if you felt so much as a spark, which clearly you did, you wouldn't have ignored it."

Cassidy sometimes found it irritating how well Marissa knew her. "I'm not shy! It's just, I don't know… It was a stupid, fluke thing. I don't know why we're even talking about it," she said defensively. She wasn't quite sure why her defenses were even up at the moment.

"You brought him up," Marissa shrugged.

"Well, it doesn't matter."

"So," Marissa chewed. "What's his name?"

"Jake." Cassidy smiled to herself.

"Mmmhmmm," Marissa hummed. "And what does Jake like to do?" she enunciated carefully.

"Dunno. We mostly talked about the game."

"Ah, that's right! Baseball and math nerd," Marissa noted.

"Hey!" Cassidy protested.

"Sorry, connoisseur," Marissa quipped. Cassidy couldn't help but chuckle.

"I mean, it's stupid that I even care. We chatted for a moment. Why is he in my head?" Cassidy groaned.

"Crushes are weird like that."

"I feel like a stupid teenager," she sighed.

"Just enjoy it! It's a fun high. Return to adulthood tomorrow," Marissa smiled. Cassidy rolled her eyes.

There was a comfortable silence. Marissa returned her attention to her dinner while Cassidy stared at the ceiling, half listening to the weatherman talk about the humidity. Her mind was in a constant loop of the events of her evening at the ballpark, and it was irritating her.

"When was your last crush?" Cassidy asked, breaking the quiet.

Marissa let out a snort. "Well, I am dating Brandon right now."

"I know, but he doesn't really count," Cassidy countered.

"Why not?"

"You never wished or waited for him. You two met, hit it off, and got together right away. It's different."

"Ahh, so you mean someone I've pined for." Marissa playfully waggled her eyebrows.

"I wouldn't use that term, but yes."

Marissa thought about it.

"Was it Mike from the soccer team?" Cassidy asked,

thinking back to Marissa's last long-term boyfriend in their junior year. Marissa had liked him since freshman year and was thrilled when they started to date two years later. The relationship only lasted six months, but - especially in the early months - Marissa had been obsessed.

"Ugh," Marissa groaned at the memory. Their breakup had been unpleasant. "Mike was probably the last one that came true - unfortunately. But I did like the guy in my psych class, senior year. Colby."

"I forgot about him. Did you two ever go for a drink?"

"No," Marissa snorted. "As far as Colby was concerned, I didn't even exist. I don't think he ever knew my name."

Cassidy sighed.

"Doesn't matter, though. I'm with Brandon and all is glorious!" Marissa said smugly.

"Very true."

"So, what are you going to do about Jakey-boy?" Marissa asked, taking a deliberate bite off her fork.

"I can't do anything. I mean, I met him once; I'm being an idiot. Jake's probably like Colby, doesn't even remember my name."

"I'm sure he does."

"Whatever." Cassidy sat herself up on the couch. "I'm going to have a drink and not even think about it anymore."

"Good luck," Marissa replied in a sing-song voice. Cassidy reached down and gave her shoulder a playful smack as she passed by.

"Ow," Marissa laughed.

"You deserved it," Cassidy smirked as she pulled an empty glass out of the cupboard.

# Chapter 10

The engine of Cassidy's blue Toyota rumbled to a halt on the left side of Art and Lynne Banker's driveway. It was the first Friday in August and Cassidy was dutifully returning home with the rest of her siblings for their family dinner. The only car she didn't see parked was Alex's, though he was often the last to arrive.

She straightened her light pink sundress as she got out of the car before walking up to the house and letting herself inside.

"Hi," she called loudly as she closed the front door behind her.

"Oh, hi, darling," Lynne called from the kitchen.

"Hi, darling," Matty parroted in a mocking, nasal tone. Cassidy entered the kitchen to see her mother stirring something on the stove while Matty casually leaned against the island with a beer in hand, smirking.

"Hi, mom," Cassidy said happily, walking over and giving Lynne a side hug. Lynne smiled and gave her a kiss on her temple as she continued to stir.

"Hello," Lynne smiled. She enjoyed having her children

home.

"Hey, babe," Cassidy said in a playful, nasal tone as she walked to Matty and gave him a gentle pat on his chin. They grinned at one another. Cassidy and Matty had never been super close, but he was always the most playful of her brothers and they had spent so much time over the years playing pranks on one another, talking in silly voices, telling dumb jokes, quoting movies, and laughing until they could barely breathe. Matty was fun. He taught tenth grade biology at the high school two towns over. He had only taught there for the last four years, but he was consistently the student body's most favorite teacher.

"Does thou lady wanteth some bubbly?" Matty asked. He had now switched to a botched English accent that caused both Cassidy and Lynne to cringe.

"I'll just get my own beer," Cassidy said in her normal voice. She opened the fridge and helped herself to a can.

"How was your week?" Lynne asked her daughter.

"Pretty boring," Cassidy said as she cracked the can open and took a sip.

"Well, isn't that special?" Matty interjected in a surprisingly good impression of the SNL Church Lady. Cassidy chuckled.

"Oh, there are my middle two," Art said as he entered the kitchen.

"Hi, Dad," Matty and Cassidy chorused.

"What are you looking for?" Lynne asked suspiciously as Art opened the refrigerator.

"Nothing. Just looking," Art replied in a bored voice.

"Dinner is going to be ready soon; get out of there!" Lynne scolded. Art gave a defeated sigh, grabbed a can of beer, and shut the refrigerator door. Cassidy and Matty exchanged

106

knowing looks.

"Who are we waiting on?" Art asked, taking a sip.

"Alex," Cassidy replied.

"As per usual," Matty added.

"Well, dinner's not ready yet anyway, so he still has plenty of time," Lynne said in defense of her eldest.

"We're still two down," Art commented, nodding towards Cassidy and Matty.

"I think they're downstairs," Lynne said offhandedly as she reached for the colander sitting in the sink. The Banker house had a half-finished basement where the kids had often been sent to watch TV or play games when their parents needed a break. It became the prime hangout spot when they were teenagers.

"Yeah, Ben's obsessed with his new Nintendo game and is thrilled that Eric will play it with him," Matty noted.

"Well, get them up here. As soon as Alex gets here, I want to eat," Art instructed. Cassidy couldn't help but smile. Her father was usually pretty passive at meal times, unless he was very hungry - which he clearly was today.

"Art," Lynne grumbled. "That's not how dinner works. Even if Alex appeared this instant, the food isn't cooked yet. We have at least fifteen minutes left on the oven timer. Here, eat some bread and go sit in your study." Lynne handed him a roll from the bread basket on the island and gave him a gentle push towards the hallway.

"He's just hungry, mom," Cassidy said in defense of her father as he ambled towards his office, munching on the roll as he went.

"He's driving me batty, is what is happening," Lynne commented before returning her attention to her vegetables.

"Okay…" Cassidy let out a low breath as she and Matty exchanged a glance. Their parents loved each other dearly, but after thirty-one years of marriage, sometimes their little quirks got under each other's skin.

"I need one of you to set the table and one of you to fill up the water pitcher," Lynne instructed.

"Pitcher!" Cassidy and Matty called in unison. They instantly locked eyes and stared at each other for a few seconds before Matty raised his fist in the air. Cassidy followed suit. With a silent nod, they both began to shake their fists. One. Two. Three. Cassidy threw scissors, Matty threw rock. Cassidy scrunched her nose in defeat as Matty tapped her fingers with his fist.

"Set that table real nice," Matty said slyly as he grinned and collected the large blue glass water pitcher from the cupboard. Cassidy sighed, but carried the dishes out to the dining room to start prepping for dinner.

Thirty minutes later, the table had been set, Alex had arrived, Ben and Eric had been lured away from their video game, the lasagna was out of the oven, and the seven Bankers were taking their seats at the dining room table. Everyone always took the spots they'd sat in since childhood, out of habit. Art and Lynne at the head and foot of the table, Matty and Eric on one side, Alex, Cassidy, and Ben on the other.

"Get those cigarettes off the table," Art warned his eldest son firmly as he picked up the serving spoon.

"Sorry." Alex quickly picked up the cardboard box from next to his fork and dropped it on the floor beneath his chair.

"Don't throw them on the floor," Lynne groaned as she helped herself to some salad.

"I don't have any pockets," Alex huffed, motioning to the

maroon gym shorts he was wearing.

"You're such a disappointment," Matty commented sarcastically.

"Shut up," Alex sighed, glaring his closest brother who was seated diagonally from him at the dining room table.

"Pass the bread around, Matty," Art ordered, handing him the breadbasket. Matty smiled proudly as he took the basket from his dad.

"Eric, any wedding updates?" Lynne asked curiously.

"Um," Eric hummed as he passed the Lasagna dish. "We're actually thinking about early next year in between our birthdays, since mine is in January and hers is in February."

"I thought she didn't want to have a snowy wedding," Cassidy said.

"Yeah, weren't you thinking summer '88?" Lynne asked.

"We were, but that just feels so far away." Eric shrugged.

"Oh, my god, is she pregnant?" Ben asked excitedly. The sound of Lynne's fork being dropped onto her plate reverberated through the room.

"No!" Eric groaned.

"He'd have to have sex to get her pregnant," Matty teased.

"You'll get there someday, bud," Alex added as Ben cackled. Eric rolled his eyes at his brothers' taunting, and Cassidy couldn't help but chuckle at her twin's annoyance.

"Boys, stop it," Lynne sighed as she took a sip of wine.

"Cassidy, you still working at the nerd capital?" Eric asked over the laughter, clearly desperate to get the attention off of him.

Cassidy scrunched up her nose and glowered at him. "I didn't say a word; don't throw me under the bus," she grumbled before shoving a forkful of lasagna in her mouth.

"Cassidy, be nice," Art said blandly. His focus was on his dinner.

"What?" Cassidy squeaked in annoyance. She caught Ben's eye, as he was sitting between her and her father, and he was grinning, thoroughly enjoying how quickly dinner had turned to chaos.

"Just asking," Eric backtracked.

"I didn't call you a virgin! But I don't think Ellie is pregnant. If she was, waiting until second trimester to waddle down the aisle would be just stupid," Cassidy reasoned.

"Thanks, I guess," Eric sighed.

"Anyway!" Lynne said loudly. "Eric, what other wedding decisions have you made?"

"I know Ellie and her sister have been looking at flowers, and invites, but I don't think much else. I guess if we are moving it up, decisions will have to be made more quickly." Eric took a bite of his dinner.

"What's the color theme?" Lynne asked curiously.

"Oh, yes, please, tell us the color theme!" Matty said mockingly. Cassidy couldn't help but chuckle. Eric shot her an annoyed look.

"I don't know, mom, I'll let you know at soon as I do." Eric turned his focus back to his meal.

"I'm just asking." Lynne shrugged.

"Ben, did you get your apartment yet? I want you moved in before classes start," Art asked pointedly. Cassidy was thrilled for the change in topic. The last thing she wanted to hear about was Eric's wedding.

"Yeah, yeah, I think Steve and I are signing the paperwork sometime this week after practice. But we definitely got in with the lottery for the upper-classmen apartments. So we'll still get to be on campus," Ben replied.

"I'm glad you've been able to stay on campus for all four years," Lynne said with a smile. "I don't want you to have to deal with driving in the city during rush hour to get to and from school."

"Mmm-hmmm," Ben agreed with his mouth full of lasagna.

"Yeah, now he can just stumble to the bar, stumble to practice, stumble to his apartment, then repeat. No driving required!" Matty said sarcastically.

"The damn classroom better be part of that stumble," Art advised.

"Excuse me, but I've been on the Dean's List every semester!" Ben pointed out.

"As through Ds get degrees," Alex said in a sing-song voice, causing all five Banker kids to chuckle.

"That's terrible advice for your younger brother," Lynne sighed. Alex shrugged, clearly unbothered.

Quickly Art changed the subject to the construction on Main Street and the closing of the local hardware store, and the rest of the meal was uneventful. Dinner and cleaning up was followed by a round and a half of Pictionary before arguments broke out, causing Art to huff off to his private study and Ben to stomp upstairs to his bedroom. Alex, Matty, Cassidy, and Eric quickly finished their beers, kissed their mom goodbye and headed back to their separate homes. They all had reached their fill of family time for the evening.

# Chapter 11

Cassidy slammed her car door as she flopped into the driver's seat of her Toyota. It had been the Tuesday from hell at work and she was beyond ready to get back to her apartment. As soon as she got out of the parking garage, she cranked up the radio as she merged onto the city street.

She had made it a mere four blocks from her office, Madonna blasting from her speakers, when she heard a loud pop and her car suddenly jerked to the right.

"Shit," Cassidy screamed, frantically weaving to the side of the road. Cars honked as she pulled off the busy street and onto the safety of the shoulder. She quickly turned down the music before switching off the engine.

"Shit," Cassidy whined, her head tilting back on the headrest. She didn't need to get out of the car to know what happened. She had popped a tire. This was absolutely the last thing she needed today.

After a long minute of feeling sorry for herself, she carefully got out of her car during a break in traffic, and scooted to the passenger side where she could safely inspect the damage to her front passenger-side tire.

It was completely flat. There was no way it could be patched and salvaged. Cassidy bit her bottom lip as she tried to process her situation. She opened the trunk of the car and saw there was a donut as well as the car jack, still in its box, that her father had bought her when she was sixteen and insisted she keep in her trunk. Cassidy sighed. She guessed it was a good thing she'd never thrown it out.

The only problem was – she had no idea what to do next.

She knew the basic principles of changing a tire, but she had never done it herself before. When Cassidy and Eric were sixteen, a week prior to their driving tests, Art had dragged them both outside to give a tire changing demonstration. Eric watched and took notes. Cassidy sat in the grass next to her twin and peeled the neon green nail polish off of her fingernails, occasionally repeating Eric's answers when Art checked to make sure they were paying attention.

As a matter of fact, she had only had one flat tire in her life. It was Easter break during her senior year of high school. Both Alex and Matty were home from college for the week and all five Banker siblings were outside and playing one of their longstanding, made-up games with ridiculous rules and many chances for injuries. This one in particular was a combination of baseball, rugby, and lawn darts. Surprisingly, none of the siblings got injured; however, during one of Ben's lawn dart throws, he had stepped out of bounds, which, according to the rules, meant he could be tackled. Unfortunately, Eric tackled him when he was in mid-throw and the lawn dart careened off course and landed squarely in the tire of the little, beat up Dodge that Cassidy drove all through high school and college. It let out a pathetic squeal and deflated unceremoniously in the driveway.

Matty, who loved cars, had stepped right in and quickly changed the tire for her before either of their parents caught them, knowing they would all be in serious trouble.

Unfortunately, at this exact moment, she did not have any of her brothers or her dad around her to rescue her. Cassidy debated taking her purse, walking into one of the nearby stores and using a payphone to call for a cab. However, she knew she'd regret having to rescue her car later. Not to mention the earful she'd receive from her father if he heard about it.

Cassidy reluctantly pulled the jack out of the trunk and opened the box, trying to ignore all the cars passing by on their way home. She tossed the cardboard box into trunk as she pulled the crisp metal device out. As she walked back around to the front of the car with the jack in hand, determined to try to figure out how to actually use it, a tan pick-up truck pulled up behind her and shut off its engine.

Cassidy sighed. The last thing she wanted was an audience to her humiliation.

"Do you need any help?" a male voice called as the truck door opened.

"Um," Cassidy hummed. She was not in the mood to interact with a stranger; however, she was not exactly in a position to turn down help if she wanted to get home anytime soon.

"Oh, hey, it's you!" the male voice called. Cassidy's head snapped up. It was the statistician from the MU scrimmage last week!

"Hi," Cassidy said, with a surprised smile. She hadn't thought she'd ever see him again. However, she had mixed feelings about him witnessing her terrible mechanical skills so early in their acquaintance.

"Cassidy, right?" he asked. Cassidy felt herself blush slightly. She was thrilled that he remembered her.

"Yeah," Cassidy smiled. "Jake?"

"Yep," Jake smiled as he walked around the car to stand next to her.

Cassidy bit her lip.

"Tire issue?" Jake asked, looking down at the flat.

"Yep," Cassidy said, trying not to sound as defeated as she felt.

"Jeez, that's a nasty one," Jake remarked. Not the uplifting words Cassidy was hoping for.

"That's what I was afraid of," Cassidy sighed.

"Well, lucky for you, I can change tires in my sleep," Jake smirked. Cassidy felt her heart give a hard thud and a tingle shoot through her body.

"Yeah?" she mumbled, like a dope.

"You have a spare, right?" Jake asked.

"Umm, I think so." She fumbled for her keys and walked around Jake to the back of her car and unlocked the trunk. She rummaged past her gym bag and the laundry basket of old towels that she'd had every intention of taking to the Salvation Army four months ago. After some shifting, she was able to locate the donut spare wheel.

"Perfect," Jake said, looking over her shoulder. Cassidy reached in to grab it at the same moment that Jake did, causing their shoulders to bump.

"Oh, sorry," they said in unison. Cassidy fought the urge to shiver. She could smell his aftershave. It was alluring.

"I got it," Jake said, reaching past her as she paused, completely lost in the moment.

115

Jake plopped the tire on the sidewalk and got to work.

"Do you know what you hit?" Jake asked casually as he started to unscrew the lug nuts from the hubcap.

"No, not a clue," Cassidy said as she crouched down next to him to watch him work. She was a sudden mix of fascinated, insanely grateful, and incredibly turned on. In short, she was completely enamored; her heart pounded as she watched him work, sliding the jack underneath the car and starting to lift it.

"Are you sure you're not a mechanic?" Cassidy asked playfully. Jake chuckled.

"No, just learned as a kid. I always thought it would make me seem cool… I was wrong," he signed. Cassidy couldn't help but laugh as he placed the old tire on the ground next to her.

"I think it's very cool," she said.

"Oh, shit, I should have been telling you what I was doing so you could learn," Jake said, looking over at her. Cassidy blushed.

"No, no, this is better," she said, causing Jake to let out a short laugh. "I was taught as a teenager. My dad insisted I learn, but the truth is, I didn't pay attention and let my brother do all of the work."

"Ahh," Jake hummed. His focus was now on getting the donut wheel screwed on. Cassidy watched him in silence for a couple of minutes.

"I am really glad you stopped for me," Cassidy said as he started to lower the jack.

"I can't stand the idea of anyone stranded," Jake replied. Cassidy felt her stomach twitch. The comment was sweet, but it also reminded her that he hadn't stopped for her specifically, he just stopped to be a good Samaritan.

Cassidy's Toyota returned to ground level and Jake pulled the jack out.

"Oh my god," Cassidy sighed happily at the sight of a functioning wheel.

"Don't drive far on it. It'll be enough to get you home and then to the mechanic's soon to get a real tire," Jake said. He gathered up the jack and the split tire and headed back to the open trunk of Cassidy's car and deposited them inside.

"Okay."

"You should be all good now," Jake said, closing her trunk with a thump.

"Thank you! Seriously! So much! How, how can I ever thank you?" Cassidy asked frantically.

"Dinner?" Jake asked nonchalantly.

"Yes, absolutely!" Cassidy gushed. She would love to spend more time with this man.

"Oh!" Jake looked surprised at her quick reply. "Really?"

"Of course!" Cassidy insisted.

"Um, yeah, okay, dinner would be great," Jake said nervously. It seemed Car Hero Jake had much more confidence than Regular Jake. She found it kind of cute and endearing. Cassidy waited a moment, but he didn't say anything else.

"I'm free Sunday," Cassidy smiled.

"Oh! Oh, yeah, um, Sunday would be good for me," Jake said.

"Great!" Cassidy grinned up at him.

"Oh, um, how about the Chinese food place on Fourth? Do you like Chinese food?" Jake asked.

Cassidy nodded. "Love it. That sounds great."

"Great, great." Jake smiled nervously. Cassidy was completely charmed by his polite nerves.

"So, I'll see you there? 7-o'clock?"

"Yeah, yeah," Jake grinned. Cassidy grinned back.

"I'll meet you out front," Cassidy said as she started to slowly walk towards her car door.

"I'll be there," Jake said. "Drive safe!"

"Thanks again," Cassidy said as she climbed in the driver's seat and Jake shut the door behind her. She heard Jake give the roof of the car two pats and she grinned as she turned the key in the ignition.

Glancing back in her rear view mirror, she saw Jake getting back into his truck before signaling and merging back onto the road.

"Holy shit," Cassidy sighed as her car rumbled down the road. "I have a date with a stranger!" She chuckled at the sudden realization that this was her first proper date since college. Cassidy swore under her breath and gave another hearty laugh as she processed what her weekend held.

# Chapter 12

Cassidy swirled the straw in her Pepsi glass with her left hand as she smoothed her dress over her knees with her right hand under the dark wooden table at the Chinese restaurant. Jake sat across from her, his wavy copper hair shimmering in the ornate red and gold light above them.

Their date had started only fifteen minutes ago and Cassidy was already having a great time. They'd met at the front door of the restaurant. She wore a knee-length purple sundress and he was in jeans, a white button up, and brown sports coat pushed up to his elbows. He looked very handsome.

They had already gotten their drinks and put in their order, and were finally able to enjoy a moment for conversation.

"Are you from Erie?" Cassidy asked, absentmindedly stirring her Pepsi.

"Oh, no, from Johnsonburg," Jake replied.

"I've heard of that," Cassidy smiled.

Jake chuckled. "Pretty small town, but it was nice. What about you? Local?"

Cassidy shrugged. "From Meadville, so not too far. I've been living in Erie since I graduated, though."

"Where did you go to school?"

"Edinboro."

"Ooo, that's a small school," Jake commented.

Cassidy giggled. "It is. Far cry from Penn State, I know," she said.

Jake looked startled. "Shit, you knew I went to Penn State? Have we already had this conversation?" he asked.

"We had a very brief conversation at the scrimmage, so it doesn't really count," Cassidy said, not wanting him to feel guilty.

"Still," Jake shrugged, taking a sip from his glass of iced tea. "What about your family, are they still local?"

"Yep. My parents are still in Meadville - same house I grew up in, actually," Cassidy smiled. "Are your parents still in Johnsonburg?"

Jake nodded. "Yeah, well, it's just my mom,"

"Oh! Has it always been just you and her?" Cassidy asked, curious.

"No, I had both parents growing up - a younger brother, too. But my dad passed away about four years ago."

"Oh, I'm so sorry," Cassidy said. She felt her heart thump. She could not imagine the unavoidable moment of losing either of her parents. It was something she truly dreaded, and hoped it would be a long way off. A very long way off.

"No, no, it's okay," Jake said with a nervous smile.

"How is it okay?" Cassidy asked.

"I mean, it's okay, I'm not sad anymore. And, well, I, um... I wasn't super close to my dad, anyway," Jake explained, looking down at his drink.

"Oh." Cassidy didn't know what to say. She often took for granted how close she was with her family, and was always surprised that other families weren't as close.

"Please, don't be sad," Jake said with a smile, clearly desperate to move the conversation to a happier topic.

"You're right. You're okay, I'm okay," Cassidy smiled back.

"Do you have any siblings?" Jake asked. Cassidy grinned. She knew the exact reaction she was going to get – it was the same every time. Ever since preschool. Four brothers is a lot to process, apparently.

"Yes, I'm one of five."

"Five, wow," Jake said. Cassidy noticed a cautious look creep onto his face.

"I have four brothers," she added. Jake's eyes bugged for a second before he quickly composed himself. Cassidy couldn't help but giggle. She loved peoples' reactions.

"Are they older or younger?"

"Two older, one younger, and one my age," she explained.

"Oh," Jake nodded, processing for a moment. "Same age? Does that mean you're a twin?"

"Yep. And I'm older by twelve minutes," Cassidy said proudly.

Jake smiled widely at her. "I always thought that would be kind of cool," he mused. "Is it?"

"Umm," Cassidy chuckled, "it's okay. I mean, I love my brother, but we're not super close."

"Ah."

"What about you? You said you have a younger brother, right?"

"Yeah, Will is one year younger than me," Jake said.

"That's nice. Are you guys close?

"Nah, not really. I mean, we get along great, but we're really different. He's in law school outside of Harrisburg, so he's about five hours away," he said.

"That's cool... I mean about the law school, well, and that you get along," Cassidy said, processing as she spoke.

"Yeah."

Before they could say anything else, a waitress arrived at their table with two heaping plates of delicious-looking food. Jake had sweet and sour shrimp while Cassidy ordered sesame chicken. They quickly thanked her before digging in and enjoying their food for a minute.

"What was it like growing up in a big family?" Jake asked as he finished his egg roll.

"It was fun! I mean, I guess I never paid much attention to it. I actually always thought our family was small since we only have a couple of cousins and they all live out of state," Cassidy said, popping a slice of carrot in her mouth.

"Five kids is a small family?" Jake playfully mocked.

Cassidy laughed, now hearing how silly it sounded. "I was used to friends at school seeing so much extended family at every holidays, or on weekends. We just didn't have that," she explained.

"Hmmm," Jake thought as he took another bite.

"What about you? Did you always feel like a small family? Or did you have a lot of extended family?"

"Yeah, my family always felt really small. My dad traveled for work a lot, so he was gone often. My brother was in sports, so my mom just drove around for that. I was either with my friends or at his games, doing the stats," Jake shrugged.

"Ooo, so the statistics love started early," Cassidy smirked.

Jake blushed a bit.

"Yeah, I was always a bit of a math nerd and frankly, it gave me something to do at Will's games," he shrugged. Cassidy watched him for a moment. There was something beautiful and raw about his words, but she couldn't quite put her finger on it. It was at that moment that she knew this was not going to be their only date.

"I love that," she said. He smiled back at her.

They spent the rest of the meal talking about work. Jake loved both teaching and working with the baseball team. Cassidy couldn't help but feel her office accountant job was quite boring in comparison. However, they both enjoyed being numbers geeks. And there wasn't a moment of silence; they both had so much to say to each other. Cassidy's cheeks hurt from smiling so much.

They finished their meal, and Jake insisted on paying. As they slowly headed outside the restaurant to the noisy street, Cassidy realized she wasn't ready for the date to end.

"Do you want to go for a walk?" Jake asked.

Cassidy perked up happily. "Would love to."

They walked the two blocks to the lake front and commented on all the odd people they came across on their way: the drunk college kids, the angry business men, the random older people out on a late walk.

"Do you want to walk down the pier?" Jake asked. Cassidy nodded.

"I haven't been out here in years," she said as they walked. The summer breeze and the sound of the lake lapping against the shore was intoxicating.

"I made the walk out here only once, and it was the day I moved out here for work. I thought it was so cool," Jake said.

"It's fun in the summer, but an absolute nightmare in the winter. My friends and I would always be daring each other to go out in the snow. How we didn't die back in college, I have no idea," Cassidy laughed. She could feel Jake watching her, smiling.

"Other than working with numbers and risking your life on a pier in the snow, what do you like to do?" Jake asked. Cassidy gave a little snort.

Cassidy turned to rest against the metal railing along the edge of the pier. "I like going to the gym, spending time with my best friend, Marissa - we have an apartment together - and, I don't know, movies, being outside, I guess. I'm pretty boring,"

"I definitely would not call you boring," Jake said, leaning on the railing next to her.

"What about you?" Cassidy asked playfully.

"I like movies, board games, beer..."

"I like beer, too," Cassidy winked.

"No - I mean, yes, but I like trying new beers," he said.

"New beers?" Cassidy asked. Her dad had been drinking the same brand of beer her entire life. She knew there were others - she'd had cheaper brands in college - but honestly, she'd never paid much attention to any of it.

"Yeah, like beer tastings, stuff like that."

"I know nothing about any of this, but I officially need to know more," Cassidy said, looking at him intently. This was the first time she had even heard of this hobby. She'd dated plenty of guys who did things she had no interest in, but she knew nothing of the world of beer tastings.

"Well, there's a festival here in a couple of weeks. We could, uh, go, if you'd like?" Jake said nervously.

124

"Here in Erie?"

"Yeah, it's like the fifth annual one or something," Jake shrugged.

"Shit, I'm really out of it," she said to no one in particular.

Jake grinned at her. "I'm happy to teach you... Well, if you'd like."

"I would like that a lot," Cassidy said.

"Good."

"Okay, let's get back to something I do know: games!"

"Yes?"

"I should remind you, I have four brothers. I'm competitive as hell. You have been warned," Cassidy smirked.

"Duly noted," Jake nodded.

"Which are your favorites?"

"Oh, anything. From good old Scrabble to Pictionary. I like Risk, Monopoly, Trivial Pursuit, Taboo, even Battleship, Clue, Sorry - honestly, whatever. Enjoy learning new ones, as well," Jake explained.

Cassidy smiled. "Nice! Monopoly and Trivial Pursuit generally end in fist fights, in my family," she added.

"Fist fights?"

"Four brothers," she reminded him.

"But no fighting for you?" Jake asked playfully.

"Oh, hell yeah," Cassidy said firmly. Jake laughed. "But I'm never the one to start the fights."

"Clearly a difference," Jake teased.

Cassidy and Jake spent the next hour telling game-playing stories from their childhoods, although Cassidy's stories revolved more around the arguments that broke out during game play than the actual games. However, Jake hung on every word she said. Cassidy was elated at how fascinated

125

he seemed to be with all of her stories. She loved his honest interest and passion for his hobbies; it was a trait she honestly wasn't used to seeing much of. Most of the people she hung out with were so nonchalant about everything. She loved Jake's enthusiasm.

As the breeze off the lake started to pick up, they slowly made their way back down the pier and into downtown, towards the Chinese restaurant where their evening had started.

"Where are you parked?" Jake asked.

"Just over here." Cassidy pointed to a street parking spot where her blue Toyota sat. They made their way over and Cassidy rested her left hip on the driver's side door.

"So, um," Jake stuttered nervously.

"I had a good time tonight," Cassidy interjected with a smile. A grateful smile spread across Jake's face.

"I had a good time tonight, too," he said.

"Yeah," Cassidy nodded, dying for him to make the next move. She was used to guys being more forward, but she was charmed by Jake's shyness.

"I'd love to hang out again… go out again," Jake corrected himself.

"Me too," Cassidy smiled.

"So, um, can I call you and set something up?" Jake asked. Cassidy felt her heart swell. She couldn't remember the last time a guy had been so nervous around her.

"Yes, let me give you my number," she said, quickly reaching in her purse. She always carried a pen with her, a trait she'd picked up from her mother when she was a little girl. Even in the little girl purses she wore for playing dress up, there'd always been a pen in her bag.

After only a couple seconds of searching, Cassidy produced

a blue gel pen and hastily pulled off the lid.

"Here, give me your arm," she instructed. Jake extended his left arm. His sports jacket sleeve was still pushed up to his elbow and Cassidy took hold of his forearm and quickly scribbled out her seven digits. "There!"

"Thanks." Jake smiled, looking down at his new marking.

"I really did have a good night," Cassidy smiled, taking half a step closer to him.

"Me too," Jake grinned. There was a pause. The air felt heavy. Cassidy gazed up into his hazel eyes as he looked down at her. Without any hesitation, Cassidy pushed herself up slightly and connected her lips to his. Instantly, she knew she had taken him by surprise. He didn't push her back, he just froze.

After a long moment, Cassidy slowly pulled back from the kiss. Her eyes fluttered open to find Jake looking pleasantly surprised.

"I," Cassidy started to explain herself, but Jake interrupted her by leaning forward and again pressing his lips to hers. Cassidy smiled into the kiss. It was nice to be kissed back. His lips were soft and warm, and she felt a tingle of electricity at their touch.

Too soon, Jake pulled back. They grinned at each other for a long moment. Cassidy's heart was racing. She hadn't felt like this on a date in a long time. Actually, she couldn't even remember the last time she'd been on a proper date like this. She loved it.

"Well, goodnight," Cassidy said, attempting to hide the giddiness in her voice.

"Well, good night," Jake repeated, reaching past her to open up her car door. Cassidy got in and waved as she started up the engine. Jake smiled and retreated towards his car.

"Oh my god!" Cassidy whispered to herself in elation before shifting her car into gear and heading home, anxious to tell Marissa everything.

# Chapter 13

Cassidy towel dried her hair after changing into her pajamas. She had immediately taken a shower after returning to her apartment, needing a moment to process her thoughts and, frankly, cool herself down a bit. Not to mention, Marissa was out, and she didn't have anyone to talk to.

She tossed her towel onto the hook on the back of her bedroom door before emerging to hear the TV on and the sound of the Cheers theme song ringing through the living room. NBC always played reruns in the late night.

"Hey!" Marissa called from the sofa.

"Hi," Cassidy smiled as she made her way into the room and plopped down on the opposite side of the couch. She pulled her feet up underneath her. "When did you get home?"

"About ten minutes ago," Marissa replied. She was still in her floral dress from her date with Brandon that evening.

"Good time?" Cassidy asked. Marissa looked at her aghast.

"Yes, but who cares? What happened?" Marissa enunciated

loudly.

Cassidy grinned. "It was good. Really good."

"Yeah?" Marissa pressed, leaning forward slightly.

"He was just so easy to talk to! I, I really like him," Cassidy admitted with a blush.

"Ahhh," Marissa gushed.

"He's a good kisser, too," Cassidy smirked.

Marissa looked at her wide eyed for a moment before leaning forward and smacking her knee. "Why didn't you open with that?!" she asked.

Cassidy guffawed. "I mean we just kissed twice, but both were really nice. Well, the second was much better," she said dreamily.

Marissa tilted her head. "I'm guessing you're seeing him again?" she asked.

"Yeah, I think so. I mean, we both wanted to, and I gave him my number, so… here's hoping he calls soon," Cassidy sighed.

"He will!" Marissa assured her. Cassidy smiled. Marissa didn't know Jake from a stranger, yet she was already defending his good intentions just because Cassidy liked him. Everyone deserved a friend like Marissa.

"I just got home like half an hour ago, so he definitely won't call tonight," Cassidy said.

"It's almost midnight. It would be creepy if he called now," Marissa said. Cassidy snorted.

"True. But I think he'll call tomorrow."

"Definitely. I'll make sure the answering machine tape is clear in case he calls while we're at work," Marissa said.

The girls stayed up and talked for another fifteen minutes, gushing about their dates and discussing the food they had eaten, one of their favorite topics, before heading to bed. They both had work the next morning.

It took Jake less than twenty-four hours to call Cassidy after their first date. They spoke on the phone Monday after work for over thirty minutes. Cassidy relished how natural conversation continued to feel with Jake. It was just easy.

Jake surprised her by inviting her to go bowling with him on Thursday and Cassidy happily accepted. She had never bowled on a date before, but Jake seemed to be ready to take on her competitive spirit, and she figured it was better to scare him off now rather than after they got attached.

Cassidy was even more thrilled when he asked if he could pick her up this time. It felt like a good sign - like he wasn't planning on bailing. Plus, she always loved riding in guys' cars.

The days seemed to drag until Thursday finally came around. Marissa even made sure she got home before Jake arrived to pick her up at six-thirty to get a chance to catch a glimpse of the famous Jake. The grin she gave Cassidy as she was leaving leaving made it clear that she fully approved.

They were now on their ninth frame and second plate of cheese fries in the large bowling alley about ten minutes west of the city. Cassidy was ahead by seven points and enjoying her lead. She had to admit, Jake held his own - not only in the game, but in the competitive spirit and playful trash talk. She could just relax and be herself.

"Wooo! Spare!" Cassidy cheered loudly as she spun around after her turn and skipped back to their bench.

"I can still catch up," Jake smirked as he stood up for his roll.

"I highly doubt that," Cassidy giggled as she sat down where he had just been and popped a cheesy fry into her mouth. Jake bowled the dark red ball down the lane and managed to topple only three pins. Cassidy laughed.

"That doesn't bode well for your score," she teased.

"I've got one more roll and one more frame," Jake grinned. Unfortunately for him, his next roll got only him an additional two pins. Cassidy tried to hide her glee.

"My turn! If I get at least five, I win - you can't catch up!" Cassidy gloated as she playfully bumped into his shoulder on her way to pick up her green ball from the return.

"You could always get a gutter ball," Jake teased.

"Oh, very unlikely!" Cassidy laughed, before rolling her ball down the lane. The ball gave a satisfying thunk as it hit the pins and knocked down seven.

"Shit," Jake laughed, as Cassidy screamed in joy. She skipped back over to him and reached up, grabbed his face with both her hands, and placed a hard kiss on his lips. Jake jolted slightly, taken by surprise. Cassidy pulled back and grinned at him.

"I won," she said in a sing-song voice.

"You did," Jake conceded with a smile. Cassidy beamed – not only at the win, but because they had had so much fun. He wasn't intimidated by her competitive spirit! He was, however, intimidated by her natural reaction to kiss him. Cassidy knew she could get him used to that.

"This was so much fun!" Cassidy said.

"What, winning?" Jake teased. Cassidy snorted.

"That was part of the fun, but I enjoyed playing with

someone else who likes to play."

"I told you, I like games," Jake said.

"You did."

Cassidy and Jake gathered their things and returned their shoes, before heading out of the bowling alley into the warm summer night air.

"What do you want to do now?" Jake asked.

"Want to go for a drive?" Cassidy suggested. What she really wanted to do was kiss him again, but she knew he was a little jumpy and she didn't want to push too hard. Not to mention, he was her ride, and she had absolutely no idea where they were.

"Sure," Jake said, leading her to the car and opening the passenger door for her.

"Thank you," Cassidy said, and smiled.

Jake started up his truck and the engine rumbled as they made their way out of the parking lot and onto the road. They drove for about fifteen minutes, happily chatting about some of the more interesting patrons they'd seen at the alley that evening.

"Where do you want to go?" Jake asked.

Cassidy chuckled. "I thought you knew where you were going,"

"Nope, just driving. Seeing where we end up," Jake admitted with a chuckle of his own.

"Well, where did we end up?" Cassidy looked around. It looked like Erie suburbs - nothing special.

"Hey, there's a diner. Up for a malt?" Jake asked.

Cassidy agreed, seeing the red neon sign glowing a top a nondescript small white brick building.

They pulled into the lot and got a seat in a corner booth

along the window and ordered two chocolate malts.

"I feel like I'm in Grease," Cassidy teased.

"Is that a bad thing?" Jake asked.

"Definitely not." She'd been to see that movie four times in theaters when it came out in her sophomore year of high school.

"Tell me something I don't know about you," Jake posed.

Cassidy raised an eyebrow. "This is our second date. There's a fair number of things you don't know about me yet," she giggled.

"Then enlighten me with something," Jake said. Their waitress walked over and placed two frosty malt glasses in front of them. They thanked her and each took a large sip. It was very sweet and chocolatey. It reminded Cassidy of her childhood.

"Something about me…" Cassidy hummed in thought.

"Could be anything! Just something I don't know yet."

"Okay, um… I actually hate accounting. Well, no, hate is a strong word. I don't care about accounting. It's just that math was always really easy for me, and I wanted a job that could be easy so I didn't have to be consumed by it and would be able to just enjoy my life." Cassidy chewed on the tip of the straw anxiously. She had never admitted that fact out loud before.

"Wow!" Jake gave her a surprised smile. "Playing the system, then, huh?"

"Never thought of it like that," Cassidy chuckled. "Alright, your turn. Tell me something new."

"Alright, well… I guess that my younger brother and I are polar opposites." He shrugged.

Cassidy scrunched up her face a bit. "That's not a secret."

"You didn't say it had to be a secret, you said something

134

you didn't know yet. You didn't know that, did you?"

"Well, no." Cassidy giggled again before taking a long sip.

"See, I played your game," Jake smirked.

"You started the game; it's your game!" Cassidy pointed out playfully.

They spent another thirty minutes at the diner enjoying their malts. The conversation flowed easily, and they ended up discussing baseball until they left.

Jake weaved through the city as they made their way back to Cassidy's apartment complex. She smiled over at him as they drove in silence, Bon Jovi crooning through the radio speaker. It felt comfortable and safe.

After about ten minutes, Jake pulled into one of the empty spaces in the complex lot and shifted the truck into park.

"I had a really good time tonight," he said, smiling over at her. Cassidy felt her heart flutter.

"So did I," Cassidy said. She leaned forward and pressed her lips to his. A spark shot through her body at the touch of his lips. It was wonderful. Jake kissed her back firmly for a few seconds before pulling back. Cassidy let out a small sigh at the loss of his lips.

"I'll call you tomorrow, but I'd really like to see you again," Jake said, reaching over and taking her hand in his. His hands were large and secure. They weren't soft, but they were not calloused, either.

"The date doesn't have to be over." Cassidy gave a playful shrug as she smiled up at him. She was more than happy to have Jake follow her upstairs.

"It doesn't?" His eyes were on Cassidy's hand entwined with his.

"You're welcome to come on up," Cassidy said, leaning

over and placing a soft kiss on his cheek. Stubble brushed against her lips. She loved it.

"No, no, not tonight," Jake said, shaking his head. Cassidy watched him for a long moment. She wasn't used to a guy not pushing for sex at the end of the second date. She wasn't sure if she found it flattering or annoying.

"Oh, um, okay," she said, trying not to sound too disappointed. Jake looked over and their eyes locked.

"I'll call you tomorrow after work," he assured her, leaning over to place a soft kiss on her cheek. Cassidy smiled.

She opened the passenger door and stepped out of the truck into the warm air.

"Good night. I had a good time," Cassidy assured him once more.

"Me too. Night."

She shut the door and made her way to the entrance of her apartment complex, stepping into the lobby without looking back – grinning widely as she went.

# Chapter 14

Cassidy paced in front of the phone in the living room, her right forefinger absentmindedly twirling in the coil cord as she listened to the ringing and waited for a pickup. She'd found Ellie's phone number in the phone book and decided to reach out. She was good at winning people over. Perhaps, the thought, she could befriend Ellie and get her on her side.

After the sixth ring, someone picked up.

"Hello?" Cassidy did not recognize the female voice.

"Hi, is Ellie there?" Cassidy asked politely.

"Yes, she is; who's calling?"

"Cassidy Banker."

"Okay, hang on."

Cassidy waited patiently. She heard the receiver being set down and a muffled conversation in the background.

"Hi, um, Cassidy?" Ellie's familiar, gentle voice sounded in Cassidy's ear. She sounded confused.

"Hi, Ellie! How are you?" Cassidy asked perkily. She knew she'd have to really sell it. There was a long pause.

"I'm great. You?"

"Great!"

There was an uncomfortable pause.

"Cassidy, why are you calling?" Ellie asked.

"Look, I know we didn't get off on the right foot, or any foot, for that matter, but you are marrying into my family, so I was wondering if you wanted to get together and talk about the wedding, maybe? You can tell me all your exciting plans," Cassidy offered.

"Oh, uh, wow," Ellie stuttered. Cassidy winced; she knew she was coming on too strong.

"Maybe next week?" Cassidy pushed gently.

"Well, I don't have a lot of things together yet. My sister and I have been looking at tons of magazines; it's getting a little chaotic. More so since we moved up the wedding," Ellie chuckled.

"I'm happy to let you bounce ideas off of me," Cassidy suggested.

"Yeah, yeah, I mean, I know you're not super into wedding stuff, but I appreciate the offer," Ellie said. Cassidy scrunched up her face, really glad they weren't having this conversation in person.

"Happy to talk through ideas," Cassidy said simply.

"Well, that's great! Um, yeah, let me talk to my sister and see what day she has free next week and I'll let you know," Ellie said. Her tone had turned from confusion to excitement.

"Let me give you my number," Cassidy offered before reciting the seven digits. The girls bid their goodbyes and hung up. Cassidy let out a sigh as she slumped into the large

138

blue chair next to the TV.

"What was all that?" Marissa asked, emerging from her room. Cassidy shrugged.

"Just thought I could reach out to Ellie, maybe get in her good graces," Cassidy said.

"Are you honestly trying to worm your way into being a bridesmaid?" Marissa asked pointedly.

"What?" Cassidy asked. She couldn't even feign confusion, though; Marissa knew her too well.

"Cassidy!" Marissa scolded.

Cassidy shrugged.

"You don't want to do this. You're going to hate being a part of that wedding, and you're going to make Eric really mad at you!" Marissa pointed out.

"Why would he be mad at me? I'm trying to be nice to his future wife. He should be happy," Cassidy argued.

Marissa sighed in defeat.

It was mid-week and Cassidy was just returning from her lunch break in the small kitchen in the back corner of the office.

"Banker," her boss, Mr. Jelif, called out curtly before she made it all the way back to her desk.

"Yes?" Cassidy asked. Mr. Jelif was a naturally grumpy man; she had learned to tune out his curtness when he spoke.

"My office," Mr. Jelif ordered. Cassidy shrugged and placed her empty lunchbox on her desk before turning to head toward his large office with the double doors.

"Private meeting, huh?" Devon crooned suggestively as

she walked past his desk.

"Luckily it's not with you," Cassidy mocked sarcastically. Devon rolled his chair back and started to stand up.

"That could be arran—"

"Not in a million years, Devon," Cassidy interrupted firmly. The thought of Devon even touching her arm was enough to make Cassidy shudder. Devon swore under his breath and rolled back to his desk as Cassidy approached the large office doors, knocked ceremonially, and let herself inside.

"Banker," Mr. Jelif nodded. He was an older man, early sixties, at least. Tall, with white hair and a beard. He almost never cracked a smile.

"Sir," Cassidy nodded in return. She liked working for Mr. Jelif. He'd taken a chance on hiring her right out of college, and held her to high standards. As long as she met every benchmark and deadline, which she always did, he never micromanaged her. Cassidy appreciated his management style and was grateful she had him as her boss.

"Close the door," Mr. Jelif ordered. Cassidy did as he asked before coming to sit in one of the brown wooden chairs in front of his large desk.

"What can I help you with?"

"I need you to look over some accounts for me," Mr. Jelif instructed.

"Me?" Cassidy asked, surprised he was reaching out to the youngest member of the accounting team.

"Yes. You are the most detail-oriented person here, and I need an eagle eye to find out if there's anything left to save," Mr. Jelif explained, handing her a large portfolio. Cassidy took it from him and opened it, giving it a cursory look to see if she had any questions before she left.

140

"Looks pretty typical of a company about to go under," Cassidy commented as she glanced over the columns of red numbers.

"No saving it?" Mr. Jelif asked. Cassidy shrugged.

"Never say never, but there would have to be a lot of changes and cutbacks. It would take a lot to get them out of the red. There's too much overhead and way too many personnel," Cassidy said, scanning the pages as she flipped through.

"I'll need you to put together a revival plan once you go through the numbers. Make this your top priority and give it your full attention," Mr. Jelif said. Cassidy looked up at him. She felt honored, but very confused.

"Mr. Jelif, what is this?" Cassidy asked.

He took a deep breath. "Our company," he admitted. Cassidy's eyes bugged.

"What?" Her heart was in her stomach and she felt like she could not breathe.

"We're going under, Banker. We have been for over a year, but I was hoping it would even out, or a miracle would happen in the market. But nothing came."

"I, I, I don't understand how we could be doing this poorly," Cassidy stuttered. She was in shock.

"This is business, Banker. Something you don't understand yet," Mr. Jelif said firmly.

"I don't know how to run a business. What do you expect me to do about this?"

"What you do is, you comb through every single line and digit with an eagle eye. I want a full report of how to turn this around - no matter what it costs," Mr. Jelif instructed.

Cassidy felt her heart thump. She willed herself to not tear up. This was not an easy assignment. "But," she started.

141

"No 'buts.' I need you to do this. And don't you even think about telling a single soul in this office. If you do, you'll be fired immediately," Mr. Jelif warned. Cassidy didn't know how to react.

"When do you need this by?" she asked timidly. She was extremely shaken.

"As soon as you possibly can. Take it home and work on it. Ideally by Friday," Mr. Jelif said.

"Friday?" Cassidy repeated. That only gave her two days.

"As you said yourself, Banker, this company is going under."

Cassidy wanted to scream; she wanted to argue. She was at a loss and her mind could not make sense of what was happening.

"Um," Cassidy mumbled.

"That is all. You are excused - but remember: not a word," Mr. Jelif reiterated firmly. Cassidy nodded. She stood up, closed the portfolio and exited the office, trying very hard to make her face look neutral.

"What was all of that about?" Devon asked, wiggling his eyes suggestively as she walked by. Cassidy hated that she had to pass him to get back to the safety of her desk.

"Nothing," Cassidy lied. Oh, how very much she would like to tell him it was about him getting fired. However, given that everyone here was about to be out of a job, it was a morbid thought.

"Oh really?" Devon asked. He started to follow her.

"Devon, I'm very busy and I have a lot of clients to tend to," Cassidy said. She took a seat at her desk and popped the portfolio in the top drawer.

"And what's that?" Devon asked, referring to the recently

hidden portfolio.

"Private client documents. Please leave and let me do my job," Cassidy said, avoiding his eyes. He drove her nuts. Thankfully, growing up with four brothers had given her a high tolerance for male bullshit.

"Oh, I bet you do a good job," Devon winked.

"You're disgusting. Go away," Cassidy grumbled.

"Just let me dream," Devon said playfully before turning and sauntering off to his desk. Cassidy rolled her eyes as she watched him go, letting out a sigh the moment he was out of her space.

Cassidy opened her desk and glanced at the portfolio. She didn't want this responsibility. Even if it could mean saving her job, she knew she would be destroying others. The weight of the situation felt like a noose around her neck.

Cassidy slammed the drawer shut and quickly opened one of her regular client folders, desperate to be distracted by monotonous work for a few minutes before taking on this monumental task.

The white wine in Marissa's glass sparkled against the side lamp in their apartment living room. Cassidy looked at it longingly. She was sprawled out on the living room floor looking through the thick company portfolio as Marissa lounged on the sofa reading a book and sipping wine. Cassidy had abstained from any alcohol that evening as she knew she had to work - and work a lot harder than usual. She'd always been quick, requiring little effort to succeed at her studies or work. But she wanted this to be exceptional. It had to be exceptional.

"Ugh," she groaned loudly. Looking at her company's books was making her mind spin. How could they be doing this poorly?

"How's it going?" Marissa asked, not looking up from her book.

"Not great."

"Can you explain something to me?" Marissa asked, lowering the paperback to her lap.

"Hmm?"

"How exactly did saving the company fall to you?" Marissa asked.

"I'm not doing this to save the company. I need to come up with a breakdown report so others that are much higher up can make informed decisions on what to do," Cassidy explained as she flipped to the next page.

Marissa raised her eyebrows.

"What?" Cassidy asked.

"I just don't understand why you specifically were chosen to do this."

"Who knows! Maybe since I've only been there two and a half years, I have the least to lose? I really have no clue," Cassidy replied, feeling even more frazzled. Why had she been chosen for this?

"Okay," Marissa said skeptically.

"You have more to say, don't you?" Cassidy knew Marissa too well to imagine she'd just roll over and accept a situation.

"Well, kind of. But also, if your company really is collapsing, I don't feel it's right for me to find more holes in the already-porous game plan," Marissa said. Cassidy let out a frustrated breath, mostly annoyed that Marissa was right. Her world was collapsing and she had no idea what was going to happen. Cassidy hadn't expected to have to search for a new job any time soon. She was comfortable, and she liked being comfortable.

# Chapter 15

Cassidy tapped her toes on the concrete steps excitedly. It was Friday night and she was standing in front of Jake's house, a half house he was renting on the east side of the city. Jake had called her a few times this past week, which had been a good distraction for Cassidy since work had been hell. Yesterday he'd invited her out for their third date at his house to play board games. Cassidy was thrilled.

"Hi," Jake said with a smile as he opened the door. He was in jeans and a blue Penn State t-shirt.

"Hey!" Cassidy smiled. Jake had told her to dress casually since they would be hanging out at his house, so she was in her comfortable yellow sundress. She appreciated the lack of formality; it made it easier to relax.

"Come on in." Jake stepped aside to let her in. Cassidy stepped into the living room, giving Jake a light peck on the lips as she walked past. Despite the fact that he had lived here for the last two years, the room was fairly stark: nothing on the walls and a few mismatched pieces of furniture. It was clean, but definitely not homey.

"Nice," Cassidy commented as she looked around. She was only half lying. There was a lot of space and everything was nice, it was just the lack of personality holding her back from loving it.

"Do you want a tour?"

"Definitely!" Cassidy beamed.

The ground floor consisted of the living room, dining room, and kitchen, all with bare walls and minimal furniture. The stairs off the dining room took them to a paneled hallway leading to three small bedrooms and a white and beige bathroom at the end of the hall.

After the tour, Jake brought her back to the kitchen to get a snack.

"I have some pizza rolls in the oven right now; they should be done in a few minutes," Jake said.

"Great," she chuckled. Total bachelor food. Not that she was mad about it.

"I've pulled a few games out in the living room. As soon as the rolls are done, we can head in," Jake said. Cassidy could tell he was nervous. She wanted him to know how happy she was to be there, so she closed the gap between them.

"We can pass the time," she whispered before pushing herself up slightly and pressing her lips to his. Jake let out a surprised chuckle, but cupped her face with his left hand and kissed her back.

Their lips moved slowly together and Cassidy's heart started to race. She loved the feeling of his lips on hers and the smell of his aftershave. She snaked her arms around his shoulders as they kissed.

The kisses were soft but firm, never deepening, but their

mouths moved with vigor and passion, both enjoying being on the cusp of something more.

They were interrupted by the beeping of the timer Jake had set on the microwave. They pulled apart with a jolt of surprise and both chuckled.

"Dinner," Jake teased. Cassidy smiled as she watched him shut off the timer before tending to the oven. She was reveling in the warmth that filled her belly. It was only going to get better as the night went on.

She wanted this night. She needed this night.

Five minutes later, they were seated on the brown shag carpet in the living room. A large plate piled high with half-exploded pizza rolls sat on the coffee table between them and Jake was setting up a game as they ate.

"I cannot remember the last time I played Parcheesi," Cassidy said, popping a hot pizza roll into her mouth.

"I love it," Jake said, focused on the set up.

"Enough to lose miserably to me?" Cassidy teased.

Jake looked up at her a smirked. "In your dreams, Banker."

Cassidy laughed. She was always pleasantly surprised at how well Jake handled her competitive nature. She liked having someone that she could be herself around. She liked having someone that wouldn't be scared away by her family. This was only the third date, but it was the start of something. Cassidy could feel it.

"How was your day?" Cassidy asked. She knew that once game play started, there was a low chance they would be having deep conversations.

"Good. I gave a test to my stats class, so there wasn't a lot for me to do," Jake said. "But I had to go over some of the books with the baseball coach after lunch to figure out some of the starters."

"Oh, cool." Cassidy was intrigued.

"Well, we'll see how it plays out on the field. What works in the books doesn't always work in real life."

"That is true."

"What about you? Did you get that report in?" Jake asked. Now that he had finished setting up the game he popped two pizza rolls into his mouth at once. Cassidy tied to hide her smile as he winced from the heat.

"Ugh," Cassidy groaned. "Yes, I did. But I have no idea what's going to happen. I was shooed out of the room as soon as I turned it in. Didn't talk to Mr. Jelif the rest of the day... or even really see him."

"What was your suggestion in the report?" Jake asked.

Cassidy shook her head frantically. "Oh, no! I didn't give any suggestions. I mean, I don't have any right to. I just had to give the facts and figures. We're spending more money than we're bringing in. I mean, like, we're hemorrhaging money."

"But you're smart, you have to have some ideas. It can't just be the end of the line," Jake said. "If it was one of your clients, you wouldn't tell them to just throw in the towel!"

"If it was one of my clients, I absolutely would. You have to cut your losses at some point if you want any hope of moving on," Cassidy groaned.

"I understand, but you have to find a next step, too, right?"

Cassidy bit her lip. "Ideally, yes. But it feels weird that I was even given this data. I'm most likely out of a job within the next year," Cassidy said glumly. She'd never put much thought into her working life. She'd always just assumed there would be a job waiting for her. She hated the realization that there might not be.

"Do you want to talk about it?" Jake offered, popping another pizza roll in his mouth. Cassidy felt her heart thud. She looked over at his sweet, sincere face. He truly cared. He was actually offering to just sit and talk. But Cassidy was tired of thinking about work. She had been looking forward to the distraction of the night and wasn't going to let anything to get in her way. Good intentions or not.

"No," Cassidy shook her head gently. "I just don't want to think about it for a bit."

"Oh, okay." He gave her a small smile, which Cassidy reciprocated.

"Hand me the dice," Cassidy said, happily changing the subject and holding out her hand.

"You know what you're doing?" Jake asked playfully.

"Definitely," she winked, and rolled the dice. Their game night was on!

Cassidy loved to play games and enjoyed being with someone who could not only keep up, but could dish out the banter like she was used to. Jake won the first game. Then Cassidy picked Guess Who for their second game, and she was able to pull out a win. Not only was Jake good at banter, he was a good competitor. He played to win, but the results didn't affect his temperament. Cassidy was similar. She liked to win, but hated playing with people who threw the board when they lost.

This was a good sign.

By the time they were packing up the game box, the pizza roll pile had been completely devoured and they were both on their third beer.

"Do you want to do something else?" Cassidy asked slyly. She had enjoyed the games, but she was ready for the real event of the evening. She was ready to sleep with Jake. She wasn't used to waiting this long, but with Jake the pace felt natural, and she wanted the moment to be perfect. Given how much fun they had been having that evening, this could definitely be it.

"Another game?" Jake asked, his attention focused on the game box.

"No. I was thinking you could come sit by me," Cassidy suggested, biting her lip in anticipation.

"Huh?" Jake asked before looking up. The instant he saw the look on her face, he knew what she wanted. "Oh! Oh, yeah," he agreed in a stutter, setting the box aside and scooting his way to the other side of the coffee table where Cassidy was leaning up against the base of the couch.

"I'm really having a good time with you," Cassidy whispered, looking over at him. Jake scooted a bit closer and slid his right arm around her shoulders. Cassidy felt a flutter in her belly.

"I'm having a good time with you," Jake replied as he leaned down and lightly pressed his lips to hers. Cassidy smiled against his lips and kissed him back.

Their kisses started slowly: playful pecks. But after a minute, they become longer, more deliberate. Cassidy felt a tingle shoot through her body. His lips tasted so good, she felt intoxicated. Suddenly Jake pressed his lips harder on hers, pushing them open. Cassidy responded enthusiastically and deepened the kiss immediately. The feeling of his warm breath and his tongue on hers was fantastic. Sparks shot up her spine. Cassidy flung her arms around his shoulder and pulled him closer. Jake moved his hands to her waist. The quick shifts caused them to teeter slightly and fall back on the carpet, Jake landing on top of her. Cassidy gave a gasp of elation at the feeling of his weight on her and kissed him with even more fervor.

Jake propped himself up on the brown carpet while leaning over Cassidy, his right hand slowly running up and down her side, their kiss never once breaking.

They kissed for many minutes. Cassidy plunged her right hand in his copper, wavy hair and held on to his upper back with her left, practically clawing at him. She wanted to be closer, she needed to be closer. The sensations shooting through her were incredible.

Jake eventually pulled back from their kiss and slid his lips down her jaw line. The touch was so light, it almost tickled, but mostly, it drove Cassidy crazy. After tantalizingly trailing his lips all along her jaw, he settled on the side of her neck, where he kissed and licked the sensitive skin.

Cassidy gasped and twitched under him. She was buzzing from his touch. She never wanted this to end. How on earth could he be affecting her so much already?

"Jake," Cassidy panted in a low voice. Jake took the hint and moved his mouth from her neck back to her lips and their passionate kissing resumed immediately.

She reached down and caught Jake's right hand, and led it down to the hem of her dress. Unfortunately, Jake didn't seize the opportunity to rip off her dress, but rather let his fingers play with the fabric along the top of her thigh. Cassidy couldn't deny this felt amazing, but it wasn't really what she was hoping for at the moment. She decided he needed another hint. She slid her hand down from his shoulder and trailed it over his chest and stomach, which felt delightfully firm even through the fabric of his tee shirt. She trailed her hand down further, to the waistband of his jeans, where she worked quickly to pop open his top button. Jake chuckled against her lips before pulling back.

"What are you doing?" he asked, amused.

"What do you think?" Cassidy smirked.

Jake shook his head with a small smile. "Not tonight, babe," he said, leaning forward and giving her a gentle peck on the lips.

Cassidy giggled. "Oh really?" she teased, moving both hands to the front of his jeans. Jake intercepted her hands in his and moved back.

Cassidy raised an eyebrow. She no longer understood this game.

"Look, I like you, and this, this, is great. But it's as far as we're going tonight," he explained.

"Sure about that?" Cassidy asked again, eyeing the front of his pants. She had been positive she'd felt a bulge. Jake sighed.

"Yeah."

"I don't understand."

"Cassidy," Jake groaned. He sat himself up and re-buttoned his pants and adjusted them.

"Jake," Cassidy mimicked, sitting herself up as well so they were facing each other.

"I just, it's too soon," Jake admitted with a shrug.

"But it's the third date," Cassidy countered.

"What does that have to do with anything?"

"I mean, generally, the third date is where things move into the bedroom… or the floor," Cassidy said with a shrug. She was actually used to this stage coming much earlier in the courtship. The waiting had been fun, but she was ready to move forward.

"That's not a law!"

"Maybe it should be," Cassidy joked, desperate for this awkward moment to end. She was in uncharted waters, and she hated it.

Jake simply stared at her for a long moment. He looked hurt. Cassidy was confused.

"Is that what relationships are all about to you? Sex?" Jake asked seriously.

"It's not the only thing, but it is an important part. I mean, don't you think so?"

"Of course I do, which is why I don't want to sleep with you tonight."

"This makes no sense to me!" Cassidy threw her hands in the air emphatically.

"Cassidy, I've been hurt before. Really hurt. I'm not ready to jump into a physical relationship immediately," Jake admitted.

Cassidy wanted to make a joke, break the tension, but the look on his face hit her. He was... sad. Vulnerable. She had never seen him look like this before. She wasn't used to seeing any guy look like this.

"Oh," she said quietly.

"What does that mean?" Jake asked.

"It means, I, I never really thought about that," Cassidy admitted.

"What are you talking about?"

"About you being hurt."

"You think no one ever gets hurt?" Jake asked. Cassidy again felt her heart thud – but this time with a twinge of shame. He looked annoyed. She felt like an asshole.

154

"No, I know people do. But like, not guys… I don't know." Cassidy shrugged.

"Is that what you want? A guy that doesn't feel anything and just wants to sleep with you all the time?" Jake asked.

Cassidy had honestly never thought about it. All of her past relationships had been fairly surface level. They never talked about feelings. She'd dated Kevin for almost two years, and while she knew almost everything about him, she'd never thought of him getting hurt. He never let her see that side of him.

"No, no, I'm just… not used to it."

"Used to what?"

"Used to hearing what a guy is feeling. I guess my relationships were never super deep," Cassidy trailed off. She was starting to feel bad for herself. Had she spent her entire life in a shallow bubble and not even realized it?

"Do you just want something light and casual?"

"No," Cassidy said immediately. She wanted a deep relationship, and it scared the hell out of her because she knew, in that moment, that Jake would hold her to it.

"I don't want something light, either," Jake said with a small, slightly embarrassed smile. Cassidy grinned.

"But does that really mean we won't… you know … tonight?" Cassidy asked playfully. She hoped he might change his mind. She was desperate to be physical with him again.

"For me, it does," Jake told her. Cassidy swallowed her disappointment.

"Okay. I can wait," Cassidy replied, telling herself as much as she was telling Jake.

"Don't look so disappointed," Jake chuckled.

"It should be a compliment to you!" Cassidy covered her

face in embarrassment.

"It is," Jake smiled, pulling her hands off of her face. Cassidy looked deep into his eyes. She knew there was no turning back, that this could be the start of something real and deep and permanent.

"Can we still kiss, or do we just start knitting now?" Cassidy teased. Jake leaned forward to press his lips gently to hers.

# Chapter 16

Cassidy turned onto her childhood street for the second time in the month of August. It was a Sunday evening and she and her siblings were all returning to their parents' house to celebrate Ben's 22nd birthday. Ben's birthday had actually been that Friday, the 15th, however, he had partied with his friends the nights before so the family was getting together on Sunday. Cassidy assumed Ben would be hungover as hell this evening, and looked forward to watching everyone annoy him by being as loud as possible, which she knew her brothers would gladly do.

She turned into the long driveway to the familiar brick house and was surprised to find most of the cars there already.

She quickly parked and grabbed Ben's present – a new Nintendo game – and headed to the house. As she approached the front porch, the door opened and Alex emerged.

"Hey," Cassidy said happily.

"Hey." Alex pulled a green lighter out of his pocket and quickly lit his cigarette.

"Does mom know you're out here?" Cassidy smirked. Their parents hated that Alex smoked so much. Cassidy didn't love it either, but she was used to it.

"No." Alex took a drag. "And don't give me away!" He nodded to the far end of the porch, out of view of the large bay window in front. Cassidy followed him to the secluded corner. They all knew about the invisible corner. Cassidy herself had used it many times in high school when returning home from dates.

"How is it in there?" Cassidy asked, leaning against the rough exterior of the house. Alex settled on the porch railing across from her.

"Eh, not bad."

"Is Ben hungover?"

"Yeah. He already took a swing at Matty for popping a balloon by his head while he was lying down on the couch."

"I'm sober and I'd take a swing if someone popped a balloon at my head," Cassidy chuckled.

"Fair point."

"Everyone's here early," Cassidy commented.

"Just waiting on you and Eric," Alex said, flicking some ash off the railing.

"Is Eric bringing Ellie?"

Alex tilted his head and shot her a knowing look.

"What?" she asked.

"I was going to talk to you about that," Alex said.

"Ellie is coming?"

"No," Alex replied, "but you need to stay away from her."

"What? Why?" Cassidy scrunched up her face.

"Cassidy, I don't know what you're playing at, but leave her alone," Alex said firmly before taking another drag.

158

"I don't know what you're talking about," Cassidy countered, although she was fairly certain she did.

"You called Ellie the other day."

"It was last week, actually, and I'm still waiting for a call back," Cassidy said sassily. Alex just watched her for a moment. He didn't look amused.

Cassidy felt a weird pang in her chest, like she was a little kid in trouble.

"Why did you call her?"

"Sounds like you already know," she said defensively.

"Do you actually want to be her friend, or are you trying to weasel your way in?"

"Weasel?" Cassidy looked taken aback. "That's low."

"It may be, but I know damn well you're pissed about the wedding and are taking things into your own hands."

"First I'm supposed to be nice to Ellie, so I reach out, and now it's a problem?" Cassidy waved her arms dramatically.

"Cassie," Alex said in a low, warning tone.

"Why is this any of your business, anyway? I can be friends with whomever I want."

"Because we know you're not reaching out to Ellie out of the goodness of your heart."

"We?"

"Ellie told Eric you called. Did you honestly think she wouldn't?"

Cassidy paused. Honestly, she hadn't thought that far. Shit. "What does that have to do with anything?

"Eric is pissed."

"Why?"

"Ugh," Alex groaned. "Because you need to just let them have their day."

"But why are you the one cornering me if Eric is so pissed?" Cassidy asked.

"Because he doesn't want to deal with you."

"Deal with me?"

"You know what I mean," Alex sighed.

"No, I don't, and I don't appreciate you taking his side," Cassidy whined, aware that she was sounding very much like a child. She hated this feeling.

"I'm not taking anyone's side," Alex assured her, stepping forward to rest his hands on her shoulders as he looked down at her.

"It feels like you are," Cassidy said in a low voice.

"Why do you say that?"

"Well, I don't know. You already talked to Eric, so clearly you got his story first," Cassidy shrugged. Alex gave her a quizzical look.

"Eric, Matty, Ben, and I meet for drinks now and then. We happened to get together earlier this week, and Eric walked in pissed. He said that Ellie just told him you called to butt in."

"He's being dramatic," Cassidy grumbled.

"Since when has Eric been the dramatic one?" Alex raised an eyebrow. Cassidy let out an annoyed huff.

There was a long pause. Alex gave her shoulders a squeeze and then stepped back to his place at the railing.

"Why did you call her?" Alex asked quietly.

"I don't know. I just offered to get together," Cassidy replied sulkily.

"And do what?"

"Look at wedding stuff. I don't even know their theme or colors!"

"Really?" Alex asked in disbelief.

"Yes, really!" Cassidy was on the defensive. "And she sounded open to it! She was going to talk to her sister to find a date. It just sounds like Eric threw a fit about it and fucked it up."

"Of course, you're blaming Eric." Alex rolled his eyes. He stubbed out his cigarette butt on the brick post and flung it into the wisteria.

"What does that mean?"

"Cassidy, he is not the sum of all of your problems."

"I never said all of them," she shrugged. Alex let out an audible sigh.

"Can you just please be nice and let Eric and Ellie have their day?" Alex asked.

"I just want to be involved in their day," Cassidy countered firmly. She could feel a lump forming in her throat.

"Ugh, come here," Alex said. He looked sad for her. Cassidy set the gift bag down and let him wrap her up in a hug. She rested her head on his chest and inhaled the familiar scent mix of smoke, Old Spice, and Doritos that had been his signature smell since he was about sixteen.

"Look, I know this sucks, and you're pissed, but if this was your wedding, would you invite Ellie to do anything?" Alex asked. Cassidy paused for a moment. It was annoying that Alex was winning this argument with logic.

"That's completely different."

"No, it's not. Ellie is celebrating her day with her sister and her friends. There is nothing wrong with that," he said. Cassidy pushed herself off of him so she could look Alex in the eye.

"But–"

"No! You know you wouldn't invite Ellie to anything.

She and Eric have been dating for years and you've hardly acknowledged her," Alex pointed out.

"Fine. Ellie didn't invite me, but neither did Eric. This worked out perfectly for him. I'm not a brother – easy option to exclude me."

"And I'm sorry about that," Alex sighed.

"So, what am I supposed to do?"

"Ignore all the politics, show up to the wedding, clap, dance, and drink. It'll be great," Alex assured her.

"It won't," Cassidy huffed.

"If it sucks, you don't have to deal with any of it."

Cassidy was silent, considering his words. They heard a car engine in the driveway and the sound of a car door slam. Eric had arrived.

"Great."

"Be nice." Alex said firmly.

"Always am."

"Bullshit," Alex smirked. Cassidy smirked back. They walked around to the front of the porch as Eric approached.

"Hey," Eric said, looking slightly suspicious at the two of them walking towards him.

"Hey," Alex said pleasantly. Cassidy simply nodded.

"What's up?" Eric asked.

"Cigarette," Alex answered.

"Oh."

"Heard you guys met for drinks this week," Cassidy mentioned airily.

"You did? That's great," Eric replied blandly. He continued towards the front door.

"Guys," Alex said in a warning tone.

"What?" Cassidy and Eric snapped simultaneously. Alex

looked mildly surprised at their joint reaction.

"Do you have anything to say to each other?" Alex asked.

"Nope."

"No."

"Really?" Alex groaned.

Suddenly the front door swung open to reveal Matty looking shocked to see the three of them standing on the doorstep.

"Whoa!"

"Hi Matty," Cassidy said with a smile, happy for the distraction.

"What the hell is going on out here?" Matty asked.

"Apparently Alex was just having a cigarette," Eric said skeptically.

Alex let out a low breath. "Okay, we all know – Cassidy called Ellie, Eric is mad, Cassidy is mad, and everyone is just being stubborn."

"Stubborn?" Cassidy and Eric asked in unison before turning to glower at each other. They so rarely spoke in unison anymore, it was weird and unnerving when it happened – especially now that they were in their twenties.

"Echo!" Matty teased, knowing exactly how irritated they were. He fed off the chaos.

"Guys!" Alex said, reaching for them both. "Let's call a truce."

Cassidy raised her eyebrow in suspicion.

"Just reset to last week. Cassidy didn't call Ellie, Eric didn't get annoyed, we're all good!" Alex suggested.

Cassidy ground her teeth in irritation. Yes, she had started all of this, but she hated that everything was her fault.

"Reset? Okay, Mr. Sci-fi," Matty mocked. Cassidy and Eric looked at each other, brows furrowed, for a long moment.

163

"Fine," Eric said with a defeated sigh. Cassidy simply grunted.

"Great!" Alex gave a forced grin.

"You're not pulling any more shit, though," Eric grumbled at Cassidy.

"Why would I do anything? I don't even exist to you," Cassidy said in a low voice.

"Heaven forbid the world doesn't revolve around you all the time," Eric said before turning to push past Matty and go inside.

"It doesn't!" Cassidy screamed after him. Suddenly, their mother, Lynne was at the front door.

"What in the world are you all doing on the porch? Get inside!"

"I'm trying!" Cassidy said defiantly.

"Try harder. I'm serious, get inside all of you. The food is almost ready and Ben is falling asleep on the couch," Lynne said in an exasperated tone.

"What a hoppin' party," Matty joked.

"Shut up, and get Ben up and moving," Lynne instructed. Matty gave their mother a nod before turning inside.

"That's not going to end well," Alex said gently.

"I know," Lynne sighed, waving her remaining children inside.

Alex and Cassidy followed her into the foyer just as Ben let out a loud scream. Cassidy bit her lip as she heard Matty's footsteps making a run for it, Ben's tread in hot pursuit.

"Boys!" Lynne screamed, marching towards the family room at the back of the house.

"You're going to be okay," Alex said, giving Cassidy a nudge.

164

"Yeah," Cassidy sighed, disheartened.

"Come on. It's Ben's birthday, he's hungover as hell, mom's pissed – this'll be great!" Alex grinned. Cassidy couldn't help but laugh.

"Best party ever." Cassidy smiled up at her eldest brother before the two made their way into the family room to join the commotion.

# Chapter 17

Cassidy was furiously punching numbers into her adding machine as she looked over third quarter reports for one of her clients when a shadow appeared over her desk. Her boss, Mr. Jelif, was standing in front of her.

"Banker," he said, as soon as she looked up. "My office, two minutes."

"Sure thing, Mr. Jelif," Cassidy said. He turned and strode away as she swore under her breath.

Cassidy quickly finished calculating the line she was on, marked her spot, and got up from her desk. She felt the eyes of her coworkers on her as she walked through to Mr. Jelif's large office at the far end of their floor. She quickly brushed her hands over her tan skirt before knocking on the door.

"Enter," Mr. Jelif called from inside, and Cassidy let herself in.

"How can I help you?" she asked.

"Take a seat." Mr. Jelif motioned to the chair in front of his large desk. Cassidy quickly sat down.

"What's up?" she asked as calmly as she possibly could.

"We've gone over the proposal you made up the other week," Mr. Jelif began.

"We?"

"The board and I."

"Ah." Cassidy felt her heart give a loud thud. She felt like there was a rock in her stomach.

"We clearly need to make some cuts."

"Oh," Cassidy gulped loudly. "Wait, am I getting fired? Did I write a proposal to fire myself?"

"Well…"

"Shit!" Cassidy swore before remembering herself. She gasped loudly as her eyes bugged in surprise. "I'm sorry!"

"You're okay," Mr. Jelif said with amusement.

"Um, thanks," Cassidy stuttered. "But, am, am I getting fired?"

"Not right now."

"Not right now," Cassidy repeated.

"Banker, I need you to let me finish a sentence or we'll be here all day," Mr. Jelif said.

Cassidy nodded frantically and brought her fingers to her lips to locked them. She realized after the fact that the gesture was childish, and probably not helpful to her hopes of staying employed.

"Go ahead, sir."

"We need to make some cuts. This is going to be the first step in trying to get us back in the black."

"What cuts?" Cassidy asked nervously.

"We need to consolidate. Drop our lowest preforming accountants, and drop all of our smallest clients. Split up the medium-to-large clients between the remaining accountants.

167

You'll all just have to adjust and work overtime," Mr. Jelif explained. Cassidy's mind was swimming.

"But if we can pay overtime, we can pay the accountants to stay," Cassidy nervously countered. The thought of her coworkers suddenly losing their jobs while she stayed on made her very uncomfortable.

"We're not paying overtime. We don't have the funds."

"But then why would people work overtime?"

"Because they want a job," Mr. Jelif said flatly.

"I don't see how this is the best option."

"Banker, come on! You saw our books. You know the situation we're in - you know we don't have any wiggle room," Mr. Jelif said firmly.

"I thought cuts would be made to the coffee station or the snacks," Cassidy said, refraining from adding "or larger salaries."

"We need to think bigger, and more long term." There was a long, awkward pause. Cassidy willed herself not to cry.

"Mr. Jelif, can I ask a question?"

"You've never held back before," he chuckled.

"Why am I looking at all these books with you? Like, how, how am I in this position?" Cassidy asked nervously. Almost everyone else in the office had more experience than her.

"Because you're smart as hell and I can't waste time worrying about seniority. I knew you were smart enough to read these books and give us a quick rundown, and you did," Mr. Jelif said plainly. Cassidy felt both honored and overwhelmed.

"Um, thank you."

"I'm going to make some phone calls, but I need you to keep pulling reports of our finances."

"How much could have changed in a few days?" Cassidy asked. She knew the money market was fickle, but she didn't want to have this responsibility.

"A hell of a lot," Mr. Jelif replied, shuffling the papers on his desk into a stack. Cassidy paused for a moment, finding the courage she needed to ask her one remaining burning question.

"Do - do I still have a job, since I'm helping?"

"For now," Mr. Jelif replied plainly. "We're going to try our best to keep this damn place afloat, but you need to work hard for me. I know you coast on your brains and natural smarts, but you'll have to put your nose to the grindstone if you want to pull through."

Cassidy gulped. She couldn't tell if Mr. Jelif meant that as a pep talk or not, but it sounded more like damnation to Cassidy. Her palms were sweating.

"Okay," she replied softly, knowing she had to at least say something.

"Go pull those reports before you leave tonight and you can do a write up tomorrow."

"And don't say a word to anyone?" Cassidy questioned.

"Not a word, or you're out on your ass, brains or not," Mr. Jelif said, motioning to the door. Cassidy nodded. Her stomach was in knots as she trekked back to her desk. She could feel eyes on her. Her coworkers must have known something was up; it was too obvious with all of the private meetings suddenly happening. She hated this feeling of secrecy so much. Generally, Cassidy enjoyed her work and office, even with creeps like Devon around. But she was coming to dread her time here. What was she going to do?

169

Jake listened intently as Cassidy regaled him with the latest developments in her work saga. They were seated in his pickup truck at the local A&W car hop for dinner. They had placed their order about ten minutes ago and were waiting for the overly perky high school girl on roller skates to bring the tray of food to their window.

"I don't know what to do," Cassidy whined, tilting her head back on the headrest of the car seat. She hated feeling so rattled.

"Is it worth starting to put feelers out for a new job?" Jake asked.

"I don't want to look for another job," Cassidy sighed.

"Well, it sounds inevitable." Jake pointed out.

Cassidy gave a low groan. "I mean, what if I can find a way to fix things?"

"Cassidy, come on. It sounds like it's already too late anyway. I don't think there's anything you can do - I think they pulled you in to help them tread water just a little bit longer," Jake said.

"I still don't want to give up yet," Cassidy told him honestly.

"Okay, that's your choice."

"You sound like you disagree with me."

"I don't know what to tell you," Jake said. "I'm not in that situation."

"Well, what would you do?"

"I'd look for a different job - but again, I'm not quite as invested as you are."

"You don't like your job? I thought you did."

"Oh, I do," Jake said. "I like my work, but I don't think Mercyhurst is my forever job," Jake said with a shrug.

"Hmmm." Cassidy wasn't sure what to think. As she

pondered, the enthusiastic sixteen-year-old skated to the truck with a tray full of food. They thanked her and took their sandwiches: a chicken sandwich for Cassidy and a burger for Jake. They shared an order of fries.

"I can't believe you came to a drive-in and didn't get a burger," Jake said playfully as he took a bite. Cassidy smirked.

"Forgive me for wanting functioning arteries," she teased, popping a French fry into her mouth.

"Yeah, that's just like eating a bowl of spinach," Jake teased nodding at her large, condiment-filled chicken sandwich. Cassidy let out a snort, knowing he was right. She enjoyed having someone to verbally spar with.

The two talked and ate happily until they had had their fill. The young car hop skated back over, took their tray and trash, Jake paid, and the truck rumbled back to life as they departed the busy parking lot.

"So, what do you want to do now?" Cassidy asked innocently. Both of them fully knew what she wanted.

"Want to go for a walk?" Jake asked as he cruised through the next intersection.

"It's 8 pm. Where would we go, other than the lake?"

"Okay, what do you suggest?"

"You can come back to my place," Cassidy offered.

Jake gave a knowing smile. "Mm hmmm."

"My roommate is home; you can properly meet her. Marissa is my best friend, you'll love her!" Cassidy offered. Marissa had been begging to meet Jake for weeks; now Cassidy could satisfy her curiosity and get a chance for some much-needed feedback from her best friend.

"Um, sure," Jake replied with a shrug.

"No, come on - it'll be fun! You'll like her," Cassidy said.

Jake gave her a quick glance and grinned.

"I'm sure I will," he said.

In less than ten minutes, Cassidy and Jake were back at her complex. He parked the truck and they headed inside. Cassidy bounded her way up the stairs with Jake right in tow before letting herself inside the red door that groaned as it opened.

"Hi!" Cassidy called loudly.

"What the hell are you doing back already?" Marissa called from the direction of the living room.

"I brought you a friend," Cassidy replied, taking Jake's hand and leading him down the entrance hall into the open living room.

"A friend?" Marissa asked excitedly. Cassidy smiled at Marissa who sprawled across the length of the sofa, leaning back on Brandon who was stretched out beneath her, resting his back on the arm rest. Marissa was resting her head on his chest. The two hardly ever let themselves not be touching when together. They were practically magnetic.

"Hey Marissa, Brandon," Cassidy greeted. "This is Jake Sullivan."

Marissa quickly clambered up and around the sofa to greet Jake.

"Jake! It's great to finally meet you!" Marissa gushed excitedly, surprising him with a big hug. Jake was clearly caught off guard, but recovered quickly and reciprocated.

"Babe, he just got here," Brandon chuckled. Marissa pulled back from Jake, but continued to beam up at him.

"Come on, sit down and tell us everything," Marissa said, gently pulling him into the seating area. Jake took a seat on the plush blue chair by the window, and Cassidy balanced herself on the wide arm of the chair. Marissa tapped Brandon's leg to sit up as she sat down next to him, pulling her legs up and crossing them.

"Want a beer?" Brandon offered. Jake nodded. Brandon got up and headed to the fridge.

"So, what do I need to know about you, Jake Sullivan?" Marissa asked playfully. She straightened her back as if she were conducting a proper interview.

"Wow, that's a question," Jake chuckled, taking the beer can Brandon offered him.

"He works at Mercyhurst - he's a professor!" Cassidy said. She had already told Marissa all of this after their very first chance meeting, but she was proud of him.

"I teach one class," Jake chimed in. Cassidy looked over at him taking a sip of beer. She didn't understand why he didn't want to brag about himself. She wanted to brag about him.

"He's really smart," Cassidy added with a big smile.

"Did you go to Mercyhurst?" Brandon asked. Jake shook his head.

"No, Penn State."

"Ooof." Brandon scrunched his nose. "OSU," he clarified.

"Ah, the enemy," Jake said with a smile. Cassidy watched the boys interact attentively. Please get along, she thought.

"What did you guys do tonight?" Marissa asked, sensing the need for a new topic.

"We had dinner at the A&W," Cassidy said.

"Oh, I love that place," Marissa said dreamily.

"Me, too," Brandon added.

"Let's go!" Marissa cheered. Brandon smiled, then leaned over and kissed her forehead. Cassidy felt her heart swell. She loved that her best friend had such a loving man in her life. How she hoped Jake would be that for her.

"Is that a concert tee?" Jake asked, nodding at Brandon's black and white shirt.

"Oh yeah!" Brandon grinned, pulling the fabric on his stomach forward slightly to look at it. "Van Halen!"

"Were you there?" Jake asked.

"Yeah, saw him in Indianapolis back in '78. Great show! I was a senior in high school and my friends and I drove into the city for it." Brandon gushed.

"That's awesome! I went to his show in Pittsburgh in '84 – my senior year of college," Jake grinned.

"I actually thought about going to that one," Brandon smiled.

"Civic arena?"

"Yep."

As the boys continued to talk about concerts, Cassidy looked over at Marissa and caught her eye. They exchanged quick, excited grins, thrilled that their boyfriends were getting along so easily.

"What was your first concert?" Brandon asked.

"Oddly enough, Sinatra," Jake chuckled.

"What?" Marissa gasped.

"Oh my god!" Cassidy said in shock, smacking his shoulder

"Seriously?" Brandon looked stunned. Jake just nodded.

"Yeah, um, he came to Pittsburgh and my parents were big fans. My brother and I grew up listening to the records, so they took us into the city for the day then we went to the show that night," Jake said.

"I can't believe this!" Cassidy said in awe.

"It was a good show. Like, I was a weird kid who grew up on oldies, so I enjoyed it, but I don't think I appreciated it as much as I should have, you know?"

"How old were you?" Brandon asked.

"Like, fourteen? It was in the fall of my freshman year of high school. Will and I were definitely the youngest people there," Jake snickered.

"Damn." Brandon sighed in awe.

Jake nodded with a smile.

"Cassidy, what was your first concert?" Marissa asked, deep in thought.

"Journey, I think," Cassidy mused. "It was the end of the last week of school, my junior year of high school. Like, I think I had finals earlier that day," she laughed.

"Drove all the way to Pittsburgh?" Brandon asked.

Cassidy shook her head. "No, no, they came to Erie - the Field House. My friends and I went. My mom was so pissed when I stumbled home at 1AM." Cassidy sighed deeply at the memory. She had been in a lot of trouble, especially since she had conveniently forgotten to mention to her parents that she was going to the city for a concert and not studying at a friend's house. She'd spent the first two weeks of summer holidays grounded for that one. The punishment had initially started at a single week of grounding, but as soon as Cassidy found out it was Ben who ratted her out, she punched him and split his lip. An additional week was tacked on.

"You guys?" Cassidy asked, nodding at Brandon and Marissa.

"Eagles," Marissa said. "My older cousins took me. I was in high school."

"Nice," Brandon said. "I think my first one was Aerosmith… Yeah that was the first one. Early high school I ended up going to three in one summer. I was hooked, loved it."

"Live music is the best," Cassidy said with a smile.

"The best," Marissa sighed dreamily.

"So, what have you been up to this evening?" Cassidy asked.

"Nothing, just hanging out," Marissa lightly, looking up at Brandon. Cassidy instantly knew she and Jake had interrupted a make-out session.

"Yeah, we watched some TV," Brandon said, looking at Marissa with a smile.

"Cassidy, do you want to give Jake the rest of the tour of the apartment?" Marissa asked slyly.

"Rest of the tour?" Jake asked, looking confused.

"Oh, um, sure," Cassidy chuckled. She knew Marissa not only wanted to regain her private time with Brandon, but also was being an excellent wing woman.

Jake raised an eyebrow. Cassidy stood up and took his hand.

"Follow me,"

"Have a good night," Marissa called as Cassidy led Jake back down the hallway toward her bedroom.

# Chapter 18

"Oh," Jake said as they stepped into the room. He looked around happily. Cassidy shut the door behind them.

"So, this is my room," Cassidy said in a low voice.

"I like it," Jake said, with a small smile.

Cassidy watched him take in the room. She slowly walked over and stood beside him, gently brushing her arm against his. Jake looked down at her and smiled at her touch.

"Hey," Cassidy whispered.

"Hey."

They slowly turned to face each other and Cassidy trailed her hands up his front to wrap her arms around the back of his neck. Jake's firm hands reached for her hips and pulled her close. Cassidy loved the feeling of his grip.

After a long moment of staring into each other's eyes, Jake lowered his head and Cassidy leaned up and pressed her lips onto his. The kiss was soft and sweet. They pulled back after a few seconds and just rested their foreheads together, tightening their hold on one another. There was electricity in the small space between them. Cassidy's heart rate accelerated.

Slowly Jake leaned down and kissed her again, over and over, sweet, slow pecks. Cassidy's body was tingling in anticipation. The kisses began to build in intensity, no longer soft and sweet, but full of passion. Before they knew it, their mouths were moving in sync. Cassidy loved the feeling of his lips on hers.

Without warning, Jake slid his tongue along her bottom lip. Cassidy gasped and Jake quickly slid his tongue into her mouth. Cassidy felt a spark shoot up her spine.

Cassidy held onto his shoulders tightly with one hand and plunged her other into his thick, copper hair. Jake kept one hand at her hip while the other slid down and cupped her ass, making Cassidy squeal inside his mouth.

After several minutes, Cassidy tightened her grip on Jake and began to walk backwards toward her bed, pulling him along with her. In a few steps, Cassidy felt her mattress hit the back of her thighs.

Jake slid both his hands under her backside and gripped firmly before lifting her off the ground. Cassidy was caught off guard; she gasped and wrapped her legs around his trim waist. They remained in that position for a few seconds, then Jake pushed forward and they crashed onto the bed. Jake landed on top of Cassidy, her legs still around his middle.

They both grunted as they hit the mattress. However, the impact only distracted them for a moment before their lips connected once more, the kiss deepening immediately. Cassidy reveled in the feeling of Jake's weight on her, especially as he ran his hands up and down her thighs. Even through her jeans, she loved the feeling of his fingers on her body. She could feel a warmth growing in her belly.

Cassidy slid her hands down Jake's back and found the fabric of his shirt, tugging it upward. She had only pulled the shirt up a few inches when Jake pulled away, leaving Cassidy bereft. However, disappointment was quickly replaced with excitement; Jake pulled the shirt off over his head and tossed it on the floor. Cassidy smiled widely at him and he grinned back. His chest was quite toned for his slim build, and Cassidy ached to touch it.

But Jake didn't give Cassidy long to eye up his body, leaning back down to kiss her once more. Cassidy reached down to the hem of her own shirt and started to tug the fabric up. Jake pulled his lips away again to help her slide her top over her head. Together, they tossed it to the side. Cassidy felt her heart give a thud. She loved the moment when clothes start to come off.

She bit her lip with anticipation as she watched Jake's eyes rove over her body before he caught her eye and grinned. Their kisses resumed with fervor. Cassidy relished the feeling of his bare stomach against hers. Sparks shot from her core to her extremities.

Jake used his left forearm on the mattress to balance his weight while his right hand began to slowly explore her body making Cassidy shiver with delight. The feeling of his fingertips deliberately sliding over her skin was intoxicating.

Cassidy wasted no time returning the favor. Her left hand ran over his strong chest and stomach, while her right hand was practically clawing his bare back with excitement. She nipped at his bottom lip with her teeth while her fingertips happily twirled through his chest hair.

They kissed deeply as their hands explored for many more minutes. Time was no longer a concept Cassidy understood;

179

she was living touch to touch. Jake's mouth and hands were addictive and exhilarating. Her body felt like it was on fire.

Cassidy brought both of her hands to Jake's shoulders, got a firm grip, and pushed him to the side, rolling them over on the mattress so she was on top. She sat up proudly on his lower abdomen, resting her hands on his chest, while Jake looked up at her in surprise and pleasure, his hands holding onto her thighs. She noticed his eyes had settled on her chest. The black bra she was wearing was lacy, floral and quite sheer. Cassidy smiled, happily allowing his eyes to linger.

Jake's gaze returned to her eyes after a long moment. They shared a smirk before Cassidy leaned down to press her lips to his. Jake immediately deepened the kiss and his hands tightened their grip on her thighs. Cassidy was soaring. She wanted more – she needed more.

Slowly, she trailed her fingers down Jake's chest and stomach, and landed on his waist. Her fingers fumbled for the button on his pants.

Without warning, Jake suddenly flipped them back over so he was on top once more. He grabbed both of Cassidy's wrists and pinned them to the mattress on either side of her head. Cassidy let out a loud gasp, practically trembling with anticipation.

"Nope," Jake whispered barely an inch above her lips. Cassidy let out a shaky breath as she fluttered her eyes open.

"Yes," she replied in a low voice. Jake continued to hold her wrists, but he propped himself up a bit so they could see each other's faces clearly.

"We've got to hit pause," he said, taking a slow breath. Cassidy gave a small smile.

"You sure?" she asked.

"Yeah."

"Well, I'm pretty sure that you're the one pinning me down," Cassidy smirked. Jake gave her a light peck on the lips before releasing his grip on her wrists. Cassidy brought her arms down and rolled onto her side, facing him.

"Hey," Jake began.

"Hey."

"We have to stop now, otherwise I won't be able to," Jake explained, reaching over and brushing her cheek lightly with his thumb. Cassidy's heart gave a thud and a shiver ran through her. His touch was electric.

"We don't have to stop ever," Cassidy insisted.

"Well, I do." Jake let out a small, embarrassed chuckle.

"Talk to me."

"I, I - I think I'm… falling for you," Jake stuttered. Cassidy gulped. She wanted to scream with excitement, but all she could seem to do was grin at him like an idiot.

"Really?"

"Yeah."

"But, then, why are we stopping?" Cassidy asked. Jake hesitated. He looked like he was trying to muster up some courage.

"Because I don't want this to end."

"I don't either," Cassidy said.

"Look, my last relationship moved quickly. Well, the physical stuff, anyway. And I fell hard, but, but, she didn't. And when she left, it … it hurt. Hurt like hell. It took me over six months to even go on another date. And that went poorly. I, just… I can't do that again," Jake admitted.

Cassidy bit her tongue inside her mouth. She hadn't known how badly he had been hurt. She hated to think of Jake ever being broken-hearted. Cassidy was suddenly aware of the silence in the room. She had to say something, to let him know that he hadn't just bared his soul to thin air.

"I don't want that to happen to you again, either."

"Oh," Jake hummed. It was a raw moment. Cassidy did not want to fuck it up.

"I mean, I won't let that happen with me. I want us to have a deep relationship because... well, I think I am falling for you, too," Cassidy admitted with a small smile.

Jake looked as if she had lifted an enormous weight off of his shoulders. Cassidy giggled as she watched him absolutely beam. She leaned forward and placed a slow, gentle peck on his lips.

"I've had so much fun these past weeks, I don't want to lose it," Jake said. Cassidy watched him for a long moment before speaking.

"Do you want to spend the night, but just... talk?"

"Yeah, I do," Jake said, leaning forward and placing a soft kiss on her lips.

"Okay." Cassidy rolled away from Jake and stood up off the bed.

"Where are you going?" Jake asked.

"I'm getting comfy for the night," Cassidy said. She walked over to her dresser and pulling her sleep shirt out of the top drawer. Cassidy turned her back to Jake in the bed and quickly unbuttoned her jeans, slid them down her legs and stepped out of them before tossing them in the hamper. She didn't turn around to look, but she could feel Jake's eyes on her. She wanted them on her. She loved the feeling.

She reached back to unhook her bra and hung it from her closet door, and was left standing in nothing more than her light pink panties with the knowledge that Jake was watching her. She pulled the grey sleep shirt over her head. The hem rested just an inch above her knees. Now dressed in her pajamas, Cassidy turned around with a smile. As expected, Jake was lying on the bed watching her keenly.

"Now I'm comfy." Cassidy smiled as she walked back over to the edge of the mattress, resting her right knee on it.

"You always know what you're doing, don't you?" Jake asked with a smirk.

"Only some of the time," Cassidy smiled back. "Give me a minute?"

Cassidy turned and made for the bathroom. She took a quick peek in the living room, but Brandon and Marissa had abandoned the sofa. She could only assume they had also moved their evening into the bedroom. Good. Cassidy didn't need any distractions at the moment. She quickly used the toilet, brushed her teeth, and splashed some water on her face before returning to her room and offering Jake the same opportunity. She had left the large bottle of Scope on the counter.

While she was waiting for Jake to return, Cassidy got herself settled under the covers on the right side of the bed, closer to the window. She let out a low, deep breath. Her mind was swirling. It had been quite a long time since she had just slept with a man. As much as she wanted to be with Jake physically, Cassidy did really want this relationship to grow. She willed herself not to toss her nightshirt on the floor before he returned.

Jake was back in her room, closing the door behind him in a matter of minutes. Cassidy bit her lip as she looked over at him. His wavy copper hair was slightly mussed and he was wearing just his dark red and black plaid boxers. He looked like a dream.

"Hey," Jake said softly.

"Hey." Cassidy smiled as he walked over and climbed into bed next to her.

She could smell him; his aftershave still lingered along with the crisp laundry scent that always seemed to be there. Cassidy loved it. As soon as he was settled in, Cassidy rolled to her side and scooted toward him. She placed a soft kiss on his lips and they smiled at each other.

"Ask me a question," Cassidy posed.

"Hmm?"

"You want us to really connect, so ask me a question. Anything you want."

Jake looked pleased. "Um, what was your favorite summer vacation as a kid?" he asked. Cassidy scrunched up her face. She'd been hoping for something more intimate.

"Well, we always went down to Kennywood in the summer, but when I was ten, we went to Cedar Point in Ohio and it was so much fun. All those roller coasters and rides! Oh, and the little beach there. We had a blast. Yeah, that was definitely the best vacation when I was a kid." Cassidy smiled at the memory.

"I've been to Kennywood a lot, too, but we never did Cedar Point."

"What about you? What was your best childhood vacation?"

"Definitely the beach. We went out to the Jersey shore for a week every summer. I loved it. We'd rent a place in Atlantic City. My parents could gamble and go to shows, and my brother Will and I played on the beach. It was the best."

"Your parents didn't like the beach?"

"They did, but they couldn't stay out on the sand or in the water all day like Will and I could. We'd all go down in the morning, but by lunch time, my mom was too hot and my dad was pissed about something, so they would go in. Will and I just had to be back and cleaned up by dinner. Easy to do." Cassidy smiled as she thought about that. The freedom Jake must have felt just enjoying the beach. Cassidy and her brothers had always been so chaotic, their parents had kept them all on tight leashes - which Cassidy had to admit, they had needed.

"Okay, next question. Something deeper," Cassidy smirked. Jake looked like he was thinking hard.

"Have you been in love before?" Jake asked. Cassidy gulped.

"I thought I was. I mean, for real thought I was. I used the word a lot when dating in high school, but I had no idea what I was talking about. But my last year in college I fell in love with my boyfriend. We dated for two years and then he left. It hurt like hell." Cassidy looked down, her eyes on the mattress. She rarely even thought about Kevin these days, and she definitely no longer had an iota of a romantic feeling for him, but the memory still stung.

"What happened?" Jake asked gently, reaching over to brush her cheek with his thumb. Cassidy tried not to focus on how good his touch felt.

"Honestly, I don't know. Maybe the writing was on the wall and I was just delusional and didn't see, but it felt very sudden to me. I was planning my future with him, and then all of that was gone."

"I'm sorry," Jake said sincerely. Cassidy slowly looked up and met his eyes. They shared a small smile.

185

"Well, what about you? Were you in love?" Cassidy asked, shifting herself slightly on the mattress.

"I thought I was."

"When?" Cassidy asked gently.

"College." Jake took a deep breath. Cassidy could see this was hard for him. "She was a girl from my dorm. It felt like it was happening so naturally. We started hanging out, then we started making out, and it progressed from there. We spent all of our time together for months - and then, suddenly, it was over."

"Why?" Cassidy asked.

"I honestly don't know. One day Dina told me that she was scared of how intense things got and - that night, she was gone."

"Fuck," Cassidy whispered. She instantly hated this Dina girl.

"I had never been serious with a girl before. At least, I thought it was serious with her," Jake said quietly. He looked so sad, like the wound was still raw, though she knew it had to have been at least three years.

"I'm sorry she hurt you."

"I mean, it's kind of the reason I don't…"

"Don't want to jump into bed immediately," Cassidy finished his thought. Jake nodded, looking slightly ashamed. Cassidy leaned forward and placed a light peck on his lips.

"Yeah," he mumbled.

"I get it, and I like that you want to be sure. That's… that's better than me," Cassidy admitted.

"Not better than you; you're brave and you put yourself out there," Jake countered.

"You're making me sound really good, and cool," Cassidy

186

chuckled.

"You are good, and very cool. You're a little intimidating,"

"Intimidating?"

"I cannot be the first person to ever tell you that," Jake chuckled. Cassidy giggled.

"Well, no, but I haven't heard it since, like, high school."

"I figured you were one of those girls."

"One of those girls?" Cassidy gasped in amused shock, smacking Jake on the shoulder. He looked proud of himself.

"You know what I mean."

"No! Explain it to me," Cassidy challenged.

"Right there! What you're doing right now – you're looking at me just right so that I back down. You do always know what you're doing!" Jake smirked.

Cassidy let out a loud laugh. "I try to make it look like I know what I'm doing, maybe," she admitted.

"You're succeeding."

"You know, I really wasn't one of those mean, bitchy, popular girls in school. I was popular, but that was because I was really good at softball."

"There was at least one other reason." Jake gave her a knowing look.

"Are you saying I was a slut?" Cassidy gave another shocked looked.

"I definitely did not say those words," Jake pointed out.

"You insinuated them."

"No, I did not! I was referencing your looks."

"My looks?"

"Oh my god, Cassidy, you know that you're fucking gorgeous. And I'm sure you were gorgeous back then, too. Come on, don't play dumb." Cassidy blushed. While she had been complimented for her appearance since childhood, it always caught her off guard.

"Gorgeous may be a stretch. That's a compliment for someone like Brooke Shields or Demi Moore," Cassidy said. "I'm pretty."

"Gorgeous," Jake insisted.

"Well, you're handsome," Cassidy smiled, kissing him lightly. Jake shook his head.

"You're in a league of your own."

"I still don't know what that means."

"It means you wouldn't have given me a second glance in school," Jake said. Cassidy rolled her eyes.

"I definitely would have, but do you know what?"

"Hmm?"

"We're out of school, and we don't even have to think about those stupid things anymore," Cassidy grinned.

"You're telling me you didn't like school?"

"Oh, I loved it! I had a blast. But it's over now. I've had to make peace with that and move on; I want to make sure that I have a good life after school," Cassidy said. This was the part of growing up she was struggling with. She didn't want to become one of those people who can only talk about the old days, because it's all they have. But she hadn't found her place yet as an adult.

"What's the best part about being out of school?" Jake asked. Cassidy bit her lip.

"You go first."

"Oh, well, that's easy. I don't live at home anymore. I get to keep my own schedule, for the most part, and I really love teaching, especially in college, because the students want to be there. I'm teaching a specialized course, and my students

188

like this shit as much as I do," Jake smiled. Cassidy smiled back, soaking up his pride and happiness.

"That's what I want."

"To teach?"

"Oh, well, I was thinking more of how content you are in life and how happily you look forward to the future."

"You don't like looking forward?" Jake asked.

"I mean, I did, especially with Kevin, but then that ended, and well... I just didn't know what my future would be. Shit, this is becoming a heavy conversation." Cassidy rolled her face in the pillow for a moment before looking back up at Jake.

"You don't want to have heavy conversations with me?" Jake asked.

"Oh, I do. You're so easy to talk to, I just find myself opening up to you. But that doesn't mean this isn't hard," Cassidy told him.

"That's fair."

"But I want to look forward with excitement, like you do," Cassidy said firmly.

"What would make you do that more often?"

"Well... um... you," Cassidy admitted, biting her lip. The moment froze. It had been a very long time since she'd been so honest with a guy. Jake just brought it out of her, in the best way possible.

"Me?" Jake looked surprised, yet quite touched.

"Yes, you."

"How did I get that honor?" Jake asked playfully, still smiling.

"You're positive and happy, and you're just... you. Unapologetically you."

189

"That's good?"

"That's wonderful. I've never met anyone like you, and that is amazing," Cassidy gushed. Jake smiled, looking slightly overwhelmed.

"Um, thanks, I guess," Jake chuckled nervously.

"Look, my words aren't right, but the feeling is. You're a good person and you make me want to be a better person. Heck, I feel like a better person when I'm around you," Cassidy explained.

"Wow, that's… wow." Jake was unable to meet her eyes, and Cassidy could have sworn he was blushing. Cassidy leaned forward and placed a soft kiss on his lips, which Jake happily reciprocated. The two shared a slow, light kiss for a long minute before pulling back and smiling at each other.

"You know, I love just getting to lie here next to you in bed. It's comfortable," Cassidy said.

"I love getting to lie next to you," Jake said softly. Cassidy snuggled into place at his side and rested her head on his shoulder.

"This is perfect," Cassidy hummed.

"Want me to shut off the light?" Jake asked.

"Sure." Jake reached over and switched off the bedside lamp. The room was engulfed in just darkness. Cassidy and Jake both let out contented sighs as they settled into place and slowly fell asleep.

# Chapter 19

The small galley kitchen of Cassidy and Marissa's apartment was busier than usual the next morning, with not only Cassidy and Marissa attempting to make coffee and scrounge something to eat before dashing out the door, but also both Brandon and Jake taking up room as they joined the busy morning shuffle.

While it was a little touch and go at times, with one bathroom and one coffee maker, all four of them managed to make it out the door on time. Cassidy was resting her left hip on the driver's side door of her car as Jake leaned over to say goodbye for the day.

"I'm glad I stayed last night," Jake grinned.

"I'm glad you did, too."

"So," Jake began.

"So," Cassidy mimicked.

"It was a little crowded this morning."

"Mmmhmmm,"

"I was thinking… would you like to come to my place

tonight?"

"Your place?" Cassidy smirked, attempting to play it cool.

"You could stay over and, well, we could have a good night, and space to ourselves and, and, maybe do a little less … sleeping," Jake said with a playful shrug. Cassidy bit her lip. She wanted to burst. To stop herself from screaming like a school girl, she leaned forward and pressed her lips firmly against Jake's.

"Is that a yes?" Jake chuckled as she pulled back.

"Definitely a yes," Cassidy gushed. "I would love to come over this evening."

"7:00? I'll order us a pizza."

"I'll bring a bottle of wine," Cassidy offered.

"Two Polacks pretending to be Italians," Jake teased. Cassidy snorted with laughter.

"It's a date, amore," Cassidy grinned.

"Have a good day," Jake said, leaning down to kiss her once more.

"You, too," Cassidy said before turning to get into her car. She buckled her seatbelt, leaned her head back on the headrest and let out a happy sigh. A part of her life was actually perfect. Completely perfect!

Cassidy had barely pulled open the large, glass door to her office when Gladys hopped up from her desk in the front lobby and hustled toward her.

"Cassidy!" Gladys said in a low, intense voice.

"What's going on?" Cassidy asked worriedly.

"Something's going down. Williams is packing up his

desk. Started a few minutes after he arrived. I think he got canned!" Gladys told her frantically. Cassidy felt her heart sink. Downsizing. How could this be happening so quickly?

"Oh no," was all Cassidy could say. She couldn't tell Gladys that she'd known this was coming, she couldn't say that she'd been spending nights looking over the books and desperately trying to find ways to save jobs. She couldn't say that she'd known this was inevitable. She really hadn't known, however, who the first target would be.

"Can you find anything out? Mr. Jelif likes you," Gladys said. Cassidy glanced down at the older woman, wanting to tell her everything. Wanting to tell her to get out while she could, wanting this burden of knowing to be taken away from her.

"I'll do my best," Cassidy lied. They nodded at each other, and then Cassidy continued through the lobby and into the bullpen filled with desks and cubicles. She had to pass Williams' desk on the way to her own. She bit down hard on her tongue as she walked by, trying to give him the dignity of respectful eye contact and a nod without staring curiously or making a horrid pity face.

Cassidy plopped down at her desk. If her stomach hadn't already been feeling unsettled, it went into a complete knot when she saw the note laying on her desk: "See me," written in thick red ink. Must have been a Sharpie. It wasn't signed, but there was no mistaking that it came from Mr. Jelif himself. Cassidy sighed deeply before standing and heading to the boss's office, summons note in hand. As she walked through the office, a hush fell. The air was thick; everyone was tense but no one dared to ask what was going on.

Cassidy was aware that there were eyes on her as she

marched, however she refused to look at anyone. She couldn't. When she finally reached Mr. Jelif's office, the door was open. He was sitting there working as if nothing was amiss. Cassidy knocked on the door frame. He looked up at her.

"You wanted to see me?" Cassidy asked, holding up the note.

"Yes, Banker, come in," he instructed. "Close the door behind you." Cassidy did as he asked and took a seat in one of the chairs in front of his desk. Behind her, the door made an ominous thud.

"What's going on?" Cassidy asked.

"I've let Williams go."

"Yeah, I see that. The whole office sees that," Cassidy replied, aware she was being far too sassy toward the guy that signed her paycheck. She bit her tongue.

"It is not something I'm enjoying. However, your cost analysis showed that he is the lowest producing employee. He has the least number of clients, and they're all small fish. I had to make the decision," Mr. Jelif explained solemnly. Cassidy appreciated that he was taking the matter seriously. She had heard too many stories on the news of companies firing whole departments without any remorse. It seemed like this was bothering Mr. Jelif, too.

"So, with Williams gone, and some cost cutting around the building, we'll just need to bring in more clients and we can, at least, finish up the fiscal year," Cassidy said, bouncing her knee anxiously. She knew this would not be the end of it, but maybe if she convinced Mr. Jelif it was possible, she could buy some time to consider other alternatives.

"Banker…"

"I think we could do it! Just give me more time," Cassidy

rambled. Mr. Jelif watched her quietly for a long moment.

"Cassidy," Mr. Jelif began. Cassidy felt her head snap up. She couldn't remember the last time he'd used her first name. "Go back to your desk. Pull yourself together and focus on your regular work today. Tomorrow we'll reconvene and look at the numbers again."

"Um," Cassidy began.

"Focus on your work," he reiterated. Cassidy nodded.

"Okay. Thank you, sir," she said, standing up and letting herself out of his office.

None of her coworkers were even attempting to hide the fact that they were watching her reemerge into the bullpen. The eyes followed her as she walked back towards her desk.

"Hey, Banker, what did he say?" Devon asked as she passed his desk. Cassidy looked over at him. For once, he wasn't leering or smirking at her, but looked genuinely concerned.

"He said to focus on my work," Cassidy replied honestly before continuing her walk. She heard Devon swear under his breath.

Cassidy once again flopped down at her desk and let out a sigh. It took almost ten minutes before she could bring herself to dive into the stack of papers in her inbox. The day was long and silent. Williams and his cardboard box of possessions departed the office by 10AM. His absence left an odd void.

# Chapter 20

Jake took Cassidy's empty plate from her and headed to the kitchen. She smiled as she watched him. They had just finished their pizza dinner – Jake had even gotten green peppers and onions on half for her, keeping the pepperoni for himself on his side. Cassidy had offered to help him clean up, but Jake insisted that she just relax at the table. Cassidy couldn't remember the last time she hadn't had to clean up after a meal, aside from going to restaurants. It was an odd feeling, but nice.

There was a sudden, loud noise that sounded like something falling in the dishwasher. "Sure you don't need help?" Cassidy called.

"No," Jake replied in a strained voice. Cassidy giggled.

Within five minutes, Jake returned to the small dining room carrying two bottles of Coors Light.

"Sorry, I'm out of wine," Jake said, handing Cassidy a bottle as he took his seat. She took the chilled bottle from him happily.

"No worries; I'm more of a beer person, anyway," Cassidy replied. They clinked their bottles and took a sip.

"I'm glad you came over. I know it was rough day in the office today," Jake said.

"Thinking about tonight is what got me through," Cassidy smirked.

"I'm honored," he chuckled. Cassidy took a long drink, feeling calmer and happier than she had all day.

"It's just nice to relax," she said.

"I want to take care of you tonight," Jake said. He bit his lip slightly as if he were a tad nervous, but recovered quickly.

"Oh yeah?" Cassidy felt her stomach flutter slightly.

"You deserve a break. Tonight, you don't have to lift a finger - or even think," Jake said as he took a sip.

"Where has thinking ever gotten us anyways?" Cassidy asked sarcastically.

"Absolutely nowhere," Jake winked. Cassidy couldn't help but laugh.

"So, what's on the table for this evening of no thinking?" she asked.

"Well, really, anything," Jake shrugged. "We can get ice cream, we can watch a movie, but, at some point, I would love to show you the new comforter I got," he trailed off as he brought the bottle to his lips and turned his gaze from her. Was he blushing? Cassidy's heart gave a hard thud.

"I would like to see the comforter now."

"Now?" Jake asked, raising an eyebrow.

"Yes, please," Cassidy grinned. Jake smiled at her for a long moment before taking a long drink of his beer and standing up from his seat. He extended his left hand toward Cassidy. She also took a large gulp before setting her half-empty bottle next to his and placing her hand in his.

Jake gave her hand a squeeze and led her out of the dining room and up the stairs.

"Oh," Cassidy said suddenly, "after this, I actually do want ice cream. But you know, after." Jake looked back at her and grinned.

"You got it."

As they hit the landing on the second floor, Jake turned to the right and into the large bedroom that took up that end of the hallway. Cassidy looked around. While it was dark in the room, the last hints of sunset shone through the large windows across from a king-sized bed that sat along the wall next to the door. The room had old-house charm, with high ceilings, long, antique windows, white walls, and dark hardwood floors.

"Nice comforter," Cassidy whispered. She could feel Jake watching her. She didn't mind in the least. After a long moment, she felt Jake's fingertips come to rest lightly on either side of her hips. She bit her lip at his touch and slowly turned to face him. Without hesitation, Cassidy leaned up and pressed her lips to his. Jake kissed her back, hard.

Cassidy wrapped her arms around the back of his neck as his grip tightened on her hips. There was a difference in his kisses tonight. No politeness, no hesitation, Jake knew what he wanted and Cassidy was happy to give it to him.

She felt his tongue slide across her bottom lip and parted her lips to let him in, his warm breath engulfing her as his tongue slid along hers.

Jake suddenly lifted Cassidy off of the ground and practically tackled her onto the mattress. He caught himself on the mattress with his left hand so only some of his weight was on Cassidy – she didn't mind, she loved the feeling of him so close, not to mention the adrenaline of his sudden movements. She brought her right foot up to the bed frame and used it to push herself back on the mattress, so they were now in the middle of the large bed.

Under her hands, Jake's hair felt thick and silky as their passionate kisses picked up their pace. Cassidy felt like she was on fire already. Jake's right hand slid from her hip, up her side, to cup her breast. They kissed with little variation for a while, Cassidy's body continued to warm at his touch and the feeling of his mouth moving with hers. She could feel sparks shooting through her body. She never wanted it to stop.

Jake moved his hand from her chest and came to the hem of her white and pink stripped t-shirt and slipped his fingers underneath. Cassidy barely had a chance to feel her heart give a loud, excited thump, when Jake rolled them to the side and quickly pulled her shirt upward. She moved her arms from around his shoulders to help him remove her top and toss it to the side. Jake sat himself up and ripped his navy blue PSU shirt over his head and thew it on the floor. Cassidy grinned up at him as Jake leaned back down and attached his lips to hers once more. She relished in the feeling of his mouth moving in sync with hers.

Cassidy slid her right hand down his chest. She could feel his muscles tense under her fingertips; she loved that she could have this kind of effect on him. Her hand trailed to the waistband of his jeans and fumbled with the buckle. Jake slid his hands from her hips and rolled to the side so he could unzip. Cassidy took the moment to unbutton her own jean shorts and shimmy them down. Jake ripped off his jeans and tossed them on the floor, pulling his socks off in the same movement. Cassidy's shorts were just past her knees when

199

Jake, in just his dark red boxers, pushed her hands aside and took over slipping her shorts off her feet. She bit her lip as they joined the growing pile of garments on the floor.

And then Jake was kissing her once more. Cassidy immediately deepened the kiss, pulling his body down on top of hers. Their kissed continued as their hands explored each other's bodies. She loved the feeling of their limbs intertwined in a feverish passion.

Slowly, Jake moved his right hand from her side to the center of her back. Cassidy knew he was going for her bra, and grinned against his lips.

"What?" Jake whispered playfully, pecking her still-grinning lips.

"You're going for the bra," Cassidy hummed.

"I am," Jake smiled as he moved to kiss her jawline.

"It won't work, though," Cassidy breathed, distracted by Jake's lips teasing her sensitive skin.

"Why's that?" Jake asked, his fingers still fumbling at her back.

"Because the clasp is in the front," Cassidy said with a smile. Jake's fingers stopped moving and he pulled his mouth off of her neck.

"Front," he repeated fuzzily. Cassidy apparently wasn't the only one distracted by kissing. She grinned wider. Jake untangled himself from Cassidy and propped himself up on his knees. Cassidy let out a shaky, excited breath as his hands came to her chest. She watched with bated breath as he eyed up her light pink bra before reaching out and slowly tracing the fabric with his fingers. From the straps, down the top of the cups, and to the center clasp, he left a trail of goosebumps in the wake of his painfully light touch. Cassidy let out a shaky breath as his fingers finally worked on the small hooks between her breasts. In a few seconds, she felt the release. Jake looked up and their eyes locked for a moment before his gaze returned to her chest. He opened up her bra and exposed her.

Cassidy smiled, watching him. He looked mesmerized. He collected himself after a few long seconds and looked back up at Cassidy's face.

"Better?" Cassidy smirked.

"Much better," Jake said, pressing his lips to hers. Cassidy sat up slightly and slid her bra off her shoulders. Jake helped her free herself from the lacy fabric, then gave it a toss before pushing her firmly back on the mattress and climbing on top of her.

Cassidy loved the feeling of her bare breasts against his chest. His chest hair almost tickled as it rubbed against her. Their kisses turned heated. Jake's hands roamed her body, and she bucked up against him whenever his fingers slid over her nipples. Cassidy's left hand gripped his hair tightly while her right hand ran along his muscular back. She was about to burst into flames. Her heart was racing and her extremities were tingling with anticipation. This was perfection.

They continued kissing for a few, long minutes, before Jake moved his lips from hers and started to work his way down. He kissed her jaw, her neck, trailed down her chest onto her left breast. Cassidy gasped as his tongue ran across her nipple. She tightened her grip on him. She was pretty sure she was hurting him, but Jake didn't seem to mind - his focus was on her body.

Jake kissed and licked the entirety of her breast before kissing his way over to her right one and repeating the process. Cassidy was soaring at his touch. She was in no way inexperienced, but this was the first time any man had paid this much attention to her breasts. She was elated, and she found she was almost panting. Once her right breast had been fully explored, Jake's mouth moved to the center of her chest, then began to slowly trail kisses down her stomach. Goosebumps broke out over her body.

Jake paused at the waistband of her grey panties. The air was heavy with anticipation.

"Hey," Jake whispered, looking up at her.

"Yeah?" Cassidy smiled as she tilted her head to look down at him.

"I want to try something."

"Hmm?"

"I want to kiss you."

"You've already done that. You already get an A for that," Cassidy teased.

"No," Jake chuckled as his fingers looped into the sides of her panties. "I want to kiss you here," he said, quickly sliding the grey fabric down her legs and tossing her final covering onto the floor with the rest of their clothes. Cassidy trembled in anticipation.

"Okay," Cassidy said in a low voice. She felt her heart give another excited thud. It had been years since a guy had gone down on her. Kevin was the last, and that was just when they first started dating. She was dying to experience it again.

Jake smiled at her as he pushed himself up and stood at the foot of the bed. Cassidy noticed the large, protruding bulge in the front of his boxers. She felt the junction of her legs start to quiver. However, she couldn't focus on it for long - Jake's hand suddenly wrapped around her left ankle and pulled.

Cassidy felt herself slide across the sheets, stopping just shy of the edge of the mattress. Before she could take a breath, Jake parted her legs, propped her heels on the low, wooden base of the mattress, and lowered himself to his knees.

Cassidy brought her hands to her sides and gripped fistfuls of the sheets beneath her as her heart pounded. There was a spark in the air as Cassidy waited. It was a pause of just a few seconds, but it felt like an eternity. Then suddenly, a touch! Cassidy inhaled sharply as she felt Jake's finger tips slowly trail the perimeter of her labia. He made three circles – his light touch driving her wild - before his fingers slid inward and rubbed across her clit. Cassidy bucked slightly into his touch. His fingers were quickly replaced by his lips. Cassidy let out an involuntary moan as Jake's mouth took over, kissing and licking her most sensitive skin. His tongue trailed across her vulva and Cassidy gasped. She tightened her grip on the sheets as he continued, needing to hold on to something. Her head tipped back as her breathing became labored and loud. Her body was heating up and a bubbly, tingly sensation was shooting the whole way down to her toes. Cassidy lost track of time, unable to process much besides the soaring feeling that was overtaking her. As his lips lingered on her clit once more, Cassidy suddenly wanted nothing more than Jake inside of her. She let go of the death grip she had on the sheets and grabbed for his hair. Jake looked up at her in surprise.

"Up," Cassidy panted. Jake grinned and quickly scrambled back onto the bed, and climbed on top of her once more. He pressed his lips against hers, sharing the new taste with her. It didn't deter Cassidy in the least. She parted her lips and Jake took advantage of the opening, deepening the kiss. He slid his left hand underneath her and cupped her backside firmly.

Cassidy gripped tightly onto his back while Jake used his knee and forearm as leverage and scooted them further up the bed until Cassidy's head hit a pillow. They kissed deeply, then Cassidy slid her hand down his chest and onto the waistband of his boxers.

"Hey," Cassidy breathed, pulling her mouth off of Jake's.

"What?"

"Why the hell are you still wearing these?" Cassidy teased, snapping the elastic waistband against his skin. Jake chucked.

"No idea," he replied, rolling off of Cassidy to slip them off. Cassidy smiled at the sight of him. He was ready to go.

"Much better!" Cassidy grinned. She brought herself up on her knees and pushed Jake onto his back, then climbed on top of him. She straddled his torso, her knees resting at his sides. Jake looked as elated and excited as she felt. He suddenly reached to his left, fumbling for the drawer on his bedside table for a moment before retrieving a small, silver packet. Cassidy took it from him, ripped it open, and scooted back onto his thighs so she could slide the condom onto him. Jake bit his bottom lip as she worked. Cassidy loved seeing him so excited. Once the condom was in place, she lifted herself onto her knees, hovering over him. Jake nodded and gripped her hips while she rested her hands on his stomach.

Jake's hold on her tightened as he lowered her onto his shaft. Both he and Cassidy gasped as he entered her. She raised herself up slightly and dropped back down, pushing Jake deeper inside. Cassidy was flushed from her face to her chest. Her breaths consisted of little gasps.

They very quickly got into a rhythm, Jake supporting and guiding the movement of her hips. They moved faster; Cassidy could feel Jake's eyes glued to her chest as she bounced.

She felt so free - full and fiery with Jake inside her. Elation overtook her every emotion. Cassidy's gasps turned into cries of pleasure; she was ready to burst. She could tell Jake was feeling the same thing. Their eyes locked in a powerful moment, and Jake began to tremble beneath her. Cassidy lowered herself down onto him one final time, and they both cried out. The sparks that had been building in her since they met finally caught, flaring into a towering inferno.

She collapsed on his chest. Jake gently helped guide her off of him as he pulled out. He turned away briefly to deal with the condom, and then his hands returned to her lower back, resting on her bare skin. Cassidy snuggled back into him, trying to soak up all the contact she could with all his skin on all of hers. It took a moment to get their breathing back to normal. But even then, they stayed in place, simply enjoying the peace and satisfaction of the moment. No talking, no distraction - just comfort. Cassidy rested her head on his upper chest, and his chest hair lightly tickled her ear. She loved it.

They lay in precious silence for about ten minutes when Jake lifted his head and placed a gentle kiss on her forehead.

"You're not getting up yet," Cassidy said in a playfully firm voice. Jake chuckled. He returned his head to the pillow and they rested peacefully for another long minute.

"That was great, by the way," Jake murmured, breaking the quiet.

"Yes. Yes it was," Cassidy agreed with a smile.

"Thank you for letting me try something new."

"That definitely was not something new for you," Cassidy giggled.

"It was! I've never done that before. It was awesome."

"Lies! You knew exactly what you were doing!"

205

"I figured it out as I went," Jake countered.

"Bull. Shit." They both chuckled. Jake placed another soft kiss on her forehead.

"We should get up," Jake said with a sigh.

"Why?"

"Because I promised you ice cream and I can't follow through if all the shops are closed by the time we get there," Jake explained.

Cassidy perked up. "Oh, yes!"

"Glad we can agree," Jake smiled.

"Kiss me first," Cassidy demanded. Jake leaned his head up and pressed his lips to hers.

# Chapter 21

Cassidy licked the black raspberry ice cream from her cone as she and Jake walked hand in hand down the sidewalk, lazily meandering through the downtown. Their conversation was easy and fun. Cassidy pointed out spots she and her friends had been to when they were in college, including the infamous storm drain that Marissa once tripped over, falling into a puddle and turning her green party dress a nasty brown. Marissa, trooper that she was, didn't let it faze her and walked into the neighboring bar, demanded a drink for her troubles and danced for another hour with dirty leaves stuck to her. Jake laughed, and Cassidy was sure to add that these days, Marissa would have gone straight home, changed into sweats, and had a drink on the sofa instead.

After thirty minutes of wandering and storytelling, ice cream now long gone, Jake gave Cassidy's arm a firm tug and pulled her from the sidewalk into a grassy patch under a tree. He kissed her. Cassidy, caught off guard by his spontaneity, took a moment to react, but then happily kissed him back.

"Cassidy?" a loud, familiar voice called, causing them to startle and pull apart. "Hey!" the voice yelled excitedly. Cassidy didn't need to turn her head to know that it was Laura.

"Who's that?" Jake asked.

"Don't worry," Cassidy assured him with a grin. Laura was bounding toward them with an excited smile. Cassidy waved, and saw that Alex was slowly trailing behind. He looked less than amused to have found Cassidy kissing a boy out in public.

"Oh, my gosh, how are you?! We didn't expect to see you here!" Laura gushed, hugging Cassidy enthusiastically.

"Hey!" Cassidy said. It might be unexpected, but she was happy to see her. Laura leaned in and put her lips an inch from her ear.

"Holy shit! You just had sex! I'm so happy for you! He's really cute!" she whispered frantically. Cassidy worked hard to keep her face neutral.

"You can tell?" Cassidy asked in a panicky whisper. Laura simply smiled.

"Yes! You're glowing, and I love it," she gushed in a low voice. Cassidy froze, unsure of how to react. Did she want everyone in the world to know what had just happened?

"Oh, sorry! Jake, this is my brother Alex and his girlfriend Laura. Guys, this is Jake," Cassidy introduced. Her stomach did a small flip. She hadn't told anyone in her family that she had a new boyfriend, and Alex was never the most welcoming – although his silent, begrudging tolerance was generally more appreciated than the teasing and tormenting that came from Matty, Eric, and Ben.

"It's so nice to meet you," Laura said enthusiastically, giving him a quick hug. Jake was clearly surprised, but recovered quickly.

"Nice to meet you," Jake smiled politely. Cassidy watched him and noticed his eyes kept flickering towards Alex, who was taking his time lighting a cigarette. Laura gave Alex a gentle nudge. He took a long drag before extending his right hand.

"Jake," Alex said with a nod.

"Alex," Jake shook his hand, a forced smile on his face. Cassidy bit the inside of her cheek. Why was Alex making this so awkward?

"What are you guys doing here?" Cassidy asked, desperate to make things feel less tense.

"Just out for a walk, it's such a nice night," Laura replied. "You?"

"I promised Cassidy some ice cream," Jake smiled. Cassidy grinned up at him.

"So, Jake," Alex began.

"We know absolutely nothing about you - tell us everything!" Laura interrupted cheerily. Cassidy was so thankful for her natural exuberance.

"Oh, there's not much to tell," Jake shrugged.

"I bet there is, especially if you caught our Cassidy's attention," Laura countered.

"Exactly how long have you known our Cassidy?" Alex asked pointedly, taking a long drag. Cassidy shot her brother an annoyed look. What was with him tonight?

"I met, or um, Cassidy and I met in early July at a baseball game, and then we ran into each other a few weeks later. I figured I better ask her out - what were the chances of running into each other a third time?" Jake said. Cassidy blushed.

"Oh wow," Laura smiled.

"Hmmm," Alex said. Cassidy knew he wanted to say

something, but she didn't really care. Jake was melting her heart more and more by the minute.

"It's been really great," Cassidy added glaring at Alex.

"What do you do, Jake?" Alex asked, flicking some ash on the ground.

"I teach stats at MU and work with their baseball team," Jake said.

"We went to college there!" Laura said, looking thrilled at the connection.

"Really? It's such a nice school," Jake smiled. Alex let out another hum, taking another drag. Cassidy bit her tongue hard. She needed a break.

"Hey, look at the time," she interjected, grabbing Jake's left wrist and pointing at his watch. Luckily, Jake picked up her cue.

"Oh, yeah, shit, I've got to get Cassidy home and I have an early class tomorrow morning," Jake said painfully. He wasn't the best liar, but Cassidy appreciated his efforts.

"No worries," Laura smiled.

"It was great to see you guys," Cassidy said.

"You, too," Laura said, giving Cassidy's arm a gentle squeeze. "Jake, it was great to meet you."

"It was," Jake said with a genuine smile. Cassidy glanced over at her brother who was busying himself with flicking more ash on the ground.

"Banker," she nodded at him.

"Banker," Alex returned the nod. Cassidy wanted to deck him. With a final wave, Cassidy entwined her hand in Jake's and dragged him down the street and back to his truck.

"Did I do something wrong?" Jake asked as they buckled their seatbelts.

"You? No, you were great," Cassidy said with a huff, resting her head on the seat behind her.

"It just, that felt… weird. I thought you and Alex got along," Jake said, turning the ignition and shifting into drive.

"We do. I have no idea what was with him tonight. Honestly, it really pissed me off," Cassidy sighed. They drove in silence for a few minutes. Cassidy was lost in her own thoughts, already planning to make an angry phone call to her brother.

"Laura seemed nice," Jake said, breaking the quiet. Cassidy smiled at him.

"She is. I hope you can meet them again when Alex is being normal."

"I'd love to meet your family," Jake replied. Cassidy's heart gave a thump.

"Really?"

"Of course. Do you want to meet mine?" Jake stuttered. The question brought with it a certain heaviness in the air.

"Um, um, yes," Cassidy smiled, completely caught off guard.

"You don't have to," Jake chuckled nervously.

"No, no - I definitely want to, but this conversation got serious quickly and I… I was surprised, that is all," Cassidy admitted.

"Oh, I mean, I just brought it up because we saw your brother, and-"

"No, no, I got it."

Jake's truck turned down Cassidy's street and then into the parking lot of her apartment complex.

"I had a good time tonight," Jake said as the car idled in front of the main entrance.

"Me too." Cassidy grinned before leaning over and placing

a soft kiss on his lips. "Thanks for the ice cream."

"Anytime," Jake smirked. Cassidy's cheeks burned as she smiled wide. She wanted to explode with joy. She waved to Jake and hopped out of the truck. She could hear the engine rumble as he drove off.

Cassidy showered and changed into an old T shirt and the shorts she used as pajamas. She paced back and forth in the living room, lightly swaying the beer bottle in her hand. Marissa was spending the night at Brandon's, so she didn't have anyone to help her sort through her feelings. She just had pure emotion. Ecstasy about the best sex of her life, joy about her time with Jake, annoyance about the weird interaction with Alex, and mix of surprise, confusion, and excitement that Jake had talked about meeting each other's families. Her mind was swirling. After another minute of pacing, Cassidy slammed her beer down on the end table, picked up the phone, and dialed Alex's number.

It only rang twice before there was an answer.

"Hello?" It was Laura.

"Laura, it's Cassidy. Is Alex there?" she asked brusquely.

"Oh, hi!" Laura had clearly been taken by surprise. "Sorry, he ran out."

"Out? You guys were just out," Cassidy grumbled. She wished she could be nicer to Laura at the moment, but she couldn't help herself.

"We got home and realized we were out of coffee for tomorrow, and he ran out to get some."

"Oh," Cassidy sighed.

"Are you calling to yell at your brother?" Laura asked playfully.

"I mean, come on, Laura, what the hell was his problem?"

"He was caught off guard."

"That's dumb."

"A little," Laura chucked, "but turning the corner to see your little sister sucking face can definitely throw off your vibe."

"Ugh, Laura," Cassidy groaned.

"I was very happy to meet Jake," Laura said, changing the subject.

"Yeah? I mean, thanks for being nice to him; he appreciated it. We both did."

"It was very nice to see you happy like that," Laura said.

"What do you mean? Like what?"

"Like you're in love."

Cassidy swallowed. "I don't know if I'd go there quite yet," she said.

"I've never seen you look at a guy like that before," Laura pointed out.

"What? You've seen me in relationships before. I was with Kevin for two years. I loved him."

"You might have thought you did, but you never looked at him like that. Trust me, this guy is different. And I support anyone that can make you look that happy."

"Hmmm." Cassidy paused, not sure how to process her words.

"That may have been why your brother wasn't too keen," Laura explained.

"What? Why?"

"Cassidy, you were glowing!"

"You said it was because I had sex," Cassidy said, blushing again at the thought.

"That was part of it."

"I didn't think it was that obvious."

"It was to people who are looking."

"Alex would not have been looking for that on me," Cassidy pointed out.

"No, but he could see how much you cared for Jake and how much he adored you."

"That doesn't mean he can be a dick, and I called to tell him that."

"Look, just because it's taking him a moment doesn't mean that he won't come around. You need to give him more than a few minutes," Laura advised. Cassidy sighed. "But I'm already a huge supporter of Jake," Laura continued.

"Yeah?"

"Yeah. So start talking! I need to hear everything," Laura ordered playfully. Cassidy smiled against the receiver.

"Alright, what do you want to know?"

"Let's start with exactly what happened before you guys came downtown and go from there."

"Laura!"

"I'm practically your sister in law - an older sister at that. I have a right to know," Laura replied fondly. Cassidy felt her annoyance melt away. She never knew how Laura was able to do that. She always had such a calming presence, even over the phone.

"Well, I went over to his house for dinner…" Cassidy began retelling her evening. Laura hung onto every word. This was exactly what Cassidy needed: someone to talk to, someone she loved. She wrapped up her tale with Jake treating her to

214

the ice cream he had promised, causing Laura to gush once more.

"I'm so happy for you!"

"I think I really am, too."

"You should be."

"Jake mentioned meeting each other's families."

"Wow."

"I know!"

"This is so perfect." Laura sighed dreamily.

"I'm trying not to get too ahead of myself," Cassidy said, biting her lip.

"Dive in, girl! Trust me, I think you'll come out swimming."

"Thanks." Cassidy felt a warmth flood through her body.

"Hey, Alex got back from the store a few minutes ago; I'm going to go hang with him."

"Oh, okay. Tell him I'm still a little mad at him."

"I will pass that along," Laura chuckled.

"Night, Laura. Thanks."

"Anytime. Night Cassidy."

# Chapter 22

The breeze flowed through the open car windows, but Cassidy's hair was, thankfully, pulled back in a ponytail - otherwise it would have looked like a rat's nest by now. She smiled over at Jake as he steered them down the old streets of his hometown of Johnsonburg, about two hours southeast of Erie. It looked like a typical western Pennsylvania industrial town. proudly featuring its historical paper mill on every sign within the town's perimeter.

It had been almost two weeks since Jake first proposed the idea of meeting each other's families. When Jake's younger brother, Will, announced that he was coming home for a long weekend, Cassidy accepted Jake's invitation to join him on the visit. The drive was beautiful, and Cassidy enjoyed seeing a part of the state she had never been to before. She was intrigued to meet Jake's small family - just his mother and brother.

Two turns later, Jake slowed in front of a dark blue sided two-story house. The street was on a fairly steep hill, common for most of the western half of the state, and a large white staircase led from the sidewalk up to the pristine porch. Two rocking chairs sat to the right of the front door, and a small table set was on the opposite side. Cassidy smiled as she climbed out of the car. She imagined years of sitting on that porch and watching everything that happened on the street. It was a cozy thought.

"You ready?" Jake asked as he reached into the bed of his truck and untied both of their backpacks from the railing.

"I'm very excited!" Cassidy said as she took her backpack from him.

"I'd lower those expectations right now," Jake teased. Cassidy gave him a playful swat.

"Let me enjoy meeting your family."

"Okay." Jake let out a deep breath, as if steadying himself. Cassidy leaned up and gave him a light peck on the lips.

"It's going to be great," she assured him. They climbed the stairs to the porch and Cassidy resisted the urge to flop into one of the rocking chairs. Jake knocked on the front door before opening it and letting himself inside.

"Mom," he called out. Cassidy followed Jake closely, keenly looking over his shoulder to get a peek at the house. They walked into a small foyer. The walls were white and everything was trimmed with a dark wood that also encased the doorframes of the rooms around them. It was clear the house was older, but in the best way possible. Original features from the turn of the century were everywhere and Cassidy drank it all in.

"Jacob?" A female voice floated in from their right.

"Yeah, we're here," Jake called, setting his backpack on the wooden bench next to the door and motioning for Cassidy to

217

do the same.

"You're here!" A middle-aged woman appeared in the entryway to what Cassidy assumed was the dining room. She gave Jake a kiss on the cheek, which he reciprocated.

"Mom, this is my girlfriend, Cassidy. Cassidy, this is my mom, Claire," he introduced. Claire was about two inches shorter than Cassidy. Her hair was dark with many strands of grey sprinkled throughout. Cassidy could tell her hair was long; it was wrapped into a large bun atop her head. She had the same green eyes as her eldest son, and while she was a petite woman, she had an air about her that said no one could mess with her - nor should they even try.

"Hi Mrs. Sullivan! Thank you so much for inviting me to your home," Cassidy said politely.

"Well, Jake said he wanted to bring home a girl he met at a baseball game, and naturally I was intrigued," Claire said flatly. Cassidy nodded and tried to ignore her lack of warmth. She remembered Jake saying she was a tough cookie.

"Yes," Cassidy smiled.

"Come on into the kitchen. I'm working on a loaf of bread and it needs more kneading." Claire gave a wave as she turned and headed to the right. They walked through a dining room that looked perfectly put-together and clearly had not been used in years, and into a bright kitchen. Dark orange counters ran along the perimeter of the room, and a large blue and silver metal table sat in the center. The style reminded Cassidy of something from a 1950s diner. The back wall, behind the large sink, was lined with windows that filled the room with light. There was a homey and well-used quality about this kitchen. Cassidy loved it.

"Cassidy, have you ever made bread?" Claire asked as

218

she walked over to the counter where a large bowl filled with dough and jars of flour were sitting in wait.

"No, ma'am," Cassidy replied honestly. "My mom has always been more of a Christmas cookie baker - or the occasional birthday cake baker, but that's about it."

"Well, time to learn," Claire said, motioning to the bowl. Cassidy looked up at Jake questioningly. He gave a defeated shrug and she walked over to join his mom at the counter.

"I'm ready!"

"Mom, she just got here," Jake said as he opened the fridge and helped himself to a can of Sprite. He turned and rested his back against the fridge as he cracked open the top.

"Oh, you boys," Claire sighed as she sprinkled flour on the counter and handed off the dough for Cassidy knead before turning to face her eldest. "You both come home and immediately want to rest!"

"Yeah, where is Will? I saw his car outside," Jake asked.

"He's in his room. Hopefully he's finally up."

"When did he get in?"

"The middle of the night," Claire scoffed. "He tells me he's leaving after his last class and will be here by 8:00PM. He then decides to go out with his friends first, and doesn't show up until 2:00AM! Scared the hell out of me, coming into the house. And now he thinks he can just sleep the day away."

"Excellent," Jake muttered in a bemused tone under his breath. Cassidy kept all her focus on the lump of dough she was kneading so she didn't laugh out loud and ruin her first impression with Claire. She made a mental note to giggle about this later with Jake.

"It was not excellent." Claire rolled her eyes.

"Then tell him to get up and make him help, rather than

subjecting my girlfriend to physical labor," Jake said, taking another sip of his Sprite.

"I'm learning something new," Cassidy interjected. While she appreciated Jake's concern, she knew she was earning points with Jake's mom. She was even kind of enjoying the process of kneading. It was a good workout.

"She is! Now keep that up," Claire instructed.

"Well, I'll go get his ass up," Jake said.

"Language," Claire scolded. Jake had taken a single step when, almost as if summoned, a loud creak from the staircase announced that Will was on his way.

"Look who's up," Jake drawled, resting his shoulder on the thick doorway between the kitchen and dining room. Cassidy did her best to turn to watch as she continued to knead.

"Look who's finally here," Will countered. While Will's voice was slightly deeper, Cassidy noticed how similar the brothers sounded. She suddenly wondered if outsiders thought that about her brothers, too. Cassidy herself thought they all sounded vastly different, but maybe that was just familiarity? Jake was patting Will on the shoulder as they entered the kitchen together. Cassidy nearly fell over. Jake and Will didn't just sound alike; they looked alike, as well. Will was maybe two inches taller than Jake and had slightly broader shoulders, but otherwise, they were identical: the same copper hair with gentle waves. The same green eyes, the same thin, but strong build. Their smiles even matched.

"Hey," Jake said to Will, patting him on the chest, "I want you to meet my girlfriend, Cassidy."

"Hi!" Cassidy smiled, abandoning the dough. Will extended his hand. Cassidy started to reach out, but quickly realized that her hands were completely coated in flour.

"Ah, sorry, I'm a mess," she said with a shrug.

"No worries," Will smirked before raising his forearm. Cassidy mirrored him and they bumped forearms in a non-traditional greeting.

"Nice to finally meet you," Cassidy chuckled.

"You, too."

"Jake told me that you're in law school," Cassidy said.

"Talk while you work the dough, please. It's not ready to proof yet," Claire directed.

"Mom," Jake protested, looking embarrassed. But Cassidy wasn't bothered. She was used to a strong-willed mother.

"I'm on it," Cassidy answered, returning to the half-kneaded dough.

"Yeah, final year."

"Where are you studying?" Cassidy asked curiously.

"Dickison."

"Oh, where's that?"

"Out by Harrisburg," Will explained. Cassidy nodded as she flipped the dough over with a thud.

"Have you been there the whole time?"

"No, no, I was at Penn State."

"You never told me that you and your brother were both there," Cassidy said to Jake.

"It's a big school," Jake shrugged.

"Yeah, I mean we only saw each other at baseball, really," Will added.

"Wait, what?" Cassidy asked in surprise. Jake never talked much about his brother, but she was shocked he'd never mentioned this before.

"I played catcher. Freshman year on JV, but I made varsity the last three," Will grinned.

"That's awesome! I played softball at Edinboro," Cassidy smiled.

"Oh, nice, what position?"

"Shortstop."

"I tried infield for a few years when I was a kid, but I covered for catcher one game when I was ten and loved it, never left," Will explained. Out of the corner of her eye, Cassidy noticed that Jake was looking a little left out and she wanted to bring him into the conversation.

"Jake and I met at a baseball game," Cassidy said, hoping to draw him into the conversation.

"Really?" Will asked.

"Jake, you didn't tell him?" Cassidy playfully scolded.

"Oh, um, well," Jake stuttered, clearly caught off guard.

"You suck, Jakey," Will smirked. Jake rolled his in annoyance and took a seat at the kitchen table.

"He does not!" Cassidy defended, giving the dough another hard shove.

"Well, I'm sorry for you, then," Will countered with an amused wink. Cassidy chuckled while Jake reached up and punched Will's arm with his left hand. If Claire was not standing in the room, Cassidy would have made another comment, but she figured best not to press her luck. Cassidy almost felt like she was back home.

"Boys!" Claire exclaimed. She pushed between them and came to stand next to Cassidy, peering over her shoulder.

"What do you think?" Cassidy asked.

"Not bad. Now shape it into a ball and put it in this metal bowl – I've already oiled the sides. It's going to proof for a couple of hours," Claire instructed. Cassidy nodded.

"So, Cassie," Will began.

"Cassidy," Jake corrected.

"Does everyone always call you Cassidy?" Will asked.

"Pretty much. Either that or Banker, but that was more in high school and college."

"Banker?"

"It's my last name." Cassidy explained, depositing the rounded dough into the bowl and making her way to the sink to wash her hands.

"My oldest brother always calls me Cassie, unless he's annoyed with me, but really, he's the only one. Kind of weird hearing it from anyone else," Cassidy said.

"Oldest? How many brothers do you have?" Will asked with a bemused look.

"Four." Cassidy turned off the faucet and dried her hands on the blue tea towel hanging from the dishwasher handle.

"Shut up!" Will exclaimed in disbelief. Cassidy was so used to this reaction that it had started to bore her.

"Yeah," she shrugged.

"Any sisters?" Will asked.

"No."

"Your parents are better than me - two was my limit," Claire chimed in. Cassidy chuckled. Will turned to Jake and gave his shoulder a playful shove.

"And you're still walking? I can see one brother maybe letting you date their sister, but not four," Will teased. Jake looked annoyed and took a long sip from his can of pop.

"I'll be perfectly fine. I just haven't met them yet," Jake said.

"Well let me know how that goes," Will chuckled. Cassidy rolled her eyes, then walked over and took a seat on Jake's lap.

"He'll be fine," she agreed. "And he has met one of them.

You met Alex," she reminded him.

"Oh, yeah," Jake nodded.

"Alex is…?" Will asked.

"My oldest brother," Cassidy explained.

"And how did that go?" Will asked suspiciously.

Jake hesitated.

"It was really quick; we just bumped into him downtown. It was like, a minute," Cassidy said quickly.

"So, he hates you?" Will asked Jake, smirking gleefully. Jake's mouth opened several times, but nothing came out. Finally, he sighed in defeat.

"Yeah, I think so," he admitted.

"Ha!" Will cheered.

"No, no, no!" Cassidy tried to interject, but she knew it was no use. The meeting had gone poorly and they hadn't addressed the subject since.

"Alright you three, out of my kitchen," Claire cut in, giving Cassidy a glare. She clearly did not appreciate her perching on her son's lap.

"Why?" Will asked.

"Because it's my kitchen and I have things to do. We're having a nice dinner tonight - this takes work," Claire said, shooing them with her hands. Cassidy climbed off of Jake and inched towards the entryway.

"Do you want help?" Jake offered.

"No, you get in my way," Claire said, giving Will a push.

"Hey!" Will whined, but he obediently followed Jake and Cassidy out of the kitchen.

Cassidy requested that Jake give her a full tour of his childhood home. Will followed them and did his absolute best to provide an embarrassing childhood story about Jake for every room they visited. Will was in the middle of a car-vomiting memory as they explored the half-finished basement that held had a pair of old sofas and a ping pong table - very clearly the boys' teenage hangout spot - when Jake, who was losing his patience with his brother, stuck his foot out and tripped him. Will, rather ungracefully, toppled onto one of the sofas before he rolled, or rather bounced, onto the floor. Jake instantly grabbed Cassidy's hand and pulled her along, dashing for the stairs before Will could get up and retaliate. Cassidy happily played along and sprinted after Jake. They ignored Claire yelling at them to stop running in the house, and quick time upstairs to Jake's old bedroom, closing the door behind them. They were laughing hysterically when they flopped down on his bed in the corner of the room.

"Jake," Cassidy scolded, still giggling, as her breathing returned to normal.

"He was annoying me. Besides, he's perfectly fine." He rolled to his side to face her.

"We came here to hang out with your family," Cassidy reminded him.

"And we're doing that. I just need a moment for just the two of us," Jake said with a grin as he leaned toward her.

Cassidy smiled as his lips gently brushed against hers. She kissed him back, soft and sweet, over and over again. Cassidy felt like she was floating. Jake had just brought his hand up to gently cup her cheek when Jake's bedroom door was violently flung open. They startled apart. Will was standing smugly in the doorway, smirking at them.

225

"Assholes," Will taunted.

"Get out," Jake groaned. Cassidy couldn't help but giggle again as Will turned to leave.

"Come on, let's go be social," Cassidy said, patting Jake's thigh as she sat up and hopped off the bed.

"What? No, why?" Jake whined. He clearly wanted to spend more time in bed.

"Because we're only here for twenty-four hours and you haven't seen your mom or brother in… what? Almost six months?" Cassidy asked, feeling a pang in her chest. She hurt at the thought of not seeing her family for such a long time. Even though they drove her crazy, they were her people.

"Ugh, fine," Jake groaned. He heaved himself off of the bed and followed Cassidy into the hallway.

"Will," Cassidy called out. "Come on, play a game with us."

"Game?" Will and Jake chorused.

"We should do something! Do you have a deck of cards?" Cassidy asked.

"Yeah, downstairs," Jake said.

"Perfect," she grinned. Will and Jake shrugged and followed her down the stairs.

Cassidy, Jake, and Will took over the large dining room table with their card game. Cassidy loved to play; it was a favorite holiday pastime among her and her siblings over the years. The trio played two hands of Rummy, followed by a spirited game of SlapJack that turned a little too violent between the brothers and caused Claire to emerge from the kitchen and angrily snap both of her sons with a dish towel. Cassidy quickly gathered up the cards to shuffle and start a new, less physical game.

"Wanna play poker?" Cassidy asked as she shuffled.

"I'm not losing all my money to you," Jake teased.

"How do you know I'll win?" Cassidy asked over the clack of the fanning cards.

"You have that air about you," Jake commented.

"We don't have to play for money," Will said with a smirk.

"I'm not playing strip poker, you dweeb," Cassidy chuckled.

"Shut up," Jake warned his brother under his breath.

"Your loss," Will winked. "We have the plastic chips, we can just play for those. That way, Jake can lose his pride instead of his money." Jake sighed.

"I'll play with the chips," Cassidy smiled. "Jake?"

"Yeah, why not," he agreed, standing to retrieve the chips from the closet in the foyer.

"Hey, Cass," Will began as Jake left the room.

"Hmmm?"

"When did you start playing ball?"

"Oh!" Cassidy was surprised at his question. "I started T-ball in Kindergarten, then moved up to softball in third grade. Played all through high school and college. You?"

"Same. Well, except I played baseball, and I stopped after I finished my undergrad at Penn State."

"Do you miss it?" Cassidy asked.

"Some days, but honestly, I'm so swamped with law school that I don't have time anyway. I wouldn't be able to enjoy it now. Or pass any of my classes," Will joked.

"I get that."

"Get what?" Jake asked, returning with the wooden box filled with poker chips.

"Being too busy now for playing baseball," Cassidy answered.

227

"Oh."

"Cass, you wanna deal?" Will asked.

"Sure."

"Cassidy," Jake corrected.

"It's okay," Cassidy smiled. She gave a final shuffle as Jake handed them each a stack of red, blue, green, and black chips.

"Did you play travel or go to tournaments?" Will asked as Cassidy dealt out the cards.

"Both," Cassidy replied, trying to keep a straight face as she spotted the three of a kind in her hand.

"Where was the furthest you traveled?" Will asked. He set two cards face down and nodded. Cassidy handed him two cards.

"Three," Jake said quietly.

"I think the furthest tournament was in Atlanta," Cassidy said, dealing Jake his card and taking two more for herself.

"Atlanta?" Will asked.

"Yeah, my freshman year of high school. It was a really good team that year, mostly seniors, and we got to go to Nationals!" Cassidy grinned, not only at the memory, but at her two new cards. They didn't give her the full house she was hoping for, but rather a four of a kind. Excellent!

"Did you win? Will asked, tossing a red chip in the center.

"Not even close," Cassidy laughed. Both she and Jake added a red chip of their own to the middle of the table.

"Really?" Will chuckled, adding two more chips to the pile.

"We were eliminated in the first round. The game was a bloodbath, to be honest," Cassidy shrugged, upping her bet to three blue chips.

"Damn." Jake matched Cassidy's chips. She winked at him, but he didn't meet her gaze.

"The trip was great, though. My oldest brother was a senior, so my family all came down to Georgia and we stayed a few extra days as a family vacation slash graduation trip for him. It was a good time. We loved downtown!"

"Nice," Will said, simply grabbing a handful of chips and plopping them in the center.

"Bullshit," Jake sighed at his movement.

"No shit," Will countered smugly.

"I'll call," Cassidy said, throwing in her own handful of chips and smirking at Will.

"Ugh, I fold," Jake dropped his cards face down on the table.

"So?" Cassidy asked Will, bouncing her eyebrows.

"Boom!" Will proudly laid down five red cards, all diamonds. "Flush!"

Cassidy hummed. "Good, but not great," she countered, setting down her hand which included four 10s. Jake let out an impressed low whistle.

"What?!" Will exclaimed.

"Read 'em and weep," Cassidy grinned, reaching forward and pulling the large pile of meaningless chips to her chest.

"Cheater!" Will teased.

"How?" Cassidy laughed.

"You dealt, obviously."

"Fine - you deal this round," Cassidy instructed, handing him the deck of cards.

"Fine." They played another hand of poker. This time, Cassidy only managed a lousy pair of fives, while Will had a full house. Jake folded early. A third game failed to materialize, as conversation took over and flowed naturally. Cassidy felt her heart soar. This visit was going so well. She hoped that she had made a good first impression with Claire, and she and Will were getting along effortlessly. The brothers and Cassidy sat and talked at the dining room table for well over an hour, swapping college dorm stories. Like Cassidy, Will had also had a weird roommate at the start of freshman year. They talked about late night practices, favorite drunk foods, and even high school prom themes. She and Will had so much in common; eventually Jake just sat back and let them get to know each other. The stories continued until Claire emerged from the kitchen asking for help to peel the potatoes.

# Chapter 23

Cassidy emerged from the large, family bathroom after brushing her teeth and padded down the hallway to Jake's childhood bedroom. Claire wasn't thrilled about the idea of Cassidy and Jake sharing a bed. Cassidy wasn't surprised, knowing Lynne would have a similar reaction. She had volunteered to sleep on the couch, but Jake insisted she take his old room.

Jake was grabbing one of the pillows from his bed to use downstairs as Cassidy entered.

"Hey there," she smirked.

"Hey."

"Are you going to sneak back up later?" she asked in low voice, wrapping her arms around his middle.

"The stairs creak," Jake replied.

"Oh," Cassidy paused in thought. "Well, we could be quick now!"

"These walls are thin," Jake said flatly.

"Come on," Cassidy pleaded playfully. "We haven't had

sex in a while."

"We had sex this morning before we left," Jake pointed out.

Cassidy was feeling increasingly frustrated. "Jake," she said sweetly in a low voice, almost begging.

"Cassidy," Jake sighed. "Let's just go to bed. It's been a long day."

"Yeah, okay." Cassidy agreed reluctantly, remembering that he had done all of the driving.

"Night," Jake said, stepping out of her embrace.

"Aren't you going to kiss me?" Cassidy asked. She was getting confused. Jake leaned over quickly and gave her the briefest of pecks before turning and departing the room with his pillow. Cassidy stood frozen in place. What the hell was going on? She chewed on her bottom lip as she listened to him descend the stairs – they really did creak loudly. Disheartened, she shook her head and climbed into Jake's bed. It had been a great day, and she didn't want to spoil it by worrying about Jake being weird just now. With that, Cassidy snuggled into the pillow, smiling at the thought of a teenaged Jake lying in the same place, dreaming of his future. She quickly fell into a deep and blissful sleep.

Loud clangs of kitchen pans and the smell of something warm and sweet woke Cassidy the next morning. She stretched in the cozy, blue sheets of the bed, smiling to herself as she remembered where she was.

She rolled over and peeked at Jake's old, round alarm clock on the bedside table. It was 7:30. Cassidy let out a yawn and a final stretch before climbing out of the bed, knowing she should get up. She hated oversleeping when she was a guest. She had promised she would attend church with Claire and the boys - and whatever Claire was making right now smelled fantastic!

Cassidy quickly freshened up in the bathroom, put on a bra, brushed her hair and headed downstairs in her pajamas, looking a very cute and polished kind of disheveled.

The smell of breakfast cooking was stronger on the main floor. She could hear Claire singing along to the radio as Bobby Darrin crooned. Cassidy noticed that the large front door was open and assumed Jake had gone for a morning run since she hadn't seen him on the sofa. She shrugged it off and made her way to the kitchen at the back of the house.

"Good morning," Cassidy said with a smile.

"Oh, good morning," Claire replied, looking surprised to see her.

"It smells great," Cassidy commented as she came to sneak a peek the large frying pan filled with eggs and pancakes.

"It'll be done shortly."

"Do you need any help?"

"No," Claire replied. Cassidy could not help notice that she sounded a little short. She took a seat at the large table, wondering how to cut the tension.

"You know, Bobby Darrin was my oldest brother's first record. He bought it with his allowance and played it non-stop for weeks," Cassidy smiled.

"Well, who wouldn't like Bobby," Claire remarked as she flipped three pancakes in quick succession. She was softening, slightly.

"No one!"

Their moment was interrupted by the sounds of the front

screen door squeaking open and crashing closed.

"Jake?" Cassidy called out hopefully.

"Oh, hey, you're up," Jake commented as he entered the kitchen. Cassidy noticed he was in jeans and one of his white Penn State T shirts rather than his usual workout clothes.

"You went out?" Cassidy asked. Claire huffed behind her.

"Packing the truck," Jake replied shortly.

"Oh, already?"

"Yeah. Um, when you get a chance, do you want to get changed and bring your bag down?" Jake asked. Cassidy scrunched up her face.

"I want to eat this amazing breakfast your mom is making us, first."

"Fine, after that," Jake sighed. Cassidy noticed he looked fidgety.

"Well come on, the food is ready. Scarf it on down since you have to leave so quickly," Claire grumbled as she pulled plates out from the cabinet next to the stove.

"Mom, I'm sorry, it's just that I forgot I have a meeting with the baseball coach at the school tonight," Jake said. He patted his mom on the shoulder. Cassidy's head whipped around to stare at Jake. She knew damn well he didn't have a meeting that night. She couldn't figure out for the life of her what was going on with him. However, she knew that pointing this out in front of Claire would be catastrophic, and she would be walking back to Erie. She didn't push.

"Oh, shoot, was that this weekend?" Cassidy asked, playing along. She hoped it might buy her points with Jake's foul mood. The shock on Jake's face nearly doubled her over in laughter. She tucked it away to enjoy later.

"Yes, it's this weekend," Jake replied tentatively.

"Jacob, I know your job is important, and I'm happy you're doing so well, but you and your brother haven't been home at the same time in months, and now that we're finally all together, you bolt in less than twenty-four hours!" Claire huffed. Cassidy bit her lip and shoveled some eggs onto her plate. What the hell was going on?

"Mom, I'm sorry," Jake sighed. He grabbed a plate to start filling.

Breakfast was a delicious, though tense affair. Cassidy did her best to keep up the conversation, asking Claire about her ladies' book club, her Bible study group at the church, and her women's hunt club that had their first meeting of the season next week.

"Too bad Will missed this amazing food," Cassidy said as they finally cleared up their plates into the sink.

"He's always been my late sleeper."

"Cassidy, why don't you go get changed," Jake said abruptly.

"Oh, doesn't your mom need help with the dishes?"

"I'll help her," Jake said. There was no emotion in his voice. Cassidy desperately wanted to ask him what was going on, but bit her tongue. They had a two hour car ride ahead of them. She would have plenty of opportunity to grill him, and she planned to.

"Okay," Cassidy agreed and headed upstairs.

Less than thirty minutes later, Cassidy was dressed and packed up. She, Jake, Claire, and Will, who had been forcefully roused by his mother, were all standing on the front porch. No one was in a chipper mood.

"Thank you so much for having me," Cassidy smiled at Claire.

235

"I'm glad you could come, even for a short time," Claire nodded. Cassidy knew that was about the best she was going to get. It was unfortunate that this early departure is what Claire would focus on when thinking of her.

"I can't believe you're bailing," Will smirked. Jake rolled his eyes and the brothers shook hands. Jake had always told Cassidy that his family wasn't warm and fuzzy, but seeing it in action was something completely different. Jake moved his attention to his mom, apologizing once more and assuring her that it had been a great visit. Will moved over to Cassidy, a large grin plastered on his face.

"Did you orchestrate all this?" he asked in a low voice.

"Not at all! I'm not dumb enough to piss off your mom," Cassidy replied in a whisper. Will chuckled.

"Fair enough."

"I'm glad we met," Cassidy said with a smile.

"Me, too. And I'm glad Jake finally started dating a girl that isn't weird."

"Thanks, I guess?"

"It's a compliment."

"Well, come see your brother in Erie; we'll go to a game or something." Cassidy nudged his arm.

"That would be a lot of fun!" Will grinned.

"Get my number from Jake. Call anytime!"

"Definitely," Will said before embracing her in a big bear hug. Cassidy wasn't sure she had won Claire over on this visit, but she was thrilled to have befriended Will. At least two of the Sullivans liked her.

"Cassidy, time to go," Jake said firmly, grabbing her arm and pulling her out of the hug.

"Ooop," Cassidy grunted. "Bye!"

"Let's go," Jake sighed as he walked around the truck to the driver's side.

Jake and Cassidy gave a final wave as the truck rumbled down the street. They drove in silence, except for David Bowie serenading from the car stereo. But as soon as Jake merged onto Route 948, Cassidy let loose.

"So, what the hell?" Cassidy asked loudly as she shifted in her seat so she was facing Jake. He looked startled by her sudden outburst.

"What?" Jake asked. Cassidy glared at him.

"Don't what me - I want to know why you dragged us out of there!"

"I just, you know, wanted to beat traffic. If we'd stayed for church, we would have had to stay for lunch, and then my mom would have found something for Will and me to fix, and, well, we wouldn't get home until after dark, and we both have work tomorrow," Jake trailed off.

"Bullshit!"

"We're going home," Jake grumbled.

"Yeah, and we have a two-hour drive ahead of us. We're going to talk about this."

"There's nothing to talk about."

"There is," Cassidy insisted firmly. "You've been weird since last night, and then I wake up this morning and you're ready to leave all of a sudden!"

"I told you!"

"Yeah, and that was a lie," Cassidy argued.

"No."

"Yes! I think I deserve an explanation. I was so excited to meet your family. Your mom is a tough cookie, and I think she would have been happy if I had joined her for church this

237

morning. Now she thinks I hate God, and I don't. I'm also a Lutheran – I thought we could bond over it.

"I didn't know you're a Lutheran?" Jake asked. Cassidy couldn't lie, she wasn't exactly a poster child for any faith.

"I'm not good about going anymore, but I go on Christmas and Easter. When I was a kid we were all at church every week."

Jake hummed.

"We're not here to argue about religion!" Cassidy said firmly.

"I'm not arguing religion, I just never knew," Jake countered.

Cassidy grunted. "Today was a really good opportunity for me to solidify a good impression with your mom. I want her to like me."

"She will!"

"She might, but right now, I'm not looking too favorable. I'm the bitch her son brought home and then turned tail and ditched her for."

"That's a little dramatic."

"Ugh," Cassidy groaned.

"Ugh," Jake groaned in mockery. Cassidy gritted her teeth. If he hadn't been driving, she would have hit him.

"Jake, you only get one chance at a first impression."

"It'll be fine," Jake said dismissively.

"At least Will and I got along. That'll give me some points. I guess this visit wasn't a total loss," Cassidy said. Jake muttered something under his breath.

"What was that?"

"Nothing."

"I think it was something,"

238

"Cassidy," Jake said in a warning tone.

"I don't understand why you have been in such a foul mood!"

"I'm not in a foul mood."

"Yesterday was great, and then you shut down last night."

"I did not shut down. I was tired."

"You, Will, and I had fun all day. I don't understand."

"Well, you wouldn't," Jake snapped.

"I seriously do not understand why you're defensive right now. Ugh, at least Will and I got along and had fun this weekend, otherwise it would have been a waste."

"Fuck Will."

"What?" Cassidy gasped in surprise.

"I'm serious, go fuck Will."

"Okay. I have so many questions right now." Cassidy's mind was spinning. Jake was normally so easy-going; why was he so angry? He had been the one to invite her.

"So do I."

"I thought you and Will got along? I know you said you weren't super close, but you seemed happy to see each other. Will was fun, we had a blast. What is going on?"

"Yeah, Will is the best," Jake said sarcastically.

"Better than you at the moment," Cassidy snipped back.

"Then date him."

"What?"

"You want to date him. I know you do. He's the one you like - you have everything in common."

"I don't want to date Will!"

"Oh come on! I saw you two together, the way you laughed, the way you looked at each other." Cassidy sat dumbfounded.

"Jake…"

"You're right. Maybe I should have let you two spend another day together. You could have gone back to Harrisburg with him instead."

"Where is this coming from?"

"Years and years of being the God's geeky older brother. I know how this works. Use me to get to him. Granted, you didn't know him ahead of time - this was just a nice surprise bonus for you."

"I don't want to date Will!!" Cassidy screamed.

"Oh please."

"I don't love Will! It's you that I love!" Cassidy spat. The words were out of her mouth before she could even process them. Jake swerved in shock, receiving a loud honk from the irritated Honda driver next to them.

"Shit," Jake said, regarding his swerve.

"Shit," Cassidy agreed, but more in shock at what she had just said.

"I'm sorry... what did you say?" Jake asked tentatively as they returned to their lane.

"I said I don't want to date your stupid brother."

"Oh," Jake said, sounding a little disappointed. Cassidy chewed her lip for a moment to muster up her courage.

"Because he's not the one I love," she added. Jake started to grin, though his focus was on the road in front of him. "It's you."

"Wow," Jake breathed.

"Wow? That's what you say after I bare my soul? Even after you yelled at me for flirting with your brother, which I did not do?! And, then—"

"I love you, too," Jake interjected, catching Cassidy completely off guard.

Cassidy was silent for a minute. "So, um, we just… said…"

"Yeah…"

"Pull over," Cassidy instructed.

"Why?"

"Because I don't want to almost die again," Cassidy sassed. Jake chuckled as he put on his blinker and slowed down. They rolled to a stop on the side of the road.

"What's up?" Jake asked as he set the parking break.

"What's up? Really?" Cassidy leaned over and pressed her lips to his for a few seconds. "I'm not having an 'I love you' moment without a kiss."

"Oh." Jake smiled before leaning in and connecting their lips once more. After a breathless moment, they pulled back and smiled at each other.

"So, we said it," Cassidy said.

"We did."

"This weekend wasn't a waste at all, then."

"No, I guess not."

"You should probably thank your brother," Cassidy smirked.

"Don't push it." Jake raised an eyebrow at her. Cassidy giggled to herself.

"But in all seriousness, that can't happen again."

"What can't?" Jake asked.

"You flying off the handle or getting all jealous or not trusting me," Cassidy told him firmly.

"Oh."

"Jake, I'm serious. I love you, but I need you to trust me and I need you to talk to me if you're feeling upset. I refuse to spend my time walking on eggshells and wondering if I'll set you off," she said honestly. Jake looked surprised and remorseful.

"I'm sorry, I didn't realize it was that bad."

"It was that bad."

"I'm sorry," Jake repeated. "Will just … ugh, I love him, but he knows how to get right under my skin. He always has."

"Trust me, I completely get strained and frustrating relationships with a brother. I do. It's okay to feel annoyed or sad, but just tell me next time. Trust me that I will take your side. Trust me that I'll take your feelings seriously."

"I do trust you, but I'm just not great at the whole trust thing," Jake admitted.

"I know you've had your trust broken. I've been there. It sucks. But you and I, we're different. This is our relationship. For this to work, we need to trust each other. Always. Even when it's hard."

"You're right."

"I know," Cassidy teased. Jake grinned at her and placed a gentle peck on her lips.

"I do love you."

"I love you, too, Jake,"

"I am really sorry I upset you today."

"It's okay. But I think you need to call your mom and say sorry to her, too."

"I will. I promise."

"Well, let's get back home," she said.

"Oh, you didn't want to…?" Jake trailed off.

"I'm not having sex in the cab of a truck on the side of the highway, Jake."

"Just thought I'd ask, you're usually the more adventurous one," he teased.

"We'll adventure when we're not on four wheels."

"Have it your way," Jake chuckled, shifting the truck back into gear and merging on the highway. Cassidy couldn't help but smile as she watched him.

"I love you," she said as she settled back in her seat and crossed her legs.

"I love you, too."

# Chapter 24

The next two weeks passed by fairly uneventfully for Cassidy. She was seeing Jake at least three times a week. And he had kept his promise, they spent a lot of time talking and he trusted her with a lot more of his emotions. Outside, the temperatures dropped as they entered the fall. Snow was just around the corner in Erie. Fall was always lovely, but short in northwest Pennsylvania; snow fell anywhere from late October to mid-April.

Work had become the part of her life that she dreaded the most. She had always enjoyed her job well enough, but now it was stressful. Two more people had been let go, and all perks, including free coffee and good toilet paper, had been taken away. Cassidy was stuck crunching the same numbers over and over with Mr. Jelif and never seeing any relief. She hated that this burden had been placed on her. While logically, she knew this meant that she would likely keep her job the longest, the stress was doing her head in. Her nails were bitten down to the quick.

Both Jake and Marissa were fantastic distractions for her,

and Cassidy knew she wouldn't be hanging on without them – she would have quit on her own. In fact, she had been toying with the possibility for a few days now.

It was a Wednesday - a normal October Wednesday - when Cassidy walked into work and got the shock of her life.

"Cassidy," Gladys wailed as she walked in. She was in tears, and Cassidy rushed over to the large reception desk where Gladys sat.

"Oh my god, what happened?"

"I had six months left until retirement," Gladys sniffled. Cassidy suddenly noticed that she was filling a box with her possessions.

"No!" Cassidy gasped in horror.

"I was so close. I've worked my whole life, I just wanted to make it 67 for full social security so I could retire and relax. Six months! My birthday is in six damn months and they gave me the axe. I've been here for decades," Gladys choked out as she added another framed picture of her family to her box.

"What happened?" Cassidy asked. Her heart and mind were racing. Was she responsible for Gladys's departure? She had told Mr. Jelif to cut back, and she knew layoffs had to happen - but not Gladys! Not the support staff who earn much less than the accountants.

"Mr. Jelif called me into his office at the end of the day yesterday. He said he was happy with my work, but that they don't have the money to keep me so I had to be let go," Gladys sniffled. "I was so shocked! I couldn't even plead my case, I just ran out in tears. When I got home, there was a message on my machine that said I could come in this morning to clear out my desk."

"Oh, Gladys," Cassidy said softly. Her heart hurt. Gladys

245

was the first person she had met there. The first face she saw when coming in for the interview. The first person to greet her on her first day. She knew all the best stories and had gossip on everyone. Cassidy adored the woman.

"No one will hire me for a lousy six months of work, especially at my age. I'll just have to take social security out early. I tried so hard to wait so I could get all the money I had earned."

"You're damn right you earned it," Cassidy agreed firmly. A man in his late thirties came in the front door.

"Cassidy, this is my son, Richard," Gladys introduced. Cassidy and Richard nodded at each other. "He wanted to drive me today. Didn't think I should be driving a car in my state."

"I'm glad he did," Cassidy said, "although you shouldn't be driving home feeling sad - you should have a party!"

"Damn straight," Richard interjected. His eyes were dark with anger, and frankly, Cassidy couldn't blame him. If she ever had to go pick up her mom after she unjustly lost her job, Cassidy would be throwing fists.

"I think I've got everything," Gladys said, looking around at the now sad, bare reception station.

"Is there anyone else you want to say goodbye to? I can bring them out here so you don't have to go in," Cassidy offered.

"No, I've said my goodbyes. I'm glad I got to see you, though."

"It was wonderful working with you these last three years," Cassidy said, giving the older woman a big hug, which she reciprocated warmly.

"Oh darling, you were a joy. You've got big things in your

future. Don't let small places hold you back," Gladys smiled. Cassidy wiped away a few escaped tears.

"The company directory is here," Cassidy said, picking up a thin, spiral bound book. "Do you need any numbers?"

"No, I've got who I want. But you keep it. My address is in there. Send me a letter sometime," Gladys grinned.

"Definitely will do."

"And don't let Devon get away with any of his garbage. My only regret is I never got to tell him to go pound sand. I was saving that for my retirement party," Gladys said. Cassidy was torn between laughing and crying.

"I can get him and you can tell him now?"

"Nah, that baton has been passed to you."

"I will definitely add it to my to-do list," Cassidy smirked.

"Goodbye, Cassidy Banker."

"Goodbye, Gladys."

Cassidy watched as Gladys followed Richard, carrying the box of her things, out the door and onto the street. She swallowed hard to bite back a blood-curdling scream.

After collecting herself, she continued into the main office, which was glum and awkwardly silent. All eyes shifted to Cassidy. They all knew she had been saying goodbye. Cassidy wished Gladys could have seen the sadness in everyone's eyes. She was going to be incredibly missed.

"Damn," the grating, deep voice of Devon exclaimed as he walked over to her. "Can't believe they fired the old lady. We're all chopped liver, apparently."

"Go pound sand, Devon," Cassidy snapped, not interested in debating the company's bleak future with him. She smiled proudly to herself as she arrived her desk. She knew she'd done Gladys proud.

# Chapter 25

Cassidy climbed out of her car as soon as she pulled into her parents' driveway. She grabbed her dress from the back seat and headed into the house.

"Hi!" Cassidy called as she let herself inside.

"Hi, sweetie," Lynne yelled back from the direction of the living room. Cassidy headed down the hall and into the living room. Lynne was sitting on the brown sofa and working on her cross-stitch.

"I brought my dress for you to hem," Cassidy said, holding up the purple dress.

"Oh, good. Set it on that chair for me, I'll get to it later."

"Thanks, I appreciate it," Cassidy smiled, hanging her dress over the chair.

"What are you up to today?" Lynne asked, concentrating on her stitching.

"Not much. I'm going to pick up a couple of subs from the pizza shop in town to bring home for Marissa and me later today," Cassidy replied.

"Mmm, sounds good."

"You?" Cassidy asked, leaning casually against the wall.

"Waiting for your dad to get home from his Booster Club meeting, then we're going over to the Richardsons for a dinner party," Lynne smiled.

"You and dad are going to a dinner party? When did you guys get so swanky?" Cassidy teased.

"It's amazing how easy life gets when the kids are out of the house," Lynne winked.

"You're hilarious, mom." Cassidy rolled her eyes.

"That reminds me, you will go to Eric's wedding, right? I need your RSVP," Lynne said.

"I'll send it in as soon as I get my invitation," Cassidy said pointedly.

"Oh, you're on ours. It's in the kitchen on the counter," Lynne said nodding in the direction of the kitchen.

Cassidy scrunched up her face. "What?" she grumbled.

"It's not a big deal, Cassidy," Lynne shrugged.

"How is it not a big deal that he can't even bother to send out invitations?" Cassidy huffed as she turned to the kitchen.

"Cassidy," Lynne sighed, setting down her cross-stitch to follow her daughter. "There are a lot of us, and they needed to save on postage." Cassidy let out a loud snort as she started digging through the pile of mail on the kitchen counter.

"First of all, that's bullshit; stamps are cheap. And secondly, Alex already told me that he and Laura got theirs." Papers were flying across the counter now.

"Would you stop making such a mess? It's right here," Lynne said, pulling out the invitation and handing it to Cassidy. Cassidy studied the blue and white floral invitation. It was lovely. She slowly turned the card over, still nestled in

249

the lip of the envelope and she saw the address line:

To: Art and Lynne Banker, and family

And family?

"What is this?" Cassidy asked.

"It's the envelope. I need to throw that out," Lynne said. She reached to take the envelope, but Cassidy pulled it back before she could grab it.

"And family?" Cassidy pushed firmly.

"Yes. You are family," Lynne replied. She was clearly already bored with her daughter's inquiry.

"But it's just that. I am and family?"

"Um, I'm not sure," Lynne lied.

"Mom, I already know that Alex got his own," Cassidy pointed out.

"I'm pretty sure it covers you and Ben," Lynne relented. Cassidy pulled a face. "I doubt Eric even knows Ben's address at school, and Ben doesn't care. He's just going to show up. Be like Ben."

"You must be joking," Cassidy said with wide eyes.

"Cassidy, do we really have to go over this again? Eric's wedding is not about you," Lynne said firmly.

"I know! I just wanted my own damn invitation. I'm already not a bridesmaid. Is a piece of paper too much to ask? Or just maybe my actual name listed on the envelope?" Cassidy clenched her jaw and threw her hands up in frustration.

"Do you want a copy of the invitation? I'll get you one," Lynne offered.

"No, that's not the point."

"Cassidy, you're being incredibly difficult and I don't know what to tell you. You'll have to talk to Eric," Lynne said. Cassidy felt something click inside of her. That was exactly what she was going to do.

"You're right. I'll go see Eric - right now!" Cassidy exclaimed.

"You will not!"

"Yes, I will. I'm allowed to go visit my brother," Cassidy insisted as she separated the invitation from the envelope, dropping the card on the counter and keeping the envelope for herself. Evidence.

"You are more than allowed to visit any of your brothers, but right now you are angry. Not to mention, you just drove all the way out here," Lynne pointed out. "Stay and calm down before getting back on the road."

"I have no intention of calming down. I want to be pissed when I get there," Cassidy huffed.

"Cassidy!"

"Thank you for your help with my dress, Mom, and I'm sorry to leave so quickly. I love you," Cassidy said as she headed for the front door.

"Cassidy!" Lynne called once more, but Cassidy closed the door behind her before another word could be said. Deep down, Cassidy felt horrible. She knew it was rude to walk out on her mother. However, at that moment, rage was driving her.

She quickly turned the ignition in her Chevy and backed out of her family's driveway. The entire drive back to the city was a blur. Cassidy wasn't even sure how she made it to her brother's - the car must have known the way. She spent the whole drive formulating arguments and rants in her head. She was ready for a fight.

Cassidy reached the city limits and pulled onto a street lined with small, white houses. She parked in front of the house her twin shared with his friend, Derek, and stomped toward the

251

front door, envelope clutched in her right hand.

Almost the moment she firmly knocked on the door, it swung open, revealing Derek, his black hair disheveled and still in pajama pants and a white tee. He had clearly not been awake long.

"Cassidy?" Derek said, looking surprised.

"Is Eric here?" Cassidy demanded.

"Um, yeah."

"Thanks," Cassidy said, pushing past him into the house.

"Hey, wait! What are you doing?" Derek asked, watching her stomp down the hall.

"Eric!" Cassidy called.

"What the hell are you doing here?" Eric asked, coming out of the kitchen. He looked less than impressed.

"We need to talk," Cassidy said, her mouth in a thin line. Eric stared at her for a long moment before giving a defeated sigh and leading her back to the kitchen. Derek disappeared back into the living room.

"Alright, what do you want?" Eric asked, resting his back on the edge of the thick, white counter. He took a sip of coffee from the mug he was holding.

"I'd like to talk to you about this!" Cassidy said, holding up the envelope.

"An envelope?"

"Yes. I stopped at mom and dad's this morning and mom asked me if I was going to your wedding. I told her I hadn't received my invite yet, and she tells me that I'm on theirs. I go to look and I find this envelope that lists mom, dad, and family," Cassidy enunciated.

Eric simply stared at her, looking quite bored with another one of his sister's rants.

"And family!" Cassidy reiterated. "Not only do I not get an invitation; I don't even get my name on the lousy envelope?!"

"You stormed in here because you need your name written on an envelope?" Eric asked, unfazed.

"It's not just that my name isn't on the damn envelope. I don't get to be a bridesmaid, I don't get an invitation - I am being completely squeezed out of this wedding!" Cassidy whined, throwing her arms in the air.

"Oh, for fuck's sake, Cassidy!" Eric groaned.

"Finally, you're noticing me."

"Cassidy! How many goddamn times do you have to be told?! This wedding is not about you!" Eric said firmly.

"I know! I'm not asking it to be about me, I'm just asking to be invited like a human adult. I am your sister, in case you forgot."

"No! You're not just asking to be invited; you're pissed that attention is on me," Eric argued.

"What the hell is that supposed to mean?"

Eric pushed himself off the counter, set his mug down, and began to pace. He was practically shaking. "You take over everything!" he suddenly yelled.

"Stop being dramatic."

"You are dramatic," Eric returned. "It's always been about you. You ignore anyone that doesn't give you all the attention. You ignore me."

"Oh, come off it," Cassidy scoffed.

"Yes, you do. You always have."

"What? When?"

"We started school and you made friends and left," Eric said.

"Oh, for fuck's sake."

"You did. You've been popular since kindergarten, and you just went off your own way. You got into softball and got more and more popular. Your life was your friends and parties and the entire world being about you!" Eric said. He was looking flushed as he ran his hand through his hair in frustration. Cassidy scrunched up her face.

"You're full of it; you don't even acknowledge me," Cassidy countered.

"You never acknowledged me. You never have!"

"Eric…"

"No! You're going to listen to me for once! You've always had all the attention. You're the only girl: extra attention! You're good at softball: extra attention! You're popular: extra attention! You complain that I don't tell people you're my twin - well when the hell was the last time you did? All through school, half of your friends didn't even know I was your brother, let alone your twin, but all of mine knew about you. The world has always been all about you and you've lapped up every moment. You always said you weren't included by our brothers, but you always were. You made the choice to spend time with your friends over us. But you'd snap your fingers or shed and a tear, and boom, the whole family is all over you. Oh, poor little Cassidy, life is so hard for her! No! It never was! It never will be! There's a reason I went to college two hours away. For once in my whole life, I didn't have to sit in the shadow of my perfect twin sister. I got to make a life for myself! And guess what? It was amazing! I've never experienced that before. I got a job back here because I missed the family. But I've worked hard to build a life that doesn't revolve around you!" Eric ranted in a full explosion of emotion that had been bubbling just below the surface finally

254

found a release.

Cassidy stood in shock. She suddenly felt like she was going to throw up. Eric took a few breaths before continuing.

"And then I met Ellie. I have a chance to have a life of my own forever. A life that's mine! Out of your shadow. But, no, you've been miserable since I announced our engagement. And yes, before you ask, of course I told her you were my twin. On our first date, actually. When was the last time you told anyone you had a twin?" Eric asked forcefully.

Cassidy swallowed hard. She couldn't remember the last person she'd told. She had told Jake, right? She felt angry and sad, with a large pang of guilt, all at once. Her heart was racing and her stomach was doing flips. Their entire relationship was rushing through her mind and there was a lot of reevaluation she needed to do. So much that it hurt.

"Ellie wanted you to be in her bridal party. Before we were even engaged, she mentioned it. She wanted to get to know you. Don't blame her. I'm the one that told her not to," Eric told her.

"Why?" Cassidy was having trouble processing everything.

"Why?" Eric repeated. "Because you always make everything about you. All the shopping and events with the girls? You would complain every step of the way. You would go out of your way to tell horrific stories about me, about all of us, to put the spotlight on how great you are. You wouldn't shut up until everyone loved you and the entire day became about you. And while I can handle you ruining my day, I won't let you do that to Ellie. I love her and I won't put her through your bullshit."

Cassidy felt like she had been punched in the gut. She could feel Eric's eyes on her, but she couldn't make eye contact.

"Even right now, this moment is about you," Eric said. Cassidy looked up at him in surprise.

"What?"

"You're thinking about who to run to because I was mean to you," Eric said, starting to pace again. "Alex is the logical option. The ultimate big brother. He'll protect you from your evil twin. He'll coddle you and make everything okay. He may even call me and tell me to stop being a dick. Matty is also a good choice. He won't baby you, but he'll cheer you up quickly and make you laugh. And if you can get him riled up enough, you two can come up with a plan to ruin the reception. He'd like a chance to make a big scene. Of course, there's also Ben. Not the obvious choice, but a good one for you. He absolutely worships you, as you expect him to, so it's easy for you to turn him against me. Your finest accomplishment. I don't think you'd go to mom and dad, though. You've been trying your hardest with them for months, and they won't give in to you. I'm shocked they haven't tried to force me to add you to the wedding party, but I do appreciate that they've taken my side for once. Thus black balling them in your books."

"What?" Cassidy repeated. Her stomach was turning painfully, and her throat was tightening. She could feel a sob looming. Eric had read her like a book.

"What?" Eric repeated, stopping his pacing right in front of her.

"Ben does not worship me," Cassidy said quietly.

"Wow, you're even too full of yourself to see your biggest fan," Eric huffed.

"What are you talking about?"

"Ben adores you. He always has. Don't you remember those years in elementary school when he desperately tried to play baseball, even though he was always the worst player on the team? He saw his beloved big sister play, and he would have done anything to be like you. Thankfully, he finally stopped. Hand-eye coordination is not his strong suit; soccer is much better for him. But he played because of you. He always stole your old jerseys to wear. Always waited up for you when you were out on dates or out at parties. The second you got into Edinboro, he said he was going there, too. He was desperate to go, to be just like you. Alex, Matty, and I talked him out of it. We told him Mercyhurst would be better for him; he'd like being in the city more. But that was a lie. The real reason we convinced him to switch was so he wouldn't learn the hard way that you weren't going to give him the time of day if he went there. You would have broken him. And MU worked out great for him. He's having fun, he's creating his own life, and Alex is just a mile away if he needs someone," Eric explained.

Cassidy stood completely frozen for a long moment. She wanted to cry, scream, throw up, kick something. Possibly all at the same time. But she refused to do it there. She swallowed hard once more. She had come to tear Eric to shreds, and he had ripped her to pieces. And the worst part was, it was all true. Eric was right. There was a heavy rock in the pit of her stomach.

"And you're right," he continued, "the invitation envelope thing was me. And that was petty. I just get so exhausted by your bullshit sometimes, Cassidy." His fists were clenched. This had clearly taken a lot out of him, as well.

"You should hate me," Cassidy said in a small voice.

"I should. But the really annoying thing is, I don't. I'm just frustrated as fuck and I want one day to myself. That's it. So, you're still invited to the wedding. I will get you a proper invitation in the mail this afternoon. One that is just for you, with your name on it and everything. All I ask is that you not act like a selfish dick. Just for one day," Eric said with a large sigh. Cassidy let out a shaky breath.

"Okay. Um, I'll let myself out." Cassidy glanced up at Eric once more. His jaw was clenched and he was holding back tears. He looked almost as wrecked as she was.

"Bye," Eric said quietly.

Cassidy turned and walked quickly back to her car. She drove in a frozen trance for a mile or so, but then the floodgates broke loose, and she started to cry. Cassidy ran Eric's words over and over in her head. She continued to think back over the years. She detested that he was making sense. Her heart hurt. She had so much to think about. She was rarely wrong. She hated that she was feeling very wrong. And for so many years. It was painful.

How she made it back to her apartment parking lot was a mystery, her eyes were filled with tears the whole way and her mind had most definitely not been on the road. After she parked, she took a few minutes to settle herself. She didn't want to walk through the lobby and up the staircase giving people a reason to stare.

Her stomach hurt. Her heart hurt. She could feel a headache coming on. Finally her tears stopped, and she wiped her nose with the back of her arm. It was gross. She gave a hearty sniffle and exited the car.

Cassidy's hands were shaking as she put the key into her apartment door and let herself in. Once inside, she dropped her purse and keys ungracefully onto the floor.

"Yes! Food time! Subs! Subs! Subs!" Marissa cheered from the living room. Cassidy felt another pang. She'd forgotten

258

lunch. Shit.

"I'm sorry, I didn't get them," Cassidy replied glumly as she made her way to the living room.

"What? Why not? Oh, my god!" Marissa said as Cassidy came into the room.

"Um, we can order something, get it delivered," Cassidy said with a shrug.

"Fuck the subs, what happened? Are you alright?" Marissa asked frantically. She grabbed Cassidy's arm and pulled her down next to her on the sofa.

"It's all my fault," Cassidy whimpered. Her breathing was choppy.

"What's your fault?" Marissa asked.

"Eric. Our relationship. My relationships with everyone," Cassidy said, tears starting to fall.

"What do you mean?"

"Eric didn't push me away. I pushed him. I'm the bad guy. And worse, I'm the bad guy who played the victim. My entire life!" Cassidy enunciated. Marissa looked confused.

"You just came up with this theory this morning?"

"No. I went to my mom's to get my dress hemmed and we started talking about Eric's wedding. Naturally, I lost it. Even more when I learned I wasn't getting my own invitation, I was just tacked on to theirs. I went crazy. I think I blacked out I was so mad. I just stormed out to confront Eric, and when I got there he went off on me," Cassidy explained. Her voice shook and tears slid down her face.

"He went off on you? But you have been excluded from everything," Marissa pointed out. Cassidy shook her head.

"No. I deserved it. He brought up how I've pushed him away over the years. And he was right. I mean, completely right. I had these blinders on and I didn't even see him. Or anyone, for that matter," Cassidy choked.

"I feel like I'm still a bit lost."

"I did this," Cassidy said firmly, staring directly at Marissa. "All of it. I have sabotaged every bit of my relationship with him, and the worst part is, I've blamed him. I've played the victim. I've bragged about being the victim. When in reality, I, I, I'm the bully."

Marissa looked at her for a long moment. There was a harsh silence in the apartment.

"Are you saying you lied?" Marissa asked carefully. Cassidy simply shrugged.

"I'm saying I learned a long time ago how to get attention and make people like me, and I've done it by standing on others," Cassidy said, wiping her eyes.

Marissa made a clucking noise. "That sounds awfully dramatic."

"See, I'm doing it again," Cassidy huffed.

"Doing what?"

"I made this about me," Cassidy said.

"But it is about you; it always is!" Marissa said. Cassidy's eyes widened and Marissa bit her lip, realizing what she had just said.

"You said - "

"No! I didn't mean it like that, it was a slip of the tongue," Marissa said, trying to recover.

"But you must've seen it. You know me better than anyone," Cassidy insisted.

"I do know you better than anyone, and I know you're not evil," Marissa said.

"Wait, who said anything about evil?" Cassidy questioned.

"I said not evil. You're just not close with your twin."

"Be honest. Have I pushed him away?" Cassidy asked desperately. Marissa sighed.

"I don't know what happened between you two growing up. In the six years I've known you, you and Eric have never been close. I never saw it as pushing him away, but you have avoided him. I only have one sister, so I'm not an expert on sibling relationships. I just assumed yours wasn't working. I mean, you and Alex are buddies, so something works," Marissa told her honestly.

Cassidy thought for a long moment. "I try with Alex, though. I just never tried with Eric. I don't know why. I mean, then more I think about it… I can't remember the last time I wished him happy birthday. And we share the same one!"

"Look, you need to take some time to reflect before making any big decisions. You have a lot to process, I am here to talk whenever you need it, but I don't know the right answers either," Marissa said honestly. Cassidy smiled at her.

"Thanks."

"Anytime," Marissa said. "Now, you sit here and try to feel less miserable, or more miserable, or whatever you're supposed to feel right now. I'll go down the street to the shitty sub shop and get us some lunch."

"There's cash in my purse; lunch was to be my treat today," Cassidy sniffled.

"No, no, you can save that and bring me the good subs the next time you're out - and don't get detoured next time," Marissa said, wagging a finger at her playfully. Cassidy let out a snotty chuckle as Marissa slipped on her shoes and left to get lunch.

Cassidy grabbed some tissues out of the box on the coffee

table and just let herself cry. She had a lot to think about, but at the moment, all she could do was cry.

# Chapter 26

It was late Sunday morning. Cassidy was in her living room perched on the large, blue chair, staring at the phone. She had spent a long time on the phone with Jake last night. He had been a good sounding board, and seemed to understand her stress. He was supportive, but definitely understood Eric's side more than hers. However, that was beneficial to helping Cassidy truly understand. There was a long road in front of the twins, but that door had finally been opened. And Cassidy was very grateful to have Jake to help her navigate it. He seemed to be honored to be brought along on the journey.

Cassidy was attempting to bolster herself to pick the phone up and dial. It had been a long, sleepless night for her, and she knew what she had to do - hell, what she actually wanted to do.

She took a deep breath, grabbed the receiver and dialed. The phone rang four times before someone picked it up.

"Hello?" She had been hoping Eric would answer, but damn, it hurt to hear his voice.

"Uh, hi Eric. It's Cassidy," she said nervously. There was

a long pause.

"Hi," he finally replied. Cassidy took another deep breath to steady herself.

"So, um, after our talk yesterday, I've, I've had a lot to think about. And, um, I wanted to say that... that, um, well, you're right," Cassidy stuttered. She bit her lip and closed her eyes anxiously as the words came out.

"Oh," was all Eric said.

"Yeah, um, so, I was just wondering if you would like to meet me for a drink sometime soon. Like, in the city, and we can talk like civil human beings - you know, like actual siblings," Cassidy stammered.

Another long pause.

"Oh, I, um," Eric started.

"I mean, I get if this is too soon, and, I um, just wanted to-"

"Yeah, let's meet for a drink," Eric interrupted. Cassidy felt like a weight has been lifted off her shoulders.

"Great! When works for you?" she asked.

"Tonight?" he proposed.

"Yeah. Yeah, tonight works."

"Cool, cool," Eric replied quietly.

"Um, where?" Cassidy asked, chewing on her lip.

"How about that new place downtown... off Third?" Eric suggested.

"Sure. I haven't been there yet, but I've heard good things," Cassidy agreed.

"Great. Meet at 8:30?"

"See you there," Cassidy said before returning the phone to the receiver and letting out a long breath. She was meeting her brother for a drink. Why the hell did she feel so nervous? Cassidy quickly shook the feeling off and hopped off the chair to go for a run. She had to get her head right.

Cassidy exited the parking garage and started the two-block walk to the bar. The cold, fall night breeze felt ominous. She made it to the large, silver door of the bar in just a few minutes and hurried inside to warm up.

"Welcome. How many?" the bored-looking hostess asked from her stool by the door. She was chewing gum with her mouth open.

"I'm meeting someone," Cassidy replied, scanning the large wood and silver room in search of her twin. The bar seats were completely filled and over half of the tables and booths were occupied. In the sea of slicked-back hair and sports jackets, she didn't stand a chance of spotting him quickly.

"I don't think anyone has come in waiting," the hostess said with an unhelpful shrug.

"Cassidy?" a familiar voice came from behind her. Cassidy spun around to see Eric smirking behind her. He was wearing a dark grey Members Only jacket and jeans. His hair was gelled back.

"Hey!" Cassidy turned and smiled at him.

"Is this who you're meeting?" the bored hostess asked. Cassidy resisted rolling her eyes.

"Yes, table for two."

"Follow me." The hostess hopped off her stool and led them about a third of the way back to a high-top table. Eric and Cassidy thanked her and climbed onto their seats.

"Sooo," Cassidy said tentatively as they were seated.

"Sooo," Eric shrugged.

"I'm glad we're doing this."

"Um, sure."

"Look, Eric, please. I'm trying here. We've literally never done this before so, you've got to give me a moment to get used to it."

"Do you think we're the only twins that can't handle meeting for a casual drink?" Eric asked with a smirk. Cassidy couldn't help but let out a small giggle. She was happy the tension had started to break.

"Probably."

"Hey! I'm Kelly, I'll be your waitress." A perky, dark haired teenager suddenly appeared at their table.

"Hi," Cassidy smiled at her.

"Do yinz need menus or do you know what you want?"

"Oh, I'll just have a Miller Light," Cassidy said.

"Corona," Eric nodded.

"No food?" Kelly asked. Both Cassidy and Eric shook their heads. "Kay, be right back."

"She's nice," Cassidy commented lamely. She just needed to break the awkward silence.

"Yeah."

"So how's work?"

"It's good," Eric nodded. "Yours?"

"Um, kind of shitty right now," Cassidy admitted.

"Really?" Eric looked surprised.

"Oh yeah."

"Haven't heard you say anything at dinners."

"Well, you know…"

"You want to be the perfect one," Eric interjected. Cassidy winced.

"You know how mom gets. She's just so frantic and she

266

obsesses over anything wrong…" Cassidy trailed off.

"Here yinz go," Kelly said in a sing song voice as she delivered their drinks to them.

"Thanks," the twins said in unison.

"If you change your mind about food or need refills, I'll be around." Kelly smiled before bounding over to her next table.

"Cassidy," Eric began before taking a sip, "you should tell the family if work is going badly."

"I'm telling you right now," Cassidy countered.

Eric let out an annoyed sigh. "I wish you would talk to us."

"What? I talk all the time!"

"About nonsense. You're too standoffish," Eric accused. Cassidy half choked on her drink.

"I'm standoffish with you, but I'm actively working on that, hence this exact moment."

"Did you tell Alex?"

"No, and I'm starting to regret that I told you."

"I get it. You were always secretive, being the only girl, but we're adults now."

"I'm not secretive," Cassidy said slowly, realizing how false that statement was as it passed her lips.

"How long has work been bad?" Eric asked.

"A little over a month," Cassidy admitted, not making eye contact.

"You could have said something the other week at dinner."

"I don't get why this is such a big deal! You just want to enjoy that things are sucky for me."

"Is that honestly what you think of me? That I'm anxiously watching and waiting for you to fail?" Eric looked a tad offended.

"Um, I mean," Cassidy stuttered; it sounded harsher when

he said it out loud than it did in her head.

"Oh come on. Stop playing the little girl victim," Eric grumbled.

"I'm, I'm-" but even Cassidy couldn't finish that sentence. "I'll work on it," she said, finally, trying to ignore Eric's smile.

"Why is work shitty?" he asked seriously.

"The company's running out of money and we're downsizing."

"I'm sorry. I know that's happening a lot of places, but it sucks that it's happening for you."

"Thanks," Cassidy replied tentatively. Maybe this wasn't so scary.

"Are you going to stay or look for somewhere else?"

"Right now, I'm staying. My boss has me helping with the number crunching, which kind of means I'm safe until the end…. But it also means I'm kind of the hatchet man."

"You have to fire people?"

"No, but I'm the one that has to say that we don't have enough money for everybody. I'm trying to make other suggestions, but we've already lost coffee, snacks, three accountants, and the secretary. The writing is on the wall."

"You should really start looking. You don't want to have to scramble when it finally collapses," Eric pointed out.

"I'm trying not to think about it."

"Unfortunately, you have to."

"Ugh, this is depressing," Cassidy said, shaking her head. "How's Ellie?"

"Oh," Eric looked surprised. "She's good! School is back in session, so she's busy."

"What grade does she teach again?"

"First."

"Aww, the littles," Cassidy cooed. Eric chuckled. "Does that mean she wants a lot of littles herself? Or has she already had her fill of them?"

"Well, you just dive right in there, don't you?"

"We have never conversed before as adults. I'm not going to get it perfect the first time around," Cassidy said playfully. Eric chuckled and rolled his eyes.

"She does want kids - we want kids - but we don't have any specific plans. Although I guess you can never fully plan."

"If you could, we wouldn't have Ben," Cassidy said.

Eric laughed. "No, we wouldn't."

"But we love him anyway."

"To Ben," Eric said mockingly, holding his beer up for a toast.

"Ben," Cassidy agreed clinking her glass against his bottle. They both chuckled as they drank.

"What about you?" Eric asked as their giggles subsided.

"Do I want kids?" Cassidy asked.

"I was going to ask if you were dating one person, or four, but sure, the kid question is fine."

"You're so funny," Cassidy said sarcastically. "I mean, ideally I would like to have a kid or two at some point. I think I would be a good mom."

"Yeah."

"But, um, I am dating someone - just one."

"Really?"

"Yes. I'm surprised Alex didn't say anything."

"He didn't. I guess that is why he's your go-to," Eric said off-handedly.

"I'm not going to apologize that Alex and I get along."

"I wasn't asking you to."

"But you should know, I didn't tell Alex a thing. Jake and I went for a walk downtown one night and we just happened to run into him and Laura. Complete accident."

"Hmm," Eric hummed in thought.

"I really haven't told anyone because I wanted to see where things were going first."

"How is it going?"

"Good," Cassidy replied, blushing slightly. "Really good."

"Do the rest of us get to meet him?" Eric asked.

"Uh, yeah, yeah, we'll, find a time," Cassidy stumbled. Eric started to laugh.

"You act like introducing a boyfriend to the family is equivalent to walking to the gallows."

"No, no, it's not!"

"Feels like it is. We're going to be perfectly civil. Everyone was very nice meeting Ellie - well, except for you."

"I wasn't mean to her, just not... super warm and fuzzy. Again, adding it to the working on it pile."

"Fair enough."

"But I want to make sure that the timing is right. He's from a really small family and we're... kind of big."

"Ellie's in the same boat. Hey, maybe they can be friends! I mean, Laura is practically one of us at this point, so she's too much of an insider."

"I love Laura," Cassidy said defensively.

"So do I!"

"Gah, I remember meeting her. I was what, a junior in high school when they started dating?" Cassidy mused.

"I know, I'm the same age." Eric stared at her looking quite bemused.

"I know."

"Anyway, what did Alex think of… what's his name? Your boyfriend?"

"Jake."

"Yes, Jake."

"Well… Laura liked him. She said I was glowing," Cassidy smiled.

"Glowing? Oh, my god, are you pregnant?" Eric hissed.

"No!"

"Thank God. I had to ask."

"Fine, but no, I am not pregnant."

"Okay, so Laura said you glowed, but not with child," Eric confirmed. Cassidy rolled her eyes. "And Alex?"

"Alex… um, he, was just…."

"Ohhh!" Eric gasped, a grin starting to appear. "Alex hates him, doesn't he?"

"Um."

"So, what happened?" Eric asked, looking positively giddy for gossip.

"You could be less excited about this, Mr. please tell us about your failing job, we're here for you," Cassidy said mockingly.

"I'm sorry. But I am wondering why they didn't get along. Alex is usually easy going."

"I know!"

"Is that why you don't want to bring him home?"

"Kind of. And Jake didn't do anything, Alex was just cranky and miserable with him. Laura likes him though."

"Hmmm."

"She does! We talked on the phone later that night. And Alex and I aren't fighting. We got along fine at dinner the other week."

"Did you talk about Jake?"

"Obviously not."

"Obviously."

"Wait, how long did you date Ellie before you brought her home?"

"We're not talking about me," Eric countered.

"We should be. You guys were together for what, almost a year before you dragged her around."

"So?"

"So, Jake and I have only been together since July! I have plenty of time," Cassidy said, taking another drink.

"Ah yes, bring him over at the holidays; that won't be stressful at all," Eric said sarcastically.

"Shit," Cassidy sighed as Eric chuckled.

"Just bring him over, sooner rather than later. You'll feel better about it," Eric advised.

"New topic!"

"We don't have very many," Eric smirked.

"Um, well… Are you planning to bring Ellie to First Friday dinners when you're married?"

"Oh!" Eric seemed surprised by the question. "I hadn't given it much thought. I guess if she would like to come, she can, but she generally uses that time to meet up with her sister."

"Does she just have the one sister?" Cassidy asked, suddenly realizing she knew nothing about her future sister-in-law.

"Yeah, Kara. She's a year older."

"Is she nice?"

"More welcoming than you've been to Ellie," Eric said pointedly. Cassidy bit her tongue at the repeated jab. "But I don't know her super well. I mean I see her at least once a month, but we don't have a ton of conversation."

"Blending families is hard."

"Yeah."

"You know," Cassidy began after a long moment, "I really would be happy to see Ellie - you know, to get to know her a bit."

"Really?"

"Yeah. I mean, I'm not making any promises, but I think if I … try, we could get along, at least a bit."

"First you will promise me that you won't hijack that whole wedding," Eric said firmly.

"Really? That's what you think of me?"

"That is what I know of you," he enunciated carefully.

"That's not fair!"

"Well."

"Eric," Cassidy sighed. "Can't you see I'm trying? I would appreciate a bit of grace here."

Eric paused. "You're right, I'm sorry."

"Forgiven." The twins smiled at each other. The peaceful moment was broken by their bouncy teenage waitress reappearing at the table.

"Yinz want another drink?" Kelly asked. Cassidy and Eric looked at one another.

"Yeah," Cassidy nodded, watching her brother.

"Yep, me too," Eric nodded with a smile.

"Sure thing. Hey, can I ask something? Are you two related or something? You really look alike," Kelly said looking between the two. Cassidy and Eric both chuckled. It had been a very long time since they had been compared.

"We're siblings," Eric said.

"Twins," Cassidy added with a smile.

"Oh wow, yep, definitely see that," Kelly said emphatically.

"That's cool you guys are adults and still hang out, so nice! Well, I'll go get those drinks for you."

"Well," Cassidy chuckled as soon as Kelly was out of ear shot.

"Oh, Kelly," Eric said with a playful sigh.

"She thinks we're friends!"

"I think that proves that we are excellent actors," Eric quipped. Cassidy laughed.

"To the theater careers we missed out on!" Cassidy raised her mostly empty glass.

"Damn straight," Eric agreed, clinking his bottle against hers before they both downed the contents.

"Can I ask you something important?" Cassidy said, leaning forward slightly.

"Hmm?"

"How have we been here for an entire drink and not discussed mom's new hair cut?"

"Oh, my god," Eric gasped. "It's terrible!"

"What is that woman thinking?"

"Absolutely no thought could have gone into that decision," Eric said.

They stayed for another couple of rounds. Cassidy and Eric talked far into the night, about everything and nothing at all. There really could be a relationship there. And both twins were thrilled.

END OF PART ONE

# *Bonus Content*

Do you share a birthday with any of the characters? Stop by Jane's Instagram @janeneagwrites to let her know!

## *January*

19th: Cassidy & Eric

## *February*

11th: Ellie

## *March*

1st: Art

30th: Laura

## *May*

6th: Jake

## *June*

1st: Brandon

## *August*

15th: Ben

## *October*

20th: Lynne

## *November*

5th: Marissa

27th: Alex

## *December*

2nd: Matty

*"Great Scott!"*
*"I know, this is heavy,"*

- *Doc Brown and Marty McFly*

*"Great Scott!"*
*"I know, this is heavy,"*

*- Doc Brown and Marty McFly*

Suddenly, Ben appeared in the kitchen, pushing past Matty to reach for the box of crackers behind him.

"Who's a nun?" Ben asked.

"Cassidy," Matty replied.

"I thought Alex said she was a hooker." Ben shrugged as he popped a handful of crackers in his mouth. Matty lit up.

"She can be anything she wants," Matty cooed, patting Cassidy's cheek.

"Ugh, get off me," Cassidy groaned, twitching away.

"Stop it, you three," Lynne scolded, stepping away from Jake and back to her vegetables. "You don't want to give Jake a bad first impression!"

"He's dating Cassidy; the bar's low," Ben teased. Cassidy lunged towards him, but Ben quickly scooted around Matty and out of the kitchen, causing Cassidy to ungracefully smack into Matty's shoulder.

"Ugh," Cassidy grumbled as she shook herself off and stepped away from her second brother. Matty made a show of rubbing his shoulder.

"Alright, alright," Lynne called over the scuffle. "Everyone out of my kitchen."

"Fine," Matty shrugged before departing.

"Do you need any help?" Jake offered politely, though he was still attempting to stifle his amusement.

"Thank you, Jacob."

"Jake," Cassidy interjected with a groan.

"But I've got everything set in here, so you are free to go," Lynne smiled.

"Okay." Cassidy noticed a little disappointment in his face. Clearly, he was looking for an excuse to hide out in the safety of the kitchen with Lynne as protection. The boys would never harm him in front of their mother.

"Come on," Cassidy said, grabbing his hand and giving it a squeeze. "I'll give you the tour."

"Okay."

"And don't worry, I'll protect you," she whispered in his ear playfully.

"Shut up."

Cassidy chuckled to herself as she led him out of the kitchen. They walked through the dining room into the large family room where Matty and Ben were both sprawled out on furniture while Ben flipped through channels with the remote.

"Well, you saw him briefly, but, Jake, this is Ben; Ben, this is Jake," Cassidy introduced.

"Hi," Jake said.

"Hey man," Ben said, twisting slightly on the couch to look over at him.

"What are you looking to watch?" Jake asked.

"Dunno." Ben shrugged.

"Isn't there a new episode of Miami Vice tonight?" Matty asked.

"Dunno," Ben said again.

"Is that all you can say?" Matty asked, looking slightly annoyed.

"Dunno," Ben said flatly, staring Matty in the face. Matty wasted no time in hurling a decorative pillow at his head before getting up and stomping over to him.

"You're always such an annoying little shit! Give me the remote!" Matty tried to wrestle the remote out of Ben's hands, but Ben was holding on for dear life.

"You guys make a great impression," Cassidy sighed before leading a rather amused Jake out of the room.

16

They went out the back door to the yard so Cassidy could show Jake where their old tree house was. She was surprised to find her dad, Alex, and Eric all seated at the large picnic table chatting and drinking beers. They all glanced over at the sound of the back storm door slamming shut behind Cassidy and Jake.

"Daughter!" Art cheered, raising his beer can to her in salute.

"Father!" she replied playfully as they walked over.

"Hi," Eric said, looking up at Jake.

"Hey! I'm Jake. You must be Eric," Jake said, holding out his hand.

"Must be?" Eric asked as they shook.

"Well, I've met Alex, and there was that whole father, daughter greeting. I met Matty and Ben inside, so by my deduction… you're Eric."

Eric watched Jake for a moment, a small smile appearing on his face.

"That was pretty funny. I'm kind of annoyed I enjoyed it so much," Eric said, looking quite amused. Jake looked positively thrilled with himself.

"You sound like your sister when I make a dumb joke she actually likes," Jake said. Both Cassidy and Eric shot him a look.

"Ooops! Lost some points there," Alex quipped as he took a sip from his can. Jake glanced at Cassidy nervously.

"Jake, this is my dad, Art; Dad, this is my boyfriend, Jake," she interjected, changing the subject.

"Hello, sir," Jake said, extending his hand. Art looked pleased with the level of respect. While Art could be playful, he was a stickler for proper behavior if the situation called

17

for it. Cassidy had previously brought home boyfriends that called him "dude," "man," and, in one unfortunate case in 11th grade, a boyfriend named Hank who would only respond with "yo!" Cassidy had actually kind of liked Hank, but when Art threatened to keep her home from junior prom if she went with him, Cassidy dumped him for her dorky lab partner in Chemistry who had been trying to woo her all year. They dated for almost two weeks. Jake was a clear improvement.

"Please, take a seat," Art said, releasing his hand and gesturing to the open spot across from him and next to Eric.

"Thank you," Jake grinned, taking his seat.

"What do you do for work?" Art asked. Cassidy smiled at Jake as she walked behind her father and took a seat next to Alex on his right.

"I work for Mercyhurst. I teach stats," Jake began. Cassidy sat back and simply soaked up the moment. The conversation flowed effortlessly between Art and Jake. Eric listened and looked fairly intrigued. As Jake was describing where Johnsonburg was off Route 6, Alex nudged her arm.

"Hey."

"Hmm?" Cassidy hummed, still looking at Jake.

"You happy?" he asked in a low voice, nudging her once more to get her full attention.

"Yeah," Cassidy said, finally looking over at him.

"Really?"

"Yes, why?" Cassidy replied, giving a confused chuckle.

Alex simply nodded. "That's what I needed to know," he said. He took a long drag from his stub of a cigarette before outting it on the wooden tabletop.

"Ew," Cassidy groaned loudly, pulling Art's attention away from Jake for the first time since they'd sat down.

"Oh, Alex," Art scolded, spotting the squashed ash residue. "Not on the table! Your mother will have a fit. Were you raised in a barn?"

"No, I was raised here." Alex rolled his eyes.

"Grange du Banquier!" Eric quipped in a French accent. Jake brought his fist to his mouth to try and hide a smile.

"Your mother is going to have a fit," Art continued, ignoring Eric's comment.

"That's why I didn't chuck it in the lawn," Alex noted. Cassidy scrunched her nose in confusion, not quite sure what point he was trying to make. Art groaned in annoyance.

"Well, I'm having your mother call you when she notices. Let you get your ass chewed out for once."

"For once?!" Alex's voice practically cracked in surprise. "I've gotten in trouble my whole life!"

"No, you haven't. That was Cassidy," Eric said smugly.

Cassidy shot him a look. "Hey! Don't hurl me under Alex's bus."

"Zero hurling occurring! Just noting that you got grounded a lot," Eric shrugged.

"Why is it my bus?" Alex asked, holding up his hands.

"The only reason you're making that notation is because Jake is sitting right here!" Cassidy said with a huff, trying to ignore how much Jake was enjoying all this.

"Not at all! It was just delightful timing," Eric smirked.

"I'm happy that worked out so nicely for you," Cassidy replied drolly.

"Alright," Art said in a warning tone. The twins nodded at each other. Truce.

# Chapter 3

The five of them sat and chatted at the picnic table for another twenty minutes before Lynne poked her head out the back door and called them in for dinner. Jake once again offered to help Lynne, which she adamantly refused. However, Cassidy knew he was winning massive points with her mom. Whether that was his game plan or not, she appreciated it.

The family took their usual places at the long dining table, Art and Lynn at the head and foot. Alex, Cassidy, and Ben sat on one side, Matty and Eric on the other. Jake had been placed between Matty and Eric, and while he was seated directly across from Cassidy, she couldn't help but find his seating assignment a little mean. Nothing like tossing him in the deep end on day one.

However, Jake was able to win himself a few more bonus points with Lynne when he recited the Lutheran table prayer verbatim along with everyone else with zero hesitation.

"So, Jake," Lynne began, after all of the serving dishes had been passed around and everyone was digging into their filled plates. "What do your parents do?"

"My mom is a legal secretary and my dad was an insurance salesman," Jake replied, taking a bite of the cooked carrots.

"Oh nice. When did your dad retire?" Lynne asked curiously.

"He didn't. He passed away," Jake answered politely. The rest of the Bankers blanched in horror as Cassidy watched him and gave him a small smile. She knew this subject didn't upset him, but she still worried.

"I'm so sorry to hear that," Lynne said in a solemn voice.

"It's okay," Jake said, trying his best to give her, and everyone, a reassuring smile. "It was years ago. I'm fine, I promise."

"May I ask how he passed?" Lynne said gingerly. Jake took another forkful of carrots.

"He had a heart attack."

"Oh, wow, and he must have been young."

"He was 55. But he was constantly wined and dined, generally on red meat and cheese, and he spent most of his time in the car driving to clients or conventions. Lots of food, lots of sitting, lots of stress. It all just caught up with him," Jake answered. Cassidy so wished she was seated next to him to at least gently pat his knee under the table.

Lynne sighed pensively. Art, however, did not.

"Now, that's the way to go," he said.

"Dad!" Cassidy scolded.

"Really?" Alex asked him reproachfully. Jake looked surprised by his comment, and Matty sat anxious, waiting for a big blow up.

"Wined and dined to death on someone else's dime while doing a job I love. There are worse ways," Art pointed out.

"Oh, my God," Cassidy groaned in shock.

"Technically if you die in the middle of any dinner, it would be free," Ben noted.

"Shut up," Eric told him.

"For Pete's sake, Art!" Lynne said through gritted teeth. Alex and Eric stared at their father in horror while Matty and Ben laughed. Even Jake started to smile.

"Don't look at me like that," Art said defensively.

"Jake, I'm so sorry," Cassidy said desperately.

"It's okay, it was actually kind of funny," Jake said sheepishly as he let out a small laugh.

"You don't have to make my dad feel better," Cassidy assured him. Jake simply shrugged.

"You're kind of dark," Ben grinned.

"Yeesh," Eric said in a low voice, clearly still processing the whole unexpected interaction.

"Maybe a new topic?" Cassidy asked loudly, giving her father a final glare.

"Why are you so upset, Cassidy?"

"What?" Cassidy practically squeaked in disbelief.

"Dad!"

"Art!"

Lynne and Alex sighed in unison.

"This is going so well," Matty added sarcastically.

"I'm upset," Cassidy enunciated. "because I bring my boyfriend home to meet my family and you start dinner by cheering on his father's passing!"

"Cheering is a bit overdramatic," Art countered, resulting in a mix of groans and laughs from his wife and sons.

"Fine. When you die, I'll make sure to find someone to celebrate it. How would you feel about that?" Cassidy asked firmly.

"Honestly, depends how I go... Cancer – no way, that's too

sad, but I don't know, if I go from something spectacular like hang gliding into a jet engine or something? Then yeah, cheer me on!" Art said as he took a bite of meat. Cassidy simply stared at him.

"Where the hell did hang gliding come from?" Alex asked.

"You've literally never done or talked about doing anything adventurous," Eric pointed out.

"You think adventure is wearing the wrong-colored shirt to the golf course," Matty smirked.

"You didn't even go kayaking with my boy scout troop when I was ten," Ben added.

"I was just saying," Art began, but he was swiftly interrupted.

"You were just going to your study to get a brandy and come back when you've finished it," Lynne snapped.

"I like that idea," Art said, standing from the table.

"Aww, daddy got put in time out," Matty cooed in a baby voice. Jake looked down and stifled a laugh with a sip of his water.

"Poor bubby," Alex said with a pouted lip.

"It's not time out, you idiots," Art grumbled as he left the room, ignoring the chorus of baby talk coos from his sons.

"Ugh," Cassidy groaned loudly. "I'm so sorry, Jake."

"It's okay," Jake assured her, shaking his head in amusement.

"Ben, how's school?" Cassidy asked, desperate to establish a new topic before her father returned.

"What?" Ben asked, giving her a very confused look. Cassidy couldn't blame him; she had never once asked him about school since his first week of kindergarten.

"I'm trying, here," Cassidy nudged him.

"Oh," Ben said, finally understanding. "Um, it's fine."

"Oh, my God, school!" Eric exclaimed loudly. Cassidy gave her twin a perplexed look – as did the rest of the table.

"Yes, school. Ben goes to school," Matty enunciated slowly. Eric ignored him.

"Jake teaches at MU. Do you guys know each other?" Eric asked excitedly, gesturing back and forth between him and Ben.

"Um, I don't think so," Jake said, looking over at the youngest Banker.

"Naw. Wait, what do you teach?" Ben asked.

"Stats."

"Definitely didn't take that," Ben said.

"Yeah, my classes are never huge."

"Wait, was Carla Gearhart in your class last spring?" Ben asked.

"Yes, actually. I have her again this semester. Curly brown hair, right? Is she a friend of yours?"

"That's her!"

"Who's Carla Gearhart?" Alex asked, his mouth half full of food.

"Hot girl from my freshman dorm. We had a few classes together over the years, but she was never super social, or at least not with any of my friends. But she showed up at Scott's end of year party last May. Turns out, she failed her last stats test and came to blow off steam. Carla got shit faced and came home with me that night!" Ben beamed proudly. "So, thanks, man!" he gave Jake a playful salute.

"Benjamin!" Lynne scolded.

"Oh, um, you're welcome," Jake said warily, conflicted on how to answer.

"You're gross," Cassidy told her youngest brother flatly.

"Not gross," Ben argued.

"Be nice, Cassidy. He'd never get a date otherwise," Matty said.

"Real funny." Ben rolled his eyes.

"You have no place to talk! You were never exactly a nun," Eric said.

"Look in the mirror when you say that," Cassidy shot back.

"Ohh, ooh, no, you still have me beat on that front, dear sister," Eric grinned.

"I beat you in a lot of fronts, my twin," Cassidy gritted her teeth in annoyance. This was not how she'd wanted this evening to go.

"Alright," Lynne called loudly over the table.

"Why don't we call a truce and declare that we're all questionable people," Matty proposed.

"You guys can all be terrible; I'm practically perfection itself," Alex joked with a puffed out chest.

"How was your last cigarette?" Lynne probed in a warning tone. Alex's face fell.

"You just got roasted by mom!" Ben cheered.

"One vice!" Alex countered. Which turned out to be a very poor move, as his siblings delightedly took turns listing his shortcomings until Art returned to the dining room carrying a tumbler. He told them all to knock it off as he took to his seat.

"Do you have any siblings, Jake?" Lynne asked.

"Yes. Just one, though," Jake smiled as he took another bite.

"Sounds delightful," Ben said.

"Sounds boring," Matty noted.

"Brother? Sister? Older? Younger?" Art asked, downing the final swig of his brandy.

"Younger brother, but only by one year."

"I have one of those," Alex said, nodding at Matty. He still looked slightly irritated at Matty's recent jabs.

"And it's been magical," Matty grinned at him.

"Can you guys let him eat for a moment before further interrogation?" Cassidy asked as nicely as she could muster. Jake was never one for the spotlight. This was a lot for him.

"We're just interested in getting to know this boyfriend that you have actually brought home to meet us," Eric said with a smirk. Cassidy bit her lip.

"I got you, Cass," Ben began, tapping her forearm with the back of his hand. "Jake, did Cassidy tell you that she lost two of her teeth because she opened up the freezer door real fast and the frozen tube of orange juice fell out and hit her in the face?"

Cassidy dropped her fork loudly on her plate and leaned over with her head in her hands in shock. The rest of the table, including Jake, erupted in laughter.

"Oh my God," Cassidy groaned.

"I forgot about that!" Alex exclaimed.

"Oh, that was horrible. She looked like she was punched in the face," Lynne said.

"Essentially, I was," Cassidy said, sitting back up and looking over at her mother.

"I'm assuming these were baby teeth?" Jake asked.

"Yesss," Cassidy replied with a long, drawn-out s, trying to ignore his very entertained grin.

"She talked with a lisp for like a week after, if I remember right," Matty added.

"She did," Eric confirmed. "My second-grade teacher pulled me aside to ask what happened to her. No one could understand her! She looked so beat up."

"I didn't know that," Lynne said.

"Now Cassidy, I have to ask," Jake said seriously.

"What?" Cassidy hummed.

"Ben said you lost two teeth. Were both taken out at once, or did you get hit by a frozen orange juice tube twice?" he asked with a smirk. Cassidy gasped in surprise. She knew he could hold his own in banter, but couldn't believe he'd joined in with her brothers' ribbing so quickly. She swallowed a swear.

A chorus of cheers rang out from her brothers, all looking quite amused.

"Okay, I like him," Matty affirmed, slapping Jake on the back. Jake looked genuinely pleased.

"Ben, how do you even remember this? You were, like, a baby," Cassidy asked, turning towards him.

"I wasn't a baby. I was at least in preschool."

"We were in second grade; he would have been in preschool," Eric nodded.

"I definitely told kids," Ben admitted. Cassidy rolled her eyes.

"Well, I'm not the only one with a dumb injury. Matty broke his ankle when he jumped from the upstairs banister onto the stairs."

"I thought I might be able to fly," Matty replied flatly. "I could not." He was completely unfazed by his sister's story. Jake laughed.

"Alex got that terrible burn when he reached into the oven to get out that pie without a mitt," Art said.

"Ugh, that was a horrible Easter," Lynne sighed as she cut her food.

"Tell me about it. It was my left hand, too. I could hardly

hold a pencil for two weeks," Alex lamented as he looked at his dominant hand in front of him for a moment before picking up his fork once more and returning to his meal.

"Why did you grab a hot pie bare handed again?" Eric asked.

"It wasn't intentional. It was Easter, all the family was here, it was chaos. Mom told me to grab the pie from the oven as I was running through the kitchen. I was trying to get out of there quickly. I just didn't think," Alex admitted.

"You were in high school at that point, you should have known better," Art grumbled.

"Eighth grade," Alex corrected. "Still technically junior high."

"Splitting hairs there, boy." Art shook his head. Alex ignored him.

"What about you?" Matty asked Jake.

"What about me?"

"What stupid injuries happened in your childhood?" Alex clarified.

"Oh," Jake choked a bit on his water. He looked caught off guard.

"Come on, everyone has one," Ben prodded.

"Well..." Jake paused in thought before letting out a small chuckle. "It's not really my injury, but I was there. Well, I kind of caused it."

"You caused it?" Cassidy asked, looking thoroughly surprised. Jake shrugged.

"Oh, I have to hear this!" Eric said excitedly.

"Yeah, spill it -- um, wait, what's your last name?" Matty asked.

"Sullivan," Jake and Cassidy answered in unison.

28

"Spill it, Sullivan! Oh, that has a nice ring to it. I like that," Matty grinned.

"Well, when my brother, Will, and I were teenagers, we were hanging out downstairs one day. I honestly don't remember what it was about that day, but we got into a fight. It happened a lot. But we were both mad and I just…. I pushed him. And, well, I pushed much harder than I thought I did, and Will went straight back and hit the wall. Went through the wall, actually. Not the whole way, but right into the drywall." Jake said.

"Wait, what?" Cassidy gaped.

"Oh my God!"

"Shut up!"

"That's hilarious!"

"No way!"

The Banker boys reacted in a loud chorus.

"Into the drywall?" Art questioned. Jake nodded sheepishly.

"Yeah. Honestly, I felt bad. I didn't think I'd pushed him that hard," Jake admitted.

"Like, did he go through to another room or just make a dent?" Ben asked.

"Kind of in between. He went into the wall, but he was kind of just …. stuck there. I had to pull him out."

Another roar of laughter broke out around the table.

"Oh, your poor mother must've been so upset," Lynne commented as the laughs trailed off.

"Yeah, that's putting it lightly," Jake said, letting out a loud breath. Cassidy winced. Jake's mom, Claire, was a tough cookie, and definitely not someone she would like to cross.

"You got in a lot of trouble?" Ben asked.

"Yeah, my mom reamed us out for a solid twenty minutes. She wouldn't let us clean anything up as she wanted our dad to see. He was also really mad when he got home that night. I remember Will and I walking on eggshells for the next two weeks."

"Did you fix the wall?" Art asked.

"No, no, I don't think they trusted us with that. My dad fixed it a couple days later. I'm pretty sure my mom made him leave it broken that long so we couldn't forget." Jake chuckled and shook his head, playing it off.

The rest of the meal was spent swapping more stories and a fair amount of laughing. Cassidy couldn't help but smile at how seamless and easy the conversation was flowing. Most of the stories were at Cassidy's expense – when she threw up in the bus on the way to school; that time she fell off the edge of the riser at the fourth-grade spring concert at school. Even the story of the first time she got caught making out on the front porch when she was thirteen. Despite the humiliating tales, Cassidy didn't mind. The time together still felt nice. Jake fit in. Perfectly.

# Chapter 4

As dinner concluded, everyone piled up their dishes and silverware to help clear the table. Cassidy hopped up to help her parents carry dishes into the kitchen. She could hear Matty start to quiz Jake on Pirates pitcher stats from their most recent dismal season.

"Cassidy," Art called as soon as they had both set their stacks next to the sink.

"Yes?"

"You like this guy?"

"Yes. Do you?" Cassidy asked, nervously biting her lip. Despite Cassidy's rebellious tendencies, she honestly did strive for her father's approval.

"He's a numbers man," Art nodded with a smile.

"Yes! Yes he is," Cassidy grinned. That was high praise from her father. Art was more vocal and exuberant with his anger than his praise, but that didn't mean he didn't give it. Small comments meant a lot coming from him, and Cassidy knew it.

Lynne appeared behind them carrying her second load of plates.

"Oh, I like him," Lynne said in an excited whisper before dropping everything in the sink with a loud clatter.

"Really?" Cassidy asked.

"Yes!" Lynne's face lit up as she turned and grabbed Cassidy's shoulders to pull her in for a hug. Cassidy's shoulders suddenly felt wet and sticky through her shirt. "Whoops," her mother chuckled, pulling back.

"Ugh, mom," Cassidy whined, frantically wiping the remnants of dinner from her sleeves.

"You'll be fine, use a dish cloth," Lynne advised as she washed her hands over top the pile of heavily used plates. Cassidy did as her mother suggested.

"I'm happy how well things are going," Cassidy commented as she dabbed at her shirt.

"You missed a spot," Art said, picking a small bit of cheese off of his daughter's other shoulder.

"Ack!" Cassidy grimaced as she quickly switched sides with the cloth.

"You're happy how well things with you and Jake are going, or how tonight is going?" Lynne asked.

"Well, both," Cassidy smiled.

"I like to hear that." Lynne smiled sweetly at her daughter.

"Thanks, mom," Cassidy said. Her heart gave a heavy thump. Both her parents' approval and a successful dinner: this night was perfect. And then Matty appeared in the opening between the dining room and kitchen.

"Cassidy? Cassidy?" He called, getting progressively louder.

"What?"

"Who'd you park in?"

"What?"

"Who's car did you park behind and therefore parked them in?" Matty asked in an overly enunciated tone.

"Eric, why? Who's leaving?" Cassidy asked.

"She's behind you, Eric," Matty said loudly over his shoulder.

"Matty?" Cassidy pushed.

"Matthew, who is leaving?" Art asked firmly as he closed the freezer door after retrieving a carton of ice cream.

"Put that back," Lynne scolded.

"We're just going to take Jake out for a quick spin," Matty replied simply.

"I'm sorry, what?" Cassidy asked, raising an eyebrow.

"We'll be back. Thirty minutes, an hour, tops."

"All of you?" Lynne questioned.

"Yep."

"Where are we going?" Cassidy asked as Jake and her brothers emerged from the dining room and headed to the front door.

"Oh, sorry, no, Cassidy. Boys only," Matty said as he walked into the foyer, his back to his sister.

"Jake, are you okay?" Cassidy asked in a frantic whisper, wondering what false promise or threat was making him go along with this.

Jake smiled at her before Ben pushed between them and Matty turned around to grab the front of Jake's shirt and pull him away.

"Alex," Cassidy groaned, reaching for his arm as he walked past.

"You can't come, Cassie," Alex said with a wink as

33

he pulled out of her grip. Cassidy turned to Eric, who was bringing up the rear of the group.

"Where the hell are you guys going?"

"Don't worry. Seriously, chill," Eric said.

"What?" Cassidy asked, stomping after him. Alex and Matty were grabbing keys while Ben was asking Jake if he knew some of his other professors.

"You boys are coming back, aren't you?" Lynne asked firmly.

"Yes," Alex answered, swapping keys with Matty.

"All of you?" Cassidy questioned. While Alex was generally pretty protective of her, and all four of them did care about her welfare, Cassidy's brothers were never the type to threaten to beat up a boyfriend. They knew Cassidy was capable and feisty enough to do it herself.

"Just go help mom," Eric smirked before turning and following the herd outside, Jake pushed along in the middle of them.

Cassidy stood on the front porch with her arms firmly crossed over her chest and watched as Alex moved his car behind hers before they all piled into Matty's Subaru. She couldn't help but wince as she watched them shove Jake into the back seat between Ben and Alex. Matty honked twice before they departed the driveway at a concerning speed. Eric grinned at her from the front seat. Cassidy swore under her breath before returning inside the house.

"Want a brandy?" Art asked calmly as he stood in the foyer eating vanilla ice cream out of the carton with a spoon.

"I thought mom took that from you," Cassidy said with a raised eyebrow.

"You better not rat me out." Art winked at her before

walking past her to his study. Cassidy smiled as he pushed his door closed and she went to the kitchen.

"Cassidy, have you seen your father? Did he go with the boys?" Lynne asked.

"He wasn't in the car with them," Cassidy replied honestly.

"Oh, he doesn't help anyway," Lynne sighed.

"Here, let me." Cassidy pushed up her sleeves and reached into the sink. She knew keeping busy would be best for her, but she also felt bad for her mom being deserted after dinner.

"I think this is a good thing," Lynne said after a couple minutes of washing and drying in silence.

"Really?"

"Yes! I don't remember your brothers ever wanting to spend time with one of your boyfriends before.... Or at least not all four of them," Lynne mused as she dried another plate.

"Thus making it more concerning. This feels like a plot to take him out to the country where an accident occurs and they bury him in a field," Cassidy said, adding more dish soap to the sponge.

"I couldn't see that. None of them are good at digging," Lynne joked, giving a side eye to her daughter. Cassidy froze and took a deep breath to avoid spitting out something she would regret.

"Ha-ha, mom," she said drolly.

"I thought it was pretty good," Lynne said with a proud smile.

"It's just weird."

"I mean… it's new. But seems like they want to be friends."

"Friends?"

"Yes! Or they just want to make fun of you without you in earshot," Lynne said.

"No, they prefer to mock me in person."

"Well, then they're hanging out with their new friend." Lynne shrugged.

"Fine," Cassidy said with a sigh. She didn't feel like arguing with her mother, or allowing herself to spiral as she thought about all the depraved possibilities.

Lynne seemed to understand and began to regale Cassidy with the drama of their neighbor's botched landscaping project and all the troubles their multiple fixes had caused. Cassidy enjoyed the distraction, as well as the story. Once they had finished cleaning up, they helped themselves to the apple pie Lynne had made and settled in the family room.

Art appeared twenty minutes later to join them. Unfortunately, he openly carried the now empty tub of ice cream to throw out and got an earful from Lynne. Despite valiant attempts on her father's part, Lynne denied him a slice of pie. Art grumbled to himself as he took a seat on the couch next to his daughter.

"Was it good?" he asked, pointing at her empty plate on the coffee table.

"Delicious," Cassidy winked. Art gave a pathetic sigh that made Cassidy giggle. The three of them watched TV in a comfortable silence for awhile until they were interrupted by the sound of the front door banging open, startling them all.

"Oh, for Pete's sake," Art grumbled as he clumsily folded his newspaper in annoyance.

"We're back!" Matty's voice rang out from the foyer. Lynne and Cassidy shared a look before hopping to their feet.

"All of you?" Cassidy asked pointedly as she walked through the dining room and into the kitchen where Matty was opening the fridge in search of a snack.

"Think so," Matty replied sarcastically. Cassidy turned to see her other brothers and Jake coming through the foyer into the kitchen. All looked surprisingly jovial. Without hesitation, Cassidy made a beeline for Jake and hugged him.

"Hi," Jake chuckled, surprised by her intensity.

"I didn't get a hug," Alex noted as he walked past the two.

"Shut up," Cassidy said as she pulled back from Jake.

"Rude!" Ben added. Cassidy ignored him.

"Are you okay?"

"Yeah, great," Jake smiled.

"Really?"

"Jeez, she really doesn't trust us," Matty said, pulling the pie out of the fridge and placed it on the island.

"Nope," Ben said, waiting plate in hand for the pie.

"Sad, really," Eric smirked. Cassidy rolled her eyes.

"Wait, wait, wait," Lynne called. She rushed into the room and intercepted the knife in Matty's hands.

"Mom?"

"I love that she still doesn't trust you with sharp knives," Alex teased.

"I trust him with a knife," Lynne sighed, slicing the pie herself, "But I don't trust the size and shape that these pieces will come out."

Matty attempted to argue his abilities as everyone tossed in jabs. Lynne dished out perfect pieces of pie to her four sons and Jake. Art once again attempted to get a slice but was swiftly rebuffed by Lynne, much to his children's amusement.

They all settled in the family room as the boys enjoyed dessert and Lynne asked Jake a lot of questions about his time at Penn State. Art even managed to convince Eric to give him the final bite of his pie when Lynne was distracted.

# Chapter 5

They were less than ten minutes from the Banker family home. Cassidy was just merging onto the interstate to head north and, other than commenting on the pie, Jake hadn't said a word. She was ready to get the full story now that they were way out of earshot of the family.

"Soooo," Cassidy hummed loudly as she turned the radio volume down low.

"What?" Jake asked, as if popping out of a daze.

"Don't play dumb, you know exactly what I'm asking."

"Oh, yes! Your parents are great!" Jake smiled.

"Jake," Cassidy whined, giving him a playful swat. "Where did you guys go? What did you do? I haven't seen any obvious bleeding."

"The blood oath is next visit," Jake said with a smirk. Cassidy held back a laugh.

"You're seriously not going to tell me? You only met them today!"

"No, duh... I'm kidding."

"We still have thirty minutes in this car together," Cassidy pointed out as she merged lanes to pass a slow-moving minivan. "Were you sworn to secrecy or something?"

"No, no. They knew I couldn't keep my mouth shut with you without getting hit," Jake chuckled.

"Come on, then! Please?" Cassidy asked sweetly.

"It was less exciting than you think. We just all got in Matty's car--"

"I saw that part."

"Yeah, and we just took these country roads – honestly there were a few moments I thought I might be killed. There were just fields around us. But a few minutes later we ended up at this lake."

"Lake? Tamarack Lake?" Cassidy asked.

"Dunno, maybe."

"If it was only a few minutes and all back roads, probably."

"But they just pulled onto the grass, and we got out. Matty opened the trunk and there was a case of beer. We just had a drink, hung out, skipped rocks on the water. It was nice," Jake explained.

Cassidy felt very confused. "What?"

"Yeah! It was nice."

"Nice?!"

"You didn't think it would be?"

"Obviously not," Cassidy said, smacking her palm on the steering wheel.

"You're upset I didn't get my ass kicked?" Jake chortled.

"No, no. I'm just … confused."

"You're confused?"

"I mean, like, they've never done that before. They've never taken my boyfriends out for beers. Not even the one I

39

dated for two years. And they just met you today and you're already hanging out with them."

"Wait, are you mad?"

"No! No, definitely not. I just was surprised they coordinated all this."

"I mean, no one is more surprised than me, but they did tell me they had this plan to leave if they hated me. They were just going to get up and go and leave us with your parents – which of course would have been fine -- but they liked me, kind of, and so I got to join."

"Liked you?" Cassidy asked.

"I think Ben's exact words were that I wasn't the 'dipstick loser' he expected." Jake grinned proudly. Cassidy couldn't help but laugh.

"That's quite a compliment coming from him."

"I felt like it was," Jake chuckled.

"So, they were just planning on escaping?"

"But apparently I didn't suck, so I got to tag along,"

"No, you don't suck," Cassidy said with a smile, leaning over to her right slightly. Jake took the hint and kissed her on the cheek. They rode in a comfortable silence for a few minutes. The sounds of Huey Lewis and Peter Frampton on the radio filled the car before Jake spoke again.

"They really love you."

"Hmm?" Cassidy asked, her focus on the cars merging from the on-ramp into her lane.

"Your family," Jake clarified.

"Oh, I know, and I love them. Even when they drive me crazy," Cassidy smiled.

"More than that. Just the way your brothers talked about you when it was just us…"

"Oh jeez, what stories did they tell you?"

"None."

"None?"

"No, not like when we were at the table. They wanted your reaction there."

"Ugh, I still can't believe they brought up half of those things." Cassidy shook her head.

"Yeah," Jake chuckled. "Like, they make the jokes, but they want you to be happy more than anything. And I know that I'm only in their good graces if you're happy."

"They're not beat you up type guys."

"Well," Jake winced. "I was actually given explicit warnings. And frankly, I believe they would follow through."

"Which one said it?"

"Kind of a group consensus."

"Jake, just remember: Alex is a pacifist, Matty is a joker, Eric is super aloof, and Ben, well, honestly, Ben may give it a hearty try, but he'd lose interest quickly," Cassidy said.

"Don't shrug them off. They'd do more for you than you give them credit for," Jake said seriously. Cassidy's heart gave a thump. She wanted to make a joke, but she couldn't. The truth was, she knew her brothers loved her. But tonight, as they took Jake under their wing, she had full proof of their respect for her. If she were alone in the car, she would cry. Tears of joy, tears of gratitude, tears of love.

"I won't," Cassidy said quietly after a long pause. Jake gave her knee a firm squeeze before changing the subject to the Steelers game coming up on Sunday. They passed the rest of the car ride happily chit chatting about sports, TV, and food. The time flew by and before they knew it, they were back in Cassidy's apartment parking lot.

"Do you want to come upstairs?" Cassidy asked, as she removed the keys from the ignition.

"I can't stay over, but I can come up for a little bit," Jake said.

"Why can't you stay over tonight?"

"Because I'm exhausted, but also, my shoes and jeans have lake water and mud on them and I really want to change. I don't want to put these back on tomorrow," Jake admitted. Cassidy grinned.

"That's very understandable," she said before leaning forward and kissing him. Jake kissed her back.

"Thank you for introducing me to your family," Jake said.

"I'm really glad you came; it meant a lot," Cassidy told him honestly, as she rested her forehead against him. "I'm just so happy that it went so well."

"Me too." Jake kissed her once more.

"I love you," Cassidy whispered.

"I love you, too."

"Are you sureeeee you can't stay over?" Cassidy asked playfully, though she knew and understood the answer.

"No," he chuckled. "But what are you doing tomorrow?"

"Marissa and I are going grocery shopping, and I'd like to go for a run, but otherwise I'm free."

"Can I come over and join you for--"

"A run?" Cassidy asked, absolutely shocked.

"Well, I started to ask that, but then I realized how embarrassing it would be."

"I'd go slow for you," Cassidy winked as she ran her thumb over the stubble on his cheek. Damn, she wanted him.

"Oh! I meant embarrassing for you," Jake quipped proudly. Cassidy pushed his chest hard and tried not to laugh, but failed miserably.

"Shut up!"

"No, seriously, running sounds horrible, but I'd love to see you after."

"I could use a shower buddy."

"Now that, I could do," Jake grinned before kissing her once more.

"How did it go, guys?" Marissa's voice rang through the apartment as soon as Cassidy entered.

"Just me," Cassidy replied as she locked the door and dropped her purse and keys in the entry.

"Just you? Uh oh," Marissa grimaced as she sat up on the couch. Cassidy took a seat at the opposite end.

"No, no, no need to worry," Cassidy said, slipping off her shoes and propping her feet up on the coffee table.

"Soooooo, how did it go?"

"Honestly, really well."

"Yeah?" Marissa smiled.

"Everyone got along well! I mean, most of the stories my brothers told were at my expense…"

"Obviously."

"But in the weirdest turn of events ever, the boys took Jake out for a beer."

"Wait, what?" Marissa asked, sitting up slightly.

"Yeah. Apparently the guys had a whole thing planned to escape if they hated Jake, but they ended up taking him with them."

"But Jake's not here now?"

"No."

"Is he dead?"

"No, he's not dead! He rode home in the car with me." Cassidy shook her head.

"Hmmm."

"What?"

"Maybe he's got head trauma?"

"He didn't look or act hurt. He said he had fun – he even defended them! He was wet and dirty from the lake and he wanted to change. I get it. He doesn't have any clothes here."

"Hmm," Marissa hummed once more. She looked as if she was in deep thought.

"Spit it out, Solomon."

"Look, I love your family, but I can only imagine how intimidating it was for Jake."

"Yeah, he was nervous on the way over. But he was having fun and laughing pretty quickly – mostly at embarrassing stories of me, but still."

"Fair." Marissa shrugged. "I'm just wondering if Jake would actually tell you if something did happen?"

Cassidy made a face as she pondered for a moment.

"Well, I'm seeing him tomorrow. I can ask him then."

"Oh, you mean when he comes over to have sex with his hot girlfriend while she has the apartment to herself?"

"It's shower sex I promised him, actually," Cassidy winked. Marissa rolled her eyes.

"Well yeah, I'm sure he'll be real honest then. Guys are known for their honesty before sex."

"Well, I'll ask him after, then," Cassidy sighed.

"Mmmhmm,"

"Maybe not. Maybe I don't care what really happened and

am happy to believe his lie?"

"Then you're lying to yourself. I know you, Cassidy. You have to know everything!" Marissa smirked at her.

"Dammit!" Cassidy groaned playfully before chucking a decorative pillow at Marissa's head, making her laugh.

"Can I just ask you one favor, in regard to Jake?" Marissa asked after a long moment.

"What's that?"

"Can you please bleach the friggin' shower and tub before I get back on Sunday afternoon?

Cassidy snorted. "Deal."

# Chapter 6

Cassidy bounded up the stairs of her apartment building, taking them two at a time. She had just finished a three mile run in under twenty five minutes. She was feeling very pleased with herself as she exited the stairwell and pulled out her key to let herself into her apartment. Marissa had been packing up for an overnight at her boyfriend Brandon's when she was departing for her run, so they had already said their goodbyes. As much as Cassidy loved coming home to her best friend, and they were both comfortable when the other had a guy over for the night, she kind of enjoyed the opportunity to have the place to herself for a few hours.

"Record time!"

Cassidy jumped slightly. She was not expecting anyone to be home, let alone hearing a male voice. She grabbed one of the long umbrellas that was resting against the wall by the door. She was ready to attack.

"Hello?" Cassidy raised the umbrella to her shoulder like a bat.

"Hey Cass-! Whoa!" Jake popped out of the living room into the hall, but stumbled back a few feet at the sight of his weapon-wielding girlfriend.

"Jake?" Cassidy dropped the umbrella with a thud. "You scared the hell out of me!"

"Sorry," Jake held his hands up in surrender, although he appeared more amused than remorseful.

"How did you get in?" Cassidy walked over and placed a light kiss on his lips.

"Marissa let me in."

"Oh."

"You called me when you were leaving for your run, so I just came right over. Glad I did, I only got here about five minutes ago and Marissa was just heading out the door. I think I scared her, too."

"You're doing great today," Cassidy teased.

"I try."

"I'm glad you're here."

"How was your run?"

"Great! Made good time."

"Ready for a cool down?" Jake asked with a smirk, gently playing with the fabric on the sides of her t-shirt. Cassidy couldn't help but grin.

"Or a warm up?"

"Yes, either or," Jake said. Cassidy gave his chest a light push and took a step back. She slipped off her sneakers and pulled her tee over her head, tossing it on the back of the sofa before turning to walk toward the bathroom.

"Coming?" she asked. She could hear Jake scrambling behind her and the thump of his shoes as she flipped on the bathroom light.

Jake's hands were on her hips by the time she crossed the threshold. She grinned, her back towards him. He spun her around so that she faced him. He had already removed his shirt. Cassidy pushed herself up on her toes and connected her lips to his in a kiss that deepened on impact. Jake's right hand cupped her butt tightly, making her heart flutter. She roughly pushed him back after a long minute. He looked a mix of shocked and concerned, but Cassidy gave him a reassuring wink and bent down to pull off her socks, which she had to admit were disgusting. She quickly balled them up and threw them back into the hall over Jake's shoulder.

"Close the door," Cassidy instructed. He kicked it closed behind him. She smirked at him as she pulled her sports bra over her head, leaving her in her dark green running shorts. She pulled back the floral shower curtain and started the water. Jake reached over and traced her bare back as she checked the water temperature. Cassidy bit her lip at the gentle touch.

"The freckles on your back look like constellations," he smiled.

"I think that's a compliment," Cassidy giggled as he continued to trace her back.

"It is," he hummed. Cassidy flipped the lever on the tap and the water streamed from the shower head. She turned and grinned at him before looping her thumbs in the waistband of her shorts and panties and pushing them to the floor. She stepped into the shower completely naked.

"Joining me?"

"It's quite a view," Jake breathed, taking her in.

"Pants off," Cassidy said, closing the curtain behind her and letting the warm water pour over her sweaty body. She had less than thirty seconds to herself before the curtain pulled back and Jake stepped in behind her. He wasted no time, placing his hand on her stomach and pulling her back against his naked body. Cassidy gasped at the feeling of all of his skin on all of her. She loved it.

Jake held her tightly with his left hand as his right slowly ran up and down her torso in an almost rhythmic fashion. From her neck, to her breasts, down her stomach, to the junction of her legs and back up. Repeating over and over as the water beat down on them. Within a minute, Cassidy's breathing was shaky, and had no chance to steady as Jake's lips suddenly attached to her neck.

Cassidy felt her legs go weak. Her body was on fire, especially now that Jake's erection was firmly pushing into her hip. She turned around to face him and grabbed the back of his head with her hands and crashed her lips onto his. She needed to taste him. The kiss deepened. Cassidy kept one hand on his head, her fingers entwined in his hair, while bringing the other to his back, practically clawing at him to hold on.

Jake wrapped his left arm around her middle, as his right went to her ass, gripping tightly and lifting her up slightly so she was on her tip toes. Cassidy was soaring. She tried to remind herself to breathe, but it was becoming more difficult between the water showering over them, and Jake's mouth moving in sync with hers.

They kissed for a long minute, then suddenly Jake picked her up and firmly pushed her back against the wall under the shower head. She clipped the edge of her back on the shower dial, causing her to grunt in pain.

"Ugh!"

"What?" Jake asked as the water hit his face.

"Dial."

49

"Shit."

"Other side," Cassidy instructed, pointing over his shoulder. Jake didn't need any more instruction. He quickly spun them around and pushed her the few feet to the back of the tub and up against the wall.

A weird hot/cold feeling came over her. Jake's back was blocking all the water and the cool tile was pressed against her back – but the heat between her and Jake was radiating.

They stared at each other for a long second, breathing heavily. And then Jake's mouth captured hers once more. Cassidy gripped his upper back tightly with her right arm as her left reached up to grab the metal bar the shower curtain hung from. She prayed it was as sturdy as she thought.

Jake used his knee to push her legs apart. His firm need for her was pushing at the junction of her legs, making Cassidy shiver. She propped one of her feet up on the edge of the tub. Jake kissed her hard as he entered her. Cassidy gasped into his mouth as he pressed her harder against the shower wall.

It took them a few moments to get a rhythm going at that angle, and Cassidy clawed at Jake's back – she was pretty sure there was going to be a deep scratch. But her mind was absorbed in the wild sensations shooting through her.

Their kisses quickly became gasps. Cassidy's eyes locked on the shower head over Jake's shoulder; it was almost hypnotic to focus on it. She no longer felt any cold from the tile. Only heat. Sparks radiating through to her extremities. Time no longer made sense and for a few moments she actually thought she was floating. The feelings were building in her and her head tilted up to let out a cry as she climaxed. Jake kissed her and pushed her even harder against the tile, holding her firmly in place. Cassidy wondered how she wasn't

50

going through the wall. He pulled out of her and let out a loud cry, spilling on the tile next to her thigh. Cassidy gasped again in gratification.

Slowly he loosened his grip on her and she let go of the shower bar – which had held its own quite nicely -- and lowered her feet to the tub floor.

Jake cupped her face and kissed her slowly, pulling her back under the warm water.

"Oh, my God," Jake sighed in a low voice. He smiled at her with the water dripping down his face.

"Oh, my God," Cassidy repeated, grinning up at him. They enjoyed a quiet moment where they didn't talk, they didn't think, they just held each other under the water and enjoyed the intimate closeness.

After a few minutes Cassidy kicked Jake out of the shower so she could actually get clean. He laughed as he exited the tub to dry off, re-dress, and return to lounging in the living room while Cassidy finished.

Five minutes later, she emerged from the steamy bathroom wrapped in a fluffy pink towel. She smiled at Jake, who was stretched out on the couch reading a magazine, his hair still damp and slightly disheveled. Her heart gave a thump at the sight of him. She loved him so much.

"Hey," he said, looking over at her. She could tell he was thinking the same thing she was.

"Hi."

"What are you doing?"

"I'm going to go to my room and get dressed."

"Can I come?" he asked. Cassidy gave a small laugh and paused a moment to consider it.

"Not this time. I'll be out in a few minutes."

"Okay."

"Okay," she smiled before going turning into her room and shutting the door. She couldn't stop smiling. How was this so perfect? Cassidy padded over to her closet and slid the door open. She looked at her wardrobe, trying to decide what to wear. She dropped the towel on the floor as she reached to grab a hanger. Cassidy paused and glanced over at her reflection in the full length mirror on the back of her door. She couldn't lie. She looked good.

"Fuck it," she said with a sigh as she returned the hanger to the rail and went to open her bedroom door.

"Jake!" Cassidy yelled, standing completely naked in the door frame. Jake popped up.

"What? -oh!" He looked pleasantly surprised.

"Get your ass in here," Cassidy said, nodding towards her room. Jake didn't hesitate for a moment. He leapt up, hurdled over the back of the couch and wrapped his arms around Cassidy. She giggled as he tackled her to the bed. They were ready for round two.

# Chapter 7

Cassidy picked up one of the small red and white bows from the large pile next to her and attached it to the top center of the 5x7 card in front of her. She was currently sitting in an assembly line on the floor of Ellie's parents' large living room helping put together wedding bulletins.

Eric's fiancé, Ellie Hammond, had reached out to her the previous week and invited her to a wedding prep evening at her parents'. Cassidy happily accepted, however the joy was waning a bit as she was forty-five minutes into ribbon gluing, which was preceded by dinner placement card writing, paper flower making, and a short-lived glitter sprinkling session. Unfortunately, while passing the glitter container down the line, there was an inexplicable, but very quick succession of slippery fingers, fumbling, attempted recovery, and finally a drop, which ended in what Cassidy could only describe as a glitter explosion. This resulted in a grievous ten minutes of vacuuming and sweeping: a low point in the evening for all involved. Though, most notably, for the Hammond family's tabby cat, Bonkers, who rolled in some of the displaced glitter before running away from the many hands trying to catch him. Bonkers retreated to the top of the stairs, where he tried to clean the sparkle off of himself, and then shortly after vomited, rather festively, on the kitchen floor. Cassidy felt for Bonkers. He was immediately whisked upstairs to the bathroom for a glitter removing bath by Ellie's mom, May, and then force-fed some medicine. He was currently on his third round of cleaning his still damp fur on the small throw rug in front of the fireplace next to Cassidy.

Cassidy decided that Bonkers was a kindred spirit. She was as over tonight's festivities as he was. She appreciated the camaraderie, even in feline form.

"Hey, last one!" Molly called out happily, waving a final invitation in the air. They all sighed with relief. While there were seven of them there, the work had been a slog. Ellie's older sister Kara was her maid of honor. Molly, Lisa, Elaine, and Mindy, her other four bridesmaids, were also there. While all of them were nice and friendly enough -- aside from Kara, who Cassidy found to be super bossy and a bit of a pill -- she knew they wouldn't leave the evening as best friends. Cassidy felt like the outsider, a feeling she was not used to, nor did she enjoy.

Once all the bulletins were prepped, pretty, and settled in a large plastic storage box for safe keeping, the girls stood up and stretched.

"Ellie, what else do we need to help with?" Elaine asked, picking a few remaining bits of glitter off of her arm.

"I think we did everything. Thank you guys so much!" Ellie grinned. Cassidy tried not to look too relieved.

"Glad we could help; this was fun!" Elaine gushed. Suddenly the room was filled with squeals and thank yous and hugs. Cassidy managed to dodge most of it, but Molly and Lisa both snagged an embrace. They all grabbed coats and purses and made their way to the front door.

"Mimosas at Shanty's next weekend?" Mindy asked the group. A chorus of yeses filled the small foyer.

"Cassidy, are you going to join us? You should!" Molly said, catching Cassidy completely off guard.

"Oh, oh, um, maybe. I need to check my book, but thank you!" Cassidy smiled.

"Good!" Elaine grinned. Cassidy was the back of the line as they filed outside. Before she crossed the threshold, Ellie caught her arm.

"Cass, you wanna stay?" she asked in a whisper.

"Oh, um, yeah," Cassidy replied with a shrug. She had no other plans that evening, and frankly avoiding the lengthy driveway chit-chat was much appreciated. Ellie closed the door behind her friends and held out her arms to take Cassidy's coat once more. They returned to the large living room where Kara and May were finishing tidying up.

"Cassidy?" Kara asked, looking surprised to see her.

"Hey!"

"I asked her to hang out for a bit – we are going to be related soon," Ellie said walking over to the large brown and tan couch and taking a seat. Cassidy followed suit.

"You look like your brother, you know," Kara commented.

"Yeah, we're twins."

"I know," Kara replied blandly. Cassidy withheld an eye roll.

"I'm glad that Ellie is going to have a sister in that family with all of those brothers." May smiled at her. She was a petite woman with long silky black hair down the middle of her back and a brown and teal headband pushing her hair out of her tanned face. Cassidy liked her a lot. She could see the joy in her face helping her daughter with her wedding. Cassidy could only imagine Lynne would love her, as well.

"Happy to be there to run defense. Maybe toughen her up a bit," Cassidy winked.

"Wax on, wax off," Ellie said with a smirk. Cassidy appreciated the movie reference and grinned at her.

"Yes, Ellie-san."

"Well, I think she's pretty tough as she is," Kara challenged. Cassidy focused hard to keep her face neutral.

"Very true."

"Cassidy, would you like some tea?" May offered.

"I'd love some, thank you, Mrs. Hammond."

"May, please! Girls?"

"Yes, please," Ellie said.

"No thanks, I'm going to go. Max said he'd take me out for drinks tonight and I want to get cleaned up," Kara responded, flipping her hair dramatically before departing. May followed her out, asking her questions about dinner the next day. Cassidy let out a low breath of relief at Kara's departure.

"You didn't say anything," Ellie said.

"Hmm?"

"With Kara, you didn't say anything. You're usually the one of the group with the best comebacks! Well, you and Matty."

"I'm honored."

"But not a word?"

"I'm a guest. I don't make sassy comments as a guest. I'm not a neanderthal!"

"You disappoint me, Banker," Ellie smirked.

Cassidy was amused. "Oh, I like you."

"Yes!" Ellie cheered playfully, pumping her fist in celebration. Cassidy laughed.

"It's fun to see you away from my brother. You're… different."

"Different?"

"Well, more relaxed, maybe?"

"I'm quite relaxed with Eric. It's just at big events… Your family is nice, but you guys kind of scare the crap out of me sometimes," Ellie admitted.

"Not the first time I've heard that."

"Really?"

"Oh yeah."

"It's getting better," Ellie said.

"I hope it does," Cassidy said honestly. The sound of the front door closing rang through the house and May appeared in the kitchen once more.

"I'm boiling the water!" she called out.

"Thanks, mom."

"Hey, I haven't seen your dad. Is he here?" Cassidy asked.

"He's at work."

"Saturday at 8PM? What does he do?"

"He's a paramedic."

"On an ambulance?"

"Yeah."

"That's really cool!"

"It is. He loves it. But the hours always suck."

"Yeah, I bet. Emergencies aren't really nine-to-five."

"Nope. He's on for forty-eight hours, off for forty-eight hours."

"Ugh," Cassidy grimaced.

"Yeah."

Suddenly a little chirp of a meow caught their attention. Bonkers had hopped up on the couch next to Cassidy.

"Hello," Cassidy smiled at the almost fully dry tabby.

"Wow," Ellie said, watching Cassidy hold up her hand for Bonkers to sniff before he leaned forward slightly, wanting pets. Cassidy happily obliged.

"Hmm?"

"He doesn't usually take to new people so quickly."

"Maybe he thinks I'm Eric," Cassidy said as she scratched Bonkers behind the ears.

"No, he doesn't really like Eric," Ellie snorted. Cassidy beamed.

"What a good kitty," she said in a playful voice.

"I'm surprised you like him."

"What's not to like? He's cute, he's friendly, he has great taste in people."

"I just thought you were a dog person."

"I like all animals! Well, not slugs, they're gross, but animals in general? I'm a big fan."

"Good to know. Eric has talked about the dogs you guys had."

"We've had two dogs. Oscar, who was a chocolate lab that my parents got while they were dating. He was nice, but he passed when I was four. And then the next year we got our dalmatian, Domino." Cassidy rolled her eyes. "He was dumber than a box of hair. I love dogs, but I'm shocked Domino didn't put me off."

"Poor Domino," Ellie chuckled.

"Don't feel sorry for him. He was a mess. And after he

passed, my mom was very adamant on not having any more animals," Cassidy explained. Bonkers, who was now purring loudly, settled down and sat his front half on her lap while his back feet remained on the couch.

"Remarkable," Ellie commented. Cassidy smiled proudly.

Cassidy and Ellie talked about work until May came over with their hot tea cups and joined them in the living room. She had a long list of questions for Cassidy. They all shared stories of childhood and school. They laughed at favorite movie quotes and talked about their favorite holiday recipes. Before Cassidy realized it, it was almost 9:30. She truly enjoyed her time with Ellie and her mom and saw why Eric loved her. After dislodging a sleeping Bonkers, she helped take dishes to the sink before, once again, putting on her coat and slinging her purse over her shoulder.

"Thank you for letting me stay, this was great," Cassidy told Ellie honestly. Ellie launched forward and hugged her tightly, surprising Cassidy a bit. She hugged her back.

"It was nice to meet you," May said, gently squeezing her shoulders.

"Thank you for the tea, and remind me once more, when are you meeting my parents?"

"Is it in two weeks?" May looked at Ellie.

"Yes, you and dad are coming to Erie and we're all having dinner at that Italian place by Eric's house," Ellie told her mom. Cassidy reached over and held onto her arm gently.

"Promise that you'll use the payphone in the lobby and call me if you need back up. I can be there in ten minutes," Cassidy winked. May let out a loud laugh.

"I will keep that in mind."

After a final goodbye, Cassidy stepped outside into the

dark and cold. It was mid-October, and in northwestern Pennsylvania, that meant snow could show up anytime from now until April. She shivered as she walked to the large, dirt driveway where her car sat. It smelled like snow. The Hammonds lived in the country on a four acre plot. It was beautiful in the daytime, but felt creepy at night. Cassidy missed the lights of the city. She was unlocking her car door when she was met with very bright lights – two car lights ambling towards her and parking to the right of her car.

"You're here?" Eric said, hopping out of his car.

"Yes, I was helping with wedding things." Cassidy smiled at her twin.

"I know, I'm just surprised you're still here," he said, rounding the car to come stand next to her.

"I was invited to stay after the others left. I really like Ellie!"

"Really?"

"Yes, really! I had a wonderful time."

"I didn't know how you'd get along with her friends."

"Oh, well, that part was just okay. Her friends are nice. Her sister is a bit of a pill."

"Hmmm," Eric hummed, which Cassidy knew meant he agreed, but would never say it so he had deniability.

"And her mother is so sweet!"

"She is. Both of her parents are really nice."

"Oh, hey," Cassidy swatted his arm. "I heard there's a parents dinner coming up. Can I please get an invite?"

"Absolutely not!"

"Ugh, but can you at least tell me everything that's said afterwards?" Cassidy asked. Eric rolled his eyes.

"I'll only tell you if mom or dad put their foot in their mouth."

"That's literally all I care about hearing!" Cassidy grinned childishly.

"Go home, Cassidy."

"Wait, why are you out here so late?"

"I'm picking up Ellie. Her friend Molly had driven her out here and I promised I'd bring her home after she had some time with her mom."

"Well aren't you the knight in shining armor," Cassidy teased.

"Yes. Yes, I am. Now go home."

"I will, and I will call Matty to let him know that we're going to have fantastic Lynne and Art out in public stories coming soon!"

"God, you're annoying."

"Drive safe, little brother."

"We're twins."

"I'm twelve minutes older than you."

"You did nothing in that time."

"How would you know? You weren't even there." Cassidy smirked as she opened her car door.

"Good night, Cassidy," Eric said, walking toward the house.

"Hey, Eric!"

"What?" Eric asked, turning around.

"Bonkers sat on my lap and purred," she said smugly.

"What?"

"It was high quality cat time."

"The last time I was here and went to pet him, he swatted me and nicked my hand with his claw."

"Best. Cat. Ever." Cassidy said as Eric groaned.

"Stupid cat."

"Be nice. Bonkers is my friend!" Cassidy yelled, then

hopped inside her car and closed the door. Eric flipped her off as she let her car idle a moment to warm up.

Cassidy smiled the whole way home.

# Chapter 8

*December 1987*

It had been a fairly uneventful month and a half for Cassidy. She and Jake were spending a few nights a week together. Over the Halloween weekend, she, Jake, Marissa, and Brandon went to a huge Halloween party at Edinboro University for the alumni. It was the best party Cassidy had been to in years. Both she and Marissa enjoyed showing the boys around their old haunts.

All four of them spent Thanksgiving with their respective families. Both Ellie and Laura joined the Bankers for their holiday meal. Alex's 29th birthday was the following day, so a combination Thanksgiving and birthday meal made for a fun and food-filled day. Given the celebratory nature of the event, only two arguments managed to break out and a single dish was broken: a holiday record for the Bankers!

Work had gone from a nice constant in Cassidy's life to a stressful and depressing daily trudge. Since Devon's firing, her office had seen three other accountants, two more office staff, and all perks - from coffee to heating - removed from the building. The fact that Cassidy remained was no longer a blessing, but a curse. Between long hours, extra reports, angry clients, general office discomfort, and the hateful glares from her remaining coworkers, all wondering when their number would be up, Cassidy was considering quitting. Both Jake and Marissa told her to look for a new job on a daily basis. While Cassidy knew they were right, she also knew that if she stuck it out to the end, and took on every crummy task Mr. Jelif assigned, he would write her a hell of a recommendation. She wanted that letter. She needed it.

It was Friday, December 4th - the first Friday of the month and her family's monthly dinner gathering. Despite seeing everyone the previous week for Thanksgiving, Cassidy was really looking forward to it. They were also celebrating Matty's 28th birthday, which had been on Wednesday. That meant ice cream cake, Matty's favorite dessert -- one he always fought for, arguing it wasn't fair he never got it, just because he had a winter birthday. Cassidy couldn't lie. He had a point.

The thought of a good, home cooked meal followed by ice cream cake was getting Cassidy through the week. She was currently eating her fifth packed turkey sandwich of the week as she opened another client folder and worked through lunch once again.

"Banker!" The familiar voice of her boss, Mr. Jelif, made her head snap up.

"Yes?"

"Oh," he noticed she was holding half of a sandwich in her left hand. "Um, finish up your lunch, then come to my office, please."

"I can come now."

"No, no, please, eat and wrap up what you're working on," Mr. Jelif gave a weak smile and nod before weaving his way through the bullpen and back to his office. Cassidy let out a low sigh, not looking forward to finding out what additional work she was about to be assigned.

Less than fifteen minutes later, Cassidy had eaten her sandwich and managed to balance the budget proposal for one of the clients she'd inherited. She closed and placed the file in her outbox, straightened her black skirt, and made her way to Mr. Jelif's office.

"Come in," he called at the sound of her knock.

"You asked for me?" Cassidy asked with a smile.

"Yeah, come in and close the door."

"What's up?" she asked, taking a seat in the chair across from him. At this point, the chair was downright familiar.

"Banker, I'm sorry," Mr. Jelif said with a sigh.

"Hmmm?"

"You've worked very hard and it's been appreciated."

"That sounds like I'm getting fired," Cassidy said lightly. Mr. Jelif looked uncomfortable.

"Oh."

"Banker… Cassidy…"

"Wh-wh-what does this mean?"

"It means you will not be working here anymore," he said. Cassidy bit the inside of her cheek to keep from swiping back with a sassy reply.

"No, I… I know what fired means, but is everyone done?"

"Um, well…"

"So, no."

"You don't need to be concerned anymore."

"Oh." Cassidy swallowed hard.

"I hope you know this is not a personal decision. You're smart as hell, and frankly if you work as hard as you have been these past few months, you'll climb your way up the ladder at your next company in no time."

"Oh," Cassidy said once more. She had known this was a possibility, she hadn't truly believed it. Her mind was swirling and she couldn't quite formulate the millions of questions she had.

"I know this is not what you had expected, at least not yet."

"No."

"Do you have questions?"

"Oh, um, yeah…" Cassidy scrambled to regain her focus.

"I would expect you have many."

"What happens to my clients? How do I get my final check? Um, do you still provide a reference letter for me to get another job, or is that gone because I'm fired?" she rambled.

"All the clients will be taken care of in-house, you don't need to do anything. We'll mail you your final check -- you'll still be at your current address, right?"

"Yeah," Cassidy nodded, suddenly considering a whole new set of concerns.

"Great. We'll get that out to you first thing next week. And yes, I will still write you a letter of recommendation. You are a reliable employee. College educated and now you have two years under your belt."

"Three," Cassidy corrected.

"Three years of experience in the work force. Your options are limitless!"

"But not here?"

"No, not here."

"Um… okay," Cassidy said. She could feel the bile rising

in her throat. There was a long moment of awkward silence.

"Cassidy," Mr. Jelif said. Cassidy looked up at him. "You really were a good employee. I could always count on you. I just wish you wanted to try harder, not just when the chips are down."

"Yeah." She felt her stomach lurch and her jaw clench.

"And I have to say, you're taking this very gracefully. I know you can be a firecracker, so I wasn't sure how this would go. You've eased my fears for a really hard task -- one I was not looking forward to, no matter the reaction," he admitted.

"What were you expecting?" Cassidy raised an eyebrow.

"I really wasn't sure. Screaming, swearing, maybe throwing a chair through the window."

"It's way too cold to break a window," Cassidy replied flatly. Mr. Jelif failed to cover his chuckle. Cassidy found herself oddly honored. Annoyed. But honored.

"If you have any follow up questions next week, you can call back in. You know my extension – five-nine-three."

"Thanks," Cassidy said in a low voice. "So, I just leave at five and never come back?"

"Well, honestly, you should take a box from the supply cupboard, take any personal items you have out of your desk and head out."

"Now?"

"Yes. I'm sorry, Banker. But it will be easier for you to leave quickly. You don't want to watch your work being divvied up. Trust me," Mr. Jelif said. Cassidy felt like she'd been punched in the gut.

"Okay." Cassidy nodded as she stood up from the chair.

"And while I don't feel like I need to say this to you, after Devon, I am required to say it to everyone: please don't steal any company property. We will take the cost of it out of your final check." Mr. Jelif said. Cassidy paused a moment before realizing she could ask without repercussions.

"What did Devon steal?"

"One of the stone flower pots out front."

"I thought that was taken out by a storm!"

"Nope."

"You charged him for it?"

"And the flowers inside."

"Thank you for telling me." Cassidy gave him a small smile.

"No problem," Mr. Jelif nodded. She gave him a final look before departing his office and going to her desk for the final time.

She was happy she didn't need a box. She was never one for knick-knacks or desk toys. After a quick search through her desk drawers, she pulled out her two packs of gum, a hair claw clip that was painted to look like a golden retriever, and a stress ball with her company's logo on it – a rather apt souvenir, she thought -- and tossed them all into her purse. She put on her coat.

After a few half-assed goodbyes from coworkers, Cassidy left the downtown building and shivered her way to the parking garage across the street.

# Chapter 9

The blue Toyota seemed to drive on auto-pilot. That's the only way that Cassidy could explain why she was turning onto her parents' street at this moment. She truly had no recollection of the forty minute drive from the city. She knew she didn't want to go back to the apartment -- she might never leave. So Cassidy drove home. She was planning to be there that evening for dinner, anyway, and she knew both of her parents would be home. Lynne was off because the school she worked at was getting a frozen pipe fixed and the school was closed. The whole ordeal had been quite a scandal among the parents of students. Art had taken a day off in solidarity, or so he said, but Cassidy knew he liked to putz around and fix things that didn't need to be fixed. And if Lynne was home at the same time, he could get her opinion before each new endeavor, rather than her coming home and yelling at him for changing something she loved and making him put it back.

Suddenly, Cassidy was pulling into the long driveway.

It wasn't until Cassidy had turned off the car that she realized she was not fully prepared to tell her parents. Fired. She never imagined she would be fired. It felt like a huge red X across her life. The bile was still lapping her throat. It made her sick. This situation made her feel sick.

After a couple minutes of unhelpful thoughts, Cassidy grabbed her purse and exited the car. She used her key and let herself in the front door.

"Knock, knock!" she called out loudly, not wanting to scare either of her parents -- or herself -- if she walked in on whatever the hell they did without a household of kids. Cassidy had never given it much thought.

"Cassidy?" Art yelled from his study. He sounded surprised.

"Yeah, hi dad."

"Why are you here?" he asked, standing up and making his way into the foyer.

"Felt like coming home a little early today."

"It's four minutes to two. What happened? Ya get fired?" Art joked.

Cassidy froze. She could feel her bottom lip start to quiver. "Oh, no, Cass," Art said, realizing what had happened and opening his arms for a hug. Cassidy didn't hesitate a moment before hugging him tightly.

"What? What's happening? Cassidy? Art, what on earth happened?" Lynne frantically asked as she came from the family room and into the foyer.

"She got the ax," Art said in a painfully loud whisper over his daughter's head before placing a light kiss on her hair.

"Ohhh," Lynne groaned. Cassidy wasn't sure if her mother's reaction was at her situation or her father's gruff announcement. Lynne was never one for kitschy expressions.

"Yeah," Cassidy sighed, pulling back from her father. She wiped her eyes and sniffled. The tears had started. Crap.

"What happened?" Lynne asked gently as she tucked some of her hair behind her ear. Cassidy shrugged.

"The company hasn't been doing great, and well… they've been downsizing really hard. Guess my number was up."

"There you go!" Art said energetically. The Banker women shot him a look. "No, no, see, you weren't fired – it was a downsizing. Still stinks, but it's the company, not you," he explained. Cassidy thought for a moment. He may have been right, but at the moment, it didn't help how she felt.

"It does stink," Cassidy sighed.

"Let me put the kettle on, we'll have some tea and you can sit down and tell me everything," Lynne said, patting her arm. Cassidy gave her a weak smile.

"Okay. But I want to put on something comfortable, at least for a bit. Is there still stuff in my old room?"

"Yeah, go on up. It'll take the water a bit to boil," Lynne said before heading into the kitchen.

"Cassidy," Art said as she was on the second step. She paused and turned to face her father.

"Yeah?"

"I've never seen you all dressed for work. You look like a professional. You're not a kid anymore. Wear this to your interview. You'll knock them dead," Art said. Cassidy grinned at her dad as a few tears slipped out.

"I think this outfit may have the stink of fired on it permanently, but I appreciate your confidence."

"Downsized, Cassidy. Say downsized."

"Either term means jobless."

"Well…"

71

"Look, I appreciate you trying to cheer me on. I do. But right now, I'm going to go change into my old clothes and just be sad for a bit before I pick my interview outfit."

"Fair enough," Art nodded. Cassidy continued up a few more stairs before turning around once more.

"Dad? Thanks."

"Anytime."

Cassidy spent a couple of hours curled up on the couch in the family room with her mom. She had found some clothes in her old room to change into. She went from professional business woman to slobby chic in a pair of black sweat pants with her high school's logo on the left thigh, a plain white T-shirt that was covered with a bulky red crewneck sweat shirt that said "Edinboro Softball" across the chest in large, white letters, and a pair of ratty pink slippers that Cassidy was pretty sure she got back in middle school. The outfit was symbolic of how she felt at the moment.

Lynne and Cassidy sat together on the large couch in the family room as they drank their tea. They started talking about work, but the conversation turned to updates on cousins, neighbor gossip, asking about Marissa and Jake. Cassidy told her about helping Ellie and Lynne gave her impressions of meeting Mr. and Mrs. Hammond – which differed a bit from Eric's telling, but Cassidy did not tell her that. The easy conversation helped, and the tea was soothing. Cassidy was glad she'd come home early.

A little after five o'clock, Lynne got up to start preparing dinner and Cassidy went upstairs to call Jake and tell him the news from the privacy of her parents' bedroom – the only upstairs telephone.

It only rang twice.

"Hello?"

"Hey, it's me." Cassidy smiled, hearing the familiar voice.

"Hey! Wait… aren't you at your parents' for Matty's birthday?"

"Yeah, I'm here."

"Oh, okay. What's up?" Jake asked.

"Well… I got here early afternoon," Cassidy began slowly.

"Uh huh," Jake gave a low hum. There was a long pause.

"I got fired today," she admitted in a low voice.

"Oh, no," he sounded sad. Cassidy wished she could hug him right now.

"So, I grabbed my stuff and left. I didn't want to go home, I just wanted to go… well, home."

"I'm glad you did," Jake said. Cassidy sniffled.

"It's like I knew it was coming, but it still sucks. I did not expect it today."

"Definitely a surprise to come today."

"It keeps replaying in my head." Cassidy flopped backwards on the bed.

"What did your parents say? Or have you told them yet?"

"I did. They were both off work today."

"So, what did they say?"

"My dad said I should say I was downsized because it's less harsh and puts the fault on the company, not me," Cassidy said. Jake gave a small laugh.

"I love Art."

"Jake," Cassidy whined.

"You don't like that term?"

"I don't know. I don't like this whole situation."

"I get that."

"What am I going to do?" Cassidy asked with a sad sigh. A few tears escaped and she brushed them away with the back of her hand.

"You're going to find a new job."

"I guess."

"Cassidy, I know you're very sad right now, and rightly so, but you'll see. It'll get better!"

"Mmmm."

"Why are you holding back emotions right now?" Jake asked curiously.

"I'm not."

"I know you, Cassandra."

"Not my name."

"I was kidding."

"Go on," she sighed.

"You never hide your feelings. That's what I love about you."

"It does suck!"

"And that you're pretty scared."

"I don't like that."

"I know," Jake said. Cassidy felt a lump in her throat.

"It feels so… embarrassing."

"Yeah, I get that."

"I just don't know what I'm going to do."

"Well, the good and bad news is, it's Friday. You can't do anything until Monday; all businesses will be closed. I'd say just rest this weekend."

"Yeah."

"So, what are you guys doing tonight?" Jake asked.

"Hmm?"

"Matty's birthday," he clarified. Cassidy appreciated a change of subject.

"Oh... probably just dinner and cake. We can't really do anything outside because it's freezing out, and indoor games... well, things get broken."

"I can only imagine," Jake chuckled.

"Well, I need to go change before everyone gets here."

"Change?"

"I was sad; I didn't want to be in the outfit I wore to work."

"You have clothes there?"

"A few left behind. I'm currently in sweats from high school."

"Sounds hot," Jake said. Cassidy snorted.

"Yeah, I'm sure Sports Illustrated will call me for their swimsuit edition any second now."

"Better hang up and not hog the line then."

"Thank you," Cassidy said in a heartfelt voice after a long pause.

"For thinking you're hot?"

"No. Well, that's nice, too, but, for being what I needed right now."

"Of course. Anytime, always."

"I love you."

"I love you, too," Jake said. "Call me when you get home tonight. Or are you staying in Meadville?"

"The only thing that would make me feel sadder than being fired--"

"Downsized," Jake interrupted. Cassidy rolled her eyes.

"The only thing that will make me feel worse than being fired," she enunciated. "is staying in my old bedroom with my parents fussing over me like I'm two."

"That's not the worst thing."

"Ugh. I know," Cassidy groaned. "I'm just feeling... shitty."

"That's fair," Jake said. "Do me a favor though, huh? Don't drive home if you aren't in the right headspace. I think we're getting some snow."

"We always have snow. And I will be in the right headspace if you agree to come over tonight," Cassidy grinned.

"Call me when you get home."

"Okay."

"Love you."

"Love you, too," Cassidy said as she hung up the phone.

At six o'clock, Cassidy was back downstairs in the kitchen, leaning on the island as she watched her mother chop vegetables for the salad. Lynne had absolutely forbidden Cassidy from helping, which was a mixture of nice and really boring.

After Cassidy talked to Jake, she changed out of the sweatpants and back into her skirt and stockings, but kept her sweatshirt on. It was chilly.

"When are they getting here?" Cassidy asked, twirling a fork on the countertop.

"You sound like your father."

"Thank you," Cassidy grinned, taking it like a huge compliment. Lynne groaned, making her daughter laugh.

"They show up whenever they show up... you all do," Lynne said pointedly.

"Hey! I'm sad."

"I know, I know," Lynne stopped chopping for a moment to give Cassidy a kiss on her temple. "And honestly, I'm so glad that you came here to us and not to some dingy bar, or dark alley, or strip club."

"What?" Cassidy looked confused.

"I don't know what you kids do," Lynne smirked.

"Well, my strip club in the dark alley got busted for crack last week," Cassidy replied smartly.

"Okay, okay, that was dumb of me."

"Only a little."

"Fine, but I'm glad you aren't blowing money in a bar when you won't have an income for a bit."

"Why do you think I'm here? The drinks are free," Cassidy winked, holding up a bottle of beer. Lynne was about to say something when they were interrupted by the sound of the door opening.

"Hi!" Matty called out. Lynne dropped the knife and hurried to the foyer. Cassidy remained in the kitchen and listened.

"Birthday boy!"

"Thanks, mom."

"Is that Cassidy's car here? She's never here first," Matty asked. Cassidy rolled her eyes.

"It is," Lynne said normally before dropping her voice to a loud whisper that wasn't as inconspicuous as she clearly hoped. "Matty, I need you to be really nice to your sister today; she's having a hard time. I don't want to make a big deal about it, but she lost her job this afternoon."

"I can hear you!" Cassidy yelled from the kitchen. She heard Matty chuckle as they both came into the room.

"Sweetie, I'm sorry. I'm just concerned," Lynne said in a

gentle voice as she tucked a lock of hair behind Cassidy's right ear.

"So, you got canned?" Matty asked, his head tilted slightly. Cassidy sighed.

"Yep."

"Just for my birthday?" he asked sarcastically, dramatically bringing his hand to his heart. Cassidy laughed despite herself.

"Sorry I didn't wrap it."

"I can put a bow on your head."

"Perfect," Cassidy smirked. Matty suddenly grabbed her shoulders and pulled her in for a too-tight hug. Cassidy grunted as she fell into him.

"Sweet, thoughtful, little sister," he cooed.

"Yeah, yeah," Cassidy sighed, firmly patting his back. He was just starting to let her go when the front door slammed and Ben bounded into the room.

"Oh, God," he gasped, shocked to see his siblings hugging. It was a rare sight, at least with Matty. "Who died?"

"No one," Cassidy pushed herself back.

"Just Cassidy's career and prospects," Matty said.

"Shut up."

"Matthew!" Lynne scolded. Cassidy punched him hard in the arm.

"Whoa," Ben breathed, surprised at the exchange.

"When's dinner?" Cassidy asked her mother, desperate for a distraction.

"Thirty minutes, at least. And not everyone is here yet."

"Eric's here," Ben said.

"Where?" Matty asked.

"Outside. We got here at the same time, but Dad asked him to help get the driveway salt out of the back of his car," Ben said.

"What? Why would he ask him to do that now?" Lynne grumbled. She quickly wiped her hands on her apron before stomping over to the door to the garage on the other side of the kitchen.

"Uh, oh," Cassidy, Matt, and Ben all hummed in unison.

"Art! What are you guys doing? Get inside, it's freezing out!" Lynne barked.

"Almost done!" Art called back.

"Hey, mom!" Eric greeted.

"Hi, sweetie."

"We'll be in soon, just giving him a head's up about… you know, and to be extra nice to her," Art said in a voice that managed to echo through the air. Cassidy rolled her eyes.

"Subtle."

"Amazing," Matty gave a low chuckle.

"Arthur! She's right here!" Lynne hissed.

"Oh," Art said in surprise.

"Just get inside," Lynne ordered. The sound of the large, double garage door whirring as it closed could be heard, and a few moments later Art and Eric entered the kitchen.

"Sorry, Cassidy," Art said sheepishly.

"Eh," Cassidy shrugged.

"Happy birthday, Matt!" Eric said cheerily before giving his sister a weak smile. Cassidy bit her tongue. She knew he meant well, but she hated feeling pitied.

"Thanks!" Matty beamed.

"Yeah, Happy birthday!" Ben patted his arm. "But what happened to Cassidy?"

"She was downsized today," Art explained.

"What?" Ben asked.

"Ben, I got fired," Cassidy said with a loud exhale.

"Downsized, it was their fault," Art interjected.

"Dad, that doesn't actually help," Cassidy countered.

"That sucks," Ben said, scrunching his face slightly.

"See, he gets it," she said, gesturing to her youngest brother. "And Matty, stop looking so happy! It's not funny anymore." She skulked off to the small powder room off the hallway.

She heard her name being called as she shut the bathroom door. She ignored everyone. Cassidy took a seat on the closed toilet seat lid and leaned forward. Placing her head in her hands and balancing her elbows on her knees.

"Lord, help me," she whispered. She could feel her body clench in frustration, humiliation, anger, and the twenty-six other emotions she was experiencing right now. After a couple of minutes feeling sorry for herself, she stood up and splashed water on her face. She looked at her reflection as she patted her face dry with the hand towel. She didn't look like herself.

"Get your shit together, Banker," Cassidy said to her reflection before flushing the unused toilet and exiting the small powder room.

Lynne was back working away in the kitchen and Art and the boys had moved to the family room where they were all lounging and arguing as Ben flipped through the channels with the remote. Cassidy decided to return to the kitchen.

"Hey mom."

"I'm sorry, sweetie," Lynne said as she opened the oven to peek inside.

"It's okay," Cassidy shrugged.

"Really? I would expect you to be a lot more upset."

"What happened to the calm down, Cassidy speech you normally give?"

"You're usually much louder, and the infraction against you much smaller," Lynne replied calmly. Cassidy shot her a look.

"Maybe I'm in shock."

"Maybe."

"Can I just ask one favor, please?"

"What's that?"

"Can you stop looking at me like I have cancer?"

"What?" Lynne asked, looking shocked.

"The pity party… I can't stand the sad puppy looks. They make me feel worse than I already do. Let me just enjoy dinner and give Matty all the attention that he loves," Cassidy said. Lynne smiled at her.

"Okay."

"Oh, and the whispering doesn't work. If you want to talk about me, wait until I'm not in the house. You're not good at being secretive."

"Alright," Lynne agreed.

"Thank you."

"You're welcome."

"So, what is for dinner tonight?" Cassidy asked.

"Matty's favorite, of course – chicken parmigiana!"

"Mmm, oh! Matty!" Cassidy gasped.

"What?"

"I never brought his gift in from the car when I got here," Cassidy said as she scurried around the kitchen island. She ran to the front door and swung it open only to be hit by a gust of cold air.

"Ugh!" Cassidy groaned before shutting the door. She opened the coat closet and grabbed the first thing she could find, which happened to be her mom's navy blue peacoat. Her shoes were still upstairs in her old room, so she slipped into her father's brown snow boots before opening the door once more and hopping out onto the porch. The shoes were big and she felt a bit like a toddler, but at least she was warm.

Cassidy hobbled ungracefully out to her car, grabbed the orange gift bag out of her backseat – three brand new cassettes -- and slammed the car door closed just as a white Honda pulled into the end of the driveway. Alex, late as usual. Cassidy held her spot and waited for him.

"Wow, love the new look there, Oscar Madison!" Alex chuckled as he got out of his car.

"You're not exactly Felix," Cassidy smirked.

"Why are you in dad's shoes?"

"Because I forgot Matty's present in my car and had to run out and get it, and it's really cold out."

"Where are your shoes?"

"My room."

"Your old room here? Why the hell were you in there?" Alex asked as they slowly walked onto the porch together. Cassidy sighed. She had to tell him. Better from her than Matty.

"Well... um... I got fired today," Cassidy said. She looked up at him, grimacing slightly. Alex looked horrified.

"Cassie, I'm so sorry."

"I mean, it sucks."

"Yeah," he said, opening the front door for them. The foyer felt delightfully warm.

"Cassidy?" Lynne asked from the kitchen. They set their presents for Matty on the steps while they removed their coats and Cassidy slipped out of her father's boots.

"Alex is here, too," Cassidy called.

"Oh, good, perfect timing!"

"Hi, mom," Alex said, but Lynne was already running the other way to get the rest of the guys out of the family room. "Has she been frantic?" he asked in a low voice. Cassidy nodded.

"Yes. Everyone has been very sad... Well, except for Matty. He's downright thrilled," Cassidy rolled her eyes. Alex scoffed before pulling her into a gentle hug.

"He's sad for you, he's just an asshole."

"It's fine," Cassidy said as she relaxed against him.

"Remember, you can stay with me and Laura before you have to move back with mom and dad."

"I appreciate that," Cassidy said truthfully. She had been trying not to think of what her housing situation might be next month. Alex rested his head on hers.

"Hey!" Matty yelled as he walked into the foyer.

"Happy birthday!" Alex smiled at him as he and Cassidy slowly pulled apart.

"Why is she nice to you? I tried to hug her today and she punched me," Matty acted offended.

"Because you crushed my organs," Cassidy pointed out as she pushed between her brothers and went into the kitchen to help her mom get everything on the table.

Dinner was delicious and a lot of fun. Jokes were flying back and forth, and, at one point, Ben's spoon. They all enjoyed hearty helpings of ice cream cake and giving Matty his birthday gifts, before moving into the family room for a game Outburst. They made it through a miraculous four rounds before their first argument, and the game didn't have to be forcefully ended until round seven. While the teams were neck and neck, the category "Things Left in Space" turned into a very surprising debate, lots of insults, and a few far-fetched conspiracy theories. However, the game ending clincher was Ben angrily throwing the game card reader into the lit fireplace and Eric punching him for doing so.

Art fished the card reader out of the fire with the tongs, but there was nothing to salvage, so he tossed it back in, despite Lynne's annoyance.

Once everything was put away, everyone started to gather their things. Cassidy ran upstairs to her childhood bedroom to retrieve her shoes, as well as her work blouse and purse. She took a moment to sit on her bed and look around her bedroom. She let out a deep sigh as she took in the familiar surroundings, listening to the chatter and chaos from downstairs.

Cassidy chewed on her lip as her mind swirled. She could find herself living back home by early next year. She tried hard to remind herself that her situation could be worse. She could be facing actual homelessness. While she was grateful for her family, it was hard to swallow the fact that sleeping in her childhood bedroom as she struggled to find a job was a very real possibility for her future. Ben was graduating from college next spring. Would he move back for a bit, too? Would she be down the hall from her baby brother once more? Who would get a job first?

Her mind started to spin faster and faster with questions she didn't want answers to. The lump in her throat formed once more.

"Ugh, fuck off," Cassidy said in a low voice, speaking to the thoughts in her head, the lump in her throat -- hell, to the whole situation.

"I didn't even say anything!"

Cassidy jolted and turned to see Matty leaning in her open doorway.

"Ah! How long have you been there?"

"Not long enough to warrant a fuck off," he said flatly. Cassidy sighed.

"What do you want?"

"I'm heading out."

"Okay." There was a long pause. "And happy birthday."

"Thanks."

"Hmm?"

"I'm sorry you lost your job," Matty said in a serious tone. Cassidy looked up at him for a moment. He wasn't sincere very often, but when he was it always hit her hard. Perhaps that was the point?

"Thanks. I appreciate that." She gave him a small smile.

"Okay, well, you'll get back on your feet. You always do."

"I hope so."

"Don't start being humble and meek now. You walk into an interview acting like a candy-ass, you'll never get a job. Not to mention, you can't really pull that look off," Matty said.

"What? Unemployed and homeless?"

"No, insecure."

"Oh. Is that a compliment?" Cassidy asked. Matty shrugged.

"More of a fact. You've always been cocky – mostly because you can back it up with skill, but self-doubt doesn't suit you. Knock it off."

"Matty, I'm sad!"

"I know."

"So, I can't be sad?"

"You can, but don't stay there."

"But—"

"Cassidy, it's my birthday and you're making me be way too nice to you," Matty said playfully. Cassidy smiled at him.

"Okay, you've served your time," she laughed.

"Okay." He smiled at her. "Now, get your shit and come downstairs."

"Why?" Cassidy asked.

"Because Alex wants to take you home, and his car is blocking most of us in."

"I have my car."

"I know, but he thinks you'll cry and not pay attention, hit some black ice and end up in a snowbank or something dramatic like that," Matty said, waving his arms emphatically.

"It's mostly highway, roads will be treated."

"Look, no one here would like to see you on the news for flipping your car and getting wedged somewhere dumb more than me. But if that happens, I will have to listen to Alex tell me that he was right for the rest of my life. And well, I cant -- no, I won't -- let that happen. So, please, get in his car and act grateful," Matty instructed. Cassidy fought hard to hold back a laugh.

"I'm coming, but I can still drive," Cassidy said as she grabbed her things and stood up.

"Shut up or I'll put you in his trunk," Matty said as he followed her down the hallway and down the stairs.

"Oh please! You couldn't fight me to get me in."

"I wouldn't fight you, I'd knock you unconscious."

"You'd still have to lift me into the trunk. That's dead weight. Ain't happening with your skinny arms."

"Bet you five bucks I could. There's a skillet in the kitchen I could hit you with," Matty said as the stepped off the bottom step into the foyer.

"No one is hitting anyone," Lynne said, overhearing the last bit of the conversation.

"And definitely not for a five dollar bet," Cassidy said pointedly.

"Name your price; bet the guys will pitch in," Matty said, pointing at their siblings.

"What are we pitching in for?" Eric asked.

"I'm not paying for any idea you have," Ben said. His nose had finally stopped bleeding, but it was still pretty swollen. Lynne had held an ice pack to it for the last fifteen minutes, and now the skin was red and irritated -- from the hit and the cold. He was looking slightly pathetic, if Cassidy was honest.

"He wants to put me in Alex's trunk," Cassidy remarked.

"I'll go in for ten," Eric said.

"Eric," Cassidy whined, reaching over to slap his chest. He already had his coat on, so it didn't faze him at all.

"I'll put her in there for free," Ben smiled.

"I can make your eye match your nose," Cassidy warned.

"Why is she going in my trunk?" Alex asked as he retrieved his coat from the closet behind them.

"None of you are going in anyone's truck," Lynne said loudly. Clearly she was ready for some peace and quiet in her house once more. Everyone got the hint that it was time to leave. Hugs and goodbyes filled the foyer as the seven of them shuffled around prior to departing. Cassidy was very aware her goodbye hugs were a little longer than usual. Her parents, even Ben and Matty. She couldn't lie, it was nice.

"Sorry, Cas," Eric said seriously.

"Thanks," Cassidy gave her twin a small smile.

"Call me sometime, we'll have a drink," Eric said.

"I'd like that," Cassidy replied honestly before giving him a hug and he headed out the door behind Matty and Ben. Cassidy stepped out on the porch and saw Alex having a cigarette, leaning on the banister.

"Come on, you're holding everyone up," Alex said, exhaling a large puff of smoke.

"I'm parked in," Cassidy said, pointing to her Toyota at the front of the line, closest to the garage door. Alex shook his head.

"Let me drive you home."

"Alex…"

"Please?"

"Why?"

"Because in ten minutes you're going to be in tears," Alex said. Cassidy bit her tongue. She was annoyed that he was right. And while she had driven while crying before, it was dark, cold, well below freezing, and the air smelled like snow. Cassidy knew that having an emotional breakdown while driving would not be in her best interest right now. And if she did crash – who would find her? How would she get ahold of anyone? It was stark driving between Meadville and Erie. Her best options were to ride with Alex or to sleep in her old room as her parents bickered and hovered outside her door. Cassidy took option A.

"Okay… But you'd better have tissues in your car," Cassidy told Alex. He smiled smugly before taking his final drag and pitching the cigarette butt into the dirt.

"There's a box in the backseat. Laura had a cold last week and I drove her to the doctor's."

"Okay." She followed Alex to his car.

Both Ben and Matty had parked behind Cassidy and were

able to drive away. Eric was parked next to Cassidy -- the only one blocked in by Alex's stalling.

"Thank God," Eric sighed seeing them walk to the car. His arms were resting on the hood of the car as he stood there, waiting to be freed.

"Sorry," Alex said, patting Eric's shoulder as he walked to his car. Cassidy gave Eric a shrug as they shared a look before both getting into their cars and out of the cold.

# Chapter 10

"It's colder in here than outside," Cassidy shivered, rubbing her arms in her coat.

"Give it a minute, it'll warm up," Alex said as they turned out of their parents' neighborhood. "I'm assuming you won't let me open the window to smoke once we get out on 79?"

"Absolutely not! You can wait forty-five minutes."

Alex groaned; Cassidy ignored him. If it was any other season, she wouldn't care, but if it was cold enough to snow, she would make him go without.

"Alex, you'll make it."

"What about you?"

"I'll be fine without a cigarette. I've smoked maybe four or five times in my life. I don't even have a habit to kick," Cassidy chuckled.

"I meant since losing your job," Alex clarified.

"I mean, it sucks."

"Yeah."

"What do you want me to say?"

"You can say whatever you want!"

"I feel like you want me to fall apart."

"I don't want you to, but it would make sense."

"Matty said you were going to drive me."

"And you took the offer," Alex said.

"Like I had a choice without throwing a fit!"

"You like throwing fits," he shrugged. Cassidy shot him a glare.

"I feel like you're baiting me right now. Pushing so I get mad."

"Cassidy, I asked how you were going to manage," Alex sighed as he put on his turn signal for the on ramp of the highway.

"Why did Matty say you were going to drive me home?" Cassidy asked.

"Because I said I was going to." The car accelerated as he merged in front of a station wagon.

"So, everyone was talking about me when I left the room?"

"About today's occurrence, yes."

"Oh."

"Cassidy, despite everything, we all do love you and we're sad that you lost your job. It's a big deal."

"No! No, its not," Cassidy said, looking out the passenger side window at the dark fields surrounding the highway. That annoying feeling was back: her stomach turning and her throat hurting. She felt herself excessively blinking. She swallowed hard.

"How is it not?"

"Because it's a job. There are people with cancer and, and..." her mind was drawing a blank. "And other real problems."

"Why are you downplaying it?"

"I'm not!" Cassidy shot back. She felt like she was being backed into a corner.

"Okay," Alex hummed in a sing-song voice.

"The heat is finally working in here. Would you be less of a dick if I told you to smoke the rest of the drive?" Cassidy growled.

"I'm going to let you have that one… but only that one," Alex warned. Cassidy swallowed hard.

"Stop. Pushing. Please." she said in a voice just above a whisper.

"I just want a simple answer."

"No, you want a really hard answer because I have no idea what I'm going to do," Cassidy choked out. A few tears escaped. She hated this feeling. Falling apart. Especially when she was falling apart because the world she knew was crumbling. Her heart hurt.

"There we go," Alex said in a kind voice, looking over at her. Cassidy knew that look. It was how he looked at her when they were kids and she wasn't allowed to do something because she was a girl, or not big enough. It was the pity face. And it went right through her. It was the face he made when he knew exactly how lousy and sad she felt. The older she got, the more she hated it. She hated looking sad or weak. The rare times she ever felt that way, she could hide it from most people. But Alex saw her. Raw and broken. She couldn't hide right now, and couldn't run, unless she was prepared for injury from tucking and rolling followed by frost bite, which she was not. Cassidy was stuck. In the car. In her emotions. In her brokenness. It sucked.

"You're enjoying this, aren't you?" Cassidy said as she started to cry.

"Not at all," Alex said. Cassidy sniffled loudly. "I hate that this happened to you."

"But…?"

"But, you can't hold it all in; it'll kill you," he said. Cassidy cried quietly, shaky breaths and sniffles, really. She felt pathetic. She continued to whimper for about a minute. An old Bee Gees song came on the radio, and Alex actively tried not to hum along. Cassidy finally took a big breath.

"But if I let myself fall apart … it is real," she sniffled.

"Cassie, it is real. Your job is gone," Alex said in a low voice. And that was it. Her heart sank. The flood gates opened and she cried. Hard. "There it is," Alex hummed sadly.

Her tears streamed as she sobbed. Alex reached back and passed her the box of tissues before turning up the radio and continuing to drive. Honestly, she appreciated it. Cassidy felt her body tremble as she cried. She hated feeling this out of control. A few heavy sobs made her think she might even throw up, but was able to settle herself.

Four songs, two radio sales jingles, and an interlude of DJ banter later, Cassidy's sobbing ceased. She was back to low sniffles as she dried her face, which was now feeling very chapped, and blew her nose, causing her to give a few, slightly pathetic coughs.

"Whoa," Cassidy sighed.

"Hmm?" Alex hummed, glancing over at her before returning his eyes to the road.

"It's snowing," she replied flatly as she looked out the window. Alex gave a snort.

"Yep."

Cassidy took a few shaky breaths and blew her nose again before repositioning so she was sitting cross-legged on the passenger seat with her feet tucked underneath her. She smoothed her skirt over her knees.

"How much longer?" she asked as she ran her fingers through her hair.

"Twenty minutes. Maybe a bit more."

"Okay."

"How do you feel?"

"Um… snotty," Cassidy answered honestly and grabbed another tissue.

"I think that's step one," Alex teased.

"Good for me," Cassidy replied sarcastically.

"You should feel lighter."

"Lighter?" Cassidy tilted her head as she looked at him. "Oh, because I'm losing so much snot?" Alex snorted.

"No. I'm not Matty."

"That is a solid Matty joke. I'll have to call and tell him it tomorrow."

"He would appreciate that," Alex smiled. A peaceful silence fell between the two for a long minute.

"You know, yeah," Cassidy began.

"What?" Alex asked. "Cassie, you can't just start talking mid-sentence, I don't live in your head."

"I know!" And thank goodness you don't Cassidy thought to herself.

"So?"

"So, I actually feel like a weight has lifted."

"Good," Alex said.

"I mean, I still feel sad… and kind of freaked out… and well--"

"Well?"

"Well, if I think about it, I'll get all worked up again," Cassidy admitted.

"I mean, it did just happen today."

"True," Cassidy shrugged. "Distract me."

"What?"

"You got your way, I cried."

"I wasn't cheering it on," Alex rolled his eyes.

"Okay, but you were right, I needed that," she admitted. "But now I need something else to think about."

"Um…"

"Tell me something that you and Laura are doing this weekend."

"We're going to go see her parents on Sunday."

"Are her parents actually hippies?"

"Cassie…"

"Sorry, but is it true they actually went to Woodstock?"

"Yeah," Alex smiled.

"Wow! They must have the coolest stories."

"Some are pretty crazy."

"Tell me one. Please? I'm sad," Cassidy said. Alex laughed before diving into Laura's dad, Gerald's, favorite story of them accidentally joining a playful mud sliding competition between a group of friends. They were trying to find their tent and when scrambling up a small hill, Gerald lost his footing and stumbled, knocking his wife, Shirley, down in the process. Shirley slid headfirst down the other side next to a man from Ohio, who was quite surprised to see her there. The group from Ohio liked her slide and invited Gerald and Shirley to join their game! Gerald and Shirley spent the next hour rolling down the hill with their new friends. Gerald managed to lose one of his shoes in the process. When making a pitstop in the river to rinse off before restarting their journey to find their tent, Gerald spotted a lone shoe on the bank and took it. He spent the rest of the festival in mismatched shoes.

The story made both Cassidy and Alex laugh, and prompted tales of childhood car trip disasters, which were plentiful. The final twenty minutes of the ride were filled with laughter and contentment, which was good, as Alex had to lower his speed considerably due to the snow. But they made it back to Cassidy's apartment in one piece.

Despite Cassidy's assurance that she would make it inside without incident, Alex walked her to her door. While Cassidy appreciated her eldest brother more than she usually showed, sometimes his overprotective nature took odd turns. What did he think she was going to do? Hurl herself down one flight of stairs?

With Alex in tow, Cassidy made her way to the second floor and let herself into her apartment.

"Hi," she called, kicking off her shoes and hanging up her thick winter coat on the hook by the door.

"Hey," Marissa said looking sad, her hand over her heart.

"What's happening?" Cassidy asked with a raised eyebrow.

"Jake told me about work."

"What?"

"Hey," Jake emerged from the far side of the living room with a small smile. Cassidy was so happy to see him.

"I thought you were coming over later," Cassidy said as she hurried over to him and hugged him, wrapping her arms around his middle. She took a deep breath, her face buried in his shoulder. Her whole body relaxed as he hugged her back.

"Well, I thought it would be nice to see you when you got home," Jake said, slowly pulling out of the hug. "Hey, Alex."

"Hey." Alex gave a nod. He didn't look thrilled to see Cassidy clinging to him, but still much friendlier than their first meeting.

"Yeah, hi, Alex, it's been forever," Marissa said, leaning over to give Alex a quick side hug which he happily returned.

"Yeah, been a while."

"Did you drive her back?" Jake asked Alex, stepping away from Cassidy. Cassidy knew he was trying not to push his luck.

"Yeah. Couldn't have her ending up in a snowbank," Alex shrugged.

"Appreciate that." Jake gave a low chuckle.

"You guys have no faith in me," Cassidy said.

"I'm sorry, but how many used tissues are in your purse right now? Thirty?" Alex asked.

"Ugh, probably. I need to clean that out," Cassidy grimaced as the other three laughed.

"Alex, are you staying for a drink?" Marissa asked.

"I appreciate the offer, but the snow is picking up. I want to get home," Alex said.

"Okay. Drive safe and thank you for the ride," Cassidy said sincerely.

"I'll call you tomorrow," Alex told her.

"Sounds good. Tell Laura I said hi."

"Will do."

"Stay for drink when it's not snowing," Marissa told him. Alex grinned.

"Definitely."

Cassidy smiled at her brother and gave a small wave. However, he wasn't looking at her, but over her shoulder. He was looking at Jake. Alex jerked his head towards the door and Cassidy looked back to see Jake nod.

"I'll be right back," Jake said, giving her a quick peck before following Alex out the door of the apartment.

"What the hell?" Cassidy asked, looking at Marissa as she walked past her into their galley kitchen.

"Oh, who knows," Marissa said with a shrug as she stood on her tip toes and pulled a bottle of wine off the top of the fridge. "Who cares, it's time for wine!"

"I care," Cassidy sighed as she came over and leaned against the counter to watch Marissa open the bottle.

"Tell me what happened."

"How much did Jake tell you?"

"Not much."

"He just showed up?"

"He called about an hour ago. I told him you weren't here yet and he asked if he could come over and wait for you."

"Oh," Cassidy said as Marissa gave a grunt, finally dislodging the cork form the bottle.

"He said you invited him over and he was worried because you lost your job today," Marissa said as she placed three wine glasses on the counter and started to pour.

"Thanks for letting him come over."

"Yeah, Jake and I are cool."

"And nice of you to pour him a glass," Cassidy smiled, taking the stem of the glass that Marissa pushed toward her.

"Hey, I'm not a complete airhead... Not to mention, he's the one that brought this bottle," Marissa winked. Cassidy laughed.

"Ahh, so, sharing."

"I'm very nice," Marissa grinned. The girls laughed as they clinked their glasses together and took a sip.

"Ugh, where are they?" Cassidy asked, leaning back slightly to try and see the door.

"Ignore them," Marissa waved, walking to the living room and taking a seat on the oversized chair. Cassidy flopped down on the couch, accidentally sloshing her wine. A few drops spilled onto her sweatshirt from home.

"Shit."

"Yeah, I have to ask about the outfit," Marissa said, taking another sip.

"Well, I was dressed nice for work. I was planning to stop here before going to my parents' place, but, well, I got fired at lunch and just high-tailed it home. Found this in my old room," Cassidy sighed.

"Fair," Marissa nodded. "Don't you have, like, a box of your stuff from your desk? I see that in TV when people are fired."

"I didn't have many personal things there. Some are in my purse, some are in my car, but not enough for a box. Thank God."

"Where's your car?"

"At my parents'. I'll see if Jake can drive me back tomorrow to grab it."

"If he can't go, I'll drive you back. I'm not meeting Brandon until dinner," Marissa said.

"Thanks," Cassidy smiled.

"Now, how did it go down?" Marissa asked. Before Cassidy could answer, there was a loud knock at the door.

"Must be Jake," Cassidy said, heaving herself off the couch

and letting him in.

"Sorry, locked myself out," Jake grinned when Cassidy opened the door. He was annoyingly cute.

"It's okay. I heard you brought wine," Cassidy said as she turned to walk back to the living room.

"And I see you've opened it," Jake teased, shutting the door behind him and following her to the couch.

"We poured you a glass," Marissa said, pointing to the counter.

"Thank you." He quickly grabbed the glass and settled in the middle of the couch. Cassidy curled up against him.

"What did Alex want?" Cassidy asked, taking another drink.

"Not much," Jake shrugged.

"Liar! Boooo!" Marissa called loudly making Jake jump slightly before looking down at Cassidy, who was grinning.

"Jeez!"

"This is why she's my friend," Cassidy replied smugly.

"Yeah," Jake hummed as he looked warily at Marissa.

"So?" Cassidy asked.

"He just asked me to keep an eye on you. He's really worried," Jake said. Cassidy knew she should be touched, but she gritted her teeth.

"I love him, but he treats me like I'm suicidal. I'm not. I swear."

"I'm glad to hear it," Jake said.

"What happened?" Marissa asked. Cassidy sighed and retold the whole story. It felt just as terrible in the retelling. However, the addition of wine was nice. Jake and Marissa listened to her saga with full attention, and sympathetic faces, which made Cassidy feel both better and worse. From her firing to her afternoon with her parents, she went over every detail. Marissa refilled their wine glasses, and Jake rubbed her back. Cassidy felt good that she only teared up twice. While Marissa had been there for multiple meltdowns and break-up cries over the years, this was her first time crying in front of Jake. He held up well.

"Want to come over next week? I can help you with your resume," Jake offered after a long pause.

"Yeah… Yeah, I guess I need to start job searching. Is the paper still here or did you throw that out?" Cassidy asked with a sigh.

"Don't look now," Marissa said firmly.

"Yeah, no. Take the weekend," Jake agreed.

"I feel like I should jump-start this," Cassidy said.

"Next week," Jake said, kissing her cheek. Marissa jumped in and changed the subject to the recent news reports that England and France were trying to dig some tunnel under the water to connect the countries. Marissa and Cassidy both found it preposterous; however, Jake was very interested how they would manage it.

Two hours later, Cassidy was showered, in pajamas, and curled up in bed in her dark bedroom next to Jake.

"Thanks for coming over tonight," Cassidy whispered.

"It's going to be okay," Jake said, rubbing his thumb gently on her cheek.

"Is it? When?"

"Well, not right now."

"Yeah."

"Cassidy, this is a set-back, not permanent."

"I just don't want to have to move back home."

"That's not the worst thing."

"It feels like a massive step back."

"It would be a small step back, and it hasn't even happened yet."

"But…"

"Babe, today sucked, but it doesn't mean your life will," Jake said. Cassidy sighed and leaned forward, resting her forehead on his shoulder. Jake held her close and kissed her cheek.

"So," Cassidy said after a long moment, bringing her head back to her pillow, "are you still going to love an unemployed mooch?"

"I think I can make that work," Jake winked. Cassidy placed a soft kiss on his lips.

"And I can find work," she said determinedly.

"Yes. Yes, you can," Jake agreed, giving her one more kiss before they both settled into comfortable positions and fell into a deep and restful sleep.

# Chapter 11

Cassidy was heading into her second week of unemployment, and she was not thriving. Jake helped her update her resume and they worked on a cover letter while Marissa helped her pick out some professional outfits. Scouring the newspaper and dropping off her resume and cover letter at multiple accounting firms and companies with finance departments had proven fruitless. The ones that were hiring gave her an unconvincing 'We'll be in touch,' and the others seemed to have zero interest in doing any hiring before the upcoming holidays. Cassidy couldn't blame them. The middle of December was not ideal for job searching.

Cassidy had returned to her parents' house the night before for dinner. She didn't have anything else to do, and she was getting anxious about eating too much food at the apartment. How was she going to afford groceries? She couldn't make Marissa pay for her share.

After a delicious meal and another emotional breakdown

from Cassidy, Art had sat her down in his office and offered her a deal. He would loan her money until she got back on her feet with a new job, and she could pay him back as she was able to. His only stipulation was that she was not to use money to go out and party or blow on frivolous shopping trips. The loan was for necessities only. Cassidy asked about Christmas. She had planned to do all of her shopping the weekend she was fired. Obviously, that hadn't worked out.

Art advised her to offer non-tangible gifts – her time and help. Everyone knew her current situation and no one would expect expensive gifts. He told her that her grandfathers and great-grandfathers, most of whom were factory workers, gave gifts of service many years when they didn't have money, and they were always greatly appreciated. Cassidy smiled at the thought. She had never met any of her great grandparents, but still had her paternal grandfather: a strong, determined, and an extraordinarily hard-working man. He had been so proud of her father – the first of the family to go to college.

She was incredibly grateful for her family, not only for her upbringing, but for their generosity. She was lucky. Not only was she not homeless, but she didn't even have to move back home. Granted, she could already hear Matty quip that they didn't want her back home. And while he could be right, Cassidy cried as she hugged her father with deep gratitude. She promised to search even harder for a job and pay him back, with interest, the second she could. Art kissed her head and said he knew she would.

Cassidy had had yet another tearful drive home from her parents, but that night, they were tears of joy and immense gratefulness.

The next day, December 15th, was the first day of Hanukkah.

Cassidy was seated in the living room with Marissa, Brandon, and Jake. Cassidy had been celebrating Hanukkah with Marissa since their first year as roommates back in 1981 -- sophomore year at Edinboro. While Cassidy was not Jewish, she liked supporting Marissa in her faith. Marissa, in turn, had attended multiple Christmas Eve services with her over the years at the Lutheran Church. Cassidy had come to truly enjoy celebrating Hanukkah, even memorizing a few of the Hebrew phrases. Not to mention, it was significantly more fun than observing Yom Kippur. That was rough. She'd made it through two years of that with Marissa before politely asking to skip future years. Marissa had taken it well.

This wasn't the first year others had joined them for holiday. Depending on when the holiday fell each year, Marissa wasn't always able to go home. Often it was during finals week at school, so she couldn't travel. This year her parents were in Ohio with her older sister, Julie, her husband, and their baby daughter to celebrate with them, as it was her niece's first Hanukkah.

Marissa invited Brandon, who was slightly confused about what the holiday entailed, but he was won over when Marissa explained what latkes were. And when Cassidy told Jake they were celebrating, he immediately asked for an invitation, citing not only the potato latkes and jelly doughnuts, but true interest in the holiday.

Despite Cassidy being home all day with nothing to do but help prep, Marissa took the day off work to cook. Cassidy appreciated the company, and the opportunity to actually do something! Although Marissa took charge and gave Cassidy more of the minor tasks, Cassidy was thrilled for an activity that wasn't job searching or wallowing.

"So, how does this go?" Jake asked Marissa now that all four were in the living room and the delicious aromas of holiday food filled the air.

"I light the menorah and then recite the Shehecheyanu. I won't make you do any chants, though."

"Darn," Brandon interjected sarcastically, causing Marissa to smack his knee.

"And then we eat, exchange gifts, and play games," Marissa finished with a smile.

"It's fun!" Cassidy grinned.

"That all sounds great, but I have to ask… what are you reciting?" Jake asked.

"Shehecheyanu."

"Sheh-what?" Jake asked delicately.

"She-hek-ee-yah-new," Marissa pronounced slowly. Both the boys spoke along slowly after her. Cassidy had to laugh. She'd done the same thing her first year (or three) of celebrating.

"Okay, okay," Cassidy cut in. "Do the honors!" She passed Marissa a box of matches. Marissa struck a match and lit the shamash before lighting the first candle.

"Do we clap?" Brandon asked in a whisper.

"No, but thank you for the enthusiasm," Marissa said as she kissed him on the cheek and then blew out the match. She recited the Shehecheyanu blessing and a prayer before they dug into the loads of food that filled their kitchen and Marissa taught them how to play traditional games. The gift exchange was done white-elephant style, which Marissa firmly insisted was not how it was supposed to be done, but since she was celebrating with two Lutherans and a lapsed Catholic, she let it slide.

The night was fun and filled with laughter, delicious food, and people Cassidy loved. It was exactly what she needed.

The next seven nights of Hanukkah were just as fun, even though Jake couldn't make a few of them. Cassidy appreciated the distraction of the holiday. She applied for more jobs in the area, all with similar results. No one wanted to think seriously about hiring right before the holidays.

Jake agreed to her suggestion of non-monetary presents, and they spent the 22nd together for their holiday celebration before he drove home the following day to see his family. Cassidy and Jake baked cookies, ate lots of appetizers, played multiple board games, drank copious amounts of beer, and spent a large amount of time naked in bed as Christmas music played in the background. The day was perfect.

Cassidy spent Christmas Eve at her parents' in the annual chaos of family, presents, food, and games before attending the candlelight service at her childhood church. The day brought comfort and joy to Cassidy. She always enjoyed her family's Christmas celebration, but this year, she realized how much it meant to her. For her gifts, she had noticed how much her brothers hated running errands, so she booked herself to help them out with multiple store and pick-up runs. Normally, Cassidy hated running errands too, but now she was thrilled to fill her time with something useful.

The holiday season came and went. Cassidy spent New Year's Eve watching the fireworks over the lake with Jake, Marissa, Brandon, and half the city. It almost felt normal, ringing in the start of 1988 with celebration, music, drinks, and fun. Cassidy knew this year would be better. It had to be.

# Chapter 12

The first full week of 1988, the world seemed to go back to the usual routine. Schools were back in session, and everyone was back to work. Cassidy had a renewed sense of determination in her job search, telling herself that she would be hired by her 26th birthday -- even if that was only two and a half weeks away.

Jake had invited her over for dinner that night and Cassidy was thrilled to have an excuse to leave the apartment. She parked in front of his house just after six o'clock and knocked on the door. There was a long pause. She was about to knock again, but suddenly the white, wooden door swung open, revealing Jake wearing a red apron and looking a tad frazzled. Cassidy grinned at the sight of him.

"Hey," Jake said a little breathless.

"What is going on here?" Cassidy said unable to hide her smile at his apron.

"Cookin'! Come on in," Jake waved her inside. Cassidy gave him a quick peck as she passed him and stepped into the living room.

"What is on the menu, chef?" she asked, taking off her jacket, hat, gloves, and boots – it was bitter outside.

"Come into the kitchen and I'll show ya," Jake smiled as he hung her winter gear on the coat tree. Cassidy followed him to the brown and white kitchen in the back of the house. She was instantly struck by the amazing aroma that filled the air.

"Smells good in here!"

"Glad to hear that."

"Pasta?" Cassidy asked, looking at one of the pots on the stove.

"Yes, with homemade sauce, and garlic bread is in the oven." He smiled proudly.

"Homemade sauce?"

"Yes!"

"Like real tomatoes and spices and the lot?"

"Yes."

"If that's Ragu simmering…"

"It is not! Old family recipe. You can check my trash can if you don't believe me," Jake smirked proudly.

"Well, wow, wow, you are full of surprises," Cassidy chuckled to herself.

"Damn straight."

"Alright, what do you need help with?"

"I'm pretty much all set in here; everything should be done in a few minutes. But if you want to put silverware and napkins on the table, we'll plate in here."

"Can do," Cassidy said, kissing him on the cheek before getting to work as he continued to monitor the stove.

"Oh, what do you want to drink?" Jake called out as Cassidy finished folding the napkins under the forks.

"Hmm, wine feels appropriate, but I'll have whatever."

"I have a bottle of white in the fridge."

"I'll pour," Cassidy said happily. Within five minutes, Jake and Cassidy were seated at the square table in his dining room with plates of spaghetti and garlic bread covered in bolognese sauce.

"This is amazing," Cassidy said, popping another bite in her mouth. Jake grinned proudly.

"I'm glad you like it."

"Is this your mom's sauce recipe?" she asked, dipping the edge of her garlic bread in the sauce.

"My mom's mom's recipe, actually. But, yeah, that side of the family."

"Well, please tell her I love it… maybe it will win me a few points with her."

"I'll make sure to mention it," Jake chuckled. Cassidy picked up her wine glass.

"I know you think it's ridiculous, but I need all the Claire points I can get." Cassidy thought back to her meeting with Claire four months prior. It hadn't gone poorly, but wasn't spectacular, either. It never hurt to score some extra points.

"I'll see what I can do."

"So," Cassidy began, setting her wine back down after a long sip. "Is there any special reason you're feeding me this delicious meal?"

"Well," Jake hastily finished chewing. "Kind of."

"Really?"

"Well, I, um, wanted to share some news."

"Hmm?"

"I've been offered a job."

"What? Really?" Cassidy asked in a mix of shock and

excitement.

"Yeah, um, yep," Jake nodded, a small smile on his face.

"When did this happen?"

"Well, actually, just before Christmas, but I, I didn't want to say anything because... well, um,"

"Oh, Jake, no, you don't have to not be happy because I had a crappy month!" Cassidy said, reaching over and squeezing his hand. She wouldn't be able to forgive herself if he missed opportunities because of her.

"No, no, I've been given time to decide. Also, it let me think about it myself some," he explained

"Okay, okay, well, you've had time to think... I want to hear all about this job and what you're thinking. Come on, spill! Tell me everything!" Cassidy said excitedly.

"Another university has head hunted me... I never thought I would be someone that was actually head hunted." Jake used air quotes and Cassidy smiled.

"You are definitely someone who should be head hunted."

"Apparently. It's similar to my current role, but I'd be teaching more classes and still working with the baseball team. Even traveling more with them."

"Wow!"

"Yeah, I mean, it's a lot. I'd be a lot busier. Responsible for a lot more. Granted, the pay is... significantly more than I'm making now."

"This all sounds fantastic! I mean look at you, you're like bouncing with excitement," Cassidy said, reaching over to take his hand that was rattling his fork against his plate. He smiled at her.

"Umm, yeah..."

"What?"

"Northwestern."

"What?"

"Northwestern University is who reached out to me with the offer," Jake said, gulping loudly before pulling his hand out of hers and stuffing a forkful of spaghetti into his mouth. Cassidy paused. She could feel her mouth hanging open in surprise, and she quickly shut it.

"Like the Northwestern in Chicago?"

"Um, Evanston, but, yep," Jake replied with a full mouth.

"Where is Evanston?" Cassidy asked.

"Just north of Chicago."

"Chicago… in Illinois?" she clarified, despite fully knowing the answer.

"That's the one," Jake nodded. Cassidy looked down at her plate for a moment. She'd gone from excited to overwhelmed in a matter of seconds. The air felt heavy. She took a big gulp of wine.

"That's, that's a good school," she said lamely before digging back into her dinner. Her mind swirled as they ate in silence for a few minutes. Finally, Jake broke the quiet.

"Cassidy, I need you to say something. Please."

"What do you want me to say?" she asked as she swallowed hard on a large bite of garlic bread.

"What are you thinking?"

"What? What? Wah?" Cassidy stuttered. Jake tried to hide a smirk which annoyed her a little bit, if she was honest.

"Simple question."

"No! No, not a simple question!" Cassidy said, dropping her fork on the plate. The loud clank was oddly satisfying. "It's a loaded question. It's a multi-layer question. It's an overwhelming question!"

113

"Okay… then go through the layers."

"Ugh! Um, okay," she began, running her fingers through her hair roughly. "I… I'm excited that you were head hunted… that is honestly really cool. But I'm less excited that you're looking at a job three states away. However, if I object to that, it sounds like I don't want you to have this opportunity. Or that I'm harboring jealously about not having a job and you getting fucking head hunted by a prestigious university three states away," she huffed, leaning her head back for a long moment.

"Oh," Jake said. Cassidy's head snapped back down as she glared at him.

"I'm going to need a hell of a lot more than that, Sullivan."

"Well, honestly, I've been racking my brain trying to figure out how you were going to respond … you fell somewhere in the middle of my guesses." Jake shrugged before taking another bite of garlic bread. Cassidy bit down on her lip, hard.

"Jake, please don't make jokes right now. This is a big thing."

"I know it's a big thing. It's huge!"

"Okay… well, did you make a decision? Or are you waiting on me to make a decision, or what?" Cassidy asked, reaching for her wine again and downing the contents. She felt like her heart was in her throat.

"I don't have a final decision yet, but, well, depending on how this," he gestured between the two of them, "goes, I really want to drive out there and meet with some people and see what it's like in person before I commit to going or not."

"Oh," Cassidy let out a heavy breath. Her mind was racing. She was mildly annoyed that Jake was continuing to eat as if they were simply talking about the weather.

"Oh?" he asked, mouth full of pasta.

114

"You… you said if this goes well, if the telling me goes well. What did you think I would do? Throw a plate at the wall and storm out?"

"Honestly, it was one of the scenarios I played out, yes."

"Really?"

"If it helps, it was in the running for worst case scenario."

"In the running? What was my worst reaction in your head?"

"Death."

"You thought I'd die?"

"God no, I thought you'd kill me," Jake said plainly.

"You really thought I'd kill you?"

"How about I answer that when you aren't holding a fork," he suggested, the hint of a smirk on his face. Cassidy leaned over and punched his shoulder with her left fist.

"Ow," he chuckled. Cassidy smiled, despite herself.

"Jake," she cocked her head slightly.

"Cassidy, look, I love you, but you are, just the tiniest bit… intense, no, passionate," he said with a wince. Cassidy knew it was true, but whenever someone else pointed it out she felt her teeth clench in annoyance.

"Fine."

"So, yeah, I played out a few different options in my head."

"And made homemade sauce," she pointed out.

"And made homemade sauce," he nodded.

"That's annoyingly good."

"Good."

"And it's pacifying me slightly," Cassidy smirked as she twirled a forkful of spaghetti before popping it into her mouth. Jake grinned.

"Well, while you're slightly pacified, I wanted to ask you

if… you wanted to head out to Evanston -- Chicago -- with me for a few days?"

"Wait, when?"

"I was thinking of driving out on Saturday. We can look around on Sunday, get a feel for the area. I'd meet with some people at the university on Monday, then we'd head back home on Tuesday."

"Oh, wow!"

"I already took Monday and Tuesday as personal days at MU next week," he said. Cassidy swallowed hard. This suddenly felt like a lot again.

"Oh, I, um, I don't know if I--" she awkwardly stuttered.

"Because you're doing what?" Jake asked flatly. It was true she had nothing else to do with her time, but it was a low blow. Cassidy shot him an annoyed side-eye and she could see him grimace. "Sorry, that, that came out wrong."

"No, it came out right," she said, absentmindedly spinning her fork on her plate.

"Cassidy, I would really, really like it if you would go with me," Jake pleaded. Cassidy didn't answer for a long moment. She could feel Jake watching her.

"I guess," she let out a loud sigh. "I guess we never really have had a trip away together before, other than visiting family. But this would be just us."

"Yes, it would be just us," Jake said. While he kept his voice calm and steady, the look on his face was absolutely beaming. She couldn't help but smile back at him. He looked so happy.

"Look, I'm excited about an impromptu trip, but I'm also freaking out a bit because, well, this is more than just a trip. Like, what are we going to do? I've never even thought about moving out of state… at least not yet. And I don't know what this means for me or for us or… Do I really want to just follow a boy? I have a life here! I, I, I…" Cassidy frantically rambled. Jake scooted his chair slightly and reached over to grab her forearms to keep her still.

"Cassidy, Cassidy, Cassidy," he said until she stopped talking and just looked at him.

"What?" she asked, her voice low.

"You're getting ahead of yourself. I mean, we're not even there yet. What if I hate the city? What if I hate the school? Or my potential boss that's interviewing me? Nothing is set in stone. We're just going to go check the place out. We won't even have a decision made by Tuesday," he assured her, gently rubbing her inner arms with his thumbs. Cassidy took a slow, deep breath.

"I know, but I just want to be prepared. This is potentially huge and I'm kind of freaking out."

"I know you are," Jake said with a chuckle.

"Jacob!" Cassidy scolded before rolling her eyes.

"Ugh."

"What? You don't like Jacob?"

"I don't dislike it, but generally, if I was called Jacob, I was in trouble," he said.

"True, I mean I could… oh, my gosh!"

"What?"

"I was about to say I could call you by your full name, but I just realized I don't know your middle name. Oh, my gosh! I'm going away for a weekend with a guy I've been dating for like six months and I don't know his full name!" Cassidy gasped. She felt a mixture of amused and horrified by that. Jake, however, started to laugh, clearly he found it amusing.

"Is it really that bad?"

"I don't know, but feels strange."

"Okay, well, my middle name is Thomas. Are you happy now?" He raised an eyebrow playfully. Cassidy nodded.

"Jacob Thomas Sullivan," she said rhythmically. Jake nodded. "Thomas after your dad, right?"

"Yep," he confirmed. Cassidy knew little about his late father, Tom. Mostly just that he had worked all the time, had been a loud, angry man, and that he'd openly preferred Will to Jake. Tom and Jake's relationship had been frosty, at best, and Jake never seemed to miss the man much at all.

"Jacob Thomas Sullivan," Cassidy repeated.

"What's yours?"

"Lynne," she smiled.

"Ah, after your mother."

"Yep."

"Our parents aren't exactly creative, are they?" Jake teased, making Cassidy laugh.

"Well, not with either of us."

"True. You have a million brothers; they can't all have the middle name Arthur."

"Only Ben does," Cassidy told him. Jake looked surprised.

"That is not the brother I would have guessed!"

"Well, apparently my parents had agreed on Alex's first name but neither liked the alliteration of Alexander Arthur. I guess it got pushed to the side until Ben came and they wanted to get it in… especially after I got Lynne," Cassidy smiled.

"Okay, well, Cassidy Lynne Banker, can we finish our dinner and start talking about our upcoming trip?" he asked, sliding his hands down to hers and giving them a squeeze. Cassidy nodded.

"Sounds good."

# Chapter 13

Cassidy slowly twirled the radio knob as the music turned to static once more. They were getting quite close to Chicago; city stations should be taking over soon. She couldn't wait. While the drive had been pleasant, the mid-song static as they drove out of range was getting old.

She and Jake had loaded up his truck and headed west before eight o'clock that morning. It was a seven-hour drive from Erie to Evanston, and their goal was to arrive by late afternoon. They had only stopped twice, once for lunch and fuel outside of Toledo, and again for a second fill up in Indiana. They were making good time and as much fun as they had been having, talking and laughing the whole trip, Cassidy was ready to be out of the truck.

"We should be close to the Illinois border," Cassidy commented after finding a station playing the Doobie Brothers and returning her attention to the map book in her lap.

"There is a sign up there." Jake pointed at a large green sign overhead that was just far enough they couldn't quite read yet.

The truck zoomed along with the growing traffic.

"Welcome to Chicago," Cassidy read as they approached. "Wow! We're in the city already?" she glanced down at her map once more.

"City limits, I'm guessing." Jake said. "But we still have to get to Evanston, which is on the north side of the city."

"But that shouldn't take that long, right?" Cassidy said. But as soon as the words were out of her mouth the red taillights of the cars in front of them started to glow, and their comfortable 70 mile-per-hour pace was down to a 30 mile-per-hour crawl.

"I think this will be the whole final hour of the trip," Jake hummed, sounding amused yet annoyed.

"Ugh. Our little city has not adequately prepared me for this big city traffic," she said, propping her right elbow on the window frame.

"It hasn't," Jake chuckled. "But I'm using my years of training from driving to Penn State games on Saturday mornings. Not a city, but those back roads don't handle the tailgating traffic."

"Didn't you live on campus?"

"When I went to school there, yes, but I grew up going to games and went to some after graduation. If you're not living there, it's a mess."

"Ahhh."

Despite the slow pace, heavy traffic, iffy merge attempts, and an absurd number of traffic lights, the drive through the city was kind of fun. Neither Cassidy nor Jake had ever been there before and they enjoyed seeing the skyscrapers, monuments, and general chaos that all big cities contain. Even with the grey winter sky and large piles of discolored snow everywhere, the city was still beautiful and captivating.

Almost a full hour after spotting the "Welcome to Chicago" sign, Jake pulled up to the large, red brick Hilton they had booked. It was only a couple of blocks from the University campus on the north edge of the city. After a slight struggle through an unpleasant underground parking garage, Jake and Cassidy took the elevator upstairs, checked in, and were given the keys to their room on the fourth floor.

"We're here!" Cassidy said happily with a breathy smile as she dropped her puffy coat, hat, and duffle bag on the bulky chair that was next to the king-sized bed.

"Yeah," Jake hummed, setting his bag and outer garments on the floor next to the chair as he took in his surroundings.

"Are you excited?" Cassidy asked, turning to face him as she rested her left knee on edge of the mattress.

"Yeah. Well, I mean, it feels surreal."

"Surreal? It's Chicago, not Paris!"

"I know, but … right now it's like a little vacation with my girlfriend. The whole reason we're here hasn't quite hit yet," he admitted with a shrug.

"Maybe that's good?"

"Ya think?"

"Maybe. I mean, you might be looking at the city more objectively… at least until your meetings on Monday," Cassidy suggested.

"Hmmm, not a bad thought."

"Do you know what else is a good thought?" she raised an eyebrow as she reached out for him. Jake chuckled as he walked forward and placed his hands on her hips.

"It's a very good plan, but I thought you wanted to be out of the car and stretch your legs."

"We are out of the car and my legs will get super stretched," she winked, wrapping her right arm around his shoulder and plunging the fingers of her left hand into his hair.

"You make excellent arguments."

"I know!" Cassidy grinned before pecking him on the lips.

"And I, personally, have never had sex in the state of Illinois before, so."

"So, that is totally a bucket list item."

"Absolutely! It's up there."

"Is this going to be our thing? We have to have sex in every new state we're in?" Cassidy asked with a laugh.

"I'm all for it," Jake said enthusiastically. "I'm not saying it has to happen the moment we cross the border, but definitely at some point during the stay."

"I love this plan." She kissed his chin. "Does that mean I need to make a checklist?"

"Oh, one hundred percent," he said, making Cassidy laugh. He kissed her on the cheek.

"I will definitely write one up when we get back to PA."

"Perfect," Jake whispered, kissing lower on her cheek. He was slowly making his way toward her mouth.

"Wait, wait!" Cassidy said, tapping his shoulders playfully.

"Hmm?"

"Do we have to spend the night or just time in the state? Because we drove through Ohio and Indiana today," she pointed out. Jake paused, looking entertained.

"I have not thought of the rules that clearly, but if you'd like, we can make a few extra stops on the drive back…"

"That's going to be a long ass trip home."

"The Indiana border is so close!"

"In distance, but we just sat in an hour of traffic to get away from that border. We'll have to be further into the state."

"Ah, real Indiana," Jake teased. Cassidy gave him a gentle shove.

"That's not what I meant."

"Or, if you suddenly want to be real efficient about all of this, we could find some place on the Indiana--Ohio border. It'll be two for one."

"That's cheating!"

"Says the girl who won't settle for Gary, Indiana," Jake said. Cassidy laughed loudly. She loved their playful banter.

"Shut up and kiss me," she said. Jake grinned before crashing his lips onto hers. The kiss deepened in seconds as her arms wrapped tightly around his shoulders and his arms circled her waist. They kissed passionately for almost a minute before Jake pushed her backwards, practically tackling her onto the bed. They broke apart laughing as they momentarily detangled and repositioned themselves on the bed so their heads were on the pillows. Cassidy snuggled close and kissed him.

"Excited to cross off Illinois?" Jake teased.

"Yes. Best welcome to a state ever!"

"Good."

"But after this, can we go out of the hotel and find someplace cool for dinner?"

"Oh, definitely," he nodded.

"This first, though?"

"This first," Jake grinned, pressing his lips to hers and rolling on top of her as her right leg wrapped around his waist.

123

The purple and grey sweatshirt selection was quite impressive. Cassidy perused the incredibly large university bookstore on campus. She was fairly certain her entire freshman dormitory at Edinboro University could fit in there. What a difference from a little state school to a massive university! Jake was currently in his interview and going into his third hour. She knew that he had a tour, multiple people to meet, and a lengthy list of questions he had prepared, so it was not going to be a quick event.

After their christening of Illinois on Saturday afternoon, Cassidy and Jake went out and walked around the few city blocks surrounding their hotel. Despite being bundled and used to cold, snowy weather, the Chicago winter air felt piercing. They found a Korean restaurant and had an amazing dinner – the first time either of them had tried Korean food. It definitely wouldn't be the last.

Sunday was a full day of exploration. After chickening out with attempting to navigate the subway, they took a taxi down to the heart of Chicago and spent the day visiting museums, the riverwalk, and even the aquarium. They had deep dish pizza for lunch, snacked on Garrett Popcorn, and went to a beautiful Mediterranean restaurant for dinner where Cassidy had lamb stew and Jake tried a grilled shrimp kebab. Both were delicious. After dinner they found a brewery where they drank a couple of beers as they chatted, relaxed, and had the most delightful people watching. Too tipsy to attempt to navigate, they took the long cab ride back north and stumbled into their hotel room a few minutes after midnight.

Grabbing coffee and a bagel for breakfast on Monday morning, Jake and Cassidy walked to Northwestern to explore the campus. It was lightly snowing, and it made the historic campus look almost magical. The students were all back from break and there was a fun atmosphere. Jake and Cassidy wandered aimlessly for a couple of hours, exploring buildings and snow covered sports fields, before grabbing a quick lunch at a sub shop. Then Jake headed to his interview. Cassidy gave him a quick good luck kiss and waved him off.

She went back to the hotel for a nap and a chance to warm up a bit. Once rested and freshened up, Cassidy returned to campus and started her exploration of the university bookstore, which honestly, she could have been happily lost in for hours.

Cassidy unfolded one of the sweatshirts and held it up to examine it. Should she buy one? Even just as a souvenir? This trip had been one of the best of her entire life. She wanted to remember it forever. She no longer knew what she wanted from Jake's interview. A few days ago, she had wanted it to fail, but she thought that might be changing. She quickly refolded the shirt and returned it to the shelf. Perhaps a "Chicago" refrigerator magnet from one of the cheesy tourist shops would suffice.

She had just made it to the overwhelming selection of hats when she heard her name called. Jake was walking quickly toward her with a big grin on his face. It must have gone well. Cassidy couldn't decide if she should cheer or just start crying. Possibly both.

"Hey!" he said, slinging his arm around her shoulder.

"Hi, how did it go?"

"Come on, let's get out of here. I'll tell you all about it."

"Okay, but where are we going?" Cassidy asked as she let him lead her out of the large store and back to the cold outdoors. She involuntarily bristled as the wind hit her in the face.

125

"Let's go get something to eat."

"It's only three-thirty," she pointed out with a giggle.

"We can get a drink and a snack, just somewhere inside where we can sit."

"Inside sounds great!" Cassidy agreed. They both zipped up their coats as far as they could go and walked as closely as they could, Jake with his arm around her shoulders, and Cassidy had her left arm around his back. It may have looked romantic, but honestly, they were both just trying to keep warm.

It was a very brisk twenty-minute walk to get off campus and to a bar and grill they had passed a few times previously. It was warm and rustic looking. The restaurant was over half full. A small TV over the bar showed sports analysts recounting last night's Blackhawks game. Cassidy and Jake were seated at a small wooden booth. They quickly ordered a beer each and a large plate of fries to share.

"Well? Are you going to tell me how it went?" Cassidy asked with a smile. Jake grinned back.

"It went… perfect," he breathed.

"Perfect?"

"Yes! Everyone was great. They answered every single one of my questions. I got a tour of the math department, met some of the heads. Then we went over to the athletic department and met the staff there for the baseball team. They have a huge staff. About three times the number of people at Mercyhurst."

"It's a significantly bigger school."

"Yeah. I just… I don't know, it went better than I could have hoped," he said. He looked slightly dazed. Cassidy willed herself not to burst into tears.

"Did you sign anything?"

"No, not yet. I have a week to decide. They told me to take a few days and think about it. They don't want to put in all the effort of bringing me on just for me to panic, change my mind and quit."

"Smart," she nodded. They were interrupted by their waitress returning to the table.

"Here you go," she set two full glasses of beer on the table. "And those fries will be out in a minute."

"Thanks," Jake smiled at her.

"Did they talk about salary? What about moving time? When would you start -- if you take the job? What about benefits? Where would you live?"

"Cassidy," Jake said calmly, reaching over and taking her hand in his. "This is a lot, I know."

"It is a lot, and you need to go over all the details," she said, picking up her glass and taking a large gulp.

"Yes, I know, and I asked a lot of questions. I thought they would think it was ridiculous, but they seemed to enjoy it."

"Okay."

"Do you want me to go over it all?"

"Obviously! We're not here to discuss anything else," Cassidy pointed out. She knew her words came out sassier than she intended.

"Fair," he smiled.

"Run it down: the good, the bad, the ugly," she said, pulling her hand out of his as she gestured. Jake excitedly pulled a yellow notepad out of his bag.

"Alright," he began, but was interrupted by another appearance by their waitress.

"Piping hot, here you go!" she said cheerily as she set down a massive basket of crispy fries and a bottle of ketchup. They sure did look delicious. Cassidy wasted no time in squeezing a dollop of ketchup out in the corner of the basket as Jake once again thanked the waitress and she disappeared.

"You were saying," Cassidy prompted, popping a fry in her mouth.

"Okay, well, the salary is great – a lot more than my current one."

"Chicago … um, Evanston, is a lot more expensive than Erie."

"I know."

"Of course, you've done the math," Cassidy smirked as she ate another fry.

"I have. But the money is good, even for out here. Benefits and days off are almost identical to what I have now. Definitely more responsibilities. I mean, it will be the same with the baseball team, but it is a much bigger program with a lot of travel."

"Do you want to do more travel?"

"I think so. It would be a cool way to see more of the country," Jake said as he reached for a few fries.

"True."

"I'd be teaching three classes."

"All stats?"

"Yes. One intro class, which they said would be mostly freshman and sophomores, and then two upper-level ones."

"What do you think about that?"

"I like the idea of teaching more, though honestly I'm not thrilled about getting freshman."

"I'm sure they won't be that bad."

"Second semester won't be, but first semester... yes. The incoming freshman that come for baseball camp each summer are like squirrels." Jake groaned making Cassidy chuckle.

"Eh, a bunch will probably drop the class in the first month, then you'll be left with the kids that want to be there."

"Yeah."

"And you like teaching the higher-level stuff."

"I really do."

"And you'll have two of those."

"Yeah."

"How often are the classes?" Cassidy asked.

"Intro is a two-hour class twice a week. Apparently, it's usually Tuesdays and Thursdays, but some semesters it can differ. And both upper levels are ninety minutes each, three days a week."

"So you'll have two classes on Monday, Wednesdays, and Fridays and one on Tuesdays and Thursdays? Sounds nice."

"I think one of the uppers is Monday, Tuesday, Thursday, but yeah, I should have a full week." Jake took a sip of his beer.

"You like the school, you like the team, what about housing? Moving? When do you have to start?"

"I would just find a local apartment to rent. As for moving," Jake checked his notes, "they offered to pay for a moving truck."

"How would you get your truck here?"

"I'd either tow it, or maybe Will can drive out with me and then fly home."

"Okay." Cassidy took a large gulp for her glass. This was feeling very real.

"But I'm not leaving next week," he assured her cheerily.

"When would you leave?"

"Summer. Well, just before."

"Summer?"

"I'd be shadowing part of the summer semester, and then helping out with the baseball camps and clinics, and then the fall semester starts."

"So, you'd hit the ground running."

"Kind of. Ideally, I'd like to have a week to move in and get my bearings, but shadowing shouldn't be too taxing," he explained as he grabbed for more fries. Cassidy watched him. He was excited. She could see the wheels turning in his head as he planned this next adventure. She should be happy for him. She should be excited with him. But his excitement was over four hundred miles from her entire world. Hell, it was in a different time zone. Cassidy didn't know what to feel or to say. She just hurt.

"Okay," she breathed.

"Cassidy, come on, I need you to tell me what you think," Jake urged before taking another drink.

"I think you've already made up your mind."

"I'm running on adrenaline right now. They told me to take the week to decide and that's what I'm going to do, but I would like some feedback."

"I…" Cassidy paused, twirling a fry between her fingers. "I think it's perfect."

"Except you sound like you would rather be at the dentist."

"Well, I'm frustrated."

"I can tell."

"Jake, this is serious." Cassidy shot him a look.

"No, no, I know it is," he held up his hands in defense.

"This is all perfect. The perfect job, the perfect everything. Except for the fact that it's in a different state and I have no idea what the hell that means for us… For me, if I'm being honest." She swallowed hard.

"You switched from 'us' to 'me.'"

"I, I, I, ugh, how am I supposed to phrase this…?"

"Look, we're still talking about all of this. I don't want anything decided tonight. But if I do take this job… I would really like you to come with me."

"Come with you," Cassidy repeated slowly.

"We can start our own life here."

"We have a life!"

"We do, but we can start something for us, a new path, new opportunities. We'll just figure it all out," he said adamantly.

"Figure it all out. On our own. In a strange city. Hours away from our friends and family."

"Yes. It's almost romantic," Jake smiled.

"It's scary as hell."

"That adds to it all. Think about the pilgrims! They traveled across the ocean for a new adventure and life together! Romantic!"

"Like, half of them died in the first year."

"And half didn't."

"I don't like this fifty-fifty-chance-we-may-die analogy." Cassidy made a face.

"Okay, okay. I'm just saying, this is something I want to really discuss this over the next few days," Jake said earnestly.

"Okay," Cassidy let out a deep breath. "We'll discuss it. Really lay it all out."

"Great, thank you."

"I mean, we do have a seven hour drive tomorrow."

"We do! With two stops. Maybe more if we dip over the Michigan border. It's only like, a five-mile detour," Jake winked. Cassidy rolled her eyes.

"Don't push your luck, Sullivan."

"Eh, we'll see."

"Okay… but we still have all evening here. Can we table the job talk and enjoy our last night in the city?" she asked.

"I would love nothing more," Jake said. He raised his glass. Cassidy held hers up and clinked it against his. They both took a long drink. She was excited to enjoy a final night downtown before reality came crashing back in.

# Chapter 14

The microwave beeped and the smell of popcorn filled the air. Cassidy poured the contents of the hot bag into a large white bowl and carried it into the living room.

"Ah, yay," Marissa said happily, reaching up for the bowl as Cassidy walked by to take her seat on the other end of the couch. Cassidy playfully pulled the bowl out of Marissa's grasp before setting it on the couch between them and they both dug in.

Cassidy had arrived back home from Evanston less than an hour ago. Marissa was just finishing dinner when Cassidy walked back into the apartment. After a quick hello, Cassidy took a much-needed shower and changed into her PJs. Now the girls were both comfy and settled on the couch. Marissa was anxious for her promised debrief of the trip.

"Alright," Marissa said as she chomped on a mouthful of popcorn. "What happened on the trip?"

"A lot," Cassidy said honestly.

"I need more than that."

"It was fantastic!"

"Your face is not relaying that."

"Because... I think Jake is taking the job," Cassidy sighed.

"He didn't have to decide there?" Marissa asked.

"No. They're giving him until Friday."

"That's nice."

"Yes, it is. They are very nice, the school is very nice, the city is very nice," Cassidy said glumly.

"Okay, again, your words and face don't match," Marissa pointed out. She tossed a kernel of popcorn at Cassidy and she gave a small chuckle.

"I'm feeling lots of things at once."

"I can tell."

"The trip was wonderful. Honestly, one of my favorites ever. Jake and I had so much fun. I loved it."

"I'm glad," Marissa smiled.

"And the interview went well. Jake loves the job."

"He's taking it?"

"He really wants to."

"Okay... so what does that —?"

"I'm still not sure what that means for me or us," Cassidy interrupted.

"Hmmm."

"We talked about it a lot."

"About the job?"

"About it all. I mean, it was a long car ride."

"Yeah, you got back later than I would have thought."

"Well... we made a few stops," Cassidy blushed. Marissa watched her for a moment.

"Oh, gah, you had car sex, didn't you? Ugh, and on the interstate?!"

"Not car sex per se..."

"Please don't tell me it was gross gas station sex?"

"Ew, no!"

"But you're not going to tell me where?"

"You won't be happy," Cassidy admitted in a low chuckle as Marissa gave a whine and covered her face dramatically.

"Ugh! Okay, perverted stops aside, you said you talked?"

"Yeah. Yeah, we did," Cassidy nodded.

"And?"

"And he's highly, highly considering taking the offer. I mean, he's talking like he's thinking about it, but I know he's decided. He wants this. He needs this. I mean, it's perfect for him."

"Mmmm," Marissa hummed as she scrunched up her nose.

"What?"

"No, no. Continue."

"You made a face like it's not a good job for him."

"I'm sure the job is great, but you're talking like it's the only perfect thing for him."

"Are you alluding to me?"

"A bit."

"Well, the job is perfect, and… Well, he wants me to go with him," Cassidy bit her lip. Marissa just stared at her.

"Move to Chicago?"

"Yeah."

"What would you do there?"

"I would have to find a job."

"So, just start over?"

"Well, it's not like I have a job here…" Cassidy said. Marissa winced.

"Shit."

"Yeah, shit." Both girls sighed in defeat. A long, heavy

pause filled the air.

"Well," Marissa began slowly. "What would you be saying if you still had your job here?"

"But I don't."

"I know that, but that is almost like pushing your hand… so, what if this happened and you and Jake had your trip and all that is the same, but you had a job here that you would need to quit?"

"Umm…"

"Just think about it."

"I don't know how to answer that."

"Would it make a difference in your decision or trepidation?"

"I want Jake to be happy."

"I get that."

"Either way, I'd have to go find a job there," Cassidy said flatly as she reached forward and grabbed a firm fistful of popcorn. It crunched slightly in her hand.

"I know."

"Marissa, what do you want me to say? I'm stressed. This sucks. No matter what I choose, I'm going to be sad."

"I know."

"Stop saying that," Cassidy snapped. Marissa sighed.

"Look, I don't want you to move. I'm going to be selfish and I'm not ready for us to move apart."

"Clearly, I'm not either."

"But," Marissa swallowed, "you've been happier with Jake than I've ever seen you."

"So, you're saying I should go?"

"No."

"So, I should stay?"

"No."

"Well, those are my two options," Cassidy pointed out. They shared a sad smile.

"When do you have to tell him by?"

"He has until Friday to make his decision, but I'm thinking he's going to call on Thursday."

"So, two days?"

"I mean, he won't move for a few months, but I'd definitely need to make a decision before he finds an apartment," Cassidy shrugged.

"What about your family?"

"They'll stay here," Cassidy quipped. Marissa rolled her eyes.

"I mean are you going to make the decision with them?"

"No. I like to know what I want before I get them involved."

"Fair," Marissa chuckled.

"I don't how I'd even tell them… either way."

"Why?"

"It's going to be a mess. I leave, they'll be sad; I stay, they'll miss Jake."

"You think Jake is part of their preference now?" Marissa smirked.

"They loved him. I think they like him more than me sometimes!"

"I wouldn't go that far."

"Okay, just Matty," Cassidy teased. Her heart felt tighter thinking about her family. What the hell was she going to do? The two friends sat in a comfortable, sad silence for a long minute.

"What do you need from me?" Marissa asked.

"Make the decision for me?" Cassidy asked with a grimace.

"I can't do that," Marissa said sadly.

Cassidy looked surprised. "What? I would have expected you to tell me I have to stay!"

"Dunno," Marissa replied lamely.

"Oh, my gosh."

"I don't want you to go, but I don't want you to mope around here for a year after he leaves, either!"

"You think I'll mope for a year?"

"You did after Kevin dumped you."

"That was a low blow," Cassidy bit her tongue.

"I'm sorry."

"I know."

"Cassidy… I can't decide for you. But you should think one year from now, what will you be doing? What will life be like, either way? You have to make your choice based on where you want to be for your twenty-seventh birthday."

"Hmmm."

"And do me a favor? Don't make a decision in two days."

"So, three or four?" Cassidy joked.

"Yes, that's exactly what I meant," Marissa replied sarcastically.

"I know what you meant."

"Just, keep me in the loop."

"Definitely."

"Do you want to watch some TV?" Marissa asked, repositioning herself slightly.

"Yeah, sure. I could use a distraction," Cassidy said as Marissa grabbed the remote.

"It's almost nine – Moonlighting will be starting soon."

"Bruce Willis will help," Cassidy smirked as Marissa flipped to the channel. Despite the distraction, her mind continued to swirl. She had no idea what she was going to do.

# Chapter 15

Jake accepted the job at Northwestern Thursday morning. She'd known he would. It was a fantastic opportunity for him. However, she still had not made a decision for herself. He took her out on Friday in a joint celebration – his new job and her birthday on the nineteenth, which was that Saturday. Despite the daunting changes on the horizon, the night was perfect. Jake took them to the Chinese restaurant where they had had their first date, followed by the movies to see Good Morning, Vietnam. It had come out at Christmas, but neither had had a chance to see it yet. The night was perfectly topped off by Jake spending the night at Cassidy's apartment. They didn't get to sleep until the wee hours of the morning.

Saturday morning, Cassidy's birthday started the same way it had every year since her sophomore year of college when she turned twenty – Marissa waking her up with a loud rendition of "Happy Birthday" as she brought her a chocolate eclair in bed and concluded her song with party popper of exploding confetti on her comforter. It was a tradition that made Cassidy laugh each year -- and one that startled the hell out of Jake. He was extraordinarily grateful that he'd decided to put his boxers back on before falling asleep. Marissa and a plate of doughnuts were suddenly on the bed with them as pink and green confetti showered over their heads.

Once Jake's heart rate had returned to normal, they finished their breakfast treats, cleaned up, got ready for the day. The three enjoyed a peaceful and happy morning together before Jake left shortly after lunch.

That afternoon Cassidy drove to her parents' house for a birthday dinner with the family for her and Eric. Cassidy honestly couldn't remember the last time she'd celebrated on her actual birthday with her family. Probably her eighteenth birthday in senior year of high school. That felt like a lifetime ago.

"Happy birthday!" Lynne called loudly, opening the front door the moment Cassidy stepped onto the porch.

"Thanks, mom," Cassidy said, hugging her.

"Twenty-six. I can't believe it!" Lynne said, pulling Cassidy inside.

"Oh, it smells good in here," Cassidy commented as the scent of the kitchen hit her nose.

"Why thank you – pot roast."

"Mmm."

"It should be ready in an hour," Lynne smiled.

"Ahh! You're here! Happy birthday!" Ellie gushed, bounding down the stairs. Eric slowly trailed behind her.

"Thanks!" Cassidy grinned at her almost sister-in-law before Ellie crashed into her with a big hug.

"It's fun having two people to celebrate!" Ellie said, pulling back.

"Oh, yes, yes," Cassidy said, looking over at her twin who was now standing on the bottom step behind Ellie. "Happy Birthday!"

"Happy Birthday," he nodded. The two shared a smirk.

"Where's Jake?" Ellie asked curiously.

"Oh!" Cassidy paused in surprise.

"You didn't dump him already, did you?" Eric groaned.

"Wait, you broke up?" Ellie asked sadly.

"What?" Cassidy tried to interject.

"You finally date someone good, but give him the heave," Eric said with a sigh.

"Guys, guys, no! I didn't dump Jake. We're great. I just didn't realize he was invited, or think to ask," Cassidy frantically clarified.

"Oh, good," Ellie smiled.

"Yes, good," Lynne agreed looking relieved before turning back into the kitchen.

"Hey," Cassidy reached over and pushed Eric's arm. "Did you really not like any of my boyfriends before?" she asked curiously.

"No. All douchebags," he replied flatly. Ellie let out a snort but quickly tried to hold her reaction back after seeing Cassidy's annoyed look at Eric. She was clearly torn on which twin she wanted to support in the moment.

"What about Mike Karlin from down the street? We all used to play together as kids."

"That's called geographical convenience – it's how kid friendships work."

"You never liked him?"

"No, he was annoying. And he got progressively more annoying for that, what, ten days you dated him in ninth grade," Eric pointed out.

"We dated for like two months," Cassidy corrected.

"My deepest apologies to that love story." He rolled his eyes.

"Oh, would you like me to give dear Ellie the run-down of all the winners you dated?" Cassidy challenged.

"We've already had that discussion and she was unfazed," Eric smirked.

"Makes sense. Lot of low cards in that hand. She has no competition," Cassidy sassed before turning to Ellie. "And I mean that with love, Ellie. You're fantastic and definitely a high card. Truly exceeded the low bar your predecessors set."

"Thanks, I think?" Ellie chuckled.

"It's a compliment," Cassidy assured her with a smile.

A loud crash from outside startled the three. They shared a quick look before pulling open the front door and clamoring out onto the porch.

"Oh my God," Eric said in a low, mildly entertained voice. There, at the end of the driveway were both Matty and Ben's cars. Matty's was horizontal across the entrance of the drive while Ben's front bumper was resting against the mailbox, which was now at a forty-five degree angle. The red pick-up flag on the side had fallen off and was sticking up right out of the snow.

"What the hell happened?" Art boomed as he pushed around the twins and Ellie and stomped off the porch. Both Matty and Ben hopped out of their cars, yelling and pointing fingers.

"I was just coming down the street and he's up my ass!" Matty complained to Art.

"We're going to the same place!" Ben held his arms out in annoyance.

"Trying not to get hit by speed racer, here, I turned in but hit ice," Matty grumbled.

"You know you're not supposed to hit your breaks on ice. That's why you spun," Ben pointed out obnoxiously.

"Do I want to go out there?" Lynne called from the kitchen, the front door still wide open.

"No," Cassidy, Eric, and Ellie replied in unison.

"Good," Lynne replied, her focus on the meal.

"And what about you?" Art asked his youngest as he had reached the end of the driveway.

"I was trying to get in and Matty starts spinning, so I had to get out of the way."

"I wouldn't have spun if you weren't an idiot!" Matty argued.

"Get out of the way into the mailbox?" Art pointed at the strained post.

"Would you rather I hit Matty?"

"A little."

"What?!" Matty asked in a loud squeak.

"You'd be fine," Art said nonchalantly, his focus and annoyance still on his youngest.

"I could be dead," Matty argued.

"Yeah, dad! Matty could be dead," Ben said, attempting to argue his case.

"Are you going to fix this?" Art asked, pointing at the tilted pole once more.

"Not immediately," Ben said.

"Why not?"

"Because there's like, two feet of snow!" Ben used his boot to kick a clump in the air.

"There's always snow! It's winter!" Art said angrily.

143

"Which is why you should know how to drive in it," Matty chimed in. Ben flipped him off. Art ignored the gesture.

"How are we supposed to get our mail?" he asked.

"The box is still here, it'll work just fine," Ben said as he dramatically opened and closed the little door on the mailbox to prove his point.

"Wow," Cassidy said in a low voice. A giant smile grew on her face. Eric shared a similar expression.

"I know. This is the best birthday present ever," he said.

"They were so thoughtful this year." Cassidy and Eric shared a look before bursting into laughter. Ellie stood on the other side of Eric looking absolutely mesmerized as she watched her future in-laws arguing about the crooked mailbox's workability. Cassidy was laughing so hard she didn't hear what made her father scream, "that is not what that means!" but she decided it was best to leave the scene. She really wanted to warm up indoors.

Eric and Ellie followed her inside and closed the front door behind them.

"Hey mom, um, don't look outside," Eric said, his laughter slowly dying out as he walked into the kitchen with Ellie in tow.

"Ugh, too late." Lynne rolled her eyes and continued chopping. Cassidy joined them in the kitchen as soon as she finished shedding her winter gear.

It was a few more minutes before Art, Matty, and Ben all came inside. Cassidy noticed that Matty's left cheek looked especially red. When she asked if he was okay Matty explained that Ben threw a snowball at him and called him a few choice words in the process. Lynne quickly put the two on a few kitchen chores. Cassidy, Eric, and Ellie happily sat at the breakfast nook in the back of the kitchen and Art huffed off to his study.

Alex arrived thirty minutes later and got a spatula lobbed at him by Ben when his opening question was, "What happened to the mailbox?"

The family birthday celebration went quite smoothly after the initial kerfuffle. Everyone shared memories of the twins, and only a few were horribly embarrassing for Cassidy, which she actually felt was a pretty good ratio. Dinner was absolutely delicious, followed by the birthday cakes – yellow cake with chocolate frosting for Cassidy and chocolate cake with peanut butter frosting for Eric. Lynne always made sure each of them felt special on their birthday and they always had specially catered treats. The rest of the family enjoyed the tradition of getting two slices of cake. Ben prided himself on managing to down four slices every year!

After dinner, presents, and three rounds of Pictionary, the evening was winding down. Cassidy went to the kitchen to help her mom clean up while the boys and Ellie went through one of the old photo albums, laughing loudly.

"Here you go, I think this is everything from the table," Cassidy said as she carried a large stack of plates into the kitchen and set them on the island.

"Thank you, darling, but you don't have to help. It is your birthday, remember," Lynne smiled.

"I appreciate that, but this honestly is preferable to the old vacation photo album."

"Ah, the one with our trip down to the Carolinas?"

"How did you know?"

"Because you always get very upset when we go through that one." Lynne failed to suppress her chuckle.

"That's because they tell the same damn stories over and over," Cassidy grumbled.

"Memories don't really come with new stories."

"I know that."

"And I know that you're overly sensitive about them teasing you for throwing up at that restaurant when we stopped for lunch," Lynne acknowledged.

"I'm not overly sensitive; they are jerks! And--"

"Cassidy," Lynne said in a light, chiding tone.

"I'm not the bad guy here."

"I didn't say that; I just think you need to let this one go. You threw up -- everyone throws up."

"I didn't feel well from the windy roads and they put us at the table right next to the kitchen and the smoking section. It turned my stomach and I couldn't stop it." Cassidy let out a loud sigh.

"I understand, dear."

"I just was really sick. I don't need them mocking me spewing."

"You hit four tables and one of the waiters."

"It was so embarrassing. They made me stand off to the side and everyone there stared at me," Cassidy said, flinching at the memory.

"Your father paid for the three other tables' meals," Lynne said.

"I don't understand why we couldn't have just left?"

"I brought you in a change of clothes. And frankly, the staff worked so hard, we felt we had to stay. We tipped, like, forty percent," Lynne said, collecting the plates from the island and bringing them over to the sink.

"Mom," Cassidy groaned.

"You brought it up," Lynne shrugged as she poured more dish soap in the sink.

"Fine."

"So," Lynne began after a moment of silence. "Any luck on the job search?"

"Um…"

"Um?" Lynne looked over at her daughter with a raised eyebrow.

"Jake got a new job," Cassidy said.

"I didn't know he was looking."

"He wasn't."

"Oh… well, can you take his old job?" Lynne asked playfully. Cassidy paused for a moment. She'd never considered that angle before. She wasn't a statistician, but she was good at math and picked things up easily. Cassidy shook the idea out of her head.

"No."

"Is he still at Mercyhurst?"

"Um," Cassidy nervously tapped her fingers on the countertop.

"Cassidy Lynne Banker, are you pregnant?" Lynne asked in alarm.

"What? No! Mom!"

"You're acting weird, I just thought you were stalling on telling me something big."

"I'm not pregnant, mom."

"Okay," Lynne hummed as she scrubbed a spot on one of the dishes.

"But it is big…" Cassidy blurted out.

"Yeah?" Lynne set the plate down and shut off the water.

"Jake got a job at Northwestern University… outside of Chicago."

"Wow, that's very impressive!" Lynne said. Cassidy gave her a strange look.

"I mean, yeah, it is."

"But that's not the point," Lynne said knowingly.

"No, it's not."

"Is he taking the job?"

"Yes."

"And?"

"And what?" Cassidy asked.

"There are a lot of 'whats' there…"

"I know!" Cassidy whined.

"Cassidy, come here, talk to me," Lynne said as she dried her hands on the dishtowel. Cassidy walked around to her side of the island and rested her back along the edge of the counter.

"I don't know what to do, mom."

"What are your options?"

"Options make this sound clinical. This is my life!" Cassidy let out a loud breath.

"Lives have options, too."

"Yeah."

"So?"

"So… I like Jake a lot."

"I know," Lynne smiled.

"Jake wants to go. Well, he is going. I mean, it's a really good job. We went out to visit the other week. It was great. But I just… don't know. I mean, he would love me to go with him, but what the heck am I going to do there?"

148

"Find a job," Lynne suggested.

"You sound like Jake."

"Hmmm."

"I'm not… well, okay. I am afraid to start over in a new city, but I don't have a job there… or here."

"Right."

"Mom, I don't want to be the girl that follows a boy. And just have nothing of my own."

"I wouldn't want you to have nothing of your own. I may have waited for your father to finish college so we could marry, but I took my school nurse certification course and started working."

"I know!"

"Cassidy, you are very smart. You can find a job."

"Clearly I haven't proven that lately." Cassidy made a face.

"You were let go right before the holidays, it was really horrible timing," Lynne said.

"Are you wanting me to go?" Cassidy asked curiously.

"Well, obviously, I love having you close. I want you to find a job and be happy and have a good life. Jake makes you happier than I've ever seen you."

"Oh."

"Cassidy, I will support you. If you find a job you love here, and want to live your life in Pennsylvania, that's fantastic! But if you find a job you love somewhere else, I won't be angry with you."

"I appreciate that."

"You also don't need to decide this exact second."

"I kind of do… Jake leaves before the summer."

"Wow."

"Yeah."

"That's still many months away."

"I don't know what to do," Cassidy gulped loudly. Lynne reached over and rubbed her shoulders.

"You'll figure it out. You're twenty-six now. A full adult! You make your own choices."

"You're not going to tell me what to do?"

"You'll just do the opposite," Lynne smirked.

"Very funny, mom."

"Cassidy, make the decision that's right for you. Not for me, or your dad, or Jake, or Marissa. You," Lynne said firmly. Cassidy nodded.

"Thanks."

"But I will say, no matter what -- and you know I love Jake -- make sure you have something for you. Other than Jake."

"Yeah."

"I love your father, and we rely on each other for love and support. That's what marriage is. However, we have shared friends and separate ones. We have our separate jobs, we have our own interests. That doesn't mean we don't spend the majority of our time together or don't love one another more than life itself. But I don't want you to be solely dependent on Jake for every single aspect of your life."

"No, I'd kill him," Cassidy said. Lynne chuckled and nodded knowingly. "That's why I don't want to just follow a boy."

"I don't want you to just follow a boy. But I don't want you to disregard the boy because he has opened up a new path," Lynne said.

"Thanks, mom."

"Anytime."

"One more thing?"

"Yes?" Lynne asked.

"Don't tell dad yet… please?" Cassidy asked. Lynne hesitated for a moment before she let out a sigh.

"Fine, but you should tell him sooner rather than later. He's going to need time to process it. If you move, he'll be sad, and if you and Jake break up, he'll be sad."

"Dad likes Jake?"

"Very much. I'm going to get an earful tonight that he wasn't here."

"I'll make sure to coordinate a playdate for them, soon," Cassidy teased. Lynne laughed before kissing her daughter on the cheek.

"Alright, now go join your brothers, or I'll make you wash dishes on your birthday."

"Thanks, mom," Cassidy smiled before turning and heading out of the kitchen to join her father, brothers, and Ellie. She felt lighter after talking to her mom. This had been a great birthday.

# Chapter 16

The day was finally here. Saturday, February 6, 1988. Eric and Ellie's wedding. It was just below freezing and hadn't snowed for two days. By all accounts, the weather was downright pleasant for an Erie winter.

Cassidy was sitting in the passenger's seat of Laura's car as they drove through the city to the church on the far east side of Erie. The rest of the Banker family had been at the church before lunch for the full day of prep.

Both Cassidy and Laura had attended the rehearsal and dinner the evening before. There were three run-throughs, and still bumps. Cassidy and Laura watched in amusement from one of the side pews. Being left out of the wedding party had turned into quite a blessing as last week Cassidy listened to the saga of the bachelorette party from the previous month. While Ellie had extended her an invitation, her sister Kara firmly insisted that everything had been perfectly planned out for just the six of them, and that Cassidy being odd number seven would mess things up. Honestly, Cassidy had been thrilled to be brutally uninvited by Kara. The last thing she needed to do was pay too much for drinks, listen to the inside jokes of Ellie and her friends, and listen to Ellie talk about sex with her brother, ugh. Most importantly, Cassidy did not need to get into a fight and give Kara a black eye. Cassidy had a short fuse on a good day, and her almost sister-in-law's older sister drove her crazy. Lynne would never forgive her if she got into a brawl with the wedding party. However, Matty would quickly deem her his favorite sibling had it happened.

But all of those events had passed. It was wedding day. The big day!

After making amends with Eric, and her mother last summer, Cassidy had dropped her crusade for a personal invitation to the wedding. She even avoided asking for a plus one. She was determined to prove that she could be supportive and simply enjoy her brother's wedding without bringing any attention to herself. Not to mention with all of Alex's groomsman duties, she would get plenty of time to hang out with Laura one on one. Something she truly enjoyed.

"Are you excited?" Laura asked as they idled at a red light.

"Um, I guess, yeah," Cassidy shrugged with a smile.

"Okay," Laura chuckled.

"I'm not mad! Honestly, I'm happy. And really excited to see Ellie's dress."

"Did she tell you anything about it?"

"I believe the term she used was poofy," Cassidy said.

Laura hummed as she accelerated once more.

"Also, Matty bet me five bucks that at least one person was going to trip down the aisle," Cassidy smirked.

"What? Last night he bet Alex ten dollars that Eric was going to fumble his lines."

"Oh jeez… guess he's covering every odd. I wonder how many bets he's made in total?" Cassidy thought out loud.

"He'll forget all about it," Laura snorted. Cassidy frantically shook her head.

"No, Matty is very alert when money is involved. And surprisingly organized. I can only imagine that he has a whole ledger in a black book somewhere."

"Do you want to make a bet on how much he's going to make by tonight?" Laura teased.

"No thanks, Matty would demand a cut," Cassidy chuckled as they turned into the narrow driveway to the church. The church was a large, dark red brick building that looked like it had been there for a century. The large, snow-covered steeple must have been almost one hundred feet in the sky. The white snow glistened in the sun. Cassidy smiled up at it as she stepped out of the car before grabbing her purse and small tote bag with her dressy heels. She was wearing her snow boots until she got inside – the last thing she needed to do was wipe out in the parking lot or on the stairs into the church. Both Cassidy and Laura hurried into the warmth of the church.

"Oh, you're here!" Lynne gushed as the girls removed their bulky coats and boots in the narthex. Cassidy appreciated the spacious coat wall with benches for changing shoes.

"Hi mom," Cassidy said with a smile. Her mother looked beautiful. Her short, blonde hair had been curled and she was in a long, grey dress and black heels.

"Oh, don't you two look nice," Lynne said, coming to hug both Cassidy and Laura. Cassidy was in a long, petal pink dress with a thick belt around her waist, gold necklace and earrings, and grey heels. Her dirty blonde hair was pulled back in a low bun, with a few fluffy strands escaping. They framed her face perfectly. Laura wore a long, navy blue dress with black polka dots and elbow length sleeves. Her shoulder length dark brown and blue streaked hair looked effortless: completely untouched yet completely perfect all at once. That summed up Laura completely.

"Thank you, Lynne," Laura grinned as she hugged her.

"How are things going here?" Cassidy asked hugging her mother next.

"Oh, my goodness," Lynne let out a dramatic sigh.

"Here, come over here," Cassidy said, leading her mom away from the coat wall and to the far side of the narthex, Laura in step.

"What's going on?" Laura asked.

"Honestly, I'm so happy I'm the mother of the groom. It's just so much -- and I've got it easy compared to Ellie's mom," Lynne said. Laura snorted while Cassidy shook her head.

"Is everything going smoothly?" Laura asked.

"As far as I can tell, yes," Lynne nodded.

"Anyone drunk yet?" Cassidy asked playfully with a raised eyebrow.

"Benjamin may be a little tipsy," Lynne rolled her eyes.

"Excellent," Cassidy smirked.

"Anything you need?" Laura asked.

"No, no, honestly, I don't have much to do other than wait for Alex's cue for Dad to walk me down the aisle to our seats."

"That's good," Cassidy smiled.

"No, it's not! I'm all hyped up and anxious for no reason."

"Your son is getting married; you're supposed to be excited," Cassidy told her.

"Very excited!" Laura added. Lynne gave a small sigh.

"I guess guests will be arriving soon."

"You can help greet," Cassidy said.

"Yes! Remember, Cassidy and I showed up forty-five minutes early because we're family. Most people won't get here until less than thirty minutes to the start," Laura added.

"Are we the first people here other than the bridal party and such?" Cassidy asked, glancing around.

"Nonna and Pap arrived an hour early, as per usual," Lynne grumbled, referencing Art's parents who had a propensity for showing up at events significantly earlier than expected or wanted.

"Nonna and Pap are here? Where?" Cassidy asked excitedly. She loved her grandparents, quirks and all.

"Yes, yes, they insisted on holding their seats." Lynne gestured toward the sanctuary. "Art is with them. I told him that he can't let Pap start talking about Jimmy The Greek to everyone that sits near them." Laura gave a snort.

"I'll go in and steer the conversation to Willie Mays," Cassidy grinned.

"That's baseball; he can easily shift the conversation," Lynne warned.

"Lynne, we've got a few minutes, want to go out and have a quick cig with me?" Laura offered, pulling the half open pack out of her purse.

"Eh, what the hell," Lynne shrugged.

"Mom!"

"Go see your grandparents, and make sure your dad hasn't taken off his shoes," Lynne instructed before hastily following Laura outside. Cassidy shook her head before turning and heading into the mostly empty sanctuary.

It was about five minutes to three and the sanctuary had filled up considerably. Cassidy and Laura were seated in the second row from the front, Nonna and Pap right behind them. Cassidy attempted to be a sound shield between Pap's commentary and her mother's ears in the front row. The right side of the church was filled with cousins, old neighbors, former classmates, and friends of Eric and the whole Banker family. There was the slightly odd paradox of Cassidy seeing people she had gone to school with from kindergarten through to twelfth grade that she knew of, but didn't know personally anymore. They had been in different social circles. And yet, here they were to celebrate her twin. There had been a few awkward waves. She really wasn't looking forward to the uncomfortable small talk later that evening.

The left side of the church was just as full with Ellie's family and friends. Cassidy and Laura played a little game of trying to guess who was who: cousins? aunts? friends? Their game of making up fake back-stories for the guests was interrupted by the sound of someone clearing their throat in the aisle next to her.

"Can I join you?"

Cassidy looked up and gasped. Jake was standing at the edge of the pew in a black suit and dark green tie. She immediately leapt up and hugged him.

"Oh my gosh! What are you doing here?"

"Your brothers invited me," he grinned as they pulled apart.

"Jake!" Laura beamed from her seat.

"Hey," he waved.

"Come sit," Laura said, scooting over slightly and patting the pew next to her. Jake squeezed past Cassidy and took a seat between the girls as Cassidy returned to hers.

157

"When did they invite you? It better not have been this morning. They are so rude!" Cassidy rolled her eyes.

"No, no," Jake chuckled. "It was after I came to dinner the other month. I got a call the next day."

"What? Why didn't you tell me?" Cassidy asked in shock, slapping his thigh playfully.

"Eric thought it would be more fun as a surprise."

Cassidy made a face, then leaned over to ask Laura, "Did you know about this?"

"No. But while Alex is many things, a scheduling savant, he is not," Laura said.

"Well, I'm glad you're here," Cassidy smiled.

"Glad to be here!"

The organ started to play a few chords and anyone who wasn't seated yet hustled to find a spot. The interlude music sounded like a familiar hymn that Cassidy simply couldn't place. The peaceful melody flowed through the sanctuary as Cassidy looked around. It was beautifully decorated in white linens with white and red flowers covering almost the entire altar. Tall red candles were lit atop the posts on either side of the pews, and a long white carpet lined the aisle.

Suddenly the melody changed and the minister appeared at the altar in white robes and a red stoll. Cassidy wondered if his color coordination with the decorations was intentional or a happy accident. Either way, it was nice. She saw him nod toward the back of the church and Cassidy turned to see her parents walking down the aisle arm in arm. Lynne was beaming. Art looked like he was trying to see who all was there; his focus was anywhere but the aisle. Cassidy grinned at them as they took their seats directly in front of her.

Next down the aisle was May Hammond, Ellie's mom. She

was being escorted by Alex. May looked quite overwhelmed, yet stunning in a deep purple dress that shimmered as she walked. Once she had been seated in the front pew opposite Art and Lynne, Alex joined Eric and the other groomsmen up front. Matty was first in line as the best man. Eric and Matty had always been the closest. Alex took his spot after Matty, with Ben just behind. Next was Derek Emig -- he and Eric had been roommates since freshman year at Pitt -- and then Jeremy Deal. Jeremy had grown up in the Banker's neighborhood and he and Eric had been friends since preschool. Cassidy smiled at her old neighbor. She hadn't seen him in years. He had gone to college down south and stayed there.

All six of them were in grey suits with red ties. Eric had a red rose and sprig of baby's breath in his front pocket. They all looked great, even Ben, who was a tad bouncy. He had definitely taken a shot or two. Cassidy watched her twin. He looked happy. He smiled at Lynne, who Cassidy could hear sniffling from the row in front of her, before he caught her eye. They shared a knowing look and a smile. This was going to be a great day!

The music changed once more and the crowd began to coo. Cassidy turned to see two young girls and a little boy, all dressed up in reds and whites, make their way down the aisle. The ring bearer and one of the flower girls were the children of Cassidy's eldest cousin. Jenny was six and Tony was four. The other flower girl was a young cousin of Ellie named Sasha. Ellie had previously mentioned that she was four, as well. Their procession went as expected. Jenny diligently tossed her flower petals while bossing the other two around to get them down the aisle. There was a brief pause as Sasha tried to pick up all the petals and put them in her basket. Jenny frantically and loudly whispered corrections to her before Sasha turned her basket over and dumped all the petals into a pile on the floor. She grinned proudly as all the guests started to laugh. Jenny shook her head in annoyance before continuing the journey on her own, proudly tossing her petals correctly and taking her seat in the front pew. Sasha then sprinted up front and was intercepted by a relative in the second row on Ellie's side. After some coaxing from the groomsmen, Tony completed his trek down the aisle, handed the pillow to Matty and ungracefully climbed up onto the pew between Art and Jenny. He grinned over the back of the pew at Cassidy who reached forward and offered him her hand in a high five which he loudly smacked before turning and sitting down.

The bridesmaids started their procession down the aisle. Mindy, Elaine, Lisa, Molly, and then Kara, all in long, scarlet red dresses with fitted bodices, A-line skirts, and poofy sleeves. As bridesmaid dresses go, they weren't bad at all. However, Cassidy was still happy she didn't have to wear one. The five bridesmaids each carried a small bouquet of white lilies and greens and all wore their hair in low buns tied with red ribbons. They all looked very pretty as they happily took their places.

The music changed a final time, the familiar wedding march began, and everyone rose to their feet. Ellie and her father appeared at the end of the aisle. Ellie looked gorgeous. Her long, black hair was in an elaborate up-do. Her diamond white wedding dress was beyond stunning. The skirt was somewhere between A-line and ballgown with lace designs along the hem. The bodice had a low neck-line and the fabric ruched to the left side of her body; a large white bow sat on her left hip. Short, puffy sleeves rested on her shoulders, but otherwise her arms were bare aside from her white satin gloves.

Cassidy gasped at the sight of her, but quickly looked back to catch the face on her brother, who looked like he was about to fall over. She giggled slightly before turning her attention back to the bride.

The service went smoothly. The mothers in the front pews both sniffled through the entire thing, and Jeremy stifled multiple sneezes; he was standing next to one of the large floral stands and was quite evidently allergic.

The church erupted in cheers at the kiss, and the music played loudly and joyfully as the couple exited hand in hand, followed by Matty and Kara, Alex and Molly, Ben and Lisa, Derek and Elaine, and Jeremy and Mindy.

The reception was held in the ballroom of a large hotel. The red and white theme continued with tablecloths, flowers, and candles all about the cavernous room.

While everyone was milling around during the cocktail hour, Cassidy was pulled out of the room by the photographer to get some family pictures with her parents, brothers and Ellie. When the photo shoot finally ended, Cassidy greeted Eric with a hug.

"Congratulations!"

"Thank you!"

"Everything went very well," she smiled as she pulled back.

"Yeah, it was weird."

"A Banker family event that ran smoothly. We need to document this!"

"I'm thrilled the ceremony went well, but I'm sure we'll find a way to make a scene here," Eric chuckled.

"Oh, come on. We've got this."

"Have you seen Ben?" Eric asked, nodding slightly behind him. Cassidy peered around his shoulder and saw Ben clip a chair with his hip and stumble slightly. He did look unsteady.

"Mom said he was tipsy before the ceremony. At this rate, he'll be shitfaced by the end of the night. He didn't drive, did he?"

"No, Mom and Dad picked him up and brought him. I don't think they trusted him getting here on time."

"Smart, but where did he get the booze?"

"Remember Matty gave him that flask for his last birthday?"

"Oh jeez," Cassidy rolled her eyes.

"There's an open bar. Everyone else will catch up to him soon, so it'll be fine."

"True." She shrugged before she was blindsided with a tackling hug from her left. Cassidy toddled to steady herself a bit.

"Sister!" Ellie squealed.

"Heyyy!! Congratulations!" Cassidy hugged her back.

"Thank you!" Ellie slowly loosened her bear hug and moved to stand next to Eric, still bouncing on her heels slightly. Cassidy loved seeing her so happy. It was contagious.

"Everything was beautiful – and you look gorgeous!" Cassidy gushed.

"Thank you! It feels like a dream," she grinned. Eric kissed her on the cheek.

"Yinz deserve it," Cassidy said honestly. She could see how happy they were -- and she was happy for them. It wasn't just avoiding the drama and stress of being in the bridal party, or the ceremony being disaster free, or even her enjoyment of watching Ben being scolded quietly like a child by Lynne after accidentally backing into a planter and knocking dirt on the carpet, but Cassidy felt real joy.

"Jake looked quite handsome," Ellie smirked.

"Yes, and, thank you guys for inviting him! I don't know why you made it all secretive, but it was a nice surprise," Cassidy said.

"We like him," Eric smiled with a small shrug.

"I do, too."

Cassidy and Jake found themselves seated at a table with Art and Lynne, Laura, Nonna and Pap, and Lynne's brother, Leo, who had never married and was currently in between girlfriends. They were seated less than twenty feet from the head table where the entire bridal party sat, which Cassidy would have enjoyed significantly more if the bridesmaid seated closest to her wasn't complaining constantly. Ellie's older sister, Kara, had a comment about everything, from decor, to food, to music, politics, fashion, and anything else she could think of. This was the fourth time Cassidy had met Kara and she enjoyed her as much as she had enjoyed working with Devon Parks.

Cassidy did her best to focus on her table. She was seated between Jake and Laura, as Art had insisted Jake sit next to him to talk with him all about sports statistics. The dinner was delicious. Cassidy, Lynne, Pap, and Uncle Leo all enjoyed the lemon parmesan chicken with rice and green beans, while Jake, Art, Laura, and Nonna selected the roast beef, smashed potatoes, and green beans choice. Everyone was thrilled and stuffed to the gills.

Matty gave a best man speech in which he managed to weave in the story of Eric spilling his blue slushie all over his date at the movies when he was in ninth grade. Cassidy had actually forgotten about that one! But after a solid laugh from the crowd, and an eye roll from Eric, Matty teased that his dating skills had obviously improved to be able to even get a first date with Ellie. The speech was sweet and everyone smiled and clapped at the end as Matty hugged the newlyweds before taking his seat once more.

Kara was up next. After a failed attempt at a shoe joke, she told a story about herself, before saying the wedding was beautiful and raising a toast. Everyone grimaced slightly as they clapped. Ellie and Eric were good sports about the whole thing, but they looked thrilled for the dancing to begin.

After the traditional first dances, the DJ turned up "Crocodile Rock" and everyone hit the dance floor. Thank you, Elton!

The Bankers and the Narleskis, Lynne's side of the family, all loved a good dance party and weren't afraid to let loose. They were very happy to find that the Hammond family joined the party without hesitation.

Jake allowed himself to be pulled along by Cassidy, and while his efforts were in full force, Cassidy -- and everyone in a five-foot radius -- were quickly made aware that he was not a great dancer. That didn't stop him though, and Cassidy appreciated that. The safety and bone structure of her toes aside, she didn't want someone who sat on the sidelines. She loved that he was out there dancing just as hard as she was, and having a great time!

After four songs, a break to hit the open bar, and another two songs, the DJ slowed it down with a Platters song. Over half the dance floor emptied, but about twenty couples stayed,

Cassidy and Jake included. He wrapped his arms around her waist and she rested her forearms on his shoulders.

"Thank God," Jake sighed.

"You missed holding me?"

"No, I was tired," he replied. Cassidy gasped in mock outrage before laughing.

"Spaz."

"I missed you, too," he smirked, placing a light peck on her lips.

"I'm so glad you're here today."

"I am, too."

"Are you having fun?" she asked as they swayed with the music.

"A lot of fun! Your family is…"

"There are a lot of adjectives you could put in there."

"Fun."

"Fun?"

"Yes. I mean it's loud and chaotic and everyone fights, but you all love each other and just make everything more fun than it would be with my family," Jake said.

"Thank you?" Cassidy giggled.

"It's a compliment."

"I like that they don't scare you off."

"Oh, they scare the hell out of me," Jake said.

"But we're fun!"

"Exactly."

Cassidy hugged him tightly to her as they continued to sway with the music. She smiled into his shoulder.

"You know, I can't remember the last time I slow danced," Jake said in a low voice next to her ear.

"Yeah?"

"I think it was high school. What about you?"

"Um, my cousin Ericka's wedding, like, two years ago," Cassidy told him.

"What song?" he asked.

"Oh, I have no idea," Cassidy chuckled.

"Really?"

"Off the top of my head, no. What song was yours?"

"We've Got Tonight."

"Bob Segar? Oh, that's a good one."

"Yes."

"Why do you still remember it?"

"Senior prom."

"Ah, you went with Molly?" Cassidy asked, pulling back to look up at him. They had talked about previous relationships. Molly was his best friend who had become his first girlfriend the last two years of high school. They parted on good terms when they both left for different colleges, and were still friends to this day.

"Yeah, we had a blast. One of our last weekends as a couple, just having fun. Because after that it was finals and graduation. We both worked in the summer and then we left for college."

"Do you miss hanging out with her all the time?" Cassidy asked. Jake shook his head.

"A bit. But not in a romantic way. She was always my friend more than anything. I was just trying to remember the last time I danced like this."

"That makes sense," she smiled. Jake leaned down and placed a sweet kiss on her lips as the final note crooned out over the speakers. They pulled back and grinned at each other.

"Wanna take a break?" Jake asked as "Walk Like an Egyptian" started up. Cassidy nodded and took his hand. They

166

weaved their way off the dance floor and out of the reception hall into the hallway.

"Wow, it's like, twenty degrees cooler out here!" Cassidy said, fanning herself.

"A lot less people."

"This place is gorgeous!" Cassidy said, slowly spinning as she took in the large corridor. "Laura and I came in with the herd; I didn't really take it all in."

"Want to take a few minutes to explore?" Jake asked, holding out his hand.

"Sure," Cassidy grinned and linked her hand in his. They walked down the beautifully decorated corridor into the spacious lobby filled with high end sofas, art, a massive glass chandelier, and a piano with a pianist, most likely hired to attempt to drown out the noise of the reception. They admired the space before continuing along toward the opposite side of the hotel with another corridor that mirrored theirs. There were a few smaller event rooms on this side. As Cassidy and Jake passed Conference Room C they heard the sound of chairs crashing. They paused and looked at each other for a moment before Jake reached out and cautiously pushed the door open. Cassidy gaped in shock when she suddenly found herself in full view of her younger brother making out with a bridesmaid. Jake gave a low chuckle. Ben and Lisa, Ellie's college roommate, were stumbling as they frantically and passionately kissed. Ben's jacket was on the floor and his white dress shirt was untucked and unbuttoned; Lisa's red bridesmaid dress was off her shoulders bunched at her waist. Her dark curly hair was frizzing out of her formerly neat bun. It took about two seconds for them to realize they had been interrupted.

"Ugh! Cassidy! Get out!" Ben said angrily.

"Shit!" Lisa said, pulling back from Ben and crossing her arms over her chest.

"Sorry, man." Jake gave a low laugh and tugged Cassidy away.

"Get lost, Cassidy!" Ben yelled. Cassidy couldn't think of a good comeback and just laughed before following Jake out of the room and closing the door behind them.

"Oh no!" she said breathily, still in shock.

"Well, he's having a good time," Jake smirked as they slowly walked away from the room.

"Seriously! Come on, let's get back to the reception," Cassidy said, taking his hand and pulling him along.

"Ready to dance more?"

"Yes, but also I have to tell Laura!" she said. Jake laughed, following her back to the large banquet hall on the other side of the hotel.

The last hour of the reception was more fun. There was lots of dancing, and lots of drinks. When Jake took breaks to talk with Art about baseball, Cassidy danced with Matty, who introduced her to a bunch of Ellie's cousins he had hit it off with –he could make friends every single place he went. He was fun!

Ben and Lisa reappeared with less than fifteen minutes left in the night. Lisa had cut her losses and pulled her curly hair up into a ponytail rather than trying to repair the neat bun. Cassidy and Laura giggled childishly as Ben walked by and he shot them an annoyed glare, which made them laugh even harder.

The final song of the night was "Shout" by the Isley Brothers. Every single person was on the dance floor. Cassidy's favorite part of the night was watching everyone do the little bit softer now part before easing back up to standing and jumping.

Once the lights were back on and the DJ was prepping everyone to see the newlyweds off, Ellie ran over to Cassidy, who was standing with Laura.

"Hi!" she grinned.

"Hi!" Cassidy said.

"Everything was perfect! Did you think it was perfect?" Laura asked.

"Yes, definitely."

"Is Kara okay? I've hardly seen her since dinner," Cassidy wondered as she spotted the maid of honor standing apart from everyone and looking annoyed. Ellie grimaced.

"Oh, I feel bad. She apparently really likes Derek, but he didn't even want to dance with her. She's taking it pretty hard. I think she thought they'd start dating tonight."

"Poor girl," Cassidy said.

"Not everyone struck out." Laura smirked and wiggled her eyebrows, making Cassidy laugh.

"What?" Ellie asked.

Laura leaned in and whispered. "Ben and Lisa."

"What?" Ellie gasped. Both Cassidy and Laura nodded.

"Yep."

"Can we have Eric and Ellie over here, please?" The DJ called over the mic.

"Oh, I've got to go, but I want to hear more!"

"You have a great time! We'll get together for drinks when you get back from the honeymoon!" Laura said.

"Really?"

"Absolutely, can't wait!" Cassidy said, giving her hand a squeeze before Ellie happily ran over to Eric.

169

Eric and Ellie were staying in the honeymoon suite at the hotel for the night so rice was tossed at them in the reception room as they ran through the parted crowd, laughing the whole way, before they were led to the private elevator by one of the staff members.

After lots of hugs and goodbyes with family and friends, and Cassidy gently asking Lynne to stop crying for the fifth time since the rice throwing, Cassidy was bundled up in her winter coat once more and walking with Jake through the dark, cold parking lot to his car.

"This was a fantastic day," she said as they reached his car.

"Yeah, it was. It was pretty perfect."

"But that's the thing! It wasn't perfect -- not at all -- but it was fantastic! And I'm so happy right now."

"I'm happy you're so happy," Jake said, leaning down and kissing her.

# Chapter 17

Cassidy stirred her peach margarita with her straw as she sat at the small, round table with Laura and Ellie. It was two weeks after Eric and Ellie's wedding, and they had only returned home from their honeymoon a few days prior. As the girls had promised at the reception, they met up for drinks -- and Cassidy was having a wonderful time. The three women had been at the restaurant for the last hour and a half, and all of them were just starting their third drink.

"Come on, what was your favorite part of Jamaica?" Laura asked, taking a sip of her wine.

"The heat!" Ellie replied with a smile. It was February in Erie. It hadn't been above freezing all week and there were five inches of snow on the ground. That Caribbean sun must have been fantastic, Cassidy thought.

"Oh, I can only imagine," Cassidy smiled.

"The heat outside or the heat in the hotel room?" Laura asked with a wink. Ellie giggled and blushed. Cassidy scrunched up her nose.

"Ellie, I'm happy you're happy, but please do not go into detail while I'm here. Please!" Cassidy begged. Laura cackled.

"Ignore her, she's scared of sex," Laura said to Ellie. Cassidy shook her head in shock.

"What the hell are you talking about?"

"Come on, you never let me talk about my sex life," Laura pointed out.

"Oh my god, you two are fucking my brothers!" Cassidy enunciated. Laura and Ellie shared a look before laughing hysterically.

"If we weren't fucking your brothers, you wouldn't get to hang out with us here tonight!" Laura pointed out. Cassidy smiled and nodded.

"Very true," she admitted. Laura laughed.

"But Eric and I did have a good time," Ellie grinned. Laura nodded and grinned back while Cassidy took a large gulp of her margarita, choosing to ignore them. She honestly was happy they were happy, and that her brothers were. She just didn't want to hear any bedroom details.

"Alright, to appease Cassidy, let's change this up slightly," Laura began.

Cassidy perked up.

"Who was your first? And was it good or bad?" Laura asked.

"Oh, boy," Ellie sighed. "I need a shot for that."

Cassidy let out a snort.

"Deal!" Laura agreed. She quickly flagged down the server and ordered three shots of rum, which were brought out a few minutes later, the three of them laughing hysterically. Clearly their earlier drinks were starting to hit. Cassidy was thrilled she didn't have to drive that night. Eric, Alex, and Jake were hanging out at the loft and had promised to pick them up after the hockey game ended on TV.

"Alright, shoot on three?" Cassidy asked, now that they each had a full shot glass in their hands.

The girls nodded, tapped their glasses three times on the table and tossed them back. All three gasped as the liquor hit.

"Yikes," Ellie laughed.

"Yeah," Cassidy agreed.

"Okay, okay," Laura said, her voice was starting to slur, which made Cassidy laugh. She was drunk.

"Okay," Cassidy teased.

"We got our shots, now we all have to tell… How good -- or bad -- was your first time?" Laura asked.

"I think weird is a better word," Ellie said with a giggle.

"Alright, Ellie, you're up first, spill," Laura pushed.

"How old were you?" Cassidy asked as she took another sip of her margarita. Her head was starting to buzz. The last time she'd been this tipsy she'd been at the club with Marissa and ended up going home with Pete. That felt like a lifetime ago, but really it had been less than a year. Damn.

"I was eighteen," Ellie began, shifting in her seat. Cassidy could see a blush coming on. "It was freshman year at Penn State. There was a huge Halloween party in my dorm. My roommate and I came dressed as the Pink Ladies from Grease. It was a great party. There was a guy from the floor above me. I saw him practically every day, he always said hi. Well, wouldn't you know it, he showed up as Danny Zucko. We spotted each other immediately and spent the whole party talking and laughing, and drinking a lot. Then he brought me up to his dorm room. His roommate was out all night so we had the room to ourselves. He kissed me the second he shut the door. I remember it all moving pretty quickly. I remember being super hot, probably from all the alcohol. Our clothes came off so fast.  He was on top of me, we were both sweaty because those dorms didn't have A/C, and even though it was late October, there were so many students there that night. It was hot as hell." Ellie sighed before taking another drink from her glass.

"And how was it?" Cassidy asked, intrigued.

"Well, I just remember that I was shocked there was no, like, warning! Just, mmmmm! He was in!" Ellie said with an accompanying hand gesture. Both Laura and Cassidy snorted in laughter.

"Mmmmm, huh?" Laura asked, still chuckling.

"I guess so. It hurt more than I was ready for and I had no idea what to expect, honestly," Ellie laughed.

"Oooof," Cassidy sighed.

"But then it was done, we kissed, and he rolled off of me, and I felt suddenly super aware that I was naked in some dude's room…" Ellie trailed off.

"Did you guys ever do it again?" Cassidy asked. Ellie shook her head.

"Nope, we just laid there for like five minutes. I sat up and got dressed, he did, too. We made out for a bit and then left and went back to the party," Ellie shrugged.

"Hmmm," Laura mumbled, clearly in thought.

"I'm not mad at him. We never dated, or had any other… encounters, but we smiled and waved at each other every time we saw each other in the halls for the rest of the year. We were both in different dorms our sophomore year, and honestly, I don't even know what happened to him."

"I think that's a pretty good first time," Cassidy said.

174

"Honestly, it wasn't bad. He was nice, and he was cute," Ellie said with a smile.

"I think it's pretty good one," Laura said before taking a sip.

"Okay, then you're up next," Cassidy nodded pointedly at Laura.

"Oh boy," Laura began with a large grin.

"Come on, you have to tell us!" Ellie pushed, smiling back.

"I don't know if Cassidy will like it," Laura shrugged. Cassidy felt her face scrunch up in confusion.

"Why?" Cassidy asked.

"Because my first time was actually with Alex," Laura shrugged, the grin not leaving her face. Cassidy's eyebrows shot up in surprise.

"Really?" Both Cassidy and Ellie asked in unison.

"Yes, really!" Laura responded defensively. Cassidy shook her head.

"No, I -- I was just surprised…" she trailed off.

"Why?" Laura asked.

"I don't know!"

"Well, tell us about it!" Ellie pushed, smacking her palm on the table.

"Just not all the details," Cassidy added.

"No, all the details!" Ellie interjected. Laura gave a hard laugh and Cassidy took another large gulp to prepare.

"Okay, okay." Laura took a sip of her drink then launched into her story.

"Alex and I met the first day of class our sophomore year at MU. We had a creative writing class together. We just happened to sit next to each other on the first day and stayed there the whole semester. We didn't have our first date for a

175

few weeks; we went out to one of the clubs downtown. But it was after our third date – we went to the movies -- that he invited me back to his dorm. His roommate had gone home for the weekend."

"That third date rule," Cassidy chuckled sarcastically.

"Yes, well, I knew something was going to happen that night, but I wasn't sure what. We had only shared a few kisses. Actually, our longest make-out session had been at the movies earlier that night. I've still never seen Death on the Nile in full," Laura admitted.

Both Cassidy and Ellie laughed and shared a smirk.

"He turned on the record player as soon as we got in the room… I looked around at all his books and posters, and suddenly he was standing right behind me. I turned around to face him and we kissed. It was pure adrenaline. But he was so sweet with me. We took our time. He just kissed me so good that night. I felt really hot and excited. I remember being oddly comfortable with him as my clothes came off. And then the moment came, we were in bed, and I knew it was going to happen. That's when my nerves kicked in, but he just cuddled me and calmed me right down. It honestly was a great night."

"Oh my God, that is so freaking sweet," Ellie gushed. "Those Banker boys."

Laura giggled, and Cassidy forced herself to not roll her eyes. She loved her brothers, but hearing about them in romantic moments was not her favorite thing.

"I, I'm, uh, glad it was so good." Cassidy took another sip.

"I'm sorry, Cassidy, I know it wasn't what you wanted to hear," Laura chuckled.

"It's what I wanted to hear!" Ellie pipped in, causing Laura to giggle.

"I'm glad you enjoyed my story, at least," Laura said.

"No, no, I'm happy. It's just, it's my brother..." Cassidy shuddered.

"I get it," Laura admitted.

"Anything else happen that night?" Ellie asked curiously.

"No, not really. I mean afterwards, we stayed in bed for like thirty minutes. Like we just rested together and shared a cigarette," Laura said.

"Awww," Cassidy said halfheartedly.

"I think it helped that he knew what he was doing, and just his general demeanor made it great for me. I remember immediately thinking that I wanted to be with him forever. And we've been together since," Laura gushed.

"Oh my gosh, I love that!" Ellie grinned. Cassidy nodded.

"Shot? Anyone?" Cassidy asked with a slight slur.

"You're shitfaced already," Laura commented with a chuckle.

"I'm drunk, but definitely not shitfaced," Cassidy countered with a hiccup, causing all three of them to burst into another fit of laughter.

"Well, before you pass out, we need your story," Ellie enunciated. Cassidy laughed and bit her lip. Her first time was not a story she readily shared. As a matter of fact, Marissa was the only person she'd ever told.

"Come on! We told you ours," Laura pointed out. Cassidy sighed.

"I've only ever told one person about it before," Cassidy blushed.

"A secret?" Ellie asked excitedly, leaning in.

"You have to tell us now! No backing out!" Laura said. Cassidy started to nervously laugh.

177

"What?" Ellie asked in a laugh, enjoying the moment.

"I fucked Alex's friend," Cassidy laughed, waving her hands in a shrug.

"Wait, what?" Ellie asked, her eyes wide as she laughed along.

"Which one?" Laura asked frantically.

"Tommy," Cassidy admitted, resting her hand on her forehead in playful shame.

"Oh, I remember him. They were friends all through high school and college, then Tommy moved out to Colorado, and we haven't seen him in years," Laura said. Cassidy nodded. She was well aware.

"Was he cute?" Ellie asked Laura.

"Very," Laura nodded. "I need to hear this story! I can't believe I haven't heard it before," Laura said excitedly.

"Honestly, it's so dumb. Tommy stopped by one afternoon in summer. Alex was still at work -- he worked at the pizza shop on North Street back then. But Tommy stayed at the house to hang out and wait for him. I'm not sure how it happened, but we ended up hanging out, just him and me. We were just talking and telling stories, then out of nowhere, he kissed me. Oh, man, I was so excited. I had such a crush on him. Suddenly, we were making out. Then he pushed me back on the bed and his hands were up my shirt. I thought I was so cool. Before I knew it, he had my shorts off, and his were, too. It didn't last long, but holy shit," Cassidy said.

"Good shit or bad?" Laura chuckled.

"I thought good. Dude, I had a million thoughts racing through my head that afternoon. I remember being excited and scared and just freaking out. I had no idea what I was supposed to be doing," Cassidy explained. "But it was done, and before I knew it and he was climbing off of me. I was very aware my shorts were on the floor and my top was pushed over my boobs. Tommy was already getting dressed, so I did, too. He pulled me in for a hug and we made out for a few more minutes. Then he said that he had to go."

"That's shitty," Ellie scrunched up her face.

"It's not shitty. I mean, honestly, the timing was good. As he was going down the stairs, Alex came in the front door from work, so we weren't caught. But we never did it again. I was always kind of hoping that we would. I stupidly thought it meant we were going to date. We never did. We went back to just him being friends with my brother and saying hi to me occasionally." Cassidy shrugged.

"Ugh," Laura sighed.

"Don't look at me like that! It's fine!" Cassidy said, looking at their pitying faces. "This is why I never tell this dumbass story. Honestly, it was good that it happened. I was home, I was safe, and I learned that real-life fairytale romance isn't real. It was good to get my bubble burst."

"How old were you?" Ellie asked.

"Sixteen," Cassidy said. "I was old enough to learn. I mean, I thought I had a chance with him. I was an idiot!"

"Only a bit of an idiot," Laura teased. All three girls burst out laughing.

"I'm glad yinz all find my dumbass teenage self as ridiculous as I do," Cassidy giggled.

"It's only funny because things are good now. Like, Jake is your fairy-tale boyfriend. So it all worked out!" Ellie said.

"Yeah, he's good. You just had to… kiss a couple of frogs first," Laura smirked.

"A lot of frogs," Cassidy sighed, rolling her eyes.

"Yeah, I remember Eric told me you were kinda slutty," Ellie commented with a hiccup. Both Cassidy and Laura gasped in shock before starting to laugh once more.

"I'm going to kill him!" Cassidy said. "That's what he says about me?"

"I think just to me, and it was a long time ago," Ellie defended her husband. "I never believed him, just assumed it was sibling humor."

"You should have believed him," Laura commented in a deadpan smirk. Cassidy turned to playfully glare at her. Laura leaned over and gave her a peck on the cheek. "But we still love you!"

"Yes! I'm so glad we're friends now. I was missing out!" Ellie added.

The girls laughed as they sipped the last of their drinks. Suddenly Eric appeared behind Ellie.

"Hey," Eric said, placing his hands on Ellie's shoulders and smirking at the inebriated state of his wife, twin, and sister-in-law.

"Hi," Ellie gushed up at him, turning to wrap her arms around his middle.

"Eric," Cassidy slurred.

"Hmm?" Eric raised his eyebrow. Cassidy could tell he wasn't taking her seriously.

"Ellie informed me that you told her that I was a slut! I can't believe that's how you talk about me," Cassidy grumbled. Laura burst out laughing while Ellie buried her face in Eric's jacket, clearly mortified.

"You've never proved me wrong," Eric grinned obnoxiously. Cassidy wanted to throw something at him. He was clearly relishing the fact that she was too drunk to fight him. If she were sober, he'd be toast.

"Such an ass," Cassidy grumbled.

"Poor baby," Eric replied half-heartedly.

"Where's Alex?" Laura asked as she finally stopped laughing.

"He's in his car out front," Eric said. "He's waiting for you and Jake's out there talking to him."

"Why'd you come in alone?" Cassidy asked.

"Because I lost rock, paper, scissors. Go get your coat on," Eric told her sarcastically.

"Okay, let's go," Laura said. Cassidy hopped off the high chair and was suddenly acutely aware of how drunk she really was. She'd been sitting and drinking for hours, and now that she was on her feet, she knew she was in trouble. Fortunately, Ellie and Laura seemed to be making similar discoveries.

"Whoa," Ellie teetered with a giggle. Eric grabbed her arm to hold her steady. With an almost comical amount of difficulty, they were able to put their coats on, grab their bags, leave cash on the table for the bill, and follow Eric through the restaurant and outside. The cold air hit them like a brick and they all let out audible gasps.

"Okay, Alex is over there," Eric said, pointing to the idling car waiting about fifty feet away. Jake was leaning over the open passenger window and chatting.

"Good," Cassidy said, happy to know she didn't have to stand out in this frigid night air for long.

"Bye girls, thanks for inviting me along!" Ellie gushed, pulling her arm out of Eric's and stumbling over to give them a hug. Cassidy and Laura immediately embraced her in a group hug.

"You're welcome out with us anytime!" Laura cheered.

181

"Definitely," Cassidy agreed. After a long moment, they pulled apart. Eric took ahold of Ellie's arm once more to steady her; she was starting to teeter.

"Bye, Eric!" Laura screamed, much louder than she needed to. Ellie laughed hysterically.

"See ya," Cassidy grinned at her twin. He rolled his eyes at her.

"Get in the car before everyone freezes," Eric instructed as he led Ellie in the opposite direction towards her car.

"Yeah, let's go!" Cassidy said, looking over at Laura shivering next to her.

"I'm freezing and I need another cigarette!" Laura grumbled. They walked as fast as they could towards the taillights of Alex's car. Cassidy wasn't sure how she made the short journey without face-planting, but she was thrilled when they reached the car. Alex climbed out as they approached.

"Can yinz walk?" he asked, looking at the two girls with amusement.

"Yes," Cassidy sighed. Jake chuckled as he walked over to her and wrapped his left arm around her shoulder.

"Oh my god!" Laura said as she got herself inside the car.

"So cold," Cassidy shivered against Jake.

"Aw, babe," Laura cooed as Alex handed her a cigarette from his pack on the dash. Cassidy rolled her eyes.

"Ready?" Alex asked.

"Yes. Night!" Laura yelled to Cassidy and Jake before rolling up the window. Alex put the car in gear and merged onto the street.

"Looks like you had fun," Jake said as they started to walk to the parking lot.

"Please tell me you didn't park far?" Cassidy shivered. Erie folk were tough in winter, but they were also smart enough to not go out if they didn't need to. This had not been one of Cassidy's smarter moments.

"Right over here," Jake said. He helped her into his truck. The engine reluctantly fired up, clearly unhappy about the cold, as well. Cassidy held her hand over the vents waiting for warm air.

"How many drinks did you have?" Jake laughed as they turned onto the street.

"Um… three? Four? There was a shot in there, too… How many drinks did you have?" she asked playfully.

"One."

"While watching hockey?"

"I know, major faux pas," Jake smirked.

"I think the faux pas is saying faux pas while talking about ice hockey," Cassidy chortled.

"Not if I was cheering for Montreal."

"Were you cheering for Montreal?"

"Absolutely not!" Jake said firmly.

"Good!" Cassidy nodded. "How was your night?"

"It was nice! Your brothers are fun."

"Yeah," Cassidy snorted. "Just the three of you at Alex's?"

"No, we went out to that sports bar by the airport and met Matty and a bunch of his friends."

"What is happening?" she asked in a low voice. Jake chuckled.

"It was a great time. Too bad the Pens lost in overtime. But we played a few rounds of darts, watched hockey, laughed a lot… Matty is a riot," he said. Cassidy watched him drive for a bit, just sitting with a smile on her face. She felt incredibly lucky.

# Chapter 18

Jake unlocked his front door and led them inside. The house was pitch black. He reached around Cassidy and flipped the light switch on the wall and his living room illuminated.

"Are you hungry?" Jake asked.

"Not really, but I do have to pee," Cassidy chuckled before dropping her purse on the ground, ripping off her coat and sprinting upstairs to the bathroom as she heard Jake laugh.

After using the bathroom and washing her hands, Cassidy ran her hands through her fluffy blonde hair as she looked in the mirror. She was still pretty tipsy, but happily she didn't look it. Her cheeks were tinged with pink, but she blamed that on the cold outside. She smiled at her reflection before departing the bathroom. The hallway was dark, but she saw a light coming from Jake's bedroom at the end of the hall.

"Hey," Cassidy said, leaning against the door frame to his room.

"Hey," he replied. He was pulling his dark green sweatshirt over his head and tossing on the foot of the bed, leaving him in his jeans and grey tee shirt.

"Damn, you look good," she said in a happy sigh. He smirked at her.

"You're not bad yourself; come here," Jake said. Cassidy walked over to him and placed her hands on his chest, immediately balling up the fabric of his tee in her fists. Jake's hands went to her lower back and held her tightly to him. Cassidy loved it. They stared at each other for a long moment before they both leaned in and crashed their mouths together, the kiss deepening on impact. Jake's left hand slid down to cup her ass through her jeans. They kissed passionately as Cassidy brought her right hand up and plunged her fingers into his copper hair. Her left hand slid down to the hem of his tee and she quickly slipped her hand underneath the fabric onto his taut skin. She let her fingers caress his chest hair as they kissed. After a long moment of their mouths moving in sync, Jake moved his hands to the base of her sweater and pulled it over her head. Cassidy wasted no time in ripping his tee shirt off of him as he slid her cami off of her. They paused for a second and locked eyes, both breathing hard with the desire they felt. Jake cupped her face with his right hand and kissed her hard. Cassidy felt her heart give a heavy thump. She wanted more. She needed more. As he kissed her, she reached back and unhooked her bra. Jake used his left hand to help pull it off her shoulders and down her arms. They were both completely bare chested. Cassidy ungracefully stepped out of the black boots she was wearing, holding onto Jake's arms for balance as they kissed. She was finally able to kick them off and slid her hands down his chest and stomach to come and rest on his belt buckle. Jake stepped himself out of his sneakers easily before pulling back and smirking at her.

185

"What?" Cassidy asked, smiling up at him. He shrugged.

"Just happy."

"Well, come here, I'm getting cold without you kissing me."

"I can tell," Jake winked as he glanced down at her. Cassidy didn't need to look to know that her nipples were rock hard. Jake's house was old and drafty. The Erie winters were rough.

"Maybe we should get warm in bed?"

"Maybe?" Jake said placing a kiss on her lips. Cassidy turned around to the bed behind her and pulled the blankets and top sheet down. She pivoted back around to face Jake. He immediately put his hands on her hips and gave her a playful shove backwards. She landed in a seated position on the bed. Cassidy laughed and rolled her eyes, knowing full well that Jake was watching her breasts.

"Come here," she motioned with her index finger. Jake grabbed her calves and pulled. She felt a jolt run through her body as her butt slid across the mattress until she was sitting directly in front of him. Her eyes were inches from his stomach.

Cassidy reached over and unbuckled his belt before opening the button and zipper. Jake took over and removed his jeans, pulling off his socks as he stepped out of his pants. Cassidy's eyes were drawn to the large, firm protrusion at the front of his light blue boxers. She immediately brought her hands to her waist and undid her jeans. They were barely down her hips when Jake grabbed the denim and ripped them off of her legs, leaving her in just her red panties.

"Come on," Cassidy nodded her head as she scooted back on the mattress and slid under the covers. Jake quickly slipped off his boxers and climbed into bed naked. They both reached for each other and pulled close. Cassidy loved the feeling of all of his skin on hers. Their lips found each other. Her left arm wrapped around his shoulders while her right hand held onto his cheek, her thumb rubbing back and forth over his five-o-clock shadow. Jake slid his right hand down her back before slipping into her panties and firmly grabbing her bare ass. Cassidy gasped into his mouth. They continued to kiss as she moved her hands down to her waist to help him remove her final covering. Once off of her ankles, Jake wadded up the red fabric and tossed them off the bed.

Cassidy stroked her hand up and down his chest and stomach a few times before taking hold of his very firm dick. He nipped lightly at her lower lip before kissing his way down her jawline to the sensitive skin on her neck.

She moved her hand slowly at first, tracing her fingertips along his length, teasing him. A few times she felt Jake buck slightly and it made her oddly proud. Cassidy tightened her hold and began to move her hand faster.

Jake brought his lips back up to hers and kissed her four times before roughly rolling them over so he was on top. He reached down and grabbed both of her wrists and pinned them above her head.

Cassidy bit her lip excitedly as she looked up at him. He smiled before leaning down and kissing her again. Slow, deliberate kisses. Again and again. He was driving her wild. The cool air from his room was nothing to combat the heat now coming from his bed.

After a few minutes, Jake released her arms. Cassidy brought them up to his shoulders. He kissed her chin before leaning over to his left and reaching for the bedside table. Cassidy could hear him rummage in the drawer, but honestly, her focus was on his tongue trailing down her throat. She gripped his shoulders tightly and let out a gasp. Her heart was pounding; she loved every feeling that was shooting through her.

Jake finished rummaging and pulled his mouth off of her throat as he hovered over her with a square, silver packet in his hand. Cassidy took the condom out of his hands and tore the wrapper open with her teeth. She tossed aside the plastic and brought her right hand under the covers. Jake helped guide her fingers as she applied the condom to his hard dick. She slowly trailed her hand back up his chest as he pressed his lips against hers in a ravenous kiss. Cassidy smiled against his mouth as she felt his knee push her legs apart. She happily complied and rested her inner thighs on his hips. Jake positioned himself at her entrance. Cassidy gripped his shoulder when he entered her. She gasped into his mouth at the contact. Jake pulled out slightly before pushing in to the hilt. He kissed her cheek as he began to move. He started slow, almost teasing her. Cassidy felt her breathing start to pick up. Her thighs squeezed against his hips. Gradually, Jake picked up the pace. Faster and faster. His breaths were heavy and loud. Cassidy felt sparks and tingling in her extremities. She was almost panting. She clawed at his back and he kissed her lips roughly. She lost track of time as he moved, her heart about to beat out of her chest. After a few more minutes of panting, thrusting, clawing, her body tingling in ecstasy, Jake kissed her hard once more. She shuddered and tipped her head back and cried out. Jake gave a final thrust and did the same.

They both went limp.

Cassidy let out a loud breath as he pulled out and rolled off of her. She turned and kissed his shoulder as he reached under the covers and removed the condom, dropping it in the waste basket off his side of the bed. They both took a moment to lie on their backs and get their breathing under control before Jake kissed her cheek and brushed a few stray strands off her face, tucking them behind her ear.

"That was good," Cassidy smirked. Jake chuckled. He placed a light peck on her lips.

"Always good."

"True."

"I love you," he said softly. Cassidy's heart gave a thump.

"I love you, too," she smiled.

Cassidy let herself back into the apartment and hung her keys on the hook. It was a little after ten in the morning on Saturday. She was just taking off her coat when she heard Marissa call out.

"Cassidy?"

"Yeah!"

"Ugh, finally!" Marissa groaned as she stepped into the hall with her hands on her hips. She looked irritated.

"What's wrong? I thought I told you I was staying at Jake's after drinks."

"Oh, you told me that," Marissa agreed. "That's not the issue."

"What's the issue?" Cassidy asked, confused. "Oh, hey, Brandon," she said, as she spotted him sitting on the couch.

"Hey." He gave a weak smile.

"The phone has been ringing off the hook all night because of your stupid brother."

"Ugh, which one?"

"Alex," Marissa huffed. She walked over and dramatically flopped down on the couch next to Brandon, her arms folded across her chest.

"I'm sorry. He's practically nocturnal and doesn't always remember most people sleep at night. I'll call him back at lunchtime."

"No! You call him back now – see how he likes it," Marissa grumbled. Cassidy winced at her friend. Marissa was generally even-tempered, easy going, and often Cassidy's voice of reason. However, when sleep deprived, she became quite stubborn and agitated. Cassidy knew she would have to make it up to her later.

"Did he say what he wanted? You should have ignored him!"

"No, it was just... Is Cassidy there? No? Dammit... Is Cassidy there? No? Dammit. Over and over. Hard to ignore."

"I answered once," Brandon chimed in. "That didn't help. He really doesn't like me."

"Ugh," Cassidy groaned. "Fine, fine, I'll call. But I don't need an audience."

"Sure," Brandon said as he stood up. "Come on, babe."

"Why?"

"Let's go lie down."

"I'm not a child, I don't need a nap," Marissa grumbled. Cassidy and Brandon shared a quick look. They seemed to both understand they couldn't make the comment they wanted to.

"I didn't say nap, I said let's go hang out in bed," Brandon said, holding his hand out for her. Marissa paused in thought for a moment before smirking and taking Brandon's waiting hand. Cassidy shook her head as she watched them head to Marissa's bedroom. Marissa stopped at the doorway and turned to look back at Cassidy.

"Make sure to tell Alex that I hate him!"

"Oh, don't worry, I will let him know."

"Okay, good! Bye!" Marissa said, shutting the door behind her.

"Good Lord." Cassidy rolled her eyes as she heard her boombox start to play The Grass Roots. She kicked off her shoes and settled on the blue chair next to the end table where they kept the phone and dialed her brothers' number.

It rang three times before answered.

"Hello?"

"Hey Laura, it's Cassidy."

"Oh, shit."

"Well, hello to you. I had a great time last night, too," Cassidy snorted.

"Sorry."

"It's okay. Where's Alex? Still sleeping? I heard he called multiple times last night. I'm appeasing Marissa by calling to wake him up this time."

"I'm sorry, Cassidy."

"What? Why?"

"I was drunk, it slipped out. I really, really didn't think it would matter!"

"What would?"

"I told Alex that you slept with Tommy," Laura admitted in a pained voice.

"Shit." Cassidy felt her heart sink. She knew he would be annoyed. Alex always wanted to be the protective big brother and care for her. However, Cassidy had always been stubborn, loud, and head strong since early childhood. She loved her eldest brother dearly but needed him significantly less than he would have liked. Cassidy always loved having him in her corner, she couldn't lie, she abused the privilege when she didn't get her way. Yet this was a moment, a private moment, that she had handled herself as a teenager. She had wanted to. She had done something grown up, she did not want to whine like a child. The interaction with Tommy was a pivotal one in her life. Both good and bad, Cassidy had learned a lot from it. The last thing she wanted to have was her brother overreacting. But now, almost ten years later, it was about to hit her like a brick. Cassidy took a deep breath.

"Yeah."

"Is he still asleep?"

"He didn't sleep much, and I can hear him putzing around in our room."

"Well, is he getting more annoyed or calming down? When would be best to talk to him?"

"I might wait... oh, hang on," Laura trailed off. Cassidy could hear noise on the other end but Laura's hand was covering the receiver and she couldn't make anything out.

"Cassidy?" Alex's voice jolted her as he took over on the call.

"Hey. You know Marissa is furious with--"

"What the hell?" he interrupted her.

"Back at you," Cassidy grumbled. This going to be painful.

"I can't believe you were sleeping with my best friend behind my back!"

"Alex!"

"I'm pissed."

"Clearly. But I don't know why. This was ten years ago, and--"

"And my sister and friend have been lying to me for a decade!"

"Please don't be so dramatic -- that's my job," Cassidy smirked, proud of her quip.

"Stop being cute."

"Stop being mad about something that happened so long ago that frankly did not involve you in the slightest!"

"Important people in my life hiding a relationship does involve me," Alex snapped. Cassidy clenched her jaw in annoyance. Of course, he was going to blow this out of proportion. Alex hated being left in the dark. He was going to make this worse.

"I don't know what Laura said, but she must have lost something in translation because she was drunk."

"Laura wouldn't lie to me."

"I'm not saying she did, but you're talking about it like Tommy and I had a love story. We did not. He really didn't want much to do with me after."

"I… I expect more from you Cassidy."

"Yeah? Well if you're determined to be annoyed, call Tommy and bitch him out."

"Don't you worry."

"Alex, I was kidding."

"You had plenty of boyfriends! You didn't need to insert yourself in our friendships just to have all the guys."

"Our?" Cassidy questioned. She was incredibly annoyed.

"You have four brothers… I doubt I was the only one who got a friend stolen."

"Wow! Alex… what the hell?"

"Who was the guy on the phone last night?"

"That was Marissa's boyfriend. And you owe her an apology because she is my friend."

"I'll apologize when you do."

"Okay. You're pissed, I get it. I don't know why you're upset, but I'm not apologizing just to shut you up. I didn't do anything wrong. This doesn't even sound like you."

"Well, you fucked up. Just… stay away from my friends," Alex spat and hung up the phone. Cassidy sat frozen for a long moment as the dial tone hummed in her ear.

"What. The. Hell?" she said to herself before huffing off to go shower. This was not what she wanted to come home to.

# Chapter 19

Cassidy spent a lot of time at the Mercyhurst University library when Jake was working. They had more resources than the community one, including newspapers from all over the country. She started combing the classifieds of the Chicago publications to help widen her job search, and see if relocating was even an option. Cassidy and Jake had been talking a lot about his upcoming move and she was quite firm that she wasn't joining him if she didn't have a job. She hated her current situation of having to rely on her parents so much. The last thing she wanted to do was shift to being a burden to Jake.

Cassidy invested in a calling card and started calling a few ads each week. Jake was making another trip to Illinois over spring break to search for a place to live and Cassidy was planning to join him for the drive out. While he apartment hunted, Cassidy hoped to line up as many interviews as she possibly could. If she didn't get a job, it definitely wouldn't be for lack of trying.

In between scouring the out of state newspapers, Cassidy was trying to improve her cooking skills. She had never been great in the kitchen, but with her sudden need to eat on a budget, she appreciated the skill more and more. Not to mention, she enjoyed making dinner for Marissa on the evenings she worked late.

Laura came over for coffee one afternoon when the school she taught at had a half day. She still felt terrible about her slip with Alex.

"I really feel awful."

"Laura, it's okay."

"You're not mad?"

"Well, I am, but you know. You didn't say anything trying to be mean."

"I really, really didn't think it would backfire this badly," Laura said earnestly.

"Is Alex still shitty?"

"Not as bad. I mean, I think he's busy with work and whatnot so it's only when I bring up your name that he starts to grumble."

"Ugh! What did you even tell him? He seems to think that Tommy and I had this long, secret relationship. I totally get how that would hurt him, but it was one afternoon -- ten years ago!" Cassidy gave a heavy sigh.

"I'm sure he'll be over it by your family dinner in a few weeks. You know him; he gets annoyed, sulks for a few weeks, then he's fine."

"Ugh, I hope. He hasn't given me that kind of shit since he first left for college and Matty helped me move his dresser into my room so I could have two."

"You stole Alex's dresser?" Laura asked with a surprised chuckle.

"Matty helped me empty it out onto his bed. I didn't throw

196

out his clothes."

"Oh my God."

"Alex came home for a visit in October and just absolutely lost it when he saw his dresser missing. That was a really long weekend. I mean, it was two days, but it felt like a decade." Cassidy shuddered slightly at the memory.

"I can imagine," Laura nodded. "But you two moved on from that, you can do the same now."

"Yeah, just um, do me a favor? Do not mention the dresser incident when you get home. The last thing I need is for him to be annoyed about two things from the past." Cassidy said. Laura stifled a laugh.

"My lips are sealed. I'm sober this time, too, so I can definitely make sure to keep my mouth shut."

"Thank you," Cassidy smiled.

It was spring break; however, the term "spring" was to be used loosely. From Erie to Evanston, the ground was covered in snow. Mid-March in the Midwest was cold and wintery. They still had another couple of weeks until the ground thawed out and flowers could start to grow. Jake and Cassidy were staying in the same hotel they did last time, and it was nice that the city felt slightly more familiar this trip.

Jake took them out to dinner at a Greek restaurant the hotel front desk had recommended to them on their first night.

"How many interviews do you have lined up again?" Jake asked as he pulled at a piece of lamb with his fork.

"I have two tomorrow, none on Tuesday, but one on Wednesday, and one on Thursday," Cassidy counted off on her fingers.

"We leave Saturday and I have to be back at work on Monday. What are you going to do if you get a second interview?"

"Well," Cassidy took a sip of her wine. "If one of the first ones go well, perhaps I can get it scheduled for Friday? But depending on when things are scheduled, I can call my dad and see if he'll wire some money so I can either stay out here for a few days next week and fly home, or I can drive back another time. I don't know… I'm trying not to think about these logistics because I don't want it to be an omen."

"An omen?" Jake asked.

"Yeah, like a sign of bad things."

"No, I know what an omen is, but how do you mean it now?"

"Jake, I'm serious. I want to have a job here if I'm moving. I hate sitting around at home now; it'd be worse in a new city. If the logistics of all this get too… kooky, I, ugh, I don't know what to do," Cassidy said seriously. Jake looked down.

"It will work."

"I hope so."

"Cassidy, I love you, and I'm pretty sure you love me."

"You know I do."

"Then we can figure out logistics," Jake said determinedly. Cassidy wanted to argue but she knew it was no use. Why burst his bubble before she had to? Why burst her bubble before she had to?

She decided to change the subject. "Tell me about your apartments?"

"I'm meeting with Rick, that agent. I forget what his title is, but he helps renters find places, not buyers."

"Ahh, yeah I remember you on the phone with Rick."

"Well, he has a few places lined up tomorrow and we'll talk and branch out from there depending on what I like and what's available."

"Are you excited? What would be your dream apartment?" Cassidy asked, attempting to sound as cheerful as she could for him. Jake listed off what he wanted in the place and all the things he had seen in the listing books that Rick had mailed him last week. She smiled as she listened. He was so excited. He was going to get the perfect place. He needed to. He deserved to!

Cassidy's first interview on Monday was spectacular! It was for a financial analyst position at an engineering firm in the city. She really liked the team that interviewed her. She gave them the phone number of the hotel where she was staying and her room number in case they called this week. However, her second interview was far less successful. The HR manager at a tax office had zero interest in hiring someone from out of state and was quite snippy about it. Cassidy could barely list all of her qualifications before she was ushered back out the door, leaving her feeling quite defeated.

With no interviews on Tuesday, Cassidy joined Jake in looking at a few apartments around the area. It was a very different experience from when Cassidy and Marissa found their place in Erie four years ago. They saw a four story walk up, a two bedroom basement apartment, and a ground floor unit in an old stone building that both Jake and Cassidy agreed they would never want to be in at night. Very creepy!

On Wednesday, she interviewed at an insurance company

199

for an auditor position. The interview went well, but it was definitely not the job Cassidy was hoping for. While the woman interviewing her was nice, the work itself sounded terrible. Cassidy returned to the hotel after the interview, ready to have a moment to herself while Jake was at Northwestern talking to his new department head. She needed a moment alone to process everything. Cassidy unlocked the hotel door and found a slip of paper on the floor when she walked in.

**MESSAGE FOR CASSIDY BANKER. ROOM 407. CALL TAKEN AT FRONT DESK – 10:42AM. DAVID PHIPPS CALLED ABOUT INVERVIEW. CALL BACK # 847-555-9322.**

It was hand-written on a piece of hotel stationary. Cassidy stared at it for a moment before letting out a squeal. David Phipps was one of the people who had interviewed her for the financial analyst position at the engineering firm on Monday.

She quickly shut the door behind her, shimmied off her coat and took a seat on the bed as she rummaged through her purse for her phone card.

The phone barely rang twice before it was picked up.

"Good Morning, Franklin Engineering, Rosa speaking. How may I direct your call?"

"Good Morning, Rosa. Cassidy Banker returning Mr. Phipp's call," Cassidy said as professionally as she could. In reality, her heart was pounding in her ears.

"Let me see if he's available," Rosa said before putting the call on hold. Classical music filled the line. Cassidy wondered if it was supposed to be soothing. It wasn't. She anxiously waited for just over a minute -- the equivalent of twelve minutes in hold music time -- before Rosa came back on the line.

"Ms. Banker?"

"Yes?"

"Mr. Phipps is ready to take your call. I'll transfer you."

"Thanks," Cassidy said. There were two loud clicks.

"Hello," a strong male voice answered.

"Um, hi, this is Cassidy Banker returning your--"

"Ah! Ms. Banker. You return calls quickly," Mr. Phipps remarked.

"Yes, yes, I try," Cassidy replied, frantically looking at her watch. She hadn't checked the time before calling. It was 11:13AM. Pretty good turn-around time.

"Well, I wanted to reach out and see if you're available for a second interview."

"Yes! Yes, thank you," Cassidy rambled before biting her lip. She had to sound professional, not like someone three months out of work and on her last prayer.

"Alright, can you come in tomorrow at 2PM?" Mr. Phipps asked. Cassidy dug in her purse once more for her mini date book. She had an interview with another tax agency at ten the same day.

"Yes, I can be there."

"Wonderful. You'll be meeting with the panel from Monday as well as one of our VPs."

"Looking forward to meeting them," Cassidy replied honestly.

"I've got you on the calendar; just check in with Rosa when you arrive. See you tomorrow."

"Thank you! See you tomorrow, Mr. Phipps," Cassidy said before hanging up the phone. Cassidy picked up a pillow and screamed into it. She couldn't wait to tell Jake!

Cassidy kept her Thursday morning interview. It was for a very similar job to her previous tax agency interview. While this one went very well, and Cassidy would honestly be quite happy to work there, there were thirteen other CPAs in the waiting room lined up for interviews. Talk about a confidence shaker.

Jake took her out to lunch and did not let her have the lunch special margarita that she desperately wanted. They walked around the city and found a park to relax in before he dropped her off for her second interview at Franklin Engineering.

Rosa led her to the same conference room she'd been in the first time and offered her a glass of water while she waited. Mr. Phipps and the rest of the panel – Mr. Tochet, Mrs. Reed, and Mr. Coomer -- greeted her warmly. She was introduced to the Vice President, Mr. Myers, an older man dressed in an expensive-looking grey suit, complete with a red bowtie. This man was old money if she had ever seen it.

The interview followed a similar pattern to the first. She answered all the questions confidently and made sure to ask a few of her own. Everyone seemed quite happy.

"Now, Cassidy," Mr. Myers began. "I do see that you have your address listed as Erie, Pennsylvania."

"Yes, sir. I am from there and currently live there, but I'm in the process of relocating to the Chicago area," Cassidy replied honestly.

"What brings you here? It can't be the weather," Mr. Myers joked. Cassidy gave a small, polite laugh.

"Well, I'm quite used to snow, so it won't scare me away."

"But what is the reason for this move?" Mr. Phipps asked. Cassidy bit her tongue. She refused to say that she was following a boy. That was not going to get her hired.

"I'm ready for a change. I'm twenty-six, and I've spent my whole life in Northwest Pennsylvania. While I love it and it will always be home, I… I want to step out of my bubble. Try something new," she said.

"That's admirable. Especially for a young person who isn't moving to New York or LA in hopes of becoming famous," Mrs. Reed said. Cassidy smiled at her.

"I definitely wouldn't make it in the entertainment world. I'll stick to numbers."

"Numbers are important," Mr. Phipps nodded. "Cassidy -- Ms. Banker."

"Cassidy is fine."

"Cassidy, can you excuse us for a few minutes, please?"

"Oh, um, sure… should I go out to reception, or..?"

"You can stay here. One of us will be back shortly," Mr. Phipps said. Cassidy nodded and smiled as she watched the five of them depart and close the door behind them. She let out a shaky breath. This was very stressful. Cassidy downed the remaining contents of her water glass in a single gulp. She wished she had something to distract her. The room had a few framed certificates of local awards and a large black and white photograph a man from many years ago – possibly the founder? Cassidy stood up and stretched as she walked over to the large window. The office was on the second floor and the window looked out over the street. While there was a fair amount of traffic, it was far from distracting enough to help Cassidy pass the time. She slowly made a lap around the conference room, reading all of the certificates and news articles that hung on the walls. She was just about halfway through a Chicago Tribune article from 1978 when the door opened.

"Thank you for your patience," Mr. Phipps said, closing the door behind him. Cassidy couldn't help but notice that he was alone.

"Not a problem. I enjoyed the reading," Cassidy lied with a smile as she retook her seat and he sat across from her.

"Well, I think the dry reading will have been worth it," Mr. Phipps smirked at her. "I spoke with my colleagues, and we would like to offer you a position here at Franklin Engineering."

"Oh!" Cassidy gasped. She felt the wind being knocked out of her. "Wow, thank you!"

"Yes, I've outlined the offer here for you to review." He passed over a manilla folder. Cassidy opened it. The first thing she spotted was the salary – almost double what she made in Erie. She tried to remind herself that the Chicago area was far more expensive, but still, it was an impressive number. The list of responsibilities and duties all fell within what they had discussed, and she felt confident that she could do or learn everything asked of her. Normal hours – Monday thru Friday, 9AM to 6PM with an hour for lunch. Honestly, she was excited for a full hour break in the day. Lunches at her last company were scarfing down food in the break room before running back to her desk to answer the phone. Everything looked perfect. There was one big question that stood in front of her, though.

"Mr. Phipps, this all looks great, but I do have to ask, when is the start date? As you know, I'm from Pennsylvania, and while I can start soon, unfortunately, it cannot be immediately," Cassidy said nervously, mentally praying this didn't knock the offer off the table.

"Yes, we are aware of your situation. We are willing to

work with you on this. If you are interested in accepting the offer of employment, we can delay your start, but would ask that you complete the training manual before starting and take an exam on it on your first day. That is why we offered a lower starting salary -- however, that has potential to increase after six months, depending on your performance," Mr. Phipps explained. Cassidy worked extremely hard to keep her face straight. That was the lowball salary? Damn!

"I really appreciate that. Everything sounds more than reasonable."

"I'm glad to hear."

"So, um, do I sign this paper? What do I need to do to accept?" Cassidy asked. She could hear her voice shake and took a deep breath to control it.

Mr. Phipps had her sign and date both her copy and his, and he signed and dated below her. After a few pleasantries exchanged, he asked Cassidy to return on Monday to pick up the training material, as they did not have that prepared at the moment. Cassidy assured him that she could easily do that. while deep down she knew she would be calling her father for another loan that evening.

She took the bus back toward the hotel and was left with just a five block walk. She could do it. She could figure this all out.

*Raymond Phipps*                 *Cassidy Banker*

3-24-88                                    *3-24-88*

Jake hopped up from where he was lounging on the bed when she walked back into their hotel room.

"So?" He asked anxiously as she closed the door behind her and set her bag down on the dresser.

"I got it!" Cassidy squealed.

"Holy shit!" Jake ran over and scooped her up in a tight hug, lifting her off the ground and spinning twice. Cassidy laughed and cried and hugged him tightly back.

"Oh, my gosh!" she said as she set her down. Her heart was beating a mile a minute. This was the first time she let herself truly react to the news.

"Does this mean you're going to move?"

"Well, I signed the offer, so I better move or it's one hell of a commute," she chortled.

"We're... we're really moving to Illinois?" he asked. Cassidy saw tears start to form in his eyes.

"Yes! Yes, I think we are!"

"I love you so much!" Jake breathed as he pulled her into another tight hug. He gave a slight sniffle. Cassidy was touched by how happy he was. She was still in disbelief.

"I love you, too!"

"Okay," Jake said, pulling back, and clearly trying to settle himself. "Want to go look at some apartments with me?"

"Yeah. Yeah, that would probably help," she grinned.

"Great! I have another appointment with my agent in an hour."

"Perfect," Cassidy smiled. "I need to be back to call my dad before it is too late there."

"He'll be thrilled."

"Um, maybe... but I have to ask for another loan to stay a couple of extra nights and then either a plane or bus ticket home next week."

"Really?"

"Yeah, I need to go in on Monday to get my training stuff. They're willing to delay my start date, so I couldn't say I couldn't wait around a few more days."

"When do you start?"

"I have up to eight weeks," Cassidy said. It sounded both really far and really near.

"Wow."

"Yes, wow!"

# Chapter 20

The city lights of Pittsburgh shone in the night sky during the plane's descent as they flew above downtown in a slow loop toward the airport. Cassidy smiled as the plane leaned slightly as it turned and she got an even better view. They'd be landing in about ten minutes so they were quite low.

She had called her father on Thursday and very anxiously asked for an additional loan. Art was quite unhappy when he heard that she was in Chicago and needed two nights in a hotel plus transportation home. Cassidy didn't want to tell him she was moving over the phone. A big announcement like this needed to be done face to face. She promised him that she would explain everything when she got home, and that she'd work out a repayment plan to start quite soon. Art graciously called the front desk of her hotel and extended her stay by two nights, although she did have to change rooms. And then he called his travel agent to book her a flight out of O'Hare. However, he had her fly into Pittsburgh as it was $100 cheaper than Erie's tiny airport. Cassidy tried to point out that it was an hour and a half drive from Meadville, while the Erie Airport was much closer to her apartment, but Art reminded her that would give her time to explain herself in the car. Cassidy couldn't lie, that was more than fair.

After a quick descent and a bit of a bumpy landing, Cassidy found herself walking down the jetway and into the airport terminal. She followed the herd toward the baggage claim. While she had only a carry-on, that was where she had promised to meet her dad. However, when she arrived in the large baggage claim area there was a familiar face waiting for her, but it wasn't her father.

"Alex?" Cassidy asked as she walked towards her eldest brother. Alex was leaning against the coffee kiosk which was currently closed as it was a few minutes after 9PM.

"Oh, hey."

"Hi."

"Did you know you can't smoke in here anymore?"

"I think they have designated smoking areas," Cassidy replied plainly, thoroughly confused as to why this was their opening topic.

"Absolute bullshit."

"It's not that bad. We'll be outside in a minute."

"Don't you have a suitcase?" Alex asked.

"Just a carry-on." Cassidy lifted her small duffle bag.

"Okay," he said, nodding toward the revolving door and walking away. Cassidy stood frozen for a few seconds before running along to follow him outside. The cold air hit her like a brick and she paused a moment to put on the winter coat that she had been carrying.

"Wait, what are you doing here? Dad was going to pick me up."

"Yeah, you're welcome," Alex said sarcastically as he lit the cigarette he had already popped in his mouth.

"Ugh. No. Thank you. I appreciate you coming to get me, I just... I was surprised not to see dad," she explained. Alex took a long drag and exhaled deeply.

"Yeah, dad threw out his back yesterday. He couldn't make the drive. I got nominated because apparently I'm the only one that's awake late."

"Wait, how did dad throw out his back?"

"Um, apparently, he was attempting to chop wood," Alex said. The two shared a look, both trying very hard not to be the first to crack a smile. Cassidy lost.

"Wha -- why was dad chopping wood? He's never done that before in his life," she asked.

"Mom said one of the neighbors was chopping and he wanted to help," Alex shrugged. They both shared a stifled chuckle before they remembered they were mad at each other.

"Come on, it's cold out. Let's get to the car," Alex said, setting off across the crosswalk. Cassidy silently trailed behind as they walked to the parking garage and found his car on the second level. Alex took the final puff of his now stub of a cigarette and flicked it out the window as they rolled out of the garage and he rolled up his window.

"Thank you," Cassidy said, thrilled to not have the March night air circling the car as they went.

"Mmmhmm," he hummed. Cassidy clenched her jaw. This was painful. She refused to ride two hours in annoyed silence.

"Can you talk to me? Please?"

"What?"

"We haven't spoken in weeks. I'm tired of you being pissed at me when you have no right to be," Cassidy huffed.

"No right to be?" he scoffed as he merged onto the northbound lane of the highway.

"That's right!"

"Cassidy… you lied to me for ten years."

"Lied?"

"My sister and my best friend… canoodling behind my back!"

"Ugh! Don't say canoodling. That's gross."

"Well, I call it like I see it."

"But you didn't see it," Cassidy said firmly as she glared at him. "It wasn't a secret relationship. It happened once when you were at work. One time, that's it. We never hung out or talked more than, hey! after that. So stop making up this narrative of an elaborate deceit."

"Oh," Alex mumbled under his breath. If he wasn't driving, Cassidy would have hit him.

"Yeah, oh! You got shitty with me because you misunderstood Laura's drunk ramblings."

"Don't be all high and mighty."

"No, I'm enjoying this. You were a jerk."

"Well, maybe it was a little too easy to believe," Alex grumbled as he changed lanes to pass a semi.

"Why didn't you even try to take my side?"

"Cassidy, your side is still not great."

"Okay, but you made up a whole fake story and got mad about it! That's not fair."

"I guess it was easy to think that way."

"Ugh, you suck," Cassidy groaned.

"I suck, but I'm the one giving you a ride?" Alex challenged.

"I didn't ask you to do that, be mad at dad."

"Jeez! I love you but you are frustrating as hell."

"Well, you won't have to suffer with me much longer."

"What in the world does that mean? Ugh, you're so friggin' dramatic," Alex grumbled.

"It means I'm moving to Chicago!" Cassidy yelled. Alex jolted and hit the breaks. The car swerved and two loud horns blared in anger. "Alex!!" she screamed as he got the car back under control.

"You're what?" he asked in disbelief.

"That's why I was there. I had a job interview, and I got it, and I'm going to move there."

"Why?"

"Why? Because I can't get a job here."

"There are other places!"

"Well, yes, there are."

"Did you and Jake break up and you're fleeing the state?"

"No! Jake will be there, too," Cassidy said.

"You're moving out of state… with your boyfriend?" Alex asked slowly. He was clearly trying to process this surprise information.

"Yeah. And I told Jake I wasn't going to go if I didn't find a job I would love. And I did. The company is great! I'm really excited."

"So, um, what--?"

"So, I got a job, and he got a job, and we found a place to live that's in our budget, and I looked up local organizations and things to do – there's a lot more than I expected," Cassidy rambled. After talking about the public transportation, the restaurants, little beaches on the lake, and the nightlife, she realized Alex was just staring straight out the windshield at the dark road in front of them.

"Care to comment?" she asked.

"I'm just… I can't believe you're leaving." He sounded sad. Cassidy's heart gave a sad thump.

"Yeah," she said in a low voice.

"When?"

"Um, like seven weeks."

"Seven weeks?"

"Yep. My new job gave me time to move – up to eight weeks. But I want to get out there a week early and get a little settled before starting, you know."

"Yeah, makes sense."

"I feel like you want to say something," Cassidy said after a long pause.

"No," Alex replied quietly.

"Alex, a few minutes ago you were ready to throttle me for being a slut."

"Um, no, you were the one ready to do the throttling."

"Fair, but… are you still mad? Are you new mad? Are we good?"

"I'm… We're… I'm going to miss you," he admitted.

"Aw, I'm going to miss you, too. But you have a phone, and I've heard rumors that Illinois also has phones," she teased, desperate to lighten the mood.

"Yeah, I heard that rumor, too," Alex smirked.

"And it's not like I'm not going to still see you," Cassidy said.

"Yeah, but it's different."

"How? I'm--" Cassidy started, but paused mid-sentence. It suddenly hit her. She wasn't going to be at the monthly dinners. She wasn't going to be at all the birthday meals. She would come home for some holidays, but the truth was, she knew she wanted to make her own traditions.

"Cassie?" Alex asked. Cassidy shook her head, not quite sure how long she had zoned out.

"Sorry, I just… I realized."

"Yeah," he nodded, knowing exactly what she meant. Cassidy gulped. As excited as she was for this new adventure, she was sure going to miss the comfortable life she had built at home.

"Ugh, can we turn on some music or you go back to being annoyed with me, or something?"

"I'm not annoyed with you," Alex snapped. They both laughed.

"Who are you going to pick fights with when I'm gone?" Cassidy asked playfully.

"I'm pretty sure I'm the passive one. You, on the other hand…"

"You yelled at me the other week!"

"You yell at everyone every week," Alex countered.

"I'm just passionate! And generally, I'm right."

"Ehhh…"

"You are such a liar," Cassidy sassed. Alex looked over at her and smiled.

"Well, it will be a lot more boring without you," he said sincerely. Cassidy felt the lump rise in her throat once more. She scooted over on the seat to lean her head on his shoulder.

"Thank you for picking me up tonight."

"I'll always pick you up."

"I'm so happy and so sad all at once!" Marissa gushed as she hugged Cassidy tightly.

"I know! Me, too," Cassidy agreed as she hugged her best friend back. Alex had dropped her off from their long journey from the airport about ten minutes ago. Cassidy was happy to be home, but then another wave of sadness hit when she realized it wouldn't be her home much longer. She had called Marissa from the hotel Saturday afternoon after Jake left to drive home and told her the big news.

"We have to do so many things before you go," Marissa began as she pulled back. "We have to go out to a club, we have to get pizza at Ziggy's, we have to go mini golfing at that place off the highway, we have to make tacos and brownies, we have to have a beer at EU with everyone from our floor of the apartment senior year like we did at Halloween. We have to have a night in and rent Jaws! Oh, and--"

"And that all sounds perfect and we have over a month. We can get all of it in, I promise," Cassidy smiled.

"I'll start making calls!"

"It's after 11PM."

"I'll start making a list of people to call tomorrow after work," Marissa said.

"Much better idea."

Cassidy arrived at her parents' house early that Friday. She wanted to talk to her father alone.

"Hi," she called out as she let herself in the front door.

"Cassidy?" Art called from his office off the foyer.

"Yeah," she replied, taking off her coat and hanging it in the front closet and kicking off her boots.

"You're early."

"I know," Cassidy said as she walked into his office. Art was sitting in his wingback chair and reading the newspaper.

"Hey."

"Hey! How's the back?" Cassidy asked, leaning over to give him a hug before taking a seat in the chair next to him.

"Easing up."

"Were you really chopping wood?"

"I was helping Doug Haller down the street."

"Dad, you've never chopped wood in your life!"

"No, but I golf a lot. It's the same thing, a swing is a swing."

"Except the axe is a lot heavier than a club," Cassidy pointed out.

"Oh, you sound like your mother," Art scoffed. Cassidy smiled at him.

"So, dad, I didn't get a chance to talk to you in the car from the airport, but I wanted to tell you: I'll be paying you back."

"I know you will be paying me back," Art said firmly.

"Yes, yes, I know, but I meant soon. I, um… I got a job!" Cassidy grinned. Art beamed proudly.

"You did? Oh, I'm so glad!" he reached over and patted her knee.

"Thanks, dad."

"Tell me all about it! I assume that's why you decided to pull that stunt and go away for a weekend?"

"Well, kind of. See, I got a job as a financial analyst for an engineering firm…"

"Oh wow, great gig. Which company?"

"Franklin Engineering."

"I don't know them."

"Well, that's because they're in Chicago."

"Their headquarters?"

"No, the whole company. I… I got a job in Chicago. I'm going to be moving to Illinois," Cassidy said with a nervous smile.

"You got a job out of state?" Art asked. Cassidy could tell he was trying to figure out how to react.

"I did."

"Well, look at you," Art said with a smile.

"Thanks. I know it's sudden and I know it's crazy, but I think this could be a really good opportunity."

"I'm not going to pretend that I'm thrilled my only daughter is deciding to pick up and leave the state, but I am proud of you for wanting to take a chance."

"It's a big chance," Cassidy said, letting out a deep breath.

"What about Jake?"

"He's going to be there, too."

"Oh, really?"

"Yeah, um… he got a job at Northwestern, and I wasn't sure about what to do, but I ended up getting a job and there's so much to do there, and -- I think it will be a good thing."

"Northwestern, really?" Art asked, looking quite impressed.

"Yeah. Basically teaching and working with the baseball team, like he does at MU, but you know … more," Cassidy chuckled.

"Well, hot damn."

"Dad," she laughed.

"Do you think he could get me football tickets? I'd love to go to a game."

"Um, I'm not sure, but… probably."

"Who do they all play? I'll need to pick someone good,"

217

Art said, clearly lost in his football dreams. Cassidy smiled. She would love to have her dad come out for a game. This could be a great tradition for them!

The Banker family was seated around the large dining room table and the serving dishes had finally made full loops around for everyone to fill their plates. Tonight they were enjoying pork barbeque, potato salad, Brussels sprouts, and corn bread. Ellie had joined the monthly dinner, having told Lynne at the wedding that she was really looking forward to it. Cassidy felt a mix of sadness at not getting to watch her full integration into the family chaos, and happiness that she had joined the crew. She was proud to pass the resident girl baton that she had carried for the past twenty-six years over to Ellie. As everyone was digging in, Cassidy decided to take advantage of the momentary silence. She had to pull the trigger.

"I got a job!" Cassidy called out loudly. Everyone looked over at her.

"Took you long enough," Matty smirked.

"Thanks, Mr. Kotter," Cassidy retorted.

"I take that as a compliment," Matty replied.

"You got a job!" Lynne cheered. She stood up, walked around Ben and gave her daughter a kiss on the cheek.

"Thanks, mom," Cassidy said as the rest of the family chorused in cheers of 'Good job!' and 'That's great!'

"Where will you be working?" Ellie asked eagerly. Alex returned to eating.

"I'm going to be a financial analyst at Franklin Engineering."

"That sounds important," Ellie said, looking impressed.

Cassidy took a deep breath to steady herself.

"It's in Chicago."

The only sound was Alex's fork stabbing one of his Brussels sprouts against the plate. It was only a few seconds of silence and everyone staring at her, but Cassidy felt it in her soul.

"Like… Illinois?" Eric asked, his face scrunched as if he were thinking quite hard.

"Yep," Cassidy nodded.

"So, you're moving?" Ellie asked cautiously.

"I am."

"Damn," Matty said, looking surprised.

"When?" Eric asked.

"In May."

"You're missing my graduation?" Ben asked, shooting her a hurt look.

"No, no, I think I'm here for it," Cassidy said, frantically trying to remember if she had budgeted her time correctly.

"May 8th… it's a Sunday," Ben said. Cassidy let out a relieved breath.

"Yep, yep, I'm here. I knew I didn't want to miss it," she told him honestly. She really could never forgive herself if she missed her younger brother's college graduation.

"Who the hell has graduation on a Sunday?" Matty asked loudly before turning to Alex, who had graduated from Mercyhurst seven years prior. "Was yours on a Sunday?"

"Hmmm, I don't think so… I think it was a Tuesday, maybe," Alex said before popping a forkful of potato salad in his mouth.

"Is the motto of the school, we hold graduation on the stupidest day of the week?" Matty quipped. Ellie laughed loudly.

"I think I've seen that engraved somewhere," Eric smirked.

"Shut up," Ben grumbled.

"I'll be there, Ben," Cassidy sat, reaching over and patting his shoulder with her right hand.

"So why are you moving?" Eric asked.

"What about Jake?" Ellie asked.

"Well, he's going, too. He got a job teaching and coaching at Northwestern, and well... it's perfect for him," Cassidy smiled.

"And?" Ellie asked.

"I'm thrilled for him. And I was on the fence about what I was going to do, but I ended up finding a really great job. I like the area, and there's a lot to do. We found a place to live! It just... it's all falling into place," Cassidy shrugged.

"Damn," Matty breathed, looking a mix of surprised and impressed. Cassidy looked over at her mother who was sniffling softly.

"Mom, no, don't cry!"

"No, no, I'm happy, I am, but I'm just realizing this is one of our last dinners," Lynne said, wiping a tear.

"Great job, Cassidy," Matty said sarcastically.

"Mom, guys, I'm not dying! Also, I don't leave for over a month. And after I do, I'll come back and visit, you guys can come and visit me. It will be fun!" Cassidy said.

"I'm sad, but I kind of like that we have an excuse for a road trip," Ellie said with a forced smile. Cassidy smiled at her.

"Are yinz going to be living, like, right downtown? Or don't they have beaches there? Are you living at the beach?" Ben asked.

"Beach?" Art asked, his mouth full of pork.

"Like the ones on Presque Isle," Eric said.

"Oh yeah," Art nodded.

"Well, my office is actually like three blocks from one of the beaches," Cassidy grinned at Ben. "But we found a townhouse in Evanston."

"Where?" Matty asked.

"It's just north of Chicago, top of the city. It's where Northwestern is. So, super close for Jake, he's only like five minutes from campus, tops."

"What about you?" Lynne asked.

"My office is in Chicago, but not far. Jake and I checked the odometer in his truck, it's just over eight miles."

"What's that in city driving time?" Art asked.

"Twenty minutes, but there are buses and trains, too. I'm going to figure it out, guys," Cassidy said.

"Alexander, I can't help but notice you're not super chatty," Matty smirked at Alex.

"I drove her from the airport on Monday. I had two hours in the car to hear all of this."

"And your sister making a life-altering move is boring now?" Lynne asked. Alex sighed.

"No, I'm, it's… good for her."

"Aw," Ellie pouted her bottom lip slightly.

"You're going to miss her," Ben sang.

"Just me?" Alex asked. "Well, that sucks for Cassie."

"We're all going to miss her," Lynne said over the chuckles at Alex's comment.

"There's a spare bedroom in our townhouse -- we can have guests," Cassidy said proudly.

"Alright, tell us about our lodging for when we come," Matty grinned. Cassidy couldn't help but laugh. She talked about their townhouse and the neighborhood they were going to live in, as well as restaurants they had found in the city. As they asked questions and talked and laughed and planned visits, Cassidy felt the weird twisty feeling once again –elated and heartbroken all at once. She had a feeling she would be feeling that a lot in the next couple of months.

# Chapter 21

The restaurant was packed and loud, filled with laughter, excited conversation, and the aromas of delicious foods. It was a Sunday evening, the first day in May. The weather finally felt like spring and everyone was out celebrating.

Cassidy sat at a large table with Jake, his mom, Claire, his brother, Will, Marissa, and Brandon. It was Jake's goodbye dinner. He had given his last final exam to his MU students last week, graded them, and finished up his paperwork and notes. He was finished as a professor there. The baseball team had two more games left in the season, but, as they were currently last in the league and Jake had been training his replacement all spring, the clipboard had been passed.

They had spent all day packing up Jake's house. He had rented a U-Haul trailer to hitch to the back of his pickup truck. The house was a flurry of packing. Tape, bubble wrap, wadded up newspapers, and boxes were everywhere. Matty had even stopped over to help for a few hours. However, he had a cookout with his friends already planned that evening and bowed out before they stopped for dinner -- although Cassidy had a strong suspicion that he was simply terrified of Claire and wanted an easy out.

After a full day of boxing and lugging, both the truck bed and the trailer were almost completely full. The only things left in the house were Jake's mattress, which was currently on the living room floor, a table lamp next to the mattress, a few pillows, two sleeping bags, a night's worth of toiletries, and clothes for tomorrow. While the place he had rented during his few years in Erie had never exactly been homey looking, it now looked sad and empty. Cassidy had teared up when they all left for the restaurant.

"This lasagna is delicious," Will remarked as he ate.

"It's so good here, we come all the time," Marissa said as she popped a forkful of ravioli in her mouth.

"Mom's lasagna is better," Jake smirked at his brother. Will rolled his eyes.

"Thank you, Jake," Claire said. "But I know you're just trying to butter me up for once again moving even further away from me."

"Ooof, that had to hurt," Will said.

"It's not like you've stayed close," Jake noted.

"Yeah, but now you're even further," Will sassed.

"You both left. Now shut up," Claire interjected firmly. Cassidy bit her bottom lip in a mix of fear and amusement, while both Marissa and Brandon stifled laughs.

"Will, what are you looking to do now that you graduated?" Cassidy asked, desperate for a subject change. Will had graduated from law school at Dickinson the previous week.

"Oh, that's right, you're a real lawyer now," Marissa said, looking impressed.

224

"Yeah, I am, sort of," Will chortled. "Um, well I did an internship at a firm in Harrisburg this past year, and they were waiting for my bar exam results. I'm also looking at the Pittsburgh area, as well as around State College."

"When do you get your results?" Brandon asked, taking a sip of his wine.

"Later this summer. It takes like eight weeks to hear back."

"Wow," Cassidy said in deep thought.

"Yeah, so I'm going to take the time and help Jakey move. And then come stay with mom for a bit, and then... well, the test results will tell where I go next," Will shrugged before taking another bite of lasagna.

"How are you holding up, Mrs. Sullivan?" Marissa asked.

"I'm getting by, like usual. It will be strange to have Will back at home for a month or so," Claire replied. She was a stoic woman. Cassidy respected her.

"I can't believe we got everything packed up so quickly," Jake commented.

"You don't have much more than the essentials; that made it easy," Brandon shrugged.

"He is not one for knick-knacks," Will snorted.

"That's good. Cassidy has a lot," Marissa added.

"I don't have that much," Cassidy said.

"Pffftt," Marissa raised her eyebrow. "Cassidy, you have so much stuff. Jake is in for a massive surprise."

"He knows what I have, and it's not going to be as dramatic as you're making it out to be."

"Mmmhmmm. Okay, just wait until you really start packing, then we'll talk," Marissa smirked proudly. Cassidy shook her head. She wasn't leaving for almost two weeks. While she had shuffled a few things in her room, Marissa was right, she hadn't really started packing yet. Once Jake was in their Evanston townhouse, she would have a lot more gusto to pack up and join him.

The six of them spent the rest of the meal talking and joking. Marissa planned everything she wanted to do on her visits, while Brandon argued for the superiority of Indianapolis, but he didn't seem to sway anyone. Will teased that he was going to decorate before Cassidy arrived, and Claire surprised everyone with stories of how messy and terribly decorated her boys' rooms were as children, making everyone laugh. Cassidy relished in every moment of the meal.

Finally, the plates were all empty, and the conversation was starting to lull. They closed out the check and made their way out of the restaurant and into the warm, dark night. There was a small parking lot across the street where they had all parked. This was the moment Cassidy was dreading. Goodbye.

"Oh my gosh, this is it, isn't it?" Marissa asked, pouting her bottom lip.

"Just until you visit," Jake said. Marissa lunged forward and hugged Jake around the middle. Cassidy smiled as he hugged her back. She knew the two of them got along, but hadn't expected them to miss each other with this move. Clearly they would.

Before she could start tearing up, Cassidy turned to Claire.

"It was so nice to see you again. We could not have gotten as much done without you," Cassidy said honestly.

"I do what I can to organize my boys," Claire smirked.

"Clearly, you do amazing work."

"Thanks," Claire nodded awkwardly. Cassidy knew this was a hard moment for her. She glanced over at her friends and saw Brandon gently pulling Marissa off of Jake.

"Come on, he's not dying," Brandon said as he pulled her back and extended a hand to Jake. "It's been fun, man."

"Yeah, great times," Jake grinned as he took Brandon's hand. As they all started talking with Will, Cassidy returned her attention to Claire.

"This is going to be great. Jake really deserves this job, and you know he's going to do so well," Cassidy said honestly.

"Yes, he will… he was always the one I knew would travel the furthest from home."

"Traveling isn't leaving. You'll visit us, right?"

"Will you visit me?" Claire challenged.

"Absolutely!" Cassidy nodded, knowing she was going to need to really juggle the holiday calendar for two Pennsylvania stops on return visits.

"I'll hold you to it."

"I would expect nothing less."

"You watch my boy out there," Claire said. Cassidy gulped, feeling the weight of Claire's request. Though she would never show it, Claire was sad and scared: two emotions she had never expected from this woman.

"He's going to do great. We're going to do great."

"You're fearless, bull headed, and fit for this challenge."

"Thank you?" Cassidy replied slowly, not sure if this was a compliment or not.

"You're welcome," Claire nodded. Apparently, it was meant as high praise. Cassidy tried to feel honored.

"Jake is ready for this, too. He may not be as … bull headed as me, but he put this all together himself. He can be quiet at times, but he's not a scared little boy."

"I appreciate hearing that," Claire smiled. Cassidy returned the gesture. "But I'm counting on you to fight off muggers or murderers or whatever those big cities all have."

"Happy to."

"I knew you would be," Claire said. Cassidy leaned forward and hugged her, despite knowing she was not a hugger. Claire patted her back and stepped away.

"What just happened?" Will asked in a low voice as his mom moved over to talk to Jake. Cassidy grinned at his amused look.

"Your mom and I get each other, that's all." Cassidy shrugged.

"Yeesh," Will sighed, making Cassidy laugh. "What time are you guys leaving tomorrow?"

"Given that we're camping on the living room floor with our mother, I doubt it will be a super fun night. So, I'm guessing we'll be up by six," Will replied with a low chuckle. "Mom's going to want to be on her way back to Johnsonburg the second we're down the street."

"That's fair. At least you guys will be there by early afternoon."

"Yeah. It should be good. I know driving through the city with a trailer will be a bitch, but better than doing it in rush hour."

"The good thing is, it's a straight shot through the city to the north and Evanston is right there."

"Good to know," Will nodded.

"You two won't have too much fun until I get there, right?" Cassidy asked playfully.

"That is yet to be determined. The last time the two of us spent this much time just the two of us was… summer before my junior year -- Jake's senior year in high school. Mom and dad went to Niagara Falls for an early an early anniversary trip," Will hummed, still looking in deep thought. Cassidy laughed.

"Well, the house is still standing, so I'm sure you'll be fine."

"Yeah."

"Have a good trip," Cassidy said, giving him a big hug.

"See you soon," Will hugged her back tightly. They smiled as they pulled back.

"We should go soon, boys," Claire said over everyone talking. Jake walked over to Cassidy and Will took his leave.

"I can't believe it's time," Cassidy said as she wrapped her arms around his shoulders. She could feel Jake snake his arms around her waist to hold her close as they talked.

"Yeah. You're coming out on the thirteenth, right?"

"Of course!" Cassidy assured him, placing a light kiss on his lips.

"I'll call you when I get out there."

"Yes, and give me our new number. Oh my gosh, our new number!" she grinned.

"Yes, our new number."

"And don't kill Will in the car. Or while moving in. He's being very helpful."

"I will not kill my brother in the car. Chicago does have a mob history though," Jake raised an eyebrow playfully.

"You dip, be nice... or I'll send your mom out there," Cassidy whispered.

"Well, shit, you play dirty, Banker."

"If I have to," she smirked.

"I'm going to miss you so much."

"I'm going to miss you, too." Cassidy buried her face in his shoulder for a moment as they hugged tightly.

"I'll see you soon," Jake said, kissing her cheek.

"And call at least twice a week until I get there," Cassidy said, pecking him on the lips.

"Definitely," Jake kissed her again.

"I love you."

"I love you, too," Jake said. They shared a last kiss for a few long seconds before pulling apart.

"Come on, Romeo," Will yelled, was climbing into the passenger's seat of the tan truck.

"Bye," Jake smiled at her before turning to climb into his truck. Marissa lovingly wrapped her arm around Cassidy's shoulder as they watched the Sullivan family drive off. Two weeks, Cassidy reminded herself. In two weeks, she would be with him and they would be starting their new lives.

"Let's go home," Marissa said as the truck turned out of sight at the second light.

"Yeah, let's go." Cassidy smiled at her best friend and they walked to her car with Brandon in tow.

# Chapter 22

"Fore!" Ben screamed as the volleyball zoomed diagonally off the heel of his palm, missing Alex's head by an inch.

"This isn't golf," Eric said.

"I thought it just meant watch out," Ben shrugged.

"In golf." Eric shook his head.

"What do you say in volleyball?" Ben asked.

"We say you're an idiot." Alex rolled his eyes as he returned from chasing the ball and tossed it back over the net at his youngest brother.

"Ha-ha-ha. I'm pretty sure this idiot just graduated, with honors, a few hours ago," Ben pointed out before serving the ball once more. This time it flew right to Laura who easily bumped it back. It was Sunday evening and the family was playing volleyball in the Banker's backyard after dinner. The day had been busy and festive after Ben's graduation earlier that afternoon. The whole family, including Cassidy's maternal grandmother and paternal grandparents, sat at the Campus Center to watch Ben and three hundred of his classmates walk across the stage and toss their caps in the air. It was a beautiful, albeit, long day of ceremony that started with Mass, broke for brunch, followed by speeches, and a full commencement program. Lynne burst into tears no less than five times; Ben was the last of her children to graduate. Her youngest baby. She kept reminding everyone that this was the last graduation she would be attending as a mom. While she really hoped to attend future graduations as a grandmother, this was the final time she would be the mother of the graduate. Cassidy honestly felt for her. Five high school graduations and five college graduations. It was the end of an era.

After lots of pictures and hugs, including a few teary goodbye hugs between Cassidy and her grandparents, the eight Bankers, now including Ellie and Laura, departed campus and the city and returned to Meadville. Dinner was a large cookout filled with laughter and arguments. Lynne insisted on cleaning up without help, but Cassidy assumed she just wanted a few moments of peace while they played a spirited game of volleyball in the yard.

"Out!" Art yelled as one of Ellie's returns landed way off to the left. Ellie shrugged, clearly unbothered. While she fit in well with the Bankers, she lacked the competitive spirit and willingness to fight for every point. Granted, that was probably a positive attribute in this environment.

"Alright, my serve," Laura said, twirling the ball in her palms. She served with a thud of her hand and it went right to Matty, who bumped it high. The volley started, one of their longest in the game. Cassidy was just jumping to set the ball over the net when Lynne called out loudly. The ball bounced off her fingertips and smacked Ben in the side of the head.

"Ow!"

"Sorry," Cassidy winced.

"Come on, dessert time!" Lynne yelled. Eric scooped up the ball and they all herded over to the patio where Lynne was setting out trays on the picnic table.

"What's all this?" Ellie asked, looking impressed. Laid out on the table were two cakes and a large plate of about five dozen cookies.

"This is a meaningful night, so we have to have the proper treats."

"Wow, mom," Cassidy smiled as she spotted the cakes. One was decorated with green and white icing and said "Congrats Ben!" with a black graduation cap perched on the C. The other was pink and blue with "To your biggest adventure, Cassidy" written in script. She felt herself tear up slightly.

"Did you make those?" Ellie asked her mother-in-law.

"Yes, I did."

"They look amazing!" Laura said in awe.

"Get a picture, quick! I'm ready to dig in," Art said, a plate already in his hand.

"I know, I know," Lynne said as she picked up the blue, rectangular camera and snapped a picture of the cakes. Then she made Cassidy and Ben stand behind each of theirs and took another snapshot.

Quickly, the cakes were cut, the cookies were loaded onto plates, and everyone took their seats to dig in.

"So, Cass, when are you going to know about football tickets?" Matty asked with a mouthful of cake.

"Honestly, no idea, but I am going to look into it for you."

"Why would we go out to see a Northwestern game? They suck," Ellie scrunched her nose.

"They do, but it would be pretty neat to see a game out

there," Art said, taking a swig of his beer.

"If we want to drive to a game, we go could to Penn State," Ellie grinned.

"Or Pitt," Eric challenged with a smirk.

"Or stay here and watch MU," Laura shrugged, making everyone laugh.

"I think the whole idea is to come visit me and Jake," Cassidy pointed out.

"No, it's definitely the football we're after," Matty quipped. Cassidy rolled her eyes.

"How's Jake doing at the new place?" Lynne asked.

"Good, good. He and Will are there and they haven't killed each other yet, so, that's something," Cassidy chuckled, popping a forkful of cake in her mouth.

"Is he working?" Ellie asked.

"He's shadowing right now. He likes it, but he said he's glad he gets time to shadow before he has to step up as it's a much bigger program."

"When does he officially start?" Alex asked.

"In July for the baseball team and then classes start in mid-August," Cassidy nodded.

"And when do you start?" Art questioned.

"Less than two weeks. I'm leaving early Thursday morning and arrive mid to late afternoon. Then I'll have all weekend to settle in and a few days to really learn my way around a bit. I'm stopping in at the office to turn in my training binders, and I'll start after that!" Cassidy smiled. She felt a mix of excited and overwhelmed. After all this waiting, it was finally happening.

"Wow. And you're not going to be back for a First Friday in... what, like, a year?" Ben commented.

"Yeah, I don't know. I, um, I just need to get through these next couple of weeks first," Cassidy replied.

"We'll see her in less than a year," Lynne said firmly. A chorus of agreement followed. Cassidy appreciated it.

"What about you, Ben? This is your day after all," Laura jumped in, forcefully changing the focus. Ben told everyone about the job he got at a psychiatric facility as an addictions counsellor. Naturally, Matty jumped in with a slew of madhouse jokes that Eric, Alex, and even Laura were quick to build on. Ellie giggled away, especially when Art threw in a joke that absolutely flopped, and Lynne put her head in her hands in embarrassment.

The family talked and laughed well after the sun was down and they were illuminated only by two tiki torches and the dimming patio light that Art had continually forgotten to change the bulb to.

It was after 9PM by the time they were back inside and cleaning up. Other than Cassidy and Ben, everyone else had to work the next day. Once the leftovers had been packed up and distributed, it was time to leave.

Which Cassidy knew was also time for goodbyes. Thankfully she could save three for later. Alex, Eric, and Ben would be helping her make the drive out. Initially it was just going to be Cassidy and Eric; however, after the decision to rent a small U-haul truck for her furniture, it became apparent that none of the family had faith in either of the twins driving a moving truck across town, let alone across multiple states. Frankly, they both found it a little offensive -- even if they were the only two Banker children to have ever had any (thankfully minor) car accidents.

Alex quickly volunteered to help, and Ben, desperate for something to do in his first week post-grad, offered to join on the stipulation that Cassidy bought him a pizza in return. She agreed, though she was a little irritated that no one seemed to have any qualms about Ben driving a truck.

Even with holding off on three of the goodbyes, she still had five painful ones in front of her tonight. Cassidy went to Ellie first.

"Oh, no," Ellie said, pouting her lower lip slightly.

"I know," Cassidy agreed with a sigh.

"I feel like we were just becoming real friends."

"Yeah, the timing kind of sucks." Cassidy gave a half chuckle.

"You're going to tell us all about it and come back and visit, right?"

"Absolutely!" Cassidy assured her. "And you're going to keep me posted on things here and come visit me, right?"

"Absolutely!" Ellie nodded. Cassidy smiled and the two hugged tightly for a long moment.

"Make sure to hold your own at the dinners. You've got to toughen up," Cassidy winked at her as they pulled apart.

"I'll do my best," Ellie grinned. Eric came to stand next to her and nodded at his twin.

"See you bright and early on Thursday?"

"Yes, thank you," Cassidy said.

"Ugh, if it wasn't the last month of school, I'd totally help you," Ellie said.

"It's okay, Matty and Laura are in the same boat. Teachers in the family have to stay until the end of the school year," Cassidy assured her.

"Eric promised to take a few pictures of your new place so I can see it when he gets back."

"Yep, I will," Eric smiled. Cassidy jolted slightly as she felt a heavy arm sling around her shoulder. She was not surprised to see it belonged to Matty.

"Hey, Ellie, what are you going to do while the old man is away?" he asked playfully. Eric rolled his eyes.

"Not too much. I'm having dinner with my friends Friday night and I might go see my parents."

"I get it. That's what you gotta say with him standing right there." Matty dramatically nodded towards Eric. Ellie laughed.

"I'm less concerned with her wanting to throw some random party while I'm gone and more concerned with her going to the animal shelter and adopting some strays," Eric said. Cassidy gasped.

"You're getting a pet?"

"Well, I really want a cat," Ellie admitted.

"Why?" Matty asked, scrunching his nose. He was a dog lover through and through.

"Aw, you should definitely get a kitten. Eric, why won't you let her get a kitty?" Cassidy smacked his shoulder.

"I never said no, we're just getting settled into the new place, still. I'd like to be a bit more organized before bringing in a small animal that we could lose."

"Won't lose a dog!" Matty interjected.

"There are small dogs… some smaller than cats," Cassidy said.

"Yeah, but they're terrible. I mean a real dog," Matty nodded and Cassidy cackled. Eric and Ellie started talking about pet adoption and Cassidy turned her attention to Matty.

"I'm bummed you won't be on the road trip out."

"Yeah… Alex and Eric are going to kill Ben when it's his turn to drive the truck. It'll be funny as hell."

"I can keep Ben in the car with me."

"And ruin everyone's entertainment?" Matty asked in fake surprise.

"I'm more concerned about my worldly possessions strewn across the highway in Indiana."

"Eh, that's fair."

"Please come visit this summer. Jake and I can show you all the cool restaurants we find – you'll love it," Cassidy smiled. She did want Matty to visit, and he was the foodie of the family so would greatly enjoy the huge selection of cuisine in the big city.

"Oh, definitely," Matty grinned. Cassidy turned toward him and gave him a big hug. Their hugs were usually quick or playful -- not that they didn't love each other, but that was just Matty's playful personality. However, this time, he held tight. Cassidy was going to miss him and hated that it would be months until she watched him play another prank. After Matty, Cassidy went down the hall and found Laura. Before she got a word out of her mouth, Laura launched herself forward and hugged her tight.

"Ugh, I'm going to miss you," Laura whispered. There was a catch in her voice that shot right through Cassidy.

"I'm going to miss you, too," Cassidy said as they hugged. There was nothing else she could say. She had known Laura for almost ten years. She had become the sister she'd always wanted.

"You'll call me every week?"

"Definitely," Cassidy assured her. After a long minute, they pulled apart.

"Drive safe, okay?"

"Yeah… make sure Alex gets some sleep before the drive on Thursday."

"I will," Laura smiled.

"Bye," Cassidy said softly before making her way back to where her parents were standing outside of Art's office. She swallowed hard. This was going to be tough.

"Well," Lynne said in a shaky voice as she reached over and brushed a stray strand of hair behind her daughter's ear.

"You guys… um…" Cassidy stuttered slightly.

"We're proud of you," Art said. Cassidy's bottom lip quivered as she looked up at her dad. He looked at her with such pride, yet such sadness. Cassidy could feel that look in her soul. She hugged him tightly.

"Thank you. Thank you so much. For everything," Cassidy cried into his shoulder. He hugged her back. She wanted to say more, but the words didn't come, so she just stayed in his embrace.

Lynne sniffed as she watched them. Cassidy pulled back and looked over at her. She had tears streaming down her face.

"Oh, mom." Cassidy stepped over to hug her. After a long embrace, Lynne pulled back and rested her hands on Cassidy's shoulders and looked her in the eye.

"Cassidy, you be smart out there."

"I will."

"This is such an opportunity and I'm so proud and excited for you, but I'm going to miss you so much," Lynne sniffled.

"I'm going to miss you, too."

"I want you to make a life out there, but I really hope you come home for at least one holiday a year."

"I definitely will. Remember, Jake's family is here, too," Cassidy smiled at her.

"Yes… but don't be running back and forth all the time."

"I won't mom. But I will always come home," Cassidy

assured her.

"Aw," Lynne hummed, reaching up to wipe a tear off of her daughter's cheek with her thumb. Cassidy smiled at the touch.

"You guys are coming to visit at some point?" Cassidy asked, looking tearfully between her parents.

"Absolutely! I want to see you place -- especially after it's decorated," Lynne nodded. Cassidy chuckled slightly.

"Yes, I'm afraid to see what Will and Jake have come up with."

"You'll have time to put your stamp on the place, too," Lynne said.

"We can come out in fall if Jake gets football tickets. Or we can just go in spring – he'll have to get us baseball tickets," Art said. Cassidy resisted an eye roll.

"You can also visit if we don't have a game to go to."

"Well, yeah," Art agreed.

"There are a lot of steak houses out there…"

"Ooo," Art smiled. Cassidy grinned.

"Cassidy, you're blocking us in," Alex said from the front door.

"Coming."

"Well, this is it… you and your brothers drive safe, and call me when you get there," Lynne said.

"Will do. You have the phone number I gave you?" Cassidy asked.

"Yes, it's on the fridge," Lynne smiled.

"Great, alright, bye… Thank you," Cassidy nodded earnestly.

"Goodbye, Cassidy," Art said. Both he and Lynne leaned in and gave her a kiss on each cheek. Cassidy gave a small wave before rushing to collect her purse from the coat tree and departing her childhood home.

She shared a quick goodbye with Alex, she would be seeing him in a few days, and climbed into her Toyota. As Cassidy pulled out of the driveway and headed down the street, she felt tears fall once more. A lifetime of memories was behind her. She wondered when the next time she would get to drive down that street and walk into her parents' house would be. Six months, at the earliest, if they came back for Thanksgiving. It was a weird feeling.

# Chapter 23

Cassidy slowly paced around her bedroom at the apartment. It was empty. The carpet showed indents from her bed, dresser, chair, and bookshelf. Her walls were now bare, with a few spots of discoloration from posters that had been tacked up for four years. She crossed her arms over her stomach. The room held so many good memories: lots of laughs, there were many kisses, there were all-night talks on her bed. There was a small black spot on the carpet by the indentation left by her dresser from when she dropped her open tube of mascara when she and Marissa were getting ready to meet a group of friends at a club three years ago. There were memories of music from her boombox playing as she cried after a break up. She could smell the take-out food, the candles, the perfume. This room that had been so filled with life, love, and emotion, was now empty. Cassidy let out a sad sigh as she took one more slow lap around the room. It was time to leave.

She exited her room and made her way down the hall to the kitchen where Marissa was standing at the counter picking at some grapes. She looked stressed.

"So, what are you going to do with my room?" Cassidy asked. She tried to sound casual, though they both felt the heaviness in the air. The guys were all outside getting things organized in the truck. Cassidy had come upstairs for a final look around to make sure nothing was forgotten.

"Dunno. Maybe make it a gym," Marissa shrugged.

"You hate the gym," Cassidy smirked.

"Yeah. Maybe I can do jazzercise or something."

"Please send me a video tape of that," Cassidy snorted.

"Honestly, it'll probably just be my closet," Marissa smiled.

"Excuses for a lot more shopping!"

"I like that."

"So, you're going to be okay here on your own?" Cassidy asked.

"Yeah, yeah. All good… it'll be quiet, though."

"Well, at least Alex won't call in the middle of the night and wake you anymore."

"Not going to lie, that will be nice," Marissa chuckled before a long quiet fell over the two friends.

"So,"

"You'll call me as soon as you get there, right?" Marissa interjected, slowly stepping towards her.

"Yes."

"Like, we don't even have to talk then, but just let me know you're there and then we can talk talk tomorrow."

"I promise, I'll call you as soon as I get in the door," Cassidy smiled. "You have my new number?"

"Yes."

"Will you come out and visit me sometime?"

"Will you come home and visit me sometime?"

"Yes." They nodded in unison, then each let out a small laugh before crashing together is a big hug. They held on to each other tightly. Cassidy took the time to remember the smell of Marissa's apple shampoo and the feel of the old, worn fabric of her favorite T-shirt she wore around the house all the time. "Camp Ramah in the Poconos – Summer 1972."

They were both trying hard not to cry, although tears did slip out. After a long minute or two, they pulled back.

"Don't cry -- you're going to make me feel bad for not being happy for you right now," Marissa sniffled.

"Well, don't you cry either, you'll make me feel bad for leaving," Cassidy retorted with a loud gulp. Suddenly they both let out a sputtering laugh. Cassidy had no idea why, but they went from crying to laughing in seconds.

"Here," Marissa said, walking over to the end table and grabbing a few tissues for them.

"Thanks." Cassidy blew her nose. "You wanna walk down with me?"

"Yeah. I want to see you off. Also, I need to make sure Brandon doesn't jump into that damn truck," Marissa said with an eye roll.

"Oh, before I forget," Cassidy said, reaching into her purse and grabbing her key ring. She fumbled with it a moment before freeing a bronze-colored key with a square head. "Here is the apartment key."

"Hmmm," Marissa hummed as she took the key. "Guess it's really official now."

"Yeah. I can't get back in." Cassidy let out a low breath. Marissa slipped the key into the pocket of her jeans shorts and they departed the apartment together for the final time.

Both the truck and car were fully packed. Both vehicles had their maps in the glove box and the drivers knew where to go. Thankfully, it was pretty much a straight shot. All four Bankers had a bottle of pop and a few car snacks. It was almost 10AM and their goal was to get to Toledo before they stopped for lunch. Knowing the U-Haul was going to need at least one more stop for gas, they still were hoping to pull up to the townhouse in Evanston before 7PM Central time. Cassidy had talked to Jake that morning and he promised to have a feast of take-out options upon arrival. She couldn't wait to see him. Jake assured her that he and Will had not killed each other, and not done any property damage yet. However, one of the dining room chairs apparently took a gnarly tumble and was now down to three legs and half a backrest. Will was determined to repair it, but Jake said it wasn't looking good. The repair project was keeping him occupied, though, so Jake let him continue, with the plan to toss the chair in the dumpster when Will returned home in a few days.

Cassidy hugged Brandon goodbye. She was going to miss seeing him around, but she was glad that Marissa had him to keep her company today. Cassidy and Marissa shared one more big hug. After a final glance around the apartment complex parking lot, she climbed into the driver's seat of her blue Toyota.

Ben was in the passenger's seat, already munching on a bag of BBQ chips. While Ben and Alex were the designated U-haul drivers of the group, they had been squabbling all morning.

Cassidy and Eric decided that, for the safety of all involved and the survival of Cassidy's possessions, they would keep them separated for at least the first leg of the journey. Alex won the coin toss and got to drive the truck first. They would reshuffle drivers after the lunch stop.

Cassidy started up her car, and shifted into drive. Ben popped in her Duran Duran cassette and turned the volume up. Cassidy honestly appreciated the distraction. She led the way for the little Banker convoy as they left Erie and merged onto I-90 West, which was going to be their home for the next seven hours.

About twenty minutes into the drive, Ben had consumed all of his car snacks and was lightly drumming along to the music on his knees.

"Hey, Ohio!" he said. Cassidy looked at the "Welcome to Ohio" sign on the side of the road. She felt her heart thump. She glanced back in the rearview mirror and saw Alex and Eric in the U-haul, and in the far left behind her, she saw the "Welcome to Pennsylvania" sign for passengers travelling the other direction.

"Wow. I really am moving away."

"Well, duh," Ben shook his head before returning to his drumming. Cassidy bit her lip, torn between crying and laughing. Instead, she simply slipped on her sunglasses and smiled.

She'd taken the leap. There was no turning around or looking back. She was ready for her new life, new adventure, and new story to tell!

# THE END

# Epilogue

## *Cassidy and Jake*

After settling into their townhouse, Cassidy sent her first postcard from the city to her old coworker, Gladys, who had written back immediately. The two remained pen pals for over a decade until Gladys's passing in 2001.

Jake proposed to Cassidy on July 4, 1988 -- their first holiday in their new city. They married on May 19, 1990 back in Erie, surrounded by friends and family.

Cassidy and Jake welcomed son, Dylan Arthur Sullivan, on April 18, 1991 in Chicago.

Jake loved his job with Northwestern -- especially traveling around the country with the baseball team. By the mid-90s he was teaching multiple classes and appointed to the academic board at the university.

Cassidy truly enjoyed her job at Franklin Engineering. She made a large community for herself in Chicago by joining a running club as well as an investment group. True to form, she made friends quickly and happily kept a very full schedule.

Cassidy ran the Chicago marathon in 1993 at age 31. Jake and two-year-old Dylan were happy to watch from the sidelines.

Dylan was a happy and social little boy. He was always involved in T-ball and then baseball from kindergarten through 10th grade. His family from Pennsylvania always attended to at least one of his games each year. He enjoyed the sport, but wasn't quite as in love with it as his parents hoped. He loved building computers and was incredibly intelligent. He got an academic scholarship and attended Penn State – much to

Jake's delight.

Both Jake and Cassidy retired in 2019. With Dylan out of the house, they decide to move back to Pennsylvania to be closer to family. Jake returned as an adjunct professor at Mercyhurst and continues to teach one class a semester. Cassidy is happily retired.

## *Alex and Laura*

Alex and Laura were married on June 10, 1989 in an outdoor ceremony at a park in Erie.

They, reluctantly on Alex's part, moved out their loft soon after the wedding, and bought a house on the edge of the city. Laura was thrilled to have a garden. Alex loved the relaxing front porch, but openly complained about having to shovel so much.

Laura continued to work as an art teacher until retirement 2018.

Alex remained a columnist with the newspaper until he published the first of his five novels in 1995.

They never had children, but love their nieces and nephews dearly.

## *Matty*

Matty continued to work as a high school teacher at Cambridge Springs until retirement.

He had multiple serious relationships over the years, but never married, nor had any interest in marriage.

As always, he continued to enjoy large friend groups and remained very social and active. He enjoyed taking a yearly trip out to Evanston to visit his sister. Cassidy and Jake always took him out to new restaurants and breweries, which he loved.

## Eric and Ellie

Two weeks after Eric returned from helping Cassidy move to Illinois, he and Ellie went to the local shelter so Ellie could pick out a kitten: a fluffy black and white cat that she named Doc. Doc was a beloved member of the family for all of his sixteen years. He passed peacefully in 2004.

Eric and Ellie welcomed their first child, a daughter named Rhea Elaine Banker, on May 10, 1992, and two years later, son Cody Aaron Banker on June 29, 1994.

Ellie continued working as a 1st grade teacher until her retirement in 2022, after which she pursued new interest in gardening and baking.

Eric continues his work in HR even today. Ellie jokes that he will never quit and just suddenly die, mid commute, when he's in his 90s.

Rhea has been obsessed with dancing since she was three. She took multiple classes over the years and participated in competitions around the state. In high school she also started to do Pilates and loved it. After graduation she took multiple certification courses and started teaching Pilates, barre, and yoga at a wellness center outside of Erie. She also teaches a jazz class for 10 year olds once a week at her old dance studio.

Cody tried a little bit of everything growing up and enjoyed almost all of it. After high school, he went to the University of Pittsburgh (much to Eric's delight) and got a degree in education. He has a job teaching fifth grade in Butler, PA, a suburb north of Pittsburgh. His college girlfriend got a job in Butler as a physical therapist and they married soon after.

## Ben

After graduating from Mercyhurst in 1988, Ben got job at a psychiatric facility in Erie working primarily with addicts.

He worked there for five years before he accepted a job in a small therapy practice in Meadville and worked there until retirement.

Ben reconnected with a former high school classmate, Sherri Nelson, at their five-year high school reunion and they started dating shortly after. Sherri works as an oncology nurse at the local hospital. They married July 19, 1991.

A few years later, they welcomed twin daughters, Shelby Lynne Banker and Abigail Suzanne Banker, born October 1, 1994.

## *Art and Lynne*

Art retired in 1990 from his financial advisor job. Lynne retired in 1992 from her work as a school nurse.

They continue to host family events, including the First Friday dinners, that have gotten significantly more chaotic with grandkids running around. Art and Lynne love spending time with their four local grandchildren, and going to Chicago to see Cassidy, Jake, and Dylan twice a year. Cassidy and her family returned these visits once or twice a year before moving back home permanently in their retirement.

## *Will Sullivan*

After he graduated from Dickinson Law and passed the bar, Will got a job at a law firm in Pittsburgh. Within a year, he started dating Nancy Woods, a woman he kept bumping into at the coffee shop next to his office. Will and Nancy married June 12, 1993 and moved to Cranberry Twp. Will drove down into the city every day for work.

They welcomed their first child, a son named Ross James Sullivan on April 25, 1994, and their second son, Ryan Andrew Sullivan, on August 1, 1997.

## Claire Sullivan

Claire remained in Johnsontown all her life. After retirement, she kept busy with a local garden club and a woodworking group.

She enjoys all 3 of her grandsons very much and visits them multiple times a year. However, her favorite is when both of her sons and their families return each summer and there is a week of chaos and fun.

## Marissa Solomon

Marissa and Brandon broke up after a disastrous Thanksgiving in 1988.

She quickly packed up and moved to a new apartment in downtown Erie to start over and really focus on her job as an interior designer.

She met Isaac Rosenthal, a bank manager, at a food festival in the spring of 1990. Marissa and Isaac hit it off instantly and started a whirlwind romance. She moved in with Issac that fall, and they quickly married on March 23, 1991. Cassidy happily, though uncomfortably, returned to Erie and stood as her matron of honor, at 8 months pregnant, in a traditional Jewish ceremony. (Calm down -- Jake drove them both ways!)
*Marissa and Isaac welcomed three sons:*

David Marshall Rosenthal (December 30, 1991), Adam Jonathan Rosenthal (February 28, 1993), and Joshua Samuel Rosenthal (November 1, 1994).

Marissa retired from interior design in early 1994 so she could stay home with her two sons, and then her third. She loved being a stay-at-home mom and felt it was her true calling.

Despite the distance, Marissa and Cassidy remained good

friends over the years. They had a weekly phone call that often lasted hours, and would get their families together at least once a year. Dylan always looked forward to hanging out with David, Adam, and Joshua!

### *Brandon Calder*

After his break-up with Marissa, Brandon quit his job, left Erie, and moved back to Indianapolis with his family to get back on his feet.

He quickly got a new job at an architecture firm in the city.

On a night out, he went home with a woman named Claudia Simmons. She called him weeks later after finding out she was pregnant. Brandon and Claudia never dated, but were able to fairly peacefully co-parent their daughter, Eva Louise Calder, over the years, living less than two miles apart.

Brandon had other relationships, but never married. His focus is always on work and his daughter, whom he loves dearly.

### *Pete Harris*

Cassidy's night club hook up -- remember him? Well, he did finally get to work as a college baseball coach – at Northwestern University. Seriously! Wouldn't that be a fun story to write? Maybe someday. And yes, Cassidy almost passed out when Jake brought her to a team banquet and introduced her to the new head coach.

Pete coached at Northwestern for six years before moving back to his alma mater, Ohio State. He worked there until his retirement and loved every minute of it.

# Where are they in 2026?

*Cassidy* - 64 years old. She has retired from work. Living in Meadville with Jake. Involved in multiple community programs. Very social. Has monthly dinners with Marissa.

*Jake* - 64 years old. Works as an adjunct professor at Mercyhurst. Living in Meadville with Cassidy. Has converted their shed into a microbrewery.

*Dylan* - 35 years old. Working in Buffalo, NY as a IT manager.

*Alex* - After successfully battling lung cancer in 2010, the cancer came back in 2021. He died during surgery in 2023. He was 64.

*Laura* - 67 years old. She has retired from teaching, but continues working part time at the theater as the art director creating sets. After her husband's passing, Laura created a memorial wall in the hospital garden that she painted with a mural and planted sunflowers all around. She hopes other patients can find peace there. She remains very close with her in laws.

*Matty* - 67 years old. Matty has retired from teaching. He is active in golfing, fishing, and foodie groups with his large friend group.

*Eric* - 64 years old. He continues working. Ellie jokes he will never stop. On weekends he will sometimes join his brothers for a round of golf.

*Ellie* - 64 years old. She has retired from teaching and has gotten into gardening and baking.

*Rhea* - 34 years old. She works at a Wellness Center as a pilates, yoga, and dance teacher. Her Aunt Cassidy attends her Tuesday morning pilates class every week - a highlight for both of them.

*Cody* - 32 years old. He works as a 5th grade teacher in Butler, PA. He's married to his college girlfriend. They welcomed their first child in 2024.

*Ben* - 61 years old. Continues to work as a therapist. Occasionally joins Matty and Eric for a game of golf. Spends most of his free time watching sports.

*Sherri* - 61 years old. She still works as a nurse, but has started to lessen her hours. Started taking cooking lessons after she and Ben took a trip to Italy a few years back, and loves trying new recipes.

*Shelby* - 32 years old. She works as an ER nurse at a hospital in Michigan. Shelby is married with two sons.

*Abigail* - 32 years old. She works as a detective in the Erie police department. Abigail is divorced with one daughter.

*Art* - Art suffered a severe stroke in 2018. He never recovered and passed two months later. He was 84.

*Lynne* - 93 years old. Lynne moved into a retirement home in 2022. While she has significantly slowed down and her hearing is poor, she is still sharp and in decent health. She gets visits from her children, grandchildren, and great-grand children multiple times a week, which she cherishes. But she also has friends in the community and plays cards and dominos often.

# Final Notes

The monthly First Friday Banker family dinners continued without a hitch over the years. Cassidy made it home for about two a year, but Art, Lynne, and the boys continued them in her absence, though she was missed -- most of the time.

The table got fuller as Rhea, Cody, and twins Abigail and Shelby were born, turning the meals from general squabbles to full-on toddler fueled chaos. Cassidy, Jake, and Dylan's visits only fueled the fire, but watching the five cousins happily play together over the years brought a joy that none of them could deny.

In 2015, Ellie and Eric took over hosting, as it became too much for Lynne. She hated the first few times not hosting, but Lynne came to love "just showing up" quite quickly. Art loved the change instantly.

Now in 2026, the remaining Banker siblings take turns picking up Lynne to come for the monthly meal.

After a couple of decades of First Fridays being full of little kids and chaos, now they are back to just immediate family, minus Art and Alex. Especially after Alex's sudden death, the five Bankers (Lynne, Matty, Cassidy, Eric, and Ben) truly cherish their time together.

However, on the occasional holiday when the entire family is there (which gets harder each year), the chaos brings joy and comfort to everyone around them. Memories of years past.

*A firm reminder that it has been a hell of a good life!*